**THE MOST HIDEOUSLY BUTCHERED CORPSES THE POLICE HAD EVER SEEN . . .**

**A GRISLY ROCK GROUP THAT HAD ROCKETED TO THE TOP OF THE HORROR CHARTS . . .**

**A GORGEOUS, SADISTIC, SEXUALLY RAVENOUS HEIRESS . . .**

**AND A CREATURE THAT CALLED THE SEWERS HOME AND THE WORLD ITS HUNTING GROUND . . .**

*What was it that bound them all together with screams of victims and streams of blood? You don't want to know—but you'll have to find out!*

# GHOUL
## is the greatest!

"As alarming a piece . . . as I've ever read in many a black moon . . . a perverted fantastic with droll skill."　　　*—The Times* of London

"Does for the mind what a roller coaster does for the body."　　　*—Australian Magazine*

"At last . . . a bloody good thriller!"
　　　*—Kerrang!* (A London rock magazine)

"Horror . . . bloodthirsty, scandalous, gory."
　　　*—Publishers Weekly*

*For more about GHOUL's*
*ghastly delights, turn the page . . .*

"A HEART STOPPER . . . the kind of roller coaster that fright fans can't wait to ride!"
—*West Coast Review of Books*

"To put it bluntly, GHOUL is not a book for wimps."
—*Fangoria Magazine*

"A very interesting supernatural police procedural."
—*Playboy*

"Those who like Stephen King or who like to go to the Saturday night horror show will thrive on this one."
—*Macon Beacon*

*And this splatterpunk feast left even more reviewers shrieking with joy. . . .*

# TERRIFYING TALES

# GHOUL

by

## Michael Slade

A SIGNET BOOK

**SIGNET**
Published by the Penguin Group
Penguin Books USA Inc., 375 Hudson Street,
New York, New York 10014, U.S.A.
Penguin Books Ltd, 27 Wrights Lane,
London W8 5TZ, England
Penguin Books Australia Ltd, Ringwood,
Victoria, Australia
Penguin Books Canada Ltd, 10 Alcorn Avenue,
Toronto, Ontario, Canada M4V 3B2
Penguin Books (N.Z.) Ltd, 182–190 Wairau Road,
Auckland 10, New Zealand

Penguin Books Ltd, Registered Offices:
Harmondsworth, Middlesex, England

Published by Signet, an imprint of New American Library,
a division of Penguin Books USA Inc.

First Signet Printing, May, 1989
10 9 8 7 6 5 4

This is an authorized reprint of a hardcover edition published by
William Morrow and Company, Inc.

 REGISTERED TRADEMARK—MARCA REGISTRADA

Printed in the United States of America

**PUBLISHER'S NOTE**
This is a work of fiction. Names, characters, places, and incidents either are the product
of the author's imagination or are used fictitiously, and any resemblance to actual
persons, living or dead, events, or locales is entirely coincidental.

for
Robert Bloch, Alice Cooper, Stephen King
with thanks

*and to*
*Howard Phillips Lovecraft*

Fetish? You name it. All I know is,
I've had to have it with me.
Ever since I was a kid . . .
—*Robert Bloch*
THE SCARF


Through vaults of pain,
Enribbed and wrought with groins of ghastliness,
I passed, and garish spectres moved my brain
  To dire distress.
—*Thomas Hardy*
A WASTED ILLNESS

# PROLOGUE

The boundaries which divide Life from Death are at best shadowy and vague. Who shall say where the one ends, and where the other begins?

—*Edgar Allan Poe*
THE PREMATURE BURIAL

# The Burial

## The Western Hills, Rhode Island
### *Friday August 20, 1971, 1:15 p.m.*

"Dig," the Grave Worm said, sucking on a joint and handing Saxon the shovel.

The younger boy stared at the spade for a moment, then shook his head.

"Don't be a fuckin baby, Hyde," the Raw-Head jeered.

"Ya wanna join The Ghouls, don't ya?" the Grave Worm asked. "A Ghoul ain't a Ghoul till he's initiated."

"Trust us," the Boogeyman said. "The club is based on trust." He was sitting on a packing crate reading *Famous Monsters Of Filmland*.

The four youths were in a field that bordered on a graveyard. They had caught a bus in Providence at nine o'clock that morning, riding it out Route 44 northwest from the city, out along what was known as the Powder Mill Turnpike during the Revolution. The city had gradually disappeared and given way to country, a land of cool dark forests, rolling fields, and rundown clapboard buildings. At Chepachet, the junction of Route 44 with Route 102, they had climbed down from the bus to hang out for a while.

Three of the boys wore jackets that turned more than a couple of heads, for Chepachet was a historic town, conservative in nature. It had been settled at the start of the eighteenth century, and even today—nestled among the rugged granite hills of inland Rhode Island—three-quarters of the original settlement buildings still remained. Studded leather jackets embellished with pictures of carrion ghouls were unwelcome and out of place.

Later they'd jumped aboard a farm truck leaving town by Route 102. The farmer had turned around in his cab

3

to see what was going on, but when Freddie "the Grave
Worm" Sterling flashed him one of his famous grins, the
man decided to play it safe and leave well enough alone.
The teenagers had abandoned the truck near the Scituate
Reservoir, Freddie stealing a shovel from the back before
jumping down.

After an hour of fooling around they had come upon
the graveyard. They'd been bopping along Ponaganset
Road above the reservoir, grooving to Black Sabbath
screaming "After Forever" from the cassette player in the
Boogeyman's hand, when they'd come across an intrigu-
ing path that branched off into the trees. Wandering
through the undergrowth they'd found an abandoned
orchard, scoffed a couple of apples then skirted a small
dense wood to a weed-choked field beyond.

It was the Raw-Head who'd spotted the crate which
led them to the graveyard, leaning up against an old
stone wall that kept the woods from eating up the long-
relinquished meadow. When he'd pointed it out to the
other boys, the Grave Worm had cracked his famous
grin.

"Initiation time," the Boogeyman had whispered, eyeing
the crate.

The boys had been clustered around the box—Saxon
leaning on the stone wall, the Grave Worm tapping the
crate with his toe, the Boogeyman digging *Famous
Monsters* out of the folds of his jacket—when the Raw-
Head first noticed the colonial cemetery. It was tucked
away in the bordering woods in a dank, dark-shadowed
clearing.

"Hey, will ya look at that?"

The boys had turned.

"It's a burial ground must be a zillion years old. Ya
can hardly see the stones."

In the early days of Rhode Island before there were
public cemeteries, it was customary to bury the dead in
small family plots. In Providence these were sunk into
the hillside behind the homes along what was then Towne
Street, now North and South Main. In the country the
dead were buried in graveyards on the family farm, including the slaves. This cemetery was ancient or it would
not have been here, for the brooks and rivers that flowed
into Scituate Reservoir were the same ones that supplied
Providence with water. Nowadays a burial ground is not

permitted within a functioning watershed—seepage from the coffins does more than spoil the taste of the water.

The Grave Worm had abandoned the crate and put down the shovel to vault the low stone wall and enter the murky woods. The Boogeyman had lit a joint and passed it around. When the Grave Worm had emerged a few minutes later his face was twisted into that often-present smirk. He'd taken the joint from the Raw-Head and picked up the stolen spade. Now he was pointing toward the ancient burial ground.

"Dig," the Grave Worm said, handing Saxon the shovel.

The younger boy stared at the spade for a moment, then shook his head.

"Trust us," the Boogeyman said. "The club is based on trust. We're like the Masons or DeMolay. Like the Alpha Delts fraternity, and all that shit." He went back to reading his *Famous Monsters* magazine. Lon Chaney was on the cover with a mouth full of sharpened teeth. *London After Midnight.*

The Grave Worm untied the rope from around the crate, brushing away some dirt to reveal stencilling on the wood: RCA Victor, and the dog listening to a Victrola, followed by the words, "His Master's Voice".

Saxon was moving away from the group when the Raw-Head grabbed him. Reuben "the Raw-Head" Levine was a muscular kid with a skin complexion that resembled a pepperoni pizza. His hair was long and greasy and he wore a Grateful Dead T-shirt.

"Where do ya think you're goin, Dickhead?" the Boogeyman snarled. He was a tall, gaunt lad with pasty-white skin and all black clothes.

The Grave Worm stood up and glared at Saxon, then grabbed him by the shirt. Freddie Sterling was a blond youth, sixteen years of age. His face was a mass of freckles surrounding two small squinty eyes and that shit-eating, aw-shucks grin. He smelled of B.O.

When the fourteen-year-old began to struggle the Grave Worm knocked him to the ground and deftly hog-tied him with the rope from the crate. Peter "the Boogeyman" Kilroy stuffed a sock in Saxon's mouth to stifle his screams. The Ghouls then crouched down on their haunches around the thrashing boy.

"Settle down," the Grave Worm said, gripping Saxon by the hair. "Ya wanna be a Ghoul, ya gotta pass the test. We all done it or we wouldn't be here now. Today yer gonna be the star."

"Depend on no one," the Boogeyman said, "except a buddy Ghoul."

"Trust no one," the Raw-Head said, "except one of yer kind."

"If you're to be in the club, we gotta trust you."

"If yer gonna be a Ghoul, ya gotta trust us."

"If we show we're straight-shooters," the Grave Worm asked, "will ya find the balls ta prove we can trust ya?"

Knowing that it was the only way out, Saxon nodded his head.

"Good dude," the Grave Worm said, flashing that famous grin. "Untie him, boys. Party time."

It was a hot summer afternoon without a breath of wind in the air. The only sound was the incessant buzzing of flies or the occasional roar of a truck gearing down for a hill on the highway far beyond the trees.

When the Raw-Head released the rope that bound Saxon's wrists together, the younger boy grimaced as he examined his skin for signs of bruising, terrified that he might be haemorrhaging inside. Once he was sure his flesh was intact he let out a sigh of relief. Then all four boys gathered around the crate.

"We let ya go," the Grave Worm said, "as an act of trust. We don't wanna cause ya no harm. What happens now is only ta show that ya trust us. If ya can do it, Saxon, yer in the club. A Ghoul's special cuz he's come back from the grave."

Minutes later, Saxon began to dig.

They christened the crate "The Lovecraft Coffin" while dragging it over the stone wall into the cemetery. The Boogeyman scratched a rectangle in the dirt and the Grave Worm ordered Saxon to remove the earth within it to a depth of four feet. "Man, yer slow," the Raw-Head said halfway through the digging, yanking away the shovel to complete the task.

Once the hole was finished all four boys lowered the packing crate into the pit. The Grave Worm knocked a knothole out of the lid and inserted a hollow three-foot pipe. The pipe was part of an old machine left rusting in the orchard which the Boogeyman had to be sent on a foray to retrieve.

"That," the Grave Worm told Saxon, "is so ya can breathe."

Then finally Saxon reluctantly stretched out in the box. After The Ghouls closed the lid, they made sure the hollow pipe stood upright for several feet before filling in the grave.

The Grave Worm called down, "Saxon, can ya hear me?"

A muffled mumble rose up from beneath his feet.

"After this is over, we'll all go back ta town. Grab us a jumbo burger and catch *Night Of The Living Dead*."

Then he shovelled the earth back into the grave and packed it down so that the pipe poked up for several inches.

"What do we do now?" the Boogeyman whispered.

The Grave Worm once again cracked his famous grin. "I saw a store a mile back. Let's go getta Coke."

"What about him?"

"We leave him down there long enough he's gonna learn the *real* creed of The Ghouls: This side of the grave there's *no one* ya can trust."

Saxon's terror began with the fact that he could hardly move. For the packing crate was six feet long, by one foot high, by two feet wide. His arms were stretched out full-length at his sides and when he tried to lift them they both struck wood. He could not bend his elbows. He could not touch his head. He could not sit up. And now his left ear itched.

Don't think about it, Saxon thought.

But the itch got worse . . .

. . . and worse until it felt like . . .

Insects crawling in!

Suddenly all his needs shrunk down to just the need to move, a desperate, overwhelming need to push back the rigid embrace of his grave by just a single inch. For even an inch would demonstrate he still had *some* control.

Saxon began to writhe and squirm and twist and thrash, smashing his head and arms against the wood of the coffin lid to try to force it open.

Stop that! his mind warned. You'll bleed to death!

Instantly he stopped.

Now Saxon lay buried beneath the ground in subterranean darkness, afraid to move and all alone . . . alone as his circling mind became more confined with each thought closing in until he knew he was going to scream . . . and scream . . . and scream until his throat tore apart.

But when he opened his mouth to shriek, his tongue and lips quivered convulsively without issuing a sound, palpitating wildly in time to the ragged thump of his heart.

It was then that he realized he was slowly smothering to death. There was no sunlight coming down the breathing tube. He panicked at the thought that the centre of the pipe must be half-plugged with mud.

Saxon's body was soaked with sweat and a prickling, tingling sensation crawled up and down his limbs.

The heat in the crate was unbearable as the sun scorched the earth above and baked the air trapped within the coffin.

His lungs were compressing and his ears began to ring with the *buzzzzzzzing* of a bluebottle fly that was buried alive with him, the buzzing growing louder and louder until it reverberated within his shrinking mind.

Saxon closed his eyes as if that would somehow shut out the sound, and for a moment had a vision of great cyclopean cities and sky-flung monoliths all dripping green ooze and covered with hieroglyphics. From some undetermined source came a voice that was not really a voice but more a chaotic sensation uttering the gibberish "*Cthulhu fhtagn.*"

Then abruptly he heard something else that made his eyelids quiver. Something that flashed an electric shiver through his brain and drove the blood from his temples back to almost burst his heart. His eyes bugged out from his head.

For unbidden there came to his nostrils the sour fumes of damp earth, putrescence, and decay. His mind grew light as he heard the rustle of movement in other graves. He thought he could see through the ground as if by X-ray vision, see skeletons crawling and boiling and seething with maggots in their coffins, see ivory skulls half-devoid of flesh and covered with grey-green mould, the skin and muscles shredded into slimy yellow strands.

Then it was dark once more on this side of the grave. Soon he sensed a hundred worms slithering and turning through the earth, drawn by the warmth of his still-living flesh. To his horror he heard them burrowing through the wood of the packing crate.

Now one by one the parasites were invading his head, crawling into his mouth . . . his eyes . . . his nostrils . . . his ears . . . sucking and chewing inside his skull at the grey cells of his brain, while his arms remained helplessly pinned at his sides, straining at the claustrophobic dimensions of the coffin.

Again he struggled to gibber and howl and this time his voice broke through, a long and wild continuous shriek that resounded and bounced within the crate but could not penetrate the earth above.

As Saxon once more relentlessly smashed his head against the coffin lid, a voice of equal terror hissed in his ears, "Don't do that, you stupid fool! We'll both bleed to death!"

"Who are *you*?" the boy screamed hysterically.

Then one minute later, Saxon Hyde was no more.

*Part One*

---

# SEWER
# KILLER

All my stories, unconnected as they may be, are based on the fundamental lore or legend that this world was inhabited at one time by another race who, in practising black magic, lost their foothold and were expelled, yet live on outside ever ready to take possession of this earth again.

—*H.P. Lovecraft*

# Looking Glass

London, England
*Friday January 3, 1986, 4:53 p.m.*

> *"I love the dead before they're cold,*
> *They're bluing flesh for me to hold.*
> *Cadaver eyes upon me see nothing . . ."*

The mirror was an antique dating from the 1850s. Its hardwood frame—now jet-black from the grime of so many years—was carved with scenes from the stories of Edgar Allan Poe. Frozen in oak was the tomb broken open in "Berenice" to reveal the corpse of a woman with all her teeth lovingly pulled out; "The House Of Usher" with its eye-like windows and pervading sense of evil twinship, incest, and decay; "The Pit And The Pendulum"; "The Tell-Tale Heart". For here in this basement room were all the victims of "The Imp Of The Perverse".

But the images carved in the wood of the frame were not as horrid as those that were reflected in the glass. For the mirror, though murky and silver-backed, with veins of black threaded through it where the coating had peeled away, still had the power to reflect the pictures and posters that were tacked to the walls of the cellar room.

> *"I love the dead before they rise,*
> *No farewells, no goodbyes.*
> *I never even knew your rotting face . . ."*

When the mirror began to move, at first all it reflected was a pale grey arm. The forearm bones were long and thick and the hands were large. Each of the big-knuckled fingers was tipped with a black-lacquered nail. Then as

13

the mirror/door creaked open with groans of protest from its hinges, the body joined to the arm was revealed in the looking glass.

The figure had grey translucent skin stretched tight over angular skull bones that leered out from behind the face. The man was six foot three in height and weighed 190 pounds. Trim and sinewy, his body was a power-house of both muscle and tendon strength. His hair, cut short at the sides but left full at the crown, was a bleached-white colour with streaks of dirty blond. His teeth were yellow and his eyes glared out from what appeared to be two giant spiders crawling across his ghoul-like face.

> *"While friends and lovers mourn your silly grave,*
> *I have other uses for you, Darling . . ."*

The figure's reflection disappeared from the mirror.

> *"We love the dead.*
> *We love the dead. Yeah."*

The cut from *Billion Dollar Babies* came to an end. The needle began a monotonous click as the Alice Cooper record continued to revolve on the turntable. Then a few seconds later the figure returned.

The Ghoul was now wearing a long grey cape over grey rubber waders that came up to his waist. Under the cape he was dressed in a heavy grey coat cinched with a belt and a safety harness. He had donned a black wig and a grey top hat, the hair hanging down around his face in dirty, coiled hanks. In one gloved hand The Ghoul gripped an electric torch, while in the other he clutched a sharp two-handed axe.

The pale grey arm reached out once more to touch the antique mirror.

Then Alice passed through the looking glass and into the sewers of London.

## 5:09 p.m.

The Ghoul made his way down a circular well on iron rungs hammered into sweating brick. The flashlight was now clutched under one arm while the two-handed axe hung from a sling tied to his belt. The light from the electric torch cast a jerky shadow across the geometrical lines of the bricks. Twenty feet below The Ghoul reached a concrete landing.

A grating set into the slimy floor led to a second shaft that descended further still. Lying in the muck beside the hole was a spiral safety lamp left behind after yesterday's dress rehearsal. The Ghoul now lifted the iron grating and carefully lowered the ignited lamp down the second shaft on a long nylon rope. This precaution was taken to check for the presence of deadly gases: carburetted hydrogen which could explode; sulphurated hydrogen formed by the putrid decomposition of the dead; carbonic acid which miners call "choke-damp". Any one or more of these gases would quickly extinguish the flame. The lamp, however, came up still burning—so The Ghoul went down.

The black hole ended in a cavernous crypt supported by crumbling pillars and arches. Along one side of the vault was a dam about twenty-five feet across, over which rising water would pour during a major rainstorm. Opposite the dam a series of tunnels angled off into the dark to become the main and subsidiary sewers that were the bowels of London. Into the narrowest of these The Ghoul now disappeared.

After travelling a distance of thirty feet he encountered a fork in the sewer and went left. Twenty feet more and there was another split. Puzzled, the figure paused a moment, then turned right.

Soon the oozing brickwork of the tunnel began to narrow. It was now necessary for The Ghoul to crouch as the egg-shaped shaft shrank to five feet in height. A stream of cold, greyish water stinking of detergent rushed knee-high against the back of his waders. The flow made him lose his balance but, pushing off the tunnel wall, he came quickly back to midstream. Beneath the water a dragging muck sucked at his boots as a dull and turbid screen of mist hovered on the surface.

At ninety feet in he stopped again for no apparent reason. A grimace of horror pulled The Ghoul's lips back from his clenched teeth. His empty hand came up to clutch his forehead sharply. Then as his eyes narrowed to slits he shook his head violently.

A frog sat watching him from a large crack in the brickwork. By this time tomorrow, the rats would make it a meal.

In less than a minute, however, the hunchbacked shadow was on the move, slipping away down the sewer, trailing words behind.

"*I . . . love . . . dead . . .*" Cold whispers in the dark.

The beam of the electric torch licked the blade of the axe.

## 5:18 p.m.

In Stonegate Cemetery fog lay thick upon the ground, seeping out of the warm wet earth to join the chill of dusk, then settling over the graveyard like a last gasp from the dead. It swirled around the chapel that stood near the summit of the hill, with its crocketed spire jutting up to starkly pierce the sky, its altar burned by vandals several years ago. It drifted down the side of the slope in a smothering gossamer ooze, groping among the branches of the yew and sycamore trees, their gnarled limbs maimed by indifferent surgery. It slithered over the monuments that were scattered about in decay: sarcophagi, obelisks, urns, and crosses, each strangled or partly submerged by the clinging undergrowth. It hovered above the catacombs that were sunk near Egyptian Row, the underground brick-vaulted passages lined with cells for the storing of coffins, each coffin sealed in its prison by a rusting iron grill. It crept over the lichen-encrusted tombstones that humped up out of the ground, with legends above in the language of death chipped into the marble or slate, and ghosts below where deep, deep down in the cold black ground 166,000 bodies lay rotting in their graves.

Then the fog reached the gate.

The gatehouse sat between two stone pillars mounted by Gothic urns. It had once contained the cemetery records and books, but now it was empty and boarded up and rumoured to be haunted. For who knew *what* lurked about in the shadows of this boneyard, with its spiked iron railings and two-foot thick walls to keep bodysnatchers out. In fact they might have been ghosts themselves, this woman and her baby.

Sylvia Pym was dressed in a long white coat with a shawl about her head, her son David asleep in a sling clutched tightly to her chest. A bitter wind foretelling a change in the weather tugged at her clothes and made her hunch against its chill. As she moved past the gar-goyled gatehouse with its broken stained-glass windows, she closed her coat around her child for extra warmth. Then Sylvia struggled up the path that wound toward the chapel.

Dusk was rapidly coming down to blacken the face of London. Through an occasional rift in the mist she could see the streets beyond the cemetery walls spread out below like a broad flat map.

Turning left, she wandered down a side-path that crossed the mouth of a tunnel leading to the catacombs. Soon the path deteriorated into a muddy track, snaking off through a wood of dead elms that still remained unfelled. Weeds and brambles had grown up to obliterate the mounds, most of which had lost their shape in the rains of a hundred years. Within this thicket, however, were also recent paupers' graves, near one of which the woman now stopped. She sank to her knees as a tawny owl watched her in silence from the branch of a dead tree.

Had it not been for the moan of the elms as the wind rose and waned, she might have heard the scrape of metal on metal nearby, might have heard the sound of the side-gate lock being smashed.

But she didn't.

"Mother . . ." Sylvia whispered tenderly, as she brushed some leaves away from the small stone cross that marked the grave. The words she then spoke were so breathless they could barely be heard even by the baby asleep at her chest. Soon the woman fell silent and bowed her head in prayer.

Close-by in the underbrush, something moved.

Without looking up, Sylvia reached out with her left hand to touch the cold headstone.

Then abruptly her eyes snapped open and her head jerked around as the axe-blade slammed against the stone, sending sparks and three of her fingers flying through the air.

Sylvia opened her mouth to scream in shock and pain.

But the force of the blow bounced the axe back off the stone, cracking her jaw and snapping the hyoid bone in her throat.

Her voice box collapsed.

Cold panic seized her gut and blood filled her mouth as

she stumbled to her feet and fled back down the muddy path.

Blinded by tears she staggered, running into tombstones, the fingers on her good hand feeling embellishments carved in the marble: anchors and urns and snakes and skulls and hourglasses and circles. The stumps on her other hand felt nothing but searing pain.

She glanced back fearfully over her shoulder to find no one there, then fled into the tunnel that led to the catacombs.

At first all she could hear was the sound of her own footsteps and the constant dripping of water. A rat squealed in anger as she kicked it with her foot. Then transfixed with terror she listened as a second set of footsteps moved into the vault, creeping towards her with a chilling *sssuck-sssuck-sssuck*. A piercing beam of light knifed across the charnel house.

Revealed now to her darting eyes was a ghastly, cape-clad monster, a spider-eyed nightmare who leered at her transfixed by the sight of the blood that dripped from her chin. The ray of light glinted off the axe in his hand.

Then the electric torch went out.

Now the echo of his tread was closing in on her. Wheezing gasps of breath bubbled through the blood in her throat as she clutched her sleeping child to her heart. She heard whispered words near her hiss, "Shall we play The Game?"

Again she bolted.

Lunging blindly away from the creature, Sylvia stumbled as her feet slipped in the muck.

The ghoulish voice came closer . . . "Game" . . . closer . . . "Game" . . . until suddenly she burst out of the vault and into the foggy night.

Then her baby woke up.

The moment the child began to howl she clamped her hand over his face to prevent him giving them away.

She whirled around to see if they were still being pursued . . . and without warning found herself slipping, sliding, falling into a pit.

Noooooooooo! her mind shrieked as her arms flailed through the dark, but the torn flesh of her throat wouldn't make a sound.

Clawing desperately at the mud in a frantic attempt to

scramble up out of the partly-dug grave, Sylvia missed a furtive movement near the edge of the hole.

As she grabbed the lip of the surface and dug deep into the dirt with her bloody fingers to grasp a solid hold, a menacing voice above her sneered:

*"While friends and lovers mourn your silly grave,
I have other uses for you, Darling."*

Sylvia's head jerked up.

Standing near the edge of the pit with both arms high in the air, the spider-eyed monster grinned down at her.

The last thing the woman saw was the wedge of the axehead as it rushed toward her skull.

## 8:30 p.m.

The watchman locked the main gate at precisely eight o'clock, then began his tour of the cemetery grounds.

Stonegate covered 37 acres. Six months earlier it had suffered a rash of vandalism. Several tombs had been defaced and monuments smashed, so Charlie O'Grady had been hired to keep an eye on the place. As he was doing now.

The fog had dissolved an hour ago and the clouds had blown away, uncovering a weak winter moon low down in the sky. It cast long shadows across the surface of the boneyard.

Half an hour into his rounds, Charlie was shocked to find blood in the catacombs.

The catacombs of Stonegate dated from the middle of the nineteenth century. A system of dank, dark tombs and tunnels burrowed beneath the ground, they wormed their way into the side of the hill that led to the summit chapel. Narrow stone-vaulted passages connected the tombs together. Sunk into the walls of each cold room were brick cells lined with wooden shelves to house the rotting coffins. The box beside which he found the blood contained a poisoned man, visible through a small glass panel built into one side. His mummified face was smoke-white and his teeth were black.

Charlie followed the blood spots from the vault to the ground beside the open grave. He winced involuntarily when his torch illuminated the large, clotting red pool partly soaked into the earth. Shining his flashlight down the hole nothing came to view, until he saw a trail of blood drops snaking away from the pit.

The trail moved toward Stonegate's western wall, then out into the street lined with abandoned tenements. Charlie noticed the smashed padlock as he passed through the gate. Sweeping his torch across the tarmac in wide expanding arcs, he discovered the trail of blood came to a halt at the edge of a manhole cover leading to the sewers. Scratches marked the asphalt where the cover had been removed.

Charlie kneeled to a crouch when the light from the torch winked back at him, for now caught in its beam and smeared with streaks of blood were the broken shards of a small looking glass.

The shattered pieces lay scattered around an old grey top hat.

# Queen Bee

**London, England**
*Saturday January 4, 11:50 a.m.*

New Scotland Yard is the headquarters of the London Metropolitan Police. The Met is made up of 26,500 cops and 15,000 civilian staff. The Metropolitan Police District is an area of 800 square miles with a resident population of seven million plus a constant flow of visitors. It is subdivided into 24 Districts. Each District has its own Criminal Investigation Department under its own Commander. These 24 CIDs are then spread among 185 police stations. There are just under 3,500 detectives in the Met.

In this city it is the CID cops in the District in which a body is found who take the shout. They will then investigate the case to its conclusion, as was happening in *this* case until the third bloodless body was fished from the Thames.

The Police National Computer is 50 million pounds' worth of sophisticated microchip technology. It provides a central data base for police throughout the country. It is housed in a fortified building at Hendon in North London. The two computers that make it up are able to store information on *every* British citizen in a number of categories:

1. The VOI—or Vehicle Owners Index—contains the name and address of each owner plus pertinent details about all 33 million motor vehicles in Britain.

2. The SSVI—or Stolen and Suspect Vehicle Index—lists not only those cars which are lost or stolen in the country, but also 41,000 vehicles "of long term interest to the police" and 9,000 that were "seen or checked in noteworthy circumstances".

3. The Wanted and Missing Persons Index contains 115,000 names. Half of these entries are in two sub-categories: "suspected", which means there is insufficient evidence to charge them; and "locate", which means they are sought in relation to unsolved investigations.

4. The Criminal Names Index lists the 2.5 million people in Britain with previous criminal records. It contains the names of crime victims as well.

5. The Fingerprint Index is programmed to hold more than 3 million sets of prints. It stores these as a series of computerized binary numbers.

All the above indexes are cross-linked.

A PNC terminal consists of a visual display unit screen (or VDU) and a keyboard connected by telephone to the Police National Computer. The PNC has what is called the Broadcast Facility. Each PNC terminal can send data to—and receive data from—any or all of the 900 other terminals that make up the network system. And four of these PNC terminals were right here in this room.

The Murder Room in C1 Central at New Scotland Yard contained thirty pale wooden desks, twenty face-to-face in a row down the middle and the rest in pairs along the right wall. Off in the far left corner was the office of Detective Chief Superintendent Hilary Rand who was in command of the Squad. Just outside the door to the DC Supt's office was the desk of Detective Inspector Derick Hone. It was set at a slight angle to denote his status and faced down the room so he could keep an eye on the other cops. Hone was a Yard specialist in the science of logistics: the movement of personnel, equipment, and supplies. So far in its hunt for the Vampire Killer over the past eight months, the Squad had taken 29,000 written statements from 114,000 persons interviewed, 1.2 million car registration numbers had been checked, 44,000 telephone calls had been recorded, and 1.9 million PNC data base entries had been indexed.

There is no Murder Squad at New Scotland Yard—at least not one in the traditional sense. The Squad which gave birth to the expression "calling in the Yard" was phased out in the 1970s. Tradition, however, dies very hard in the London Met Police, so when it was decided last July that C1 Central would take command of the Vampire Killer case, the cops assigned to the manhunt were dubbed the new Murder Squad. Today the 34 detectives crammed into this room were the spearhead of 300 more out there in the field.

Two men were conversing near the door as Winston Braithwaite entered the Murder Room.

"You'd have thought we were there for a breach of the peace, not a murder collar," one said. "Right couple of bastards they were. I tell you, Sarge, one of them got right up my nose."

"Irish, was he?"

"No, a coon. He came within an ace of getting his fucking nig-nog head slammed against the wall."

"Yes, the sooties do go on. Some of our own coonstables, too."

"I mean, who the fucking hell do they think they are?"

"Well, they've got to be taught, you see. You can't let it start. If you let it start, you don't know where it will stop, do you? The Brixton mess. Tottenham. We don't want the razor blades thinking they—"

"Sssh! A challenger."

Both cops turned and stared at Braithwaite. The Sergeant nodded and they parted company. Braithwaite paused to look around for DC Supt Hilary Rand.

Born in Bridgetown, Barbados, Winston Braithwaite was the son of two black sugarcane-cutters. A wiry man of forty who played cricket very well, the doctor wore horn-rimmed glasses and a smile punctuated by one gold tooth. He was impeccably dressed in a tailored blue blazer and grey slacks with a sharp crease, sporting a white shirt and a red-striped tie. An unmarried man, his life was his work.

Braithwaite's academic standing had brought him to Britain as a Rhodes scholar twenty years ago. By the age of twenty-four he had an MBChB from Oxford University. At the Maudsley Hospital in London his research for his MD had been in the field of forensic psychiatry. The doctor's thesis was titled *The Personality Structure Of The Violent Sociopath*. He was now a psychiatric advisor to the Home Office and the Metropolitan Police.

Braithwaite spotted the DC Supt at the far end of the Murder Room in the alcove where the PNC terminals were housed.

As he walked toward Rand he saw several cops studying a bulletin board which ran the length of the room. This board was cluttered with overlapping information.

A Met District map, pinned and flagged. Documents and photographs culled from promising Criminal Record Office files. A glossy snapshot of three men standing outside a pub, one man's head encircled with a halo of red crayon. A list of official interpreters and the Fingerprint Officer's duty roster. Identikit and Photofit mock-ups of wanted men, some developed from psychics and others from witnesses under hypnosis. Divisional Crime Information sheets to update the Squad on prisoners arrested overnight. Personal messages phoned in for specific detectives. PNC tips from the provincial forces. A copy of *The job*, the Yard's fortnightly newspaper. Plus several sheets of data sent over from C11, the Central Intelligence and Surveillance Branch of the Yard.

Telephones rang as typewriters clattered and personal radios squawked.

As he moved along the rows of desks, Braithwaite overheard snippets of conversation.

" . . . a man can't get on with his governor, that's his problem, isn't it? Find someone with bottle and search that drum . . ."

"Crawford, come 'ere! You got the name right, but you left out the offence . . ."

" . . . that number plate again, love . . ."

"Next to other people's wives, Smith, more good men have got into bother in this job over . . ."

"Ah, Mr Braithwaite," Rand said. "How good of you to come. I was just about to have a sandwich and a pot of tea. Care to join me? There's coffee if you prefer."

"Tea would be fine."

"Good. You've read the morning papers?"

Braithwaite nodded his head.

"Then may I suggest we talk over lunch?"

Hilary Rand was a tall, thin woman, fifty-four years of age. She was dressed in a grey flannel suit with a plain white blouse. Her face was devoid of make-up but for a touch of red lipstick and her hair was conservatively short. Yet despite her thinness she was anything but frail—a tough lady with shrewd, piercing, china blue eyes.

It's as if she knows what you're thinking, the doctor thought. She watches intently for some slight subconscious giveaway, until the pressure of her stare and absence of conversation will surely make you give away what she's watching for.

Rand's office off the Murder Room was a rectangle fifteen feet by twenty-five. To the right of the door stood an old oak desk in front of a blackboard above which was a rolled-up projection screen. Six chairs in two ranks of three were lined up in front of the desk. The long wall opposite the door was a bank of windows that looked out on Victoria Street. Heavy grey clouds weighed down the sky and threatened snow. A bulletin board as cluttered as the one outside covered the wall opposite the windows while a trophy case gleaming with brass stood to the left. Because Rand held the rank of Detective Chief Superintendent she had the luxury of a carpet and a leather armchair.

"Quite a change," the doctor said, "since I was here last summer." He was studying the pictures pinned to the bulletin board.

"Yes," Rand agreed. "Sometimes I feel my job is more akin to horror fiction than it is to the world of fact."

Braithwaite smiled.

"Detective, you sound like—"

"Hilary. Please," she said.

The psychiatrist nodded, flashing his gold tooth.

"All right. Hilary, you sound more like one of my patients than you do a homicide detective. You should give my profession a try. It's *all* fantasy."

"Thank you, doctor, but—"

"Winston. Please," he said.

"Thank you, Winston, but your offer I decline."

Hilary Rand closed her office door and crossed to a tea tray on her desk. She poured two cups from a pot nestled in a tea cosy. Three sandwiches were wrapped in see-through plastic. "Egg, cheese and onion, or beef," she said. "Take your choice."

"Egg," Braithwaite replied.

As he pulled a chair up to the desk the psychiatrist suddenly realized how very cold it was in the room. Had the detective shut off the heat, either to keep her own thoughts crystal clear or anyone else in the room focused and wide awake? It was not an environment one would want to waste much time in.

For a while they ate in silence, studying each other. Rand was trained, Braithwaite could see, in the Yard detective's art of giving nothing away. British cops neither look nor act like ordinary people. Through conscious effort they learn to prevent the muscles around the mouth from showing normal feeling. The face then becomes expressionless, throwing others on the defensive by allowing them no clue as to the policeman's inner thoughts.

Finally, sipping the last of her tea, Rand placed the china cup on its saucer and wiped a few crumbs from her lips.

"Winston," she asked, "do you know the meaning of the term 'Queen Bee'?"

"That's Yard slang for a senior female officer."

Rand raised an eyebrow.

"I keep my ears open," the doctor replied.

"Well, Winston," Rand said bluntly, "I need your help. And your discretion, so I'll be frank with you. The Yard—as you might suspect—is not an open and friendly place for a woman."

"No doubt," Braithwaite agreed.

For he knew only too well that the chain of promotion to this office would not have been an easy one. Rand would have had to do twice the job just to stay even with the other CID officers at C1, let alone rise in rank. All his life the doctor had carried a similar cross.

"Most senior policemen," Rand continued, "have never worked with, or for, a well-qualified woman. They have known us simply as secretaries, lovers, and wives. It was only recently that WPCs were integrated into the force."

"The Little Sister Syndrome," Braithwaite said.

"Yes," she replied. "Bad enough when a man encounters sudden danger, but harm to a female officer is unthinkable. Some *still* say police work is unsuitable for a woman."

"God may have given her brains, but he didn't give her brawn."

"Precisely."

"So how did you advance?"

"First I used matron duty—in my case a trip to the loo with an important suspect's worried and talkative girl-friend—to crack a contract murder case. Then as Token Woman of the seventies, my quick promotion was good for public relations. And lastly because I'd like to think I do the job well—and humbly, of course—which makes the men at the top look good."

"Why were you put in command of the Murder Squad?" Braithwaite asked.

"Because at the time there were only three victims, all pre-teenage girls. The men on the eighth floor thought me a natural for the job."

"I see," the doctor said.

"But you and I know," Rand continued, "that women—and *ethnic* minorities—have not gained acceptance within the Yard to the extent the public is led to believe they have."

Braithwaite recalled the conversation he had just overheard at the door to the Murder Room. And recently he had been called "that nigger voodoo witch doctor" by a disgruntled Detective Sergeant who had not liked his diagnosis of insanity in a case where a Constable had been assaulted.

"Even for a man," Rand said, "the system is not set up so talent and qualifications are the only characteristics that determine who moves ahead. So I suppose I've been lucky. At least up until now."

"Ah . . ." Braithwaite sighed, nodding his head. He was catching on.

"Was it G. K. Chesterton who said, 'Society is at the mercy of a motiveless murderer'? Well," the detective added, "so, it appears, am I."

"You're about to be sacked from the Vampire Killer case?"

"Yes. And soon. Which some of the men on the eighth floor think will put me back in my rightful place as a woman and restore natural harmony."

"That Ol' Natural Harmony," Braithwaite said. "Where would we be without it?"

"Heaven only knows."

"I do think Chesterton was wrong, however, Hilary. There is always a motive for murder once you understand what motivates the murderer. It would have been better for him to say, 'Society is at the probable mercy of the *irrational*-motive murderer.'"

"Good point, Winston," Hilary Rand said. "Which happens to be the reason why I've asked you here today."

"Ah . . ." Braithwaite sighed again, and grinned.

Not long ago the question of motive was considered to be the exclusive province of policemen. But these are the days of the Yorkshire Ripper, Son of Sam, the Night Stalker, Zodiac, the Headhunter, the Boston Strangler,

the Black Panther, the Moors Murderers, the Manson
Family, the Green River Killer, the Hillside Strangler,
and Dennis Nilsen's "House of Horrors". Motive, therefore, has become the territory of the forensic psychiatrist.

"What I need," Rand told Braithwaite, "is to get a
better idea about this killer. When you were last here in
the summer our hunt was full of leads. As a result,
naturally, you gave us a cautious and conservative hypo-
thetical psychiatric opinion."

"That I did."

"At that time, Winston, I'm sorry to say, you were not
given *all* the facts. As usual in this type of case the Yard
was playing its cards close to its chest."

"For fear of a copy cat killer," Braithwaite said.

"Yes. That and other reasons. The more people who
know all the facts, the weaker the trap that can be set if
an arrest is made. A detail that slips from a prisoner's
mouth which only *we* know can ensure an air-tight charge."

"I understand," the doctor said.

"Yes, I'm sure you do. But when your back is against
the wall, such caution becomes a luxury. So here is a
précis of what we know to date."

Rand handed Braithwaite several papers which he began to read.

Between May 13 and August 12, 1985, the bodies of eight young girls were found floating in the
water by the Thames River Police. They were
discovered between Blackfriars Bridge to the west
and the East India Docks downstream. Diatom
tests of their internal organs at autopsy, plus
lack of water in the lungs, showed none of them
had drowned. It has now been almost five months
since the last victim was fished from the river.

The girls ranged in age from seven to eleven.
All were found naked but none had suffered a
sexual assault. In each case the victim's body
had been completely drained of blood by means
of a deep wound to the neck. Each victim's heart
had also been cut out. In christening this murderer "the Vampire Killer" the *Mirror* chose a
very apt name. (See autopsy reports attached.)

Braithwaite flipped to the back of the sheaf of papers.

He read each autopsy report once, then skimmed them all again. That done, he tented his fingers into a steeple that just touched his lower lip. After some concentrated thought he pulled his hands apart as if his flesh were magnetized.

"How strange," he said. "Each neck wound is to the artery, not the vein."

"And cut with precision," Rand added. "Not in a frenzy."

"Yes. That tells a lot."

For there was evidence to show the bleeding from each neck wound occurred while the victims were still alive. All the internal organs were pale and devoid of blood. In each case the brain was almost white. If the bleeding had occurred *after* each death the organs would have retained their blood and been flushed at the autopsy.

In addition, there was bruising and bleeding into the soft neck tissues surrounding the wounds to each carotid artery. That would not have happened if the victims were already dead.

The conclusion reached in all eight autopsy reports was that death resulted from rapid loss of blood. Each exsanguination took place *before* the victim died, then after each killing the murderer cut out his victim's heart.

Like a *coup de grâce*, Braithwaite thought.

What intrigued the doctor most, however, was the MO of the slayings. Open a vein—as is done when a person volunteers blood—and the blood will slowly flow out. This is because you have tapped a vessel that *returns* blood from the organs to the heart and is therefore under low pressure. But open a major artery and the blood will spurt for a good distance. This is because you have tapped a vessel that *takes* blood to the organs under full pressure from the heart.

Rapid loss of blood will cause a victim to go into hypovolemic shock. The body will respond through its homeostatic mechanism to constrict its vessels in an attempt to maintain blood pressure.

A twelve-year-old girl would have approximately five to six pints of blood. That is about seven per cent of her body by volume. If she lost half of her body's blood rapidly she would die. Her heart would stop beating and her blood pressure would cease. As a result a portion of her remaining blood would stay in the body. Yet in each of these cases the corpse was almost *completely* devoid of blood. Which meant that after the point of each girl's death the blood that stayed in her body was vacuum-sucked out.

Braithwaite frowned.

"You'll note," Rand said, "that the blood types are not all the same."

"Yes," the doctor replied. "Five Type O. Two Type A. One Type B. That's a little off the percentages in the general population, but not by much."

"Any conclusions?"

"Yes, a few."

The psychiatrist tapped his fingers on the desk and thought a moment. "First, the killer wants to collect *all* of each victim's blood.

"Second, the killer wants to do this in the most *dramatic* way, through conscious choice of the carotid artery over the equivalent vein.

"To my mind this shows that the killer has a psychological obsession with human blood. This is confirmed by the cutting out of the hearts."

"Is there a psychiatric condition to conform with your conclusions?" Hilary Rand asked.

"Yes. Haematomania. But first let me finish reading your report."

Outside, snow was now falling heavily from a leaden sky. The traffic around New Scotland Yard did not adapt well. As the ground turned white, three cars slammed each other in front of the Yard's revolving sign.

Several minutes later, Braithwaite handed the report back to Rand.

"Not much there," he said, shaking his head.

"No," the detective agreed. "We've mounted the largest investigation since the Yorkshire Ripper and the Black Panther, but still we do not have a suspect. All the victims, so far as we know, were chosen totally at random. . . . except for one detail. It does appear that all come from fairly well-off upper middle class families. But beyond that we cannot find a connection."

"I'm surprised the PNC did not serve you better," Braithwaite said.

The "Crime Pattern Analysis" system developed by the Home Office in 1983 was designed to recognize similarities among crimes recorded by different police forces in the PNC's data banks. The hope was that offences committed by the same perpetrator might be revealed.

"We've fed the PNC every detail available on each girl's background and pattern of day-by-day life," Rand said. 'Except for the common MO of the crimes in the method of the killing, what we have discovered to date is not very much.

"First, all eight girls disappeared during the day in different parts of London. They simply seem to have vanished into thin air. Some from the streets. Some from the parks. Some on their way to and from school."

"So the killer is either unemployed or works a night shift," Braithwaite said.

"Or is his or her own boss and does what he or she pleases. Even if that's not the case and the killer does work nine to five, what's to say that he or she doesn't phone in sick or work on the road?"

"You have no idea how the killer kidnapped all eight girls without detection?"

"None. Until now."

"Ah . . ." Braithwaite said thoughtfully.

"We know that each girl was off by herself when she vanished. We've received several thousand tips about motor vehicles noticed near the location where each was last seen alive. But none have been of any use.

"An interesting feature, however, is that every crime occurred during a light rain. We have assumed that this was so the killer could mask his or her appearance without suspicion."

"But now you think," Braithwaite anticipated, "this was so your police dogs couldn't trace either the killer's or the victim's scent to the sewers?"

"Winston," Rand said, as she swept her hand across a map tacked to the bulletin board, "I am told that if a person knows his way around down in that maze, it is possible to go from one side of London to the other *entirely* underground."

"So now you're hunting a sewer killer?" the doctor said.

"Yes," Rand replied.

"Okay, let's come back to that. But first tell me what else you've turned up."

"Not very much," the detective said. "There are no common physical features among the victims to establish a pattern. Blue-eyed blondes, that sort of thing. Two of the girls took ballet lessons, but at different studios. Two had shopped at Hamleys within three weeks prior to their deaths. But then half of London goes through that toy shop every year. And that's about it."

Braithwaite blinked.

"Incredible, isn't it?" Hilary Rand said. "Perhaps Chesterton was right after all."

"You said the girls had families that were fairly well-off. No ransom demands?"

"None."

"No business connections? Some source for revenge?"

"No. So far as we can find there is no motive common to all the families."

The doctor shrugged. He had run out of questions.

"More than 200 cranks have confessed to the crimes," Rand said. "On the chance that there might be a medical link in the method of the killings we have examined the health professions as best we can. Doctors. Nurses. Students. Biologists. And researchers. Again with no results.

"Every child molester in the CRO who we can find has been questioned. Still no positive leads.

"We've done surreptitious funeral photographs to see who attends to watch the mourning.

"We've tried hypnotism of witnesses and psychic impressions. Nothing again.

"Media coverage has yielded tens of thousands of tips none of which has worked out."

"I see," Braithwaite said. "So now everyone wants a scapegoat to help vent their frustration."

"Yes," Rand agreed.

"How much time do you think you have?"

"Perhaps a few days. Three at most. Last night will certainly heat things up. Opinion on the eighth floor is that the case has grown too big for a woman."

"Can your Squad be trusted?"

"Just Derick Hone. No one wants to back a loser and go down with her."

" 'When the hunt is on, all dogs bark'."

"Hundreds of officers working for me, yet I feel as if I'm alone with some computers."

"You're never as alone as when you're in a crowd."

"I knew you'd understand."

"So what do you want from me?"

"Support," Rand said. "I'm desperate, Winston. This job is my life."

The doctor got up from the desk and pressed his face against the window. The stark fluorescent lights in the room reflected off the glass. Down in the street the snow looked blue and traffic was in a snarl. Three recovery trucks and seven PCs were trying to sort out the mess the accidents had caused.

Braithwaite knew only too well the sacrifice Rand had made in order to advance against the tide in her chosen field of work. Her sex and his colour exacted a vicious price. He was both flattered by her request and more than a little concerned. Flattered because New Scotland Yard is about as tight a closed shop as can be found in Britain today, yet this woman had breached the ranks to confide in *him*. Concerned because if he didn't help, or if his help didn't hit the mark, Hilary Rand would be, in a way, *his* casualty. To a good man the burden of protecting himself is never as onerous as the moral obligation to protect someone else.

Braithwaite had heard a story once about Hilary Rand. It was said that she had run foul of a senior officer with the independent City of London Police. The man had dealt with the conflict by saying, "There's nothing wrong with you, Hilary, that a good fuck wouldn't cure."

Rand, it was said, had replied, "That may be, Inspector. But then *you* wouldn't be the man."

Nigger voodoo witch doctor, Winston Braithwaite thought.

He turned from the window.

"All right," he said. "Count me in. Besides, I like the challenge this killer presents. We British will never outdo the Americans when it comes to volume killing, but for sheer perversity there's something about our murders that makes us unique. As a nation I think we do murder very well."

"Yes, Winston," Rand said. "*We* do, don't we."

# The Language of Flowers

When Jack Ohm looked out on the world he saw it as an image on a cathode-ray tube.

For Jack Ohm perceived his mind as a room with stainless steel walls. One wall of this metal box was taken up entirely by a giant computer screen. Set against the wall to its left was a DEC VAX 11/780 hardware system. The VAX was housed in a cabinet six by fifteen feet. Its panel lights were now lit up to show that it was running the Berkeley UNIX software programme. Across the room, facing the screen, stood a single stainless steel straight-back chair. In front of this was a large desk into which were built a computer terminal and several electronic security systems. There was a PG–2000 with a camera that worked much like a vidicon tube, its 100–x–100 cell array capable of identifying a person by reading the lines on the palm of the hand; an EyeDentifyer with a Type II error rate of 0.005 per cent, able to use its binoculars to analyse the one-of-a-kind blood vessel patterns on the retinas of the eyes; an Identimat with strips of photocells to measure the geometry of the hand; plus a voice recognition system from Texas Instruments.

Jack Ohm, no doubt about it, was a *very* cautious man.

There'd been a time when Ohm was certain someone else had hacked into his computer system, an alien intelligence bent on zapping subliminal messages deep into his mind. This was shortly after he had read Vance Packard's book *Hidden Persuaders* and heard about the film *Picnic*'s 1957 screening in New Jersey.

Scientists have long known that the subconscious human mind is able to absorb information that is imperceptible to the conscious flow.

According to what Jack Ohm had heard, spliced into Kim Novak's celluloid performance in *Picnic* were split-second messages urging the audience to buy popcorn and soft drinks. As a result, it was said, the theatre refreshment stand that day was mobbed by ravenous viewers.

Jack Ohm—on hearing this—had convinced himself that *he* was the victim of a sinister computer hacker's attack upon his subconscious mind.

Since he viewed the world out there from a computer screen, was he not left wide-open to subliminal brainwashing?

Could someone not be feeding him the deadly message: "Don't be afraid of gays?"

You bet, Jack Ohm had thought.

And so it was that Ohm had spent the next few days security-sweeping the wires of his mind, searching for a hack-in that could zap and tap his brain. It was true that he had found nothing so his fears were laid to rest—at least for the moment—but just to be on the safe side against a future attack, the next day he had purchased his computerized defence. And ever since, like tonight, Jack Ohm had felt safe.

In fact *"safe"* was the buzzword of Jack Ohm's life.

"Buy you a drink?"

"Huh."

"Want another beer?"

"Oh . . . uh . . . no thanks. I haven't finished this one."

"Mind if I sit down?"

"Uh . . ."

"Don't be shy, bonar boy. Let's explore the beads."

And with that the man in the Roman toga sat down at the table.

Jack Ohm was convinced that most of the people he encountered thought of him as a nerd. His self-image was of a short, fat man who was not God's gift to women, a shy and retiring scholar with a nondescript face crowned by a balding fringe of dull brown hair and centred on weak brown eyes. But that didn't mean he didn't have his points.

For had he not been the highest ranking male in his senior year at Harvard? And had he not taken the Texaco Prize for his thesis at MIT: *Microtubules—The Cell Computer Protein Network In The Human Brain?*

Jack Ohm knew he had.

So why, he had asked himself at least a hundred times, did most people think that he should be ignored?

Most people, that is—but not this man tonight.

The man in the Roman toga was already half-cut. His breath stank of Charrington IPA. A chubby individual somewhere in his forties, he had three or four chins and a nose constructed of lumpy paste mixed with cracked blood vessels. His watery eyes were now locked on Jack Ohm's crotch and his leg was pressed against Ohm's knee.

"I saw you watching the tubs, cupcakes, from over at the bar."

The man's words were soft and heavily slurred, with a North American accent.

"Staring out the window with buff-light in your eyes. How about coming over with me and having yourself a new experience *in depth*?"

The man gave him a wink and added, "If you get what I mean."

" 'Tubs'?" Ohm said.

"Sweet thing, come on, let's quit bumping pussies. Our lady of the vapours is calling out to you. Come along with me and let's slip in the back door."

The man winked again and said, "If you get what I mean."

Jack Ohm was catching on.

When he tried to pull his knee away, the toga man moved closer.

When he turned to look out of the pub window and ignore the drunk's advances, he felt a sweaty but intimate hand brush against his balls.

"Nice basket, sonny boy. Plump accoutrements."

And when he made an attempt to get up and abandon the table, he found himself face-to-face with yet another man dressed in a Roman toga.

"Don't mind Alphonse," the new man said, a North American too. "He's bisexual. He likes *both* men and boys."

"Let me by!" Ohm said.

"Don't be afraid, son. You look a little pale. Time to bring you out, boy. I see it in your eyes."

"Change over, cutie," Alphonse said. "Boys look just

the same as girls when taken from the rear. Meet Mr
Three-Way. The man's a cherry splitter. Just what *you*
need."

"Maybe the guy's cash-ass?" Mr Three-Way said. He
looked like a football player gone to seed.

"We got money," Alphonse said.

"We'll pay to bruise your fruit."

"A real body job, son, before we flip you over."

"Hell, cupcakes, it's time to bait the hook. Getting laid
is no worse than shitting backwards."

Both men laughed as Jack Ohm broke away and headed
for the bar.

"Damn," Alphonse said. "Such nice buns."

"Forget it," Mr Three-Way grinned. "Down your beer,
sir, and let's have a steam. All boys with brown eyes
have a shitty view of life."

Jack Ohm waited at the bar until the men departed. A
woman next to him was telling a tourist from Wisconsin,
"There are only two types of beer in the world—the
English kind and the kind that everybody else drinks."

The Roman Bath was unlike any other pub in London.
It was in Cousin Lane near the Cannon Street Station,
close to where the Walbrook joined the River Thames.
Here the Roman conquerors had built their capital and
called it Londinium. The floor was made of thick glass
held up by metal trusses. The ruins of a Roman bath
were revealed by spotlights down amid the building's
foundations. Tonight, however, the crowd crammed into
the pub hid this archaeological find from Jack Ohm's
sight.

Ohm was now absorbed in reading the lead story in a
copy of today's *Express* left on the bar. The story was
about the crime in Stonegate Cemetery and New Scotland Yard's subsequent investigation. The headline shouted
"FINGERS FOUND".

So, Jack Ohm thought, fighting down his anger. Some
bastard thinks he can steal my press. Trying to copy cat
me? Well, my friend, we'll see about that.

Sitting mentally at the desk in the steel room of his
mind, Ohm reached out in front of him and punched
several buttons. One of these activated the dual remote-
control cameras that were actually his eyes. A moment
later the image on his mental wall screen slowly began to
pan the interior of the pub.

The barmaid . . . heavyset and buxom . . . flesh-coloured bra . . . uncapping a Guinness and scratching at her once-broken nose . . . how many bottles behind her . . . hanging upside down . . . glass teats of Teacher's Scotch and Lemon Hart Rum . . . of Beefeater Gin and Russian vodka waiting to be milked . . . hand-pumps with pottery handles continually in use . . . tapping an IPA or Old Peculiar off the wood . . . a murky jar of Scotch eggs sitting on the bar . . . the Lincrusta ceiling revealed above as the cameras came around . . . lots of cut and frosted glass . . . a stained-glass window . . . curved leather-covered seats arranged along one wall, joined together in order to form several shallow niches . . . two more Roman togas sitting and drinking in one of these . . . a man with his hand up under a skirt laughing in the next one . . . and then the table where Ohm had sat looking out the window before he'd been chased away.

Jack Ohm punched another button to close up the shot. Then he hit a second one to shut off the noise in the pub. Instantly total silence filled his head.

Now the cameras were tracking as he pushed through the crowd, making his way to the table that looked out on the street which ran in front of the pub. Luckily no one had taken his place since he had abandoned the chair, so he sat down beside the window once more and looked outside. A winter storm was blowing snow down Cousin Lane.

The streetlamps along the road cast an eerie bluish light. Blue-white covered the pavement and the umbrellas passing by, while red-eyed taillight monsters glared back from the moving cars. The only other colour was a sign across the street. *The Roman Steambath* it announced in garish purple neon. *Gentlemen Only* blinking under that. Then *Toga Party Every Saturday Night*.

Jack Ohm smiled. For as he sipped his beer and savoured it while staring out the window, Alphonse and Mr Three-Way entered the "tubs" across the street. They were followed by two other bundled-up men with togas under their coats. Then a delivery van arrived.

Good, Ohm thought.

The delivery van was small and of Japanese make. As it did not have the weight required to cope well with the snow, it fish-tailed and skidded slowly down the street, coming to an abrupt halt at the kerb in front of the baths.

A Pakistani delivery boy jumped down from the van and entered the building with a package under his arm. He emerged a minute later empty-handed.

Ohm watched as the lad climbed back in the van and it pulled out into the street. Then he followed the vehicle down the road on his mental computer screen. As one of the streetlamps cast its light on a side panel of the van, Ohm read the illuminated words *McGregor's East End Florist*.

Satisfied, Jack Ohm got up and quickly left the pub.

Outside the air was cold enough to chill and crack his bones, so he warmed himself around the heat of a single burning thought: Those aren't the only flowers that will arrive tonight.

## *11:19 p.m.*

Lee Gibson was trying to hail a taxi in Upper Thames Street, her collar up around her neck to protect her from the snow, her feet stamping the ground in a useless effort to keep warm, when suddenly there was a flash of white like a blinding lightning bolt. Everything seemed to come out of the ground beneath The Roman Steambath—bodies, boilers, pieces of pipe, chunks of broken tile—erupting like a volcano spewing into the air. When a leg slammed down to land in the snow within three feet of her—ripped off at the point where it had once joined someone's groin—Lee let out a scream that was loud enough to wake the dead. She screamed a second time as the streetlamps went out.

Reggie Douglas and his wife were strolling down the pavement, casually enjoying the snow on their way to Cannon Street Station, when there was a terrific bang like Concorde's sonic boom. Up ahead of them a man with a toga beneath his coat was about to enter The Roman Steambath when he spun around abruptly and sank to his knees. In the silence that followed the blast Reggie heard him groan, and saw him holding his guts in as blood poured through his hands. A second later the road was showered with metallic rain.

Across the street the windows of the pub caved in.

Flames now shot up from the baths to a height of twenty feet.

There was smoke everywhere.

Hysterical people rushed about in the falling snow, shocked and stunned and lost in the vapour that swirled about The Roman Steambath from several ruptured pipes.

Cars turned over and gore sprayed the ground.

A man in rags sat down on the kerb to bury his face in his hands.

Jack Ohm was several streets away when the bomb went off. He didn't hear the noise of the blast for the sound switch on the computer panel within the steel-walled room of his mind was still shut off. He just kept walking.

Ohm had gone to a lot of trouble to make sure the explosion would get his point across. He had packed the foundations of the baths with plastic dynamite, an adhesive and putty-like combination of nitroglycerine and nitrocellulose. Then he had connected the blasting caps to a remote-control device, which was tuned to the radio frequency of the high-tech instrument that Ohm held in his hand.

In the real world, Ohm was now walking along the street with his finger still pressed down on the button that had triggered the explosive blast.

But that's not what Jack Ohm presently *thought* he was doing.

For in his imagination he was locked away safely back home within that steel-walled room of his mind, sitting and staring at eight small hearts floating in eight glass jars.

# Whodunit

London, England
*11:46 p.m.*

*Psychiatry basically recognizes three major types of mental abnormality—psychosis, neurosis, and character disorder.*
*But you know most of this, Braithwaite said.*

*Assume I don't, Rand replied. Then we won't overlook anything important.*

*Of these, Braithwaite continued, the psychotic is the most disturbed. He would correspond to the layman's term "crazy". The distinguishing feature or symptom of psychosis is that there has been a break with reality. In other words, because of the pressure of the illness, the psychotic has replaced some important aspect of the real everyday world with a creation of his own deranged mind.*

*Schizophrenia is the most common kind of psychosis. One out of every hundred people will develop some form of this condition. Schizophrenia literally means a split mind.*

"*Split mind*" *as in the books* Sybil *and* The Three Faces Of Eve? *Rand asked.*

No, Braithwaite replied. Those are examples of the rare neurotic condition of split personality. *Only a hundred verified cases of that disorder have been reported and it rarely leads to crime. Sybil Dorsett and Chris Sizemore—Eve—are the most famous examples.*

*In split personality, what happens is this. A child suffers severe emotional and/or physical trauma within the first five years of life when its personality is forming. Because the trauma is something with which its mind cannot cope, it uses the mental technique of multiple personality to split off the traumatic experience from the general consciousness. It insulates itself by constructing a separate personal-*

41

*ity around some aspect of the upsetting experience. The new personality arising from the trauma is then left to deal with the experience and release the general mind of the "core personality" from the terror of the act with which it cannot deal. Any number of personalities may arise from the initial trauma.*

*So how does that differ from schizophrenia?* Hilary Rand asked.

*Multiple personality,* Braithwaite replied, *is not a psychosis because there is no actual break with reality, although the patient often imagines each personality as being physically different from the real self. But still there are no psychotic delusions as such, just parallel "islands of personality" stealing time from one another which results in memory gaps.*

*Schizophrenics generally do not have two or more separate personalities to flip back and forth among. They have one personality with a brain disease on top of that. The "split mind" of schizophrenia means the splitting of the basic functions of the personality, namely the separation of feeling and thought. The mind turns away from external reality toward the self, toward fantasy, and toward imagination. In some aspect it completely breaks with reality.*

*The most common form of schizophrenia is the paranoid type. The "mass murderer" is usually a paranoid schizophrenic. The "serial killer" is often either a paranoid schizophrenic or a sexual psychopath.*

*The main diagnostic symptoms of paranoid schizophrenia are as follows:*

*1. Hearing your own thoughts aloud as you think them, or hearing hallucinatory voices discussing you and commenting on your actions;*

*2. Believing that you are being controlled by uncanny powers and that your thoughts are not your own. This psychiatrists call "thought insertion". A good example is Son of Sam. David Berkowitz shot several people in New York because he thought a neighbour's dog contained the spirit of a 6000–year-old demon that ordered him to kill. Referring to the murders after his arrest he said: "It wasn't me. It was Sam working through me . . . Sam used me as a tool."*

*3. Delusional perception. A delusion is a belief that has no basis in reality but is nonetheless unshakably held despite evidence to the contrary. The classic illustration is the fellow who thinks he's Napoleon.*

*Is there any particular age at which this disease is prevalent? Rand asked.*

*No. Paranoid thinking may develop in adolescence, but usually it reaches a peak between the ages of twenty and thirty.*

*Is the cause environmental or passed on in the genes as an organic disease?*

*Both, Braithwaite replied.*

*Are psychotic delusions usually of the persecutory type?*

*Yes, he said. The schizophrenic often believes that he is being plotted against and persecuted by a particular group. Such psychotics will misinterpret reality so that everything going on around them is in some way related to them. For instance, if three men walk by a male psychotic and they all have beards he will think it prearranged to let him know that he is a fool for not growing one. Sexual anxiety and concerns about homosexuality are common. These thoughts psychiatrists call "ideas of reference".*

*The best way to imagine psychosis, I think, is to see it as stated by an American, Harry Stack Sullivan. Compare it to walking down the stairs in pitch dark and suddenly finding that the next step is missing.*

*If the Vampire Killer is psychotic how do we spot him? Rand asked.*

*That will be difficult if he's an "Imposter", the doctor replied. The "Imposter", as we call him, is a dramatic form of schizophrenic illness. He's our psychiatric version of Dr Jekyll and Mr Hyde, except that in Stevenson's story the process was externalized, whereas we are talking about transactions totally contained within the human mind.*

*The Imposter—like an actor—is not bound by a sense of his own identity, but rather assumes the role and status of any part that he may wish to play. In many respects his entire life is the wearing of a mask.*

*The danger of the Imposter is that people around him relate to the mask and not the psychotic personality beneath. "Fish see the worm, not the hook", the Chinese say.*

*It may be, Braithwaite continued, that the Vampire Killer has created an Imposter within his own deranged mind, then has psychologically assumed the role of that Imposter and subconsciously buried and forgotten the personality*

*that created the mask. Should the hidden killer ever want
to act, he takes control of the body and shuts down the
Imposter's artificial awareness until he—the unrecognized
psychotic personality—slips back into hiding once again.
At that point the awareness of the Imposter will reappear
and know nothing about what has happened while he was
shut down mentally.*

*In other words, Rand said, our man could be living a
normal life and not even know he's the Vampire Killer
himself.*

*Yes, the doctor replied. And truly be outraged by such a
preposterous suggestion.*

*Do you think our killer is psychotic? Rand asked.*

*Perhaps, Braithwaite said. Or a psychopath.*

Now as she stoked the fireplace alone in her London
flat, Hilary thought back on her discussion with Braithwaite
earlier on in the day. Outside, the wind was howling and
the snow blew in gusts. Ice crystals rapped on the win-
dowpanes like the knuckles of Jack Frost.

Hilary Rand lived in a small and intimate flat near
Shepherd Market in Mayfair. From her sitting room windows on a normal day she could see the ring of trees that
circled Crewe House in Curzon Street. The flat had been
bought with money from her father's estate.

The sitting room was in darkness with only the light
from the fireplace to enrich its antiques. Beside the hearth
was a Regency breakfront bookcase filled with volumes
on the history of Scotland Yard and archaeology. A
Victorian highbacked armchair stood next to a chess-
board set with figurines depicting the Battle of Culloden
in 1746. Spread out on a table in front of the chair was
*The Times*, folded to the crossword puzzle, and a jigsaw
all the pieces of which were entirely white. A small settee
was near the window beside a rolltop desk. Crowning the
glowing hearth, an ornate overmantel backed two pictures in silver frames.

One picture was a wedding photograph of her parents.
Rand's mother had died at Coventry during the German
bombing attack in 1940. Her father had been a Yard
detective, as had *his* father before that. Hilary had nursed
the old man to his lingering death in 1963 from Alzheimer's
disease. To this day her greatest fear was of slowly going
mad.

The second photograph was of Rand's fiancé, Philip

Moore. It had been taken three days before the car crash in which he lost his life. That too was in the summer of 1963.

As she now stood up from stoking the coal on the hearth, Rand glanced at Philip's picture and felt a familiar wash of dull grey pain. So many years, but it would never go away. It seemed like only yesterday that she had opened the door on a rainy August night to receive the shocking news from a fellow PC. Her subsequent illness, the hospital, the miscarriage of their baby—she turned away from the picture before all that came flooding back.

The summer of 1963 was the lowest point in her life.

Just as right now was the lowest point in her career.

Rand went into the kitchen and poured herself a small Drambuie. This she carried back to the sitting room and placed on a table beside the armchair. For a moment she contemplated turning on the light and reading a while—Alec Guinness's autobiography, *Blessings In Disguise*—but instead she crossed to the stereo and put on one of her favourite records. It was Ray Anthony, *The Soul of Big City Rhythm and Blues*.

As the soothing notes of the trumpet solo in "I Almost Lost My Mind" softly filled the room, Rand sank into the armchair and closed her eyes. More and more these past few months she had thought herself a fool to have buried herself in her job while the best of her life slipped by. Though she now willed her mind to drift away on the wings of the soaring trumpet, still it kept floating back to close around the Vampire Killer case. Finally Hilary Rand gave in and let it have its way.

*Psychopathy comes under your third division of character disorder, does it not?*

*It does, Braithwaite replied. In the case of the psychopath, the person afflicted with the disease—rather than developing a psychotic symptom like seeing or hearing hallucinations, or a neurotic one like the various phobias— fails to develop a normal moral sense of what is right and what is wrong. Right becomes whatever the psychopath feels like doing for his personal gratification with no concern whatsoever for its effect on anyone else. He cannot resist impulsive urges whatever they may be. The psychopath cannot learn from mistakes but repeats them again and again. Such a personality is internally cold and cal-*

lous in human relationships. That is why sadists often fit the psychopathic mould and why begging, beseeching, and imploring have no effect on them.

The important point, however, Braithwaite said, is that both the deeply-repressed psychotic and the over-controlled aggressive psychopath may appear perfectly normal on the surface but be seething with illness underneath. If either disease breaks out in murder the results can be horrific.

You allude to mutilation, Hilary Rand said.

Yes, Braithwaite replied. Neville Heath and Ian Brady are two fine examples.

Earlier I asked if you could give me a psychiatric condition to fit the facts of the Vampire Killer case. You said you could. Haematomania.

Correct, the doctor agreed. But first let me explain.

In life there is no such thing as normalcy. There is only the appearance of normalcy. As psychiatry has developed we have come to realize that the healthy and the sick mind have more in common than they do in contrast. We all have perversions to a differing degree.

A mania develops when a person's mind has upset or lost its natural balance with the appearance of normalcy. In other words, it no longer keeps its skeletons in the closet where most of us do. Instead, the mind develops an obsessive concentration upon some type of object or substance as a fetish. A fetish is any inanimate thing or nongenital part of the body that causes a habitual erotic response and is linked to sex. This we call a fixation.

Haematomania is the obsession with human blood.

It is a psychiatric condition akin to vampirism which can be found in both psychotics and psychopaths.

Examples of it are well documented.

Gilles de Rais was a French nobleman who fought with Joan of Arc. He actually drank human blood before battle in the belief that it would give him courage. Later he was involved in Black Magic practices and used the blood of young children as an invocation to the Devil. He was tried and executed in 1440 for the deaths of almost fifty victims.

Countess Elizabeth Báthory was a Hungarian noblewoman who kept hundreds of girls chained in a dungeon so she could milk them daily of blood like human cows. The woman was obsessed with the belief that blood was good for her skin so she bathed in it every morning.

Fritz Haarmann of Hanover would pick up destitute

*boys at the railway station and kill them for blood by biting them on the neck. He then sold their flesh to haus-fraus as ordinary meat in a shop below his living quarters. At his trial in 1924 more than twenty victims ranging in age from thirteen to twenty-one were mentioned. He used to enjoy carrying buckets of blood around his flat.*

*Peter Kürten—convicted of nine murders as "the Monster of Dusseldorf"—was driven to ejaculation by the sight of human blood. He considered a blood-red sunset to be an omen of good fortune. On one occasion when he was unable to immediately find a human victim he seized a sleeping swan, cut off its head and drank its blood. Just before his execution in 1931 he told Dr Karl Berg, the psychiatrist studying him, that his final pleasure would be to hear the gurgle of his own blood running into the basket as the guillotine cut off his head.*

*John George Haigh—the English acid bath murderer of the late 1940s—was also called the "Vampire Killer" by the press. He confessed to tapping a wineglass full of blood from each of his eight victims' necks, then consuming it.*

*Haigh had a blood obsession most of his life. He said it began when he was spanked by his mother with a hair-brush which broke the skin. Sucking the blood this drew off his finger, he acquired a taste for it. As a choirboy he used to sit in Wakefield Cathedral at twilight and gaze for hours at the figure of Christ bleeding on the cross. During the war he suffered a head injury that caused blood to pour into his mouth. After that he had recurring murder-inciting visions of forests spouting blood.*

*Why, Rand asked, would our killer's victims all be pre-pubescent girls?*

*That, Braithwaite replied, depends upon the source of his haematomania.*

*If our subject is in fact schizophrenic, one of the major symptoms is a turning away from the external world toward an internal world of fantasy and hallucination. This we call "autism". The fantasy content is then what rules the psychotic killer's mind and determines his choice of victim.*

*If our subject is a psychopathic sadist, then the normal sex drive has gone into reverse. His emphasis is no longer on orgasm, but now on cruelty. That's why the Moors Murderers—Ian Brady and Myra Hindley—kept tape recordings of the screams of their victims for later use. To a sadistic killer satisfaction is only obtained through destruc-*

*tion or mutilation, which need not necessarily be of a
sexual nature. Jack The Ripper is the classic example. He
savagely carved up five prostitutes in the East End of
London, removing internal organs and carrying them away.
Our case is similar in the bloodletting and the cutting out
of the hearts.*

*The important point, however, Braithwaite said, is that
serial killers of both types are often driven by a fierce
all-consuming hate. It is this hate that compels them to kill
again and again. The object of the hate—or its symbolic
stand-in—is made to suffer horrifically while the killer
savours the power of being the cause of that torment. The
murderer wants to actually feel the victim's suffering with
his own hands and experience the thrill of life being drained
away.*

That fits, Rand thought as she got up to pour a second
Drambuie.

*Modus operandi* plays an important part in police investigation. For like most of us, criminals are basically
creatures of habit. They are apt, once a particular method
has proved to be successful, to go on repeating it. That is
why the Yard keeps an MO file on certain methods of
operation—motive, technique, time, and individualistic
traits—in the PNC.

MO was also the reason why the recent graveyard
incident did not mesh with the previous acts of the Vampire Killer. For, as Rand now thought, The latest victims
are wrong.

The night before Scotland Yard had found several sites
of bloodletting in Stonegate Cemetery. The largest of
these was the clotting pool beside the open grave. But
there were also two smaller sites in the catacombs near
Egyptian Row and off in the woods leading to the western gate. Four feet from a recently chipped tombstone
that marked the location of this latter spray of blood, a
Yard detective had found three severed fingers.

The fingers were from a young woman with a minor
police record for soliciting. Fingerprints led the Yard to
identify the victim as one Sylvia Pym. The grave near
which the digits were found turned out to be that of her
mother, Celia Pym. Mother, like daughter, they discovered, had been a prostitute.

Sylvia Pym had an ongoing case before the London

courts; the social services were attempting to apprehend her eight-month-old son. According to legal records, the woman was unstable. She believed that her mother was haunting her because she had died all alone in the streets on Christmas Day two years before while Sylvia was drunk and prostituting herself. To atone for this transgression, the court records said, Sylvia went to her mother's grave every night during the twelve days of Christmas. She would arrive at precisely the time that it was thought Celia Pym had died.

It was on such a vigil the previous night that Sylvia Pym and her baby had both disappeared.

Now as Ray Anthony began the first notes of "Since I Met You Baby" soft shadows cast by the dancing flames of the fire moved around Hilary Rand. As she sipped the Drambuie her mind ticked off the differences between Sylvia Pym and the other victims in the Vampire Killer case.

1. Sylvia was in her twenties and her baby was a boy. The girls had all ranged in age between seven and eleven.

2. Pym, it would appear, was killed at the cemetery, *then* her body removed. The girls had all been abducted *before* they were slaughtered.

3. The prostitute's body had not yet turned up. Neither had her son's. The girls had all been found floating in the Thames. But then the graveyard crime had only occurred last night, so perhaps the killer needed a little more time.

4. The "Sewer Killer"—to use the name Braithwaite had coined—had left behind a top hat and a shattered hand mirror. If these were consciously left behind and not just dropped in the heat of the moment, what did the abductor intend them to mean?

Rand's stomach now began to knot in anxious tension. This she saw as a sign of her subconscious fear of failure, and of the knowledge that her days at the helm of the investigation were numbered. Such a long and public fall would finish her career, which meant the shattering of the focus of her life.

Rand took a larger sip of Drambuie. When her lower teeth touched the glass they set the rim of the crystal singing. The liqueur warmed her stomach and soothed her nerves.

Is it worry that the Vampire Killer case has struck a

dead end that makes me want to find a connection with the graveyard crime? she thought.

Is that why I would rather see Stonegate as a change in MO than as an offence committed by a different person?

Were the bodies of the butchered girls actually dumped in the water from a boat, a bridge, or the Thames Embankment? Or did they, as I now suspect, emerge from the sewer outfalls opening on the river?

Assuming the "Sewer Killer" to be a different individual raised even more questions in the detective's mind:

1. How could he use the sewer system—a vastly complicated maze of interconnecting tunnels and vaults and underground rivers—unless the abductor knew his way around down there? Did that mean he was either a sewer worker or someone with ready access to such knowledge?

2. Why carry off Sylvia Pym's corpse after she was surely dead, judging from the amount of blood the Yard had found? And why take her baby?

3. How did the killer know there would be someone in the graveyard at such a late hour in such inclement weather? Did he know the victim, or haunt the cemetery and notice Sylvia Pym's daily ritual?

4. Were the top hat and mirror meant as some sort of insane taunt at the police?

As Hilary Rand considered all this the flames dwindled to embers. The shadows that danced about on the walls began to fade away. "Troubled Mind" had come and gone, as had "Goodnight My Love", and Ray Anthony's trumpet had long since fallen silent.

All right, Rand thought, so they're different villains. Then what alternatives are there for why the Vampire Killer has stopped his crimes?

1. He (she?) has not in fact stopped killing, just stopped dumping the bodies in the river—or else they've not been found. How many thousand runaway girls are there in Britain? Some 83,000 families are homeless, 73 per cent with children. A few of those girls might have become his victims.

2. The killer has moved somewhere else or changed his MO. (Why do I keep coming back to the graveyard incident?)

3. The killer's mental illness is now in remission. Like Zodiac in San Francisco who is still around but hasn't murdered for years.

4. The killer has died, committed suicide, been committed to a mental hospital or jailed for some *other* reason. Like Jack The Ripper, or more recently the Thames Nude Killer of 1964–65.

Of these alternatives Rand thought the last the best. She knew that serial killers belong to that class of criminal that rarely stops of its own choosing. Murder becomes habitual, and each subsequent offence is easier to do. As Braithwaite had quoted this morning from a man named L. C. Douthwaite, "Murder grows by what it feeds upon."

Is suicide the reason why the Vampire Killer has stopped? Rand wondered.

Wouldn't it be ironic if my career went down the drain and the killer was already dead?

Why else have we not—

The telephone rang abruptly, jarring her from her thoughts.

She put down the Drambuie, got up, and crossed to her desk.

Four minutes later, in a rush, Hilary Rand left her flat.

# The Slaughterhouse

**Vancouver, British Columbia**
*9:46 a.m.*

Trouble was waiting for him as he broke into the slaughterhouse.

The trouble was in the form of a man six foot three with greasy blond hair shaved in a mohawk cut. A small metal skull on a chain dangled from one of his ears. He was wearing a blue jean jacket with the sleeves torn off, open over his chest to expose a massive tattoo—a scene of hell where demons were eating and torturing human beings. One look at the man told Zinc Chandler he was high on crack.

"Fuck off," Mohawk snarled, as Chandler came swiftly down the corridor hung with slabs of beef.

It was dark inside the abattoir and the smell of shed blood and decaying flesh was heavy in the air. The only light came from the moon which stabbed silver shafts through the windows high above where the walls met the ceiling. The sides of beef spiked on iron hooks cast lurking, sinister shadows.

As he came down this grisly aisle of death, Zinc Chandler loosened his jacket for access to the Smith and Wesson .38 holstered at his waist. He heard the snap of a switchblade even before he saw the knife.

Mohawk was moving fast for he was jitterbugged by the drug. Quickly raising his arm in the air, he rushed along the aisle of carcasses to engage Chandler in a fight. The razor-sharp steel of the switchblade stuck down from the base of his fist like a dagger.

Zinc Chandler was a muscular man six foot two in height and weighing 195 pounds. His powerful shoulders and large strong hands had come from working the family farm back in Saskatchewan when he was a boy. Now thirty-seven, Chandler had natural steel-grey hair that had been that colour since birth. This characteristic was responsible for his given name.

Zinc was a ruggedly handsome man with sharply-chiselled features. His eyes were the colour of his hair as was the two-inch scar along his right jaw-line. He had the look of a benign predator. Smart people sensed on meeting him that he should not be provoked, grasping instinctively that this man thought well under pressure and would be most dangerous when the knife was at his throat.

Mohawk, however, was not a smart person.

Now just three feet away, the biker was bringing the switchblade down from above his head in a forceful, plunging stab.

Chandler could not chance a shot as yet—it was too soon for that. So he slammed his heel down hard on the other man's instep, using pain to break the force of the blade's descent. He blocked the stab with his left forearm and swung his right hand in an upward arc behind the biker's arm holding the now-motionless knife. Locking his right palm over the back of his own left hand, adding the strength in his shoulders to the force of his onward motion, Zinc wrenched Mohawk's arm back until he heard a sharp *crack*! At the sound of the snapping bone he drove his right knee hard into Mohawk's groin.

The knifeman let out a shriek of pain and was crumpling toward the floor when Chandler slammed his fist down hard in a rabbit punch that finished the biker off.

At the far end of the aisle of carcasses stood a sliding glass partition beyond which a narrow, darkened corridor continued on toward the rear of the slaughterhouse. There was a closed door halfway down the hall.

Gun now drawn, Chandler yanked back the partition and moved silently down the corridor where he put his ear to the door.

He listened a moment to the conversation in the room, then satisfied the timing was right, crossed the floor and pinned his back against the opposite wall.

Pushing off with both hands, he catapulted across the hall with his right knee raised and rammed his foot hard against the wood just to one side of the knob.

As the door burst open and into the room, Chandler followed close behind and threw himself to the floor.

Eight feet in front of his eyes, a flash of yellow exploded from the muzzle of a .357 Colt Python Magnum.

The rush took hold too quick, too hard, and she knew she was overdosed.

First came a wrenching, sickening, world-turning-upside-down, poisoned-food jolt to the gut that made her want to throw up. It wasn't the feeling of coming all over—the orgasm of the stomach—that she had expected.

Then she felt a cool hand of skeletal bones slip slowly inside her rib cage and gently squeeze her heart, just enough to let her know that Death was at her side.

What's in this shit! her mind cried out—but the sound that came from her throat was no more than a moan.

Soon the room got dark around the edges as if ink were seeping into her eyes, each face, each detail blotted out beneath the spread of black. As her eyes rolled back in their sockets she glimpsed a hypodermic needle clinging to her right arm like a hungry glass leech. Then her face turned blue.

Up, up, up shot her mind, for this was a borderline fix. There was now enough smack in her veins to push her right through the ceiling between life and death itself.

Then a sudden crash of thunder made her body react with a jerk. The utter surprise of the loud *boom*! galvanized her to her feet.

Jennie Copp stood up.

Zinc Chandler had burst in upon a heroin transaction.

The room in the rear of the slaughterhouse was fifteen feet square, its plaster walls covered with posters of smiling cattle and pigs, their bodies segmented with dotted lines to show the cuts of meat. There was also a picture of two men with their arms around each other, while in the background a sulking woman was wiping one eye with a tissue. The caption for the poster read *A real man prefers beef to fish.*

The only furniture in the room was a table and three chairs. But what was on the table was worth two hundred thousand bucks.

Several small packets of fine white powder lay spread out on the surface. Beside the table was a bucket filled to the brim with blood and animal brains. One of these brains was now on the table top in a stainless steel tray, a slit through the flesh revealing another plastic packet inside. Also set out on the surface were the paraphernalia necessary for capping up heroin—a thousand Benadryl capsules emptied of their powder, the clear halves to one side, the pinks to another; jars of Manitol and Epsom salts for cutting; scales; a sifter; a rolling pin; hundreds of brightly-coloured balloons to receive the restuffed caps in bundles of twenty-five; and—strangely, Chandler thought —a gleaming butcher's cleaver.

Seated at the table to the right was the largest Chinese Zinc Chandler had ever seen, a massive Buddha of quivering flesh who would have broken a set of scales calibrated no higher than 300 pounds. A large mixing bowl was on the surface in front of him.

Jennie Copp was sitting across from the giant, one of her sleeves rolled up as a single bubble of red blood dotted her inner elbow crease. In her hand she held an empty hypodermic needle. Though in fact her age could not have been much more than twenty, junk had ravaged her face enough to make her look forty years old. Right now the glaze on her eyes told Zinc that Jennie was off somewhere several light-years from this room.

Across the table from the door sat a second man dressed in bike leathers glittering with chains. Though his body silently stated "I pump iron", his face was painted so he looked like a whore. Between eyelids shaded purple and lips smeared red, each of his cheekbones blushed with a streak of rouge. A crest stitched to his jacket read *Headhunters Motorcycle Club*.

As Chandler came crashing through the door, Leathers had grabbed the .357 Colt Python Magnum stuck down the front of his pants.

The first shot fired off in haste missed Zinc's head by inches. It blew a chunk of plaster from the wall beyond the smashed-in door.

As the muzzle flared a second time, Chandler threw himself into a body roll off to his left.

Leathers' second shot ripped a hole in the floor the size of a golf ball, the wood erupting in splinters where Chandler's head had been. The sound of the Magnum filled the room like a blast from a cannon. Jennie Copp jumped from her chair in shock at the roar of the dual explosions.

In reflex, Zinc had rolled so the woman was now

between his position and that of the gunman. Leathers' third shot directly at Chandler's head was intercepted by Jennie's body. The slug slammed into her side, hit her spine, veered off its original trajectory, and blew out an exit wound of blood and gristle and bone. The force of the blast hurled her body right overtop of Zinc.

Now on his stomach, Chandler pulled off four rapid shots from his .38.

Leathers was rising to his feet as the first slug caught him above the groin, the second in the stomach, and the third in the heart. The fourth and final shot took the biker in the head.

Leathers crashed back against the wall, smashing the only window as Buddha lumbered towards Chandler with the meat cleaver gripped tight in his ham-hock fist.

Hit his head, Zinc thought, or this guy won't go down. It would take a .44 just to cut the flab.

Buddha was upon him before he could aim the .38.

The fist with the cleaver was rising as he grabbed Chandler's gun hand and yanked him from the floor. Zinc got off a single shot that hit the giant Chinese in the chest. Totally ignoring it, Buddha wrenched Chandler's hand away so the muzzle of the pistol was pointing at the wall.

Reaching across with his free right hand, Chandler grabbed the Smith and Wesson from his left.

"Cocksucker," Buddha hissed, spitting in his face.

With a quick and powerful right jab Zinc punched the pistol barrel into the man's open mouth, ramming down hard on the gun grip to raise the muzzle angle.

You son of a bitch, he thought. Suck on this.

Then he pulled the trigger.

As thick as the giant's skull was, it wasn't thick enough to stop a mouth-shot blast from the Smith. The .38 slug ripped up through the bone pan that cradled Buddha's brain, tearing the soft grey tissue before it burst out through the crown of his head amid a spray of splintered skull.

Chandler jerked back not a moment too soon as the cleaver dropped from Buddha's fist to *thunk* into the floor. Now released from the giant's grip, Zinc sank to the ground as the massive weight of the Chinese slowly levered back.

The man hit the table behind him sending the mixing

bowl full of junk and cut spinning from its surface. The
air in the room whitened like a haze of powder snow
while the floor turned red as with a crash Buddha flattened the bucket of gore beside the table. A spew of
animal brains and blood gushed around Zinc Chandler.

"Fuck," Zinc gasped. Then he sat up on the floor and
let the tension dissipate.

Seventeen years on duty with the Royal Canadian
Mounted Police, and tonight was only the second time
he'd been forced to fire his gun.

As the fingers of Death let go of his spine Inspector
Zinc Chandler's hands began to shake.


## London, England
### *Sunday January 5, 1:10 a.m.*

When Hilary Rand arrived in Cousin Lane the Anti-
Terrorist Squad was having problems.

First the street was in darkness because the power lines
had blown. Then the portable arc lights brought in by the
Yard were not sufficient in number to cover the area.
And finally the snow and wind were blowing so fiercely
the cops could not lay down the usual grid with a 200
metre radius to guide a systematic search of the blast
debris for forensic clues. In fact the storm was so bad
that Rand had been forced to travel here by tube.

Two men bundled in overcoats were conversing outside a pub with the windows blown in. Large tumbling
white flakes were rapidly transforming them into animated snowmen. One was with the Special Branch and
the other the Murder Squad. As they spoke their breath
plumed in the freezing night air like comic dialogue bubbles. Both men turned toward Rand as she came through
the snowfall, shivering with the cold.

"Hilary."

"Jim. Derick."

"Chief."

"Not the IRA?"

"Doubt it," the Special Branch man said. "In light of
what has happened."

"What's all this about flowers, Derick? I'm a little too
old for secret admirers."

Detective Inspector Derick Hone clutched the throat of his overcoat in a feeble effort to keep warm. He was approaching middle age and plagued by baldness. Whenever discreetly possible, Hone wore a hat. Tonight he was wearing a fur cap of Canadian beaverskin.

"Shortly before I rang you, a bouquet of flowers arrived at HQ.

"When I read the accompanying message I telephoned the proprietor of the florist shop that sent them. His name is Alan McGregor. McGregor's East End Florist.

"Mr McGregor said that in Friday's post he received several ten pound notes and a written request to send two bouquets of flowers tonight. The letter was signed by one Elaine Teeze, a woman unknown to the proprietor.

"The first bouquet, he was told, must contain trefoil and be sent to The Roman Steambath in Cousin Lane at 10:30 p.m. on Saturday night.

"The second must contain Hydrangea and arrive at a given street address shortly after that. The order did not specify this address as New Scotland Yard.

"Mr McGregor was unable to obtain either plant at this time of year so he substituted as best he could.

"It was while I was chatting to him that the shout came in on this bombing at The Roman Steambath in Cousin Lane. The same Roman Steambath as the destination for the first bouquet. That's when I rang you."

Detective Chief Superintendent Hilary Rand frowned and shook her head. "Were notes to be sent with the flowers enclosed with the instructions to the shop?"

"Yes," Hone replied. "McGregor received the tenners, the order and delivery instructions, plus two sealed cards to be delivered with the flowers. The second bouquet was not directed to a personal designate. Just an address. HQ had to open the card to see whom they were for."

"Where's the card now?"

"On its way to the lab. But I have a photocopy."

Reaching into his coat pocket, the Detective Inspector removed a sheet of paper which he handed to Rand. The man from Special Branch shone his pocket torch on the note so the DC Supt could read its contents:

> Hilary—
>     Kill em all
>         Jack

# The Outsider

"This guy Chandler. He's fucked up before."

"If he had, Cal, we wouldn't have put him on the job."

"Don't bullshit me, Burke. I've read his file. What do you call Mexico ten years ago?"

"That wasn't a fuck-up."

"Ah, come on. His partner was shot six times in the back of the head. That sounds like a major fuck-up to me. Chandler missed the meet."

"That was because of the actions of one of *your* colleagues back in Ottawa."

"Sure. Shift the blame to us."

"Your man made them vulnerable. He should have known that a Mexican cop might be on the take. What the hell was he doing contacting the Mexican police? The U.S. Drug Enforcement Agency was coordinating that one."

"Who says that's the way it went down?"

"Look, a Mexican cop gave Chandler the wrong time, didn't he? Zinc missed the meet and his partner got shot. Your boys were the ones who brought in the Mexican bulls."

"You ever been to Mexico, Burke? You ever actually *worked* with those people? They run their police the same way they do their telephone system. It could have been a simple misunderstanding."

"That's crap, Cal. We've both seen the Department of Justice directive. You know the information in it wasn't the same as the Mexican cops passed on."

"That's according to Chandler. Maybe *he* blew it and later said that to cover his tracks. I'd say this effort with Hengler shows he's a hothead. *And* a fuck-up."

"Zinc's a good cop."

"Good cops don't tube million-dollar drug busts to save some burnt-out junkie."

"You don't know the job, Cal. The force can't keep informants without some loyalty. You can't just sacrifice them to the so-called 'greater cause'. Loyalty is currency in the pocket of a cop. The same with a partner. Zinc knows that."

"Is that how you justify his little revenge sortie into the Mexican jungle in 1975? Loyalty? *Loyalty?* His partner Ed Jarvis was already dead. I call such an escapade 'settling the score'. *And* he could have blown *that* bust in the process."

"Zinc's a man of principle."

"Sure. Tell me another. Loyal to his partner. Let it cost the bust. Loyal to this junkie. Who cares if a million taxpayers' bucks get flushed down the toilet. Loyalty can be a drawback in a cop."

"Fuck off, Waechter. You just don't understand."

Cal Waechter was a Crown prosecutor with the federal Department of Justice. A short slight man with curly blond hair and wire-rim glasses, he was considered the local expert on the law of wiretaps. A few years ago Ottawa passed the Protection of Privacy Act. The stated intention of this statute was to insulate Canada's citizens from unjustified police electronic intrusion. What in fact occurred, however, was just the opposite as wiretaps mushroomed. Set something down in black and white and cops will use it to the absolute limit.

Cal Waechter used the law to the limit to further his own career. For Waechter had made a cottage industry out of wiretaps.

"Let's back-burner Zinc for a moment," the Crown attorney said. "Give me an update re the bugs on Hengler's phones."

"Still negative on drugs, positive on films."

"Damn. Once again the provincial boys get all the luck. Even if it's a chickenshit porno bust."

"You're a bitter man, Cal."

"And you're pretty bloody blasé, my friend, for a Mountie Superintendent."

"Bitter and full of crap."

"Oh, is that so? Well let's run the laundry through again and see what dirt comes out."

Burke Hood had been a Horseman for twenty-nine years. He was a stiff-lipped man who looked like the Duke of Edinburgh, the sort of cop who thought that *every* lawyer was a weasel.

The Superintendent had once been told by a detective with the NYPD that there are only three types of criminal attorney: The Old Farts, who are cast in the Clarence Darrow mould; rapidly-aging artifacts who still pull at suspenders though belts hold up their pants. The White Shoes, or slick types, in blue three-piece pin-striped suits; the sort of shark for whom the law is a big-money business. And The Punk Rockers, post-Vietnam/Watergate kids who inherently know the system sucks and there ain't no rules in a knife-fight.

Burke Hood thought Cal Waechter was the bureaucratic version of a slick White Shoes.

"Okay, Burke," Waechter said. "Let's wash the laundry.

"Point one, we know Ray Hengler is deeply into drugs. We're not talking Number Three Red Chicken here, or crap like that. His stuff is China White, plain and simple. 92 per cent pure.

"Point two, we know his junk is middled by the Headhunters cycle gang. We also know Hengler is into porno flicks. VPD Vice say the rumour is he actually produced a snuff film late last year. On that they've no hard evidence, but he's before the courts on other assorted fuck-film beefs.

"Point three, as yet we've been unable to connect Ray Hengler to the cycle gang.

"And Point four, without that we can't bust him for drugs.

"So what do we do, eh? Call in the Midas Top Guns? Call in The Man From Glad? No, we call in *me*.

"Working with the provincial boys, I get a joint porno/drug tap sucked onto Hengler's phones. That gets us lots of skin flick crap but sweet fuck-all for drugs.

"So what do we do, eh? Call in the U.S. Marines? The Texas Rangers? Batman and Robin? No, the ball goes to you to produce the perfect undercover to break into Hengler's scam. And who do you come up with? Why, Zinc Chandler. He's our man.

"So Zinc flies in from . . . where was it, Burke? London? Yeah, London. The Man From Special X. What do I know, eh? You're the Mountie boys. It's your type of game. All I've got is my ass on the line and about a million tax bucks tied up in this thing. Who am I, eh?

"Anyway, into town comes Zinc as a bucks-for-drugs-big-spender. He sniffs around and somehow gets onto this junkie, Jennie Copp. Seems Jennie gives good head to some member of the gang—though I thought the Head-hunters were all supposed to be fruits.

"Jennie lets Zinc know that maybe she can help him. That she's got connections. But later she turns and gets cold feet. Smells him for a cop, huh? So he twists her arm.

"How'm I doin', Burke? I got a bing. I got a bong. What say I try for another bing?

"By now Zinc has Jennie dead on smack possession. Not to mention a couple of traffickings. Jail time, baby. Poor junkie chick squirming around on the floor. So why not be smart instead and play out this little charade?

"Jennie's a bright girl, of course, cause junkies have no choice. Yes, she'll tell Zinc when the deals go down and let him get to Hengler. She'll be a body-roller for the Mounted Police. Then after it's all over, she can fly away. No charges. New name. Mountie relocation and a pay cheque every month.

"Look, Burke, the girl knew what she was buying and she made her own decision. You and I will never know exactly what went wrong. She was the tester for the drugs cause none of the gang was using. That's how Zinc knew she'd hear about the shipments. When the call went out for a test, the bikers had new product. Maybe the gang had already decided that she knew too much. In any event, word goes out the broad is to be terminated. Dead meat, eh?

"Now, Burke, I'm not the cold-hearted asshole you think. But I do believe that in this life you get what you pay for.

"Zinc, by then, through Jennie Copp, had already made contact with the cycle gang. Some of the drugs coming in yesterday were to be sold to him. He could then have worked the size of the sales right up to Hengler.

"Jennie Copp had done her bit when she gave him the introduction. Sure, Zinc might not have known when a *particular* load of junk was coming in, but that was irrele-vant cause we weren't ready to move in yet. Not without Hengler. So yesterday all his meet with the broad could possibly have done was get him useless information that—"

"Fuck you, Waechter!" Hood interrupted. His face was now cherry-red and moving on to purple. I've had just about enough of this posturing prick, he thought. "Hengler might have showed when the drugs were being capped!"

"No way!" Cal Waechter snapped in reply. "Hengler's too well insulated to blow it all like that."

"Oh sure! Would *you* leave a junk investment that size in undependable hands? Even Al Capone didn't cut himself off from the hard product of his trade. Drugs do not mix with trust."

The lawyer shook his head.

"What the fuck does that mean, Burke, in the larger scheme of things? Jennie Copp had already told our boy Zinc that a deal was going down soon at the slaughterhouse. So what if he didn't know just *when* that deal would be? With the information he already had Chandler could have suggested that you set up a surveillance. And we would then have seen Ray Hengler if he'd showed.

"So why the fuck does Chandler go and give away the ballgame? Because he'd set up a useless meet and then when Copp didn't show he began to suspect that something might be wrong? Because he went to the slaughterhouse on his own and found her purse dumped on the ground outside near one of the parked cars? Because he thought *maybe* she might have herself a little trouble inside? Is that why he burst into the place, killed two people outright and injured another, blew a million-dollar drug bust—*and* in the process got Jennie killed as well?

"We were damn close, Burke. So damn close. And then this fucker tubes the show all for some two-bit, burnt-out junkie in way over her head. No matter how you cut it she was not worth the bust!"

A look of disgust crept into the Mounted Policeman's eyes.

"You're right about one thing, Cal," he said. "I do think you're an asshole. Chandler, plain and simple, is a damn good cop."

"Not yesterday he wasn't."

"I think he was. Just like he was a good cop in '75 when he smashed the Mexican Brown Connection and—"

There was a sharp knock at the closed door to Burke Hood's office.

Inspector Zinc Chandler was standing outside.

## Monday January 6, 7:02 a.m.

¡Hijo de tu puta madre! ¡Trinquinuela! *one snarls.*

¡Hijo de la chingada! *another replies, as Zinc Chandler watches from his hiding place in the bushes fifty feet away.*

The Mexican who feels cheated at cards is now rising from the table, a machete in his hand. He is tall and thin with wide Indian cheekbones and a shaggy handlebar moustache dangling under his beak of a nose. His upper face is lighter than his lean tanned jaw, for his eyes are masked from the sun by the shade of a large sombrero.

The other man sits perfectly still at the table opposite him, cards in one hand and tequila in the other, squinting at his adversary trying to stare him down.

Slit Eyes puts his cards on the table and slowly reaches out to place one hand on the rotting stump of a guayacan tree. He raises the tequila to his lips and snaps the fiery liquid straight down his throat. Finished, he too picks up his machete.

Slit Eyes, Chandler observes, is much brawnier than most of the local men. His facial features are of Aztec ancestry: prominent cheekbones, thin-lipped mouth, long black hair, and dark close-set eyes. A sweat-soaked guayabera clings to his frame while a snakeskin bandana circles his forehead.

Chandler now uses binoculars to study the two men. He runs the glasses around the outline of each Mexican's body, checking for a telltale bulge to indicate a weapon. Satisfied that they are armed solely with machetes, he sweeps the binoculars twenty-five feet to the right.

A third man is leaning against a large zapote tree, taking a standing siesta with an automatic rifle cradled in his arms. He has yet to stir from slumber at the sound of Sombrero's anger.

This man's features are Spanish, not Indian; his colouring much lighter and his skin a mass of freckles. His unshaven jaw is covered with spiky orange stubble. Two other rifles are leaning against the trunk of the zapote tree that supports his weight.

Zinc Chandler assesses the scene.

He knows that you have to be careful with what you think you see in the jungle: that seeing in the jungle is an art to be learned. For here light filters through a ceiling of dense, thick foliage overhead to form small dazzling patches *of brilliance against a background of deep shade. In turn this fragmented sunshine breaks up the jungle shapes into random patterns of dark and light the same way that army camouflage is meant to do. As a result you might see things that really are not there—or even worse, miss things that actually are.*

*Zinc must be sure the men who killed Ed are only three in number.*

*The colours of the jungle are too intense to be real— greys and browns in the trunks of the trees; reds and yellows in the rotting fallen leaves; cool greens in the underbrush and in the epiphytes; bleached greens high above in the canopy of branches. What strikes him most, however, is the weird jungle silence.*

*He studies the undergrowth to seek out the presence of a fourth hidden man. Satisfied when he finds no one he turns his attention back to the three Mexican drug-runners. Now lying prone on the ground, he rolls slightly to one side to remove his .45. He fingers off the safety and brings the pistol from his waist to a point directly in front of his eyes, lining the muzzle-sight up with the heart of the man who is holding the automatic rifle.*

*Clang!* The sound of steel on steel ripples through his thinking as Slit Eyes and Sombrero clash in a fight. Machetes flash in anger, reflecting glints of sun.*

*Red Beard jerks from slumber at the noise of the weapons, dropping the automatic rifle to his waist.*

*Zinc grips the .45 outstretched in both his hands, elbows steadying.*

*Then he pulls the trigger and his world goes mad.*

*For suddenly Red Beard is no longer a light-skinned Mexican, but rather his partner Ed with six red holes through his head. When the shot from Zinc's gun strikes Ed's face it shatters into pieces, leaving a bloody maw that shrieks,* Chandler, you bastard. You killed me!

*No,* Zinc whispers.

*Yes,* his mind replies.

*Now Slit Eyes and Sombrero are running toward Chandler, each wielding a cutlass as if they are two pirates intent on plundering him.*

*The .45 bucks and bucks again, roaring in his ears, as both men tumble backward, crashing to the ground.*

*Then Slit Eyes rolls over and laughs at him as . . .*

*. . . as his headband comes alive.*

*Chandler freezes in disbelief. He breaks out in a sweat
and his heart begins to pound. From high in the leafy
canopy comes the shrill of a cicada. The hum of a thousand mosquitoes is electric in the air. Sombrero and Slit
Eyes are bubbling blood that soaks into the ground, while
within the* hissss *of the headband snake is Jennie Copp's
raspy voice accusing,* Chandler, you bastard. You killed
me too!

*No,* Zinc whispers.

*Yes,* his mind replies.

*Now the snake is moving and slithering his way, ever so
slowly uncoiling from around Slit Eyes' head. Paralysed,
Zinc watches as it slips across the ground, knowing he
should shoot it but unable to raise his hand. The .45 seems
to weigh at least a hundred pounds.*

*The snake is a bone-tail, a* rabo de hueso. *It raises its
russet brown head to expose a belly that is dirty ivory
white. There are black Vs down its spine and its tail is
pinched out to form a thin bony spike.*

*Zinc closes his eyes as he feels the reptile bite.*

*Yes,* he whispers in assent. *Your deaths belong to me.*

*Pain surges from his bitten leg into his vital organs,
making his heart race while his skin turns clammy cold.
He feels his body betray him as his blood bursts its bounds,
both flash-flooding his mouth and trickling from his nose,
then sweating out through his skin as*

"Jesus!" Chandler gasped, and he sat up in bed.

It took him several seconds to realize just where he
was, a short unsettling interval in which his heart continued to beat wildly in his chest and rivulets of perspiration
dripped from his face. Then as the horrid dream began to
fade from his mind, he swung his legs out of the covers
and stumbled to his feet in an effort to orient himself.

Zinc was up on the eighth floor of the Westin Bayshore
hotel.

Glancing at his watch he thought, *I slept thirteen hours.*

Then clad in only pyjama bottoms he crossed to the
window, yanked back the curtains and opened the balcony door.

The sounds of Vancouver coming to life quickly assailed his ears: the garbled roar of a seaplane taking off
from the Inner Harbour, drowning the chug of tugboat
engines idling out on the water; the swish of morning
traffic on the causeway through the park; the sea-gulls

squawking above the crunch of joggers' shoes on the gravel footpath eight floors below.

Grabbing the blanket from the bed, Chandler wrapped it around his shoulders and dialled for room service.

As he listened to the phone ring he ran his hand across the stubble on his face. Even through the blanket, the cool sea breeze from the window had him shivering sharply as his sweat evaporated. Fumbling through the pockets of his shirt draped over a nearby chair, he found that once again he was out of cigarettes.

A warm efficient voice answered the phone.

Zinc ordered: "Coffee. Black . . . and a pack of Benson and Hedges."

Then he hung up the receiver and walked back to the balcony.

A chill snap in the morning breeze slapped him across the face, making his eyes water. He squinted against the sunlight and willed himself to relax. His body was stiff and his muscles ached from over-sleep, but in spite of all that heavy rest he felt as drained as he had the day before.

Across the Inner Harbour stood the majestic North Shore mountains with their peaks of dazzling snow. The morning sun was breaking through the low Pacific cloud to splash the Lions and Cypress Bowl with streaks of orange and gold. Sun dogs flashed and sparkled off random ice crystals high up on the ski slopes.

The grey-green sea at the foot of the mountains rippled, bobbing the boats like Halloween apples in a barrel. Lions Gate Bridge took a step across the narrows to span the mouth of the harbour, with one foot on the North Shore and the other in Stanley Park.

Chandler was interrupted by a loud knock at the door.

Zinc had registered in this room when he was still undercover as a well-to-do high-roller. It was here the Headhunter bikers first made telephone contact with him, so although he was sure that outside the door was a waiter from Room Service—still, with what had gone down at the slaughterhouse on Saturday evening, he couldn't be too careful.

Chandler gripped his .38 beneath the blanket as he opened the door, standing to one side away from the obvious line of fire.

A pimple-faced kid with a silver tray bearing coffee and cigarettes looked in at him.

"Your breakfast, sir," he said.

Outside, Zinc thought. That's what I am. I feel as if I've lived my life on the outside looking in.

Thinking back, he turned the shower on full-force and closed his eyes.

First Ed Jarvis. Now Jennie Copp.

At least your partner Ed had some sort of choice. He took on the danger when he joined up with the force. What choice did Jennie have? You'd nailed her to the wall.

*You—you're a cop! . . . Oh, Jesus Christ!*

*Keep your voice down, Jennie. If other people hear, the threat's to you. Not me.*

*But a cop!* she whispered. *Oh my God!*

*You act like you've never been around the block before.*

*Not like this.*

*Well, then it's time you learned.*

*Please, Zinc. Don't let—*

*Shut up and listen. You've got two options. Either I bust you right now and you'll sweat cold turkey in a cell till your guts squirm up your throat, followed by one, two, three years, thirsting for the needle. Or I let you go and you work for us. Give me what I want and you get relocated. Screw me around and I'll put the word out on the street—Jennie Copp's a rat of her own free will.*

*You—you wouldn't do that.*

*Don't bet on it.*

*I don't feel so good,* she said, turning away. Then she threw up on the cafe floor until Chandler got up and pushed her out the door.

*Zinc, I've got to see you.*

*One week later. Day before last.*

*What's the matter, Jennie?*

*I'm afraid.*

*Does the deal go down tonight, just as you sus—*

*Help me, Zinc! Please!*

And the phone went dead.

*Pow!*—an hour later Jennie takes a .357 slug to the heart. Because—go on, admit it—*you* set her up.

First Ed Jarvis. Now Jennie Copp.

Wallow in shit most of your life and some of it's going to rub off.

The full force of the shower would not wash his guilt away.

*8:43 a.m.*

Chandler was having breakfast in a rundown greasy spoon near the Public Safety Building at 312 Main.

Police work in this city is not done by the RCMP as it is in most of the suburbs. Vancouver has the VPD, its own private force. Zinc was waiting for one of the city bulls working out of Vice, a man named Howlett who had promised to bring him the Hengler wiretaps.

The detective was late.

There was nothing quite as depressing to Chandler as morning on skid row. At the table next to him sat two longshoremen coming off a drunk, talking in hoarse whispers that were barely audible above the sizzle of breakfast cooking in the kitchen. One wore a tartan hunting hat and the other a baseball cap. Both were dressed in lumberjack mackinaws and Dayton boots with steel-covered toes. They were discussing the pros and cons and cost of getting laid.

Close-by, across a carpet black with grime from the streets, a wino with orange-stained fingertips slouched, rolling a cigarette. His unshaven face was a road map of cracked blood vessels, his eyes blue puffy bags weighed down by sagging cheeks. He was waiting for that time of day when his stomach could handle the bottle of Aqua Velva shaving lotion in his pocket.

"Know why Aqua Velva comes in three colours?" Zinc heard one of the longshoremen ask, glancing at the bottle.

"No," the other replied.

"So the bums on the row can mix B52s."

Out beyond the window was a jungle of broken dreams. A line of derelicts huddled in hand-me-down overcoats, waiting outside a welfare door that was just beyond the Courts. A tired old man pulled two makeshift carts along the sidewalk in front of the Public Safety Building, each waggon filled with the knick-knacks that comprised his worldly possessions. A weirdo on the corner was screaming at himself.

"Want more coffee?" the Chinese waitress asked.

Zinc nodded his head.

As she filled his cup he stared at the spoon in his hand. His reflection in its concave bowl was upside down. Just like you, he thought.

The longshoreman nearest Chandler cracked another joke.

"Hear about the woman who went on a date with ten fishermen?"

"No," his friend said.

"She came home with fifty bucks. And a red snapper."

The door to the restaurant opened and a man walked in, followed by two glass-eyed kids with a ghetto-blaster blaring "Desperado". From its speakers The Eagles were telling Zinc and everybody else to let somebody love them before it's too late.

Howlett approached the table and sat down opposite him. He was the Robert Mitchum type, sleepy eyes and all, but with two fingers missing from one of his hands.

"I'm late," the VPD cop said. "But what can you do? You know how it is?"

"Sure," Zinc replied.

He looked at the binder of wiretaps Howlett was holding in his good hand.

"These are the bugs transcribed up to late yesterday. Hengler's office, home, and Fantasy Escort Service which is one of Hengler's fronts."

Zinc took the binder. "Thanks," he said.

"You got a real hard-on for this guy. Wanta tell me why?"

"Unfinished business," Zinc replied.

## 10:59 a.m.

One block from the restaurant in a rundown Main Street room, Chandler sifted through the binder Howlett had given him. The wiretap conversations concerned film and video deals, escort arrangements, but nothing on drugs.

Zinc put the binder down and moved to the window that looked out across Main Street at the Courthouse doors. A beefy cop named Caradon sat stakeout with a mounted camera and telescopic lens focused on the sidewalk in front of the Courts. Aged somewhere in his late thirties, Caradon had long reddish-brown hair, a well-kept beard, and a taste for junk food. Egg McMuffin wrappers were scattered about him on the scuffed linoleum floor.

"Anything of interest?" Chandler asked.

"Just a black hooker with a nice set of tits and a truly spectacular ass."

"But no sign of him?"

"Not yet," Caradon replied as a third man entered the room.

Within the Royal Canadian Mounted Police there are several secret units. Special O is one of these, and so is Special I.

Special O is short for Special Observation. The ten men who make up its central core are police surveillance experts. They talk in a language of terms like "front tail", "side tail", "flood pattern" and "three-car plan". These are techniques refined and tested by British, American, and Israeli Intelligence networks. The men of Special O, however, have a few tricks of their own: for computers, homers, satellite bounces, infrared cameras, and gyroscopically-mounted binoculars are their stock in trade. It is not uncommon for Special O to send a hundred members out after a single suspect, and more if necessary. Bill Caradon was a cop with Special O.

The man who just entered the room was Ken Behnes of Special I. A good-natured cop with large ears, blue eyes, and sandy blond hair, he was raised in the Yukon and served in the Arctic before being retrained and posted to Vancouver. Special I—short for Special Investigation—controls the electronic ears of the force.

"Moisture's sealed the window shut," Behnes said. "That means we can't use the parabolic mike. I tried to find a place downstairs where I'd not be seen. It's too risky, Zinc."

"Then let's do without it," Chandler said.

"What do you hope to get from this guy? I peg the hog queens as strictly lower level. With what went down in the slaughterhouse on Saturday night, don't you think Hengler is going to run for cover?"

"Yeah," Chandler said. "But he won't sever his one remaining link to the motorcycle gang until he's sure we don't suspect him. That sort of loose thread can't be ignored if he wants to stay in business and out on the street. We can make a few mistakes. He can make just one."

"So how'll it go down?" Caradon asked, keeping his attention focused through the mounted camera lens.

"I want a picture of the guy when he comes out the door. If Hengler's lawyer comes out with him, get him in the shot. Then set up a visual surveillance on Hengler's video business, his home, and Fantasy Escort Service. Photos of everyone going in or coming out. And while you're at it, tap the lawyer's phone."

Ken Behnes whistled. "That's dangerous, Zinc. Lawyer-client privilege."

"Not if the lawyer himself is criminally involved. Besides, I'm not looking for evidence. I'm looking for a lead."

"It's your case," Behnes said. "And *your* ass in the wringer."

"I'll take the chance," Zinc replied.

Caradon sat up sharply and began snapping pictures. "They just came out," he said.

As a cockroach scurried along the windowsill, Chandler trained a pair of binoculars on the two men who were now standing in front of the Courthouse doors. One held a barrister's briefcase in his gloved hand and wore an expensive dark ranch mink coat with matching Russian Cossack-style fur hat. The second man, hair cut in a mohawk, shivered inside a black leather jacket.

Zinc could see their lips move as their breath froze in the air. He could see the stubble where Mohawk's hair had grown a little during his brief stint in the city jail. He could see the outline of the broken arm in a sling beneath the biker's leather jacket. For Zinc had now penetrated their world as he waited on the outside.

Someone must pay for Jennie Copp, Chandler thought. And Hengler, I don't see why it should be just me.

# Water Foul

London, England
*Tuesday January 7, 4:25 a.m.*

H. P. Lovecraft's collected works lay on the cellar floor, one volume open at his story "The Call Of Cthulhu".

From behind the closed Poe mirror/door that led to the sewers came a faint stench of shed blood and rotting human flesh.

The hum of a generator vibrated in the basement room, the walls washed blue with the flickering light cast by a TV screen.

The Ghoul punched his VCR to "hold" when the tape of the Hitchcock movie reached the scene where a farmer was sprawled in the corner of a bedroom.

The cellar wall beyond the television screen was plastered with a collage of five hundred overlapping posters, pictures, and film stills of horror fantasy.

At the centre of this collage was a large painting of a monster with an octopus-like head whose face was a mass of slimy, gelid, many-tentacled feelers.

The monster was Great Cthulhu—Lovecraft's vulval creation. His Freudian vaginal nightmare representing a young boy's castrating mom.

When The Ghoul glanced up from the TV screen at the picture of Great Cthulhu, his lips whispered the single word, "Mother."

*7:11 a.m.*

Edwin Chalmers QC was thinking about his mistress and trying to forget his wife.

Thinking about Molly was an easy thing to do, for he had just spent the last eight hours in the sack with her,

73

drinking champagne from her bellybutton and from the
deep valley that ran between her science-fiction breasts,
playing a hundred other games that sprang from Molly's
delicious Cairo-sewer mind. Forgetting Florence, however, was *not* an easy matter.

Edwin Chalmers QC was a thin and meticulous man,
wearing a suit from Savile Row beneath a Burberry overcoat. A white silk scarf was looped about his neck while a
mink hat purchased in Moscow adorned his oversized
head. His clothes reflected the fact that he was the senior
counsel in chambers dealing with lucrative civil actions.

Chalmers had told his wife that he was having dinner
at the Middle Temple, one of the Inns of Court which
have been a preserve for lawyers since the fifteenth century. He had said he might be late, but not this late. So
now he stood on the Victoria Embankment with the Inns
of Court before him and the Thames at his back, with his
balls empty and his belly full of wine, concerned that
Florence might suspect. . . . no, might *accuse* him outright of philandering.

Lawyer though he was and therefore used to such
things daily, even Edwin Chalmers QC did not feel up to
flinging the bullshit necessary to mount his own defence.
So turning away from the spiked iron railing which ran
around the Inns of Court, he meandered along the Embankment, trying to think of an excuse that Florence
might swallow without a gag reflex.

The fact he was piss-drunk certainly didn't help.

Dawn was breaking in the east and London was now
coloured a brilliant bronze. To Chalmers' right the river
was a shimmering molten flow. Up ahead both Tower
Bridge and St Paul's dome were blinding to his eyes.

The snow which had fallen on Saturday still lingered
on the ground in dirty white pockets. This morning,
however, the air was warmed by the weak rays of the sun
so the earth gave off great breaths of mist as if from a
thousand frozen, buried lungs.

Chalmers stumbled along the river bank, still lost in
worried thought, moving from one veil of mist into another, cloaked in the eerie atmosphere created by gnarled
and barren branches reaching down to strangle him from
the plane trees to his left, watched silently by the black
cast-iron serpents that wound around the lampposts on

the retaining wall to his right. His umbrella tapped the paving stones in counterpoint to his stagger.

Chalmers passed the black hulls and white bridgehouses of *H.M.S. Chrysanthemum* and *H.M.S. President* moored to the bank of the Thames. He puffed up the sloping ramp toward Blackfriars Bridge with its squat red pillars and its span of white latticework and bright blue arches, the skeletal form of a double-decker bus now moving across the blazing ball of the eastern sun. He passed a concrete blockhouse pumping station jutting out of the water, the pilings supporting its wooden dock green with water slime. He carefully made his way down the stairs to the Blackfriars underpass, then weaved in underneath the bridge itself. The noise of light traffic crossing the span seemed amplified down here as his umbrella tap-tap-tapped in syncopation with his drunken stagger. He was closing on the pilings of the train bridge up ahead . . . when a strangely disembodied voice cried out, "My God! I don't believe it!"

Edwin Chalmers QC stopped dead in his tracks.

He looked as far ahead as he could see along the underpass, but there was no one there.

He turned and searched behind him, but he was still alone. Off in the distance Old Scotland Yard's spires were silhouetted against the sky beyond Waterloo Bridge.

Old boy, you're soused, Chalmers thought. You're hallucinating.

Perplexed, he crossed to the Embankment wall and peered over the side.

Twenty-five feet below him at the base of the stone-block bank was a rocky, debris-laden portion of the Thames river-bed. It stretched eight feet from the foot of the wall to the water's edge and was hidden from view of the river traffic by the superstructure of Blackfriars Bridge. The bed of the Thames was only exposed during the lowest low tides.

Standing on the stones below looking back upstream through a pair of binoculars was an excited young man wearing a blue knitted cap. Chalmers could not see his face, just the top of his head.

The young man looked up suddenly and called out to the lawyer, "Thank God, I heard you walking by. Come down quickly. I need you as a witness."

"What *are* you talking about?" asked the barrister, frowning.

"You can't see it. It's under the pier."

"*What* is under the pier?"

"The bird, man, the bird! The only North American Tricoloured Heron *ever* spotted in London."

"Oh, good show," Chalmers replied.

"Use the ladder," the young man said, turning the binoculars back upstream.

Four feet away to the barrister's left, fixed to the top of the Embankment wall, was a wire mesh cage designed to discourage pedestrians from trying to descend a ladder which ran down to the river bottom below.

If Chalmers had not been drunk and dreading going home, he would have ignored the young man's request. But he *was* drunk and here was a reason to put off facing Florence at least for a little while. So the lawyer grabbed hold of the cage and swung one leg over the wall. . . . and in his inebriated condition almost fell to his death on the rocks below.

As he now climbed down the ladder a sudden foul stench assailed the barrister's nose. Glancing to his right he saw the massive outfall where the Fleet Sewer emptied into the River Thames. A heavy metal hinged door fifteen feet high was set into the face of the stone-block Embankment wall. It weighed at least a ton and it only opened outward. A wheelbarrow which had come down with the sewer water flow had jammed the outfall door partly open; the hinged cover had closed before the barrow had completely exited. A trickle of foul sewer water was seeping out.

"Here," the young man said as he passed the binoculars to Chalmers. "The water fowl is under the pier attached to the pumping station."

The lawyer looked at the birdwatcher and involuntarily shivered, for on closer inspection the man had a creepy face. His lucid skin was as pale as blackboard chalk, stretched tight over the bones of his skull. The pupils of his hard brown eyes were dilated as if by drugs. Well over six feet tall, he was wearing a navy donkey jacket and kid-leather gloves. The woollen cap on his head was pulled down over his ears, and stitched to his jacket was the crest of the American Audubon Society. Chalmers put him near thirty.

"With you as a witness," the young man said, "they'll *have* to believe my sighting. So please take special note of the markings on the bird."

The lawyer looked back upstream toward the pumping station dock. Thin wisps of gauzy morning mist curled above the water. The stern of *H.M.S. President* loomed beyond.

"Use the binoculars," the birdwatcher said.

Chalmers put them to his face but couldn't see a thing.

"It's like a game, isn't it?" the American whispered. "I'm glad you want to play."

"All I see is black."

"Turn the centre knob and they'll come into focus."

So Chalmers felt for the dial and gave it a twist.

The sharp snap as the knives released was like the breaking of a dry autumn twig. The force of the springs set into each lens drove the pointed six-inch blades through his eyeballs to pin his brain against the back of his skull. The spike-tips slammed against the bone to jerk back Chalmers' head, while the scream that came from his startled lips was smothered almost instantly as one of The Ghoul's gloved hands clamped across his mouth. The lawyer dropped the binoculars which tumbled to the rocky beach as ocular fluid mixed with blood fountained out from the two slits in his eyes. Then he crumpled to the riverbed as the young man let go of him.

Within five minutes, The Ghoul had disappeared. He was now inside the outfall door the wheelbarrow had wedged open. A noose was looped around the neck of Edwin Chalmers' body and his corpse was being dragged up over the exit lip into the sewer tunnel.

Left behind on the rocky beach exposed by the River Thames were four small ceramic birds and the pair of binoculars.

Blood ran down the sharp steel jutting from each lens.

Less than a mile away in the wall of a rundown basement room, the door backing the Poe mirror stood open to await the return of The Ghoul.

The mirror reflected a TV screen that flickered with the frozen image of a farmer sprawled in a bedroom with his eyes pecked out.

# 999

The 999 came into the Yard at 8:13 that morning.

In October of 1984 the Metropolitan Police unveiled their new central command complex which cost 30 million pounds. At the centre of this system is a Command and Control computer linked to 800 terminals in the metropolitan area. It is this computer that responds to 999 calls, for it can handle 400 emergencies simultaneously. The Yard now deals with urgent incidents by means of U.S. technology developed to fight the war in Vietnam.

The nerve centre of the C + C is the control room at New Scotland Yard. Here between twenty and twenty-five white-shirted operators sit at VDU terminals arranged in semi-circles like the rims of broken wheels. Each is equipped with computer, radio, and telephone links. When a 999 call comes in, the details of the report are typed directly into the C + C.

Right now at one of these terminals, the console activated. A button flashed to indicate the call was a 999.

"Scotland Yard," the operator said. "Where's the emergency?" He was wearing a telephone headset with a single earphone and a mouthpiece close to his lips.

"Under the north end of Blackfriars Bridge. At the foot of the Embankment wall."

"Please hold on," the operator said.

His fingers moved to the keyboard in front of the VDU. As he typed, the dark green screen filled with glowing green letters. The C + C told him the incident had not already been reported with a response underway.

"What's the emergency?" the operator asked.

"A surprise," the voice replied, and the line went dead.

Unfazed, the operator continued typing.

The C + C already contained information giving up-to-date locations for all Met police cars and their present assignments. This information had come from the routine HQ calls that motorized cops must make on their radios periodically. The C + C gave the operator the nearest car to the site of the 999. It also provided him with a list of the equipment the officers had. The operator could respond to any situation for the special tactical and surveillance groups at the Yard, plus the police arsenal, were at his fingertips.

The C + C, however, did more than that.

Contained within its memory banks was a computerized street index for London; in effect an electronic map. By typing in a place name, the name or nickname of a building such as a pub or restaurant, the telephone number from which a call had been made, a statue or monument or any other landmark, the Yard operator could rapidly pinpoint any place in the city. The C + C would—as it did now—respond with a full street address and an accompanying six-figure map reference.

Within fifteen seconds of the call the Yard was on the move.

The Marine Police were formed in 1798 to combat river crime. Originally the force used galleys to patrol the River Thames and visit the various docks. Then in 1839 all municipal forces—with the exception of the City of London Police—were amalgamated as one. The Marine Police became the Thames Division of Scotland Yard, and so they too now responded to the 999.

By the time the boat eased in under the span of Blackfriars Bridge, the tide was on the rise and less than three feet from the Embankment wall. The sound of patrol car sirens echoed down from the street above.

Spotting blood on the rocks of the riverbed, the cop at the bow of the boat jumped into the muddy Thames as a constable descended the ladder from the Embankment above. Two knife blades were sticking up out of the water a foot and a half from shore. The marine cop pulled on a glove as he bent down and reached into the river to pick the binoculars up. Traces of diluted blood still ran down the blades.

Because he was a cautious man trained well for his job, the officer reached back into the water and scooped up a handful of the stones on which the binoculars had stood.

Among the rocks in his hand were four small ceramic birds.

# Mother Superior

## Providence, Rhode Island
### *8:16 a.m.*

Another morning, Mom. Another step closer to you.

I forgive you not loving me then as you love me today.

So what do you think of your son now that you see all? See what I mean? *The wolf also shall dwell with the lamb . . . and a little child shall lead them?*

I can barely see you, Mom—your blissful light's so blinding. But I hear His breathing and sense the truth of your message in the pulse of the universe. Do all the stars really outline the face of God?

I promise your niece shall suffer the Fate for what she's done to you. *Lot's wife looked back on Sodom, and she became a pillar of salt.*

To celebrate your First Coming on January 11, she who has taken from you and yours that which rightfully does not belong to her shall be punished for her sins.

*And with the breath of His lips shall He slay the wicked.*
Amen, Mom.

# Alter Ego

By the time Deborah Lane's last class was finished the streets were white with snow . . . and still it came down.

She stood on the steps of the high school, a young woman wrapped in a cosy down parka gazing out with a smile at the monochromatic hush. For of all the seasons, Deborah loved winter best.

There was something about a snowfall that made her feel safe and secure. She liked the anonymity in bundled-up layers of clothes, and the way the plumes of frozen breath hid her face like a Japanese fan, while about her the soft cocoon of flakes turned everyone else to shadow. Winter brought peace and tranquillity that made the rest of the world go away. And that left Deborah free to live in a world that was her own.

"Have a nice weekend, Miss Lane," a voice behind her said. The door had just opened and one of her students had left the library.

"Thank you, Mary. Same to you."

She watched as the girl descended the steps and turned up Angell Street. Then she hunched her shoulders against the cold, adjusted her scarf and went down the steps herself. As always it sounded so very strange to be called "Miss Lane" by someone who was only nine or ten years younger than she was. Twenty-five, Deborah thought, and I might as well be middle-aged.

Deborah Lane's apartment was less than six blocks from the school. She unlocked the front door with her key to find Mr Nibs waiting patiently in the hall for her return. He trotted over to greet her, tail in the air and motor purring. "What a nice welcome, you silly old thing."

Poor old Nibbers, he was looking rough these days. But eighteen cat years made him what—126?

"How are the eyes today, Nibs?" Debbie asked. For her pet's vision was clouded by advancing cataracts.

He replied with one of his loud cheeky meows.

She prepared them both a cheese omelette which was her cat's favourite food, dividing it fairly between two plates before switching on the kitchen radio. She sat down on the tile floor to eat her meal with him as the Beatles were asking a question about all the lonely people, where do they all come from?

When later she entered the bathroom to fill the tub, Mr Nibs followed at her heels like a shadow. These days he seemed to want to follow her everywhere.

"If you don't start cleaning your pelt again, cat, you'll *join* me for a bath."

Nibs climbed up on the toilet seat, put his front paws on the sink and yowled for her to turn on the tap for a drink. He'd been so demanding these past few weeks.

As Deborah removed her clothes and hung them on a hook, she glanced at her reflection in the bathroom mirror.

Lane did not think of herself as attractive; in fact she played down her looks as much as she could. The image she caught in the glass, with honey-blonde shoulder length hair and deep blue eyes, resembled a young Liv Ullmann in face and figure. Her body was lithe, full-breasted, healthy, and graceful. Naked she exuded an image of ordinary perfection which her lack of make-up and choice of clothing were subconsciously designed to hide.

Deborah sank into the bathtub and for the next half hour languished in its soothing warmth. Nibs stretched out on the bathroom rug and purred contentedly.

Climbing out, Deborah dried herself briskly then put on her faded blue jeans and her Opus Penguin sweatshirt. Entering the living room, she rummaged through the record rack and selected Mozart's *Concerto for Flute, Harp and Orchestra in C Major*. As she placed it on the turntable and the first notes filled the room, Mr Nibs crossed to his favourite place between the speakers where he curled up happily.

"I love you, cat," Deborah whispered as she sat down in front of the word processor on her desk.

Outside the window behind her the snow continued to

fall. It clung to the bare branches of the trees like blue-white cotton wool.

Deborah switched on the Kaypro and adjusted a small oval mirror on the desk so that it reflected the winter scene out beyond the windowpane. To one side of the glass she had taped a full-length picture of how she imagined Corinne Grey to look. Now as Deborah joined her heroine in her latest peril, Corinne was out there somewhere hopelessly lost in the snow.

# Daddy's Girl

Rosanna Keate was thinking about the day she murdered her father.

That was July 23, 1984.

She remembered that scorching afternoon beside the pool near the sea in Newport, Rhode Island. Ronald Fletcher, her father's lawyer, was sweating enough to fill the swimming pool himself as he sat on a deck chair by her feet and looked up her long legs. Rosanna was wearing a string bikini, the tanned flesh of her body glistening with coconut oil. She lay on her back worshipping the sun, arms stretched above her head and feet a foot apart to drive the attorney crazy. Ronnie was leaning forward on his elbows to hide his growing erection.

Poor Ronald Fletcher. What a horny fool.

Fletcher was a ruddy-faced man in his late fifties, with slicked-back silver hair and a body so short and fat that he had a radius. Ronnie did all the legal work for Rosanna's wealthy father. Every time she fucked him he took less than a minute to come. Rosanna kept trying to shorten his record to amuse herself.

Her father, Enoch Keate, however, was a different matter. Sometimes she thought he would never get off.

On the days when she and her father had sex, Rosanna would spend the morning studying pictures of her mother to get the make-up right. Then she would select a revealing dress from among the copies a Newport seamstress had made for her from the gowns in her mother's aging wardrobe. She would later hike the skirt up to her waist with nothing underneath, and her father would lie on top of her body and whisper her mother's name in her ear.

"Enoch, my darling," Rosanna would say as she slowly rocked her hips. "How silly of you to think me dead. I could never leave you."

Her father would always cry for a while after he climaxed, just as he had done earlier on that afternoon of his death.

"Do you think he suspects anything?" Fletcher asked.

"Of course not, Ronald. He changed the will, didn't he?"

"Yes, sure, but not without a little help from . . . from his legal adviser. Rosanna, he was drugged and wasn't rational at the time."

"You and I may know that, but no one else does. It'll stand up in probate, you said so yourself. And speaking of standing up, Ronald, look at your shorts."

Rosanna sat up on the lounge chair and slowly stretched forward to touch her toes, giving Fletcher a good look down her bikini top at her oil-glistening breasts. She just loved this sort of game—teasing the young, the old, the ugly with her sex.

One day when Rosanna was sixteen and the servants weren't around she had led a new paperboy by the hand down to the Chinese Teahouse where the Atlantic Ocean touched the Keate Estate. There she told the twelve-year-old to remove his pants while she taped two lines on the marble floor thirty inches apart. She had him stand with his toes touching one of the lines, then she stroked his rigid penis with the promise that if he could spurt past the second mark she'd give him a lesson in female anatomy he'd never forget.

At the height of the sexual revolution in 1971, Rosanna, then eighteen, hostessed a pool party that Newport's rich youth talked about for months.

The Keate Estate cabana house had twenty-four rooms, twelve on each side of a long hall with an exercise parlour at the far end by the swimming pool. Rosanna hung a bedsheet so it completely covered the open gym door, then cut out a circle one foot in diameter two and a half feet up from the floor.

First the thirty girls at the party drew secret numbers from a hat, each number corresponding to one of the forty rooms in the Keate Mansion as outlined on a map, except for numbers 1 to 12 which were the cabana rooms along one side of the hall. Each in turn then left the ballroom for her private destination. When the last girl had departed, a boy was sent with a master key to lock all twelve doors in the cabana house.

On his return to The Mansion he dropped the key into a vase on the patio table. The boys then drew numbers to follow the same procedure, except for the youth who picked bathhouse number 24. When it came his turn to leave the ballroom he took the master key from the vase. On arriving at the cabana house he too went to his room, then later at the sound of a bell emerged to lock cabana room doors 13 to 23. Finally, he locked himself in and pushed the master key back out under his own door.

Five minutes later, a second bell rang in the poolhouse. That was the signal for each locked-in girl to search above the door to her room for a key. The one of the twelve who found it then removed her clothes below her waist and went out into the hall where she picked up the master key. This she took with her down to the exercise room and went behind the sheet.

When a third bell rang, the boys did the same. The youth who found a key came out into the hall to find an anonymous girl's buttocks and pussy framed and waiting for him in the hole cut in the sheet. They had half an hour for fun and games before the next bell sounded.

When it rang the spent boy went back to his room. After he had closed the door, the girl with the master key came out from behind the sheet and unlocked all the cabana doors before returning to her own room where she would eventually leave the key behind.

Then one by one at intervals the poolhouse people opened their doors and crept back to The Mansion. They entered the ballroom along with the others who had remained in the house and were drifting back from their scattered locations.

The party that followed was a smashing success. The whole world loves a mystery, and everyone at the dance that night was wondering either who'd been fucking whom or whom they'd been fucked by. Rosanna Keate went down in Newport teenage social history as the premier hostess of 1971.

"Your father's coming out," Ronald Fletcher whispered. Sweat was dripping in big fat drops from his pudgy, beet-red brow.

Rosanna turned on the lounge chair and looked back toward The Mansion.

Rhode Island—the island, not the state—is in Narragansett Bay southeast of Providence. Newport lies at its southern tip with Land's End at the southern point of the city itself. It was here, twenty-eight miles from Providence looking out over Rhode Island Sound and then the Atlantic Ocean, that years ago the New England wealthy built their summer homes. The Keate Estate, however, predated all of them. For the Keates were among the religious dissenters who came with Roger Williams from Massachusetts in 1636 to found a new colony for "persons distressed in conscience".

Newport was the birthplace of the American Navy. From The Mansion a broad green lawn reached down to the swimming pool by the sea where a succession of sandspits, cliffs, and barren beaches was backed by salt ponds and lagoons. As Enoch Keate walked from the house toward the pool, boats bobbed lazily out on the Sound. To the southwest the Benton Reef Light Tower winked.

Enoch Keate was sixty-one and heir to the family fortune. A vacant-eyed man with thinning hair and sagging jowls, he walked with the assistance of a silver-handled cane. As he neared Rosanna's lounge, which was four feet from the pool, his daughter swung her legs around and knocked him off his feet.

"Look out, Daddy!" Rosanna cried, grabbing his ankles as she jumped into the air.

Enoch Keate's head hit the concrete deck with the sound of a squashing melon. Then his body slipped into the swimming pool.

"Jesus!" Ronald Fletcher wheezed, struggling to his feet. "What are you doing?"

"Why, Ronald," Rosanna said. "I thought you understood. Now get the hell out of here and I'll call you later."

As she watched the body of her father sink deep into the pool, the azure swirl of the water obscured his outline like a dream and then became the image of herself reflected in the bedroom mirror of her North Vancouver suite.

At thirty-two Rosanna dripped sex appeal, and in her own opinion resembled a young Joan Collins or Elizabeth Taylor, the sort of vamp Joan's sister Jackie made millions writing about.

Her body was luscious, her breasts full, her face, with its high prominent cheekbones, elegant. Her green eyes were set in a pampered skin without a trace of wrinkle or blemish, and framed by long black lashes. Her nose had a slight but provocative flaring of the nostrils, her bee-sting lips sensual over white, even teeth with a hint of overbite. Her hair was black and stylish and cut close to her head.

As Rosanna slowly pirouetted in front of the mirror, a small gold cross around her neck moved gently away from her throat with the force of the turn. Its perpendicular finger-like shaft pointed down as if to accentuate her cleavage. Lower still—but just above where tanned skin met white at her bikini line—a tattoo of a cherry was engraved on her left buttock.

The room reflected around her reeked of elegance and money. It was a lair of sophistication and taste designed by the sort of indulgent female for whom designer labels and the finer things in life are invented. The walls of subdued silver were hung with erotic nudes, each draw-ing of either a naked man and woman or two naked women in a passionate embrace. Stretched out beneath these drawings was a king-sized waterbed with black satin sheets. The speakers set into the headboard purred with the sultry voice of Madonna singing "Like A Virgin". Rosanna herself was one of the figures in each of the charcoal prints that hung above the bed.

Turning now from her reflection in the silver-framed mirror, she studied the female outlined on the canvas set up on her easel.

Picking up a stick of charcoal she spent several minutes sketching her own features into the figure's face. That done she was starting on the rough outline of a second nude when a sudden wave of tiredness washed over her. Unable to continue, she put the charcoal down.

Dammit, Rosanna thought angrily. How much longer until I am rid of this disease?

Anger, however, only served to weaken her even more.

Stooped with exhaustion she crossed to an ebony ward-robe and removed a black silk negligee. Rosanna found expensive clothes a sure cure for depression. Feeling slightly better she sat down at her dressing table.

The table was of silver set with black onyx. Spread out across it were two large books. Rosanna touched one of the volumes and read the words engraved on its cover: *Fantasy Escort Service. Pick The Man Of Your Dreams.*

Opening the book she began to examine the models inside. All were physically attractive men with ruggedly handsome faces. Each was dressed in a pair of skin-tight briefs. In the second portfolio the models were bikini-clad women.

Rosanna closed the book and set the volumes side by side.

Man or woman? she thought with a smile. Which will it be this time?

Rhythmically she began to move her index finger from book to book.

"Eenie, meenie, miney, moe; catch a tiger by the toe," Rosanna whispered softly, mimicking Madonna's voice cooing in the background.

Then she went to the telephone and dialled Fantasy Escort Service.

# Overwhelmed

Providence, Rhode Island
*Wednesday January 8, 3:03 p.m.*

She saw it in the vet's eyes before he spoke the words.

Deborah had put a litter box in the bottom of a wicker picnic basket to transport Mr Nibs to the doctor's office. Since the day he was born her cat had had a sixth sense that told him when he was on his way to the vet's—and this knowledge had always caused him to piss all over her. Doctors meant needles, and that was *the bad thing*.

Mr Nibs now lay on the table as Dr Burnett skilfully examined him. The cat's body moved up and down rapidly with his terrified breathing while he stared at Debbie with a forlorn look in his saucer eyes.

"It's his kidneys," the vet said. "Both appear to have failed. He's a very sick cat, Deborah. I could do some tests, but I think the kindest thing would be euthanasia."

There was a long, long silence as the doctor's words sank in. Deborah tried to imagine life and her lonely apartment without her closest friend. Finally she whispered, "Is he suffering?"

"Yes," the vet replied.

"Will you do it right now?"

"I think that best."

The next words choked in her throat so she merely nodded her head.

Deborah bent down and picked Mr Nibs up and cradled him in her arms. She looked into the clouded cataracts that covered the poor thing's eyes, gave him one last hug that came straight from her heart and said, "You've been better to me, Nibbers, than any human being. Oh God, I'm sorry. I love you so."

Tears welling, she put him down gently, smoothed his fur, and quickly walked out of the room.

The nurse out front took one look at her and said not to worry about the account, she could come back later. Deborah thanked her for her kindness and left the vet's, alone.

For an hour she aimlessly walked the streets of Old Providence. The city was magnificent in its robe of pure white snow, and all the people passing by had smiles upon their faces.

In Market Square to the east of the Great Bridge over the Providence River, the sun shone down from a clear blue sky on Market House and beyond that the ancient roofs and belfries of College Hill. It gleamed off the small-paned windows and fanlights set high over double flights of steps with wrought-iron railings, blinding white in its reflection off the steeple of The First Baptist Church in America.

Here Providence Indiamen used to anchor before setting sail on the triangular route of colonial trade, shipping rum to Africa and slaves to the Caribbean, bringing molasses home to distil before shipping out again.

From this spot, it was rumoured, tunnels were sunk deep into College Hill, either as part of the underground railway to help the slaves escape, or to move slaves to work certain homes after the trade was banned.

Right now, however, all this was far from Deborah's mind as she remembered a tiny, playful kitten a long time ago.

Without you, Nibs, Deborah thought, how would I have survived the hell years in that house?

After a while she made the mistake of scaling the Hill by wandering up College Street. For the route only reinforced memories that depressed her even more. On the southeast corner where College crossed Benefit Street loomed the Greek Revival façade of the Providence Athenaeum established in 1753. Here, at one of the oldest libraries in America, Edgar Allan Poe had courted Sarah Helen Whitman. And for Deborah, Poe meant *him*. Then on the northwest corner of College and Prospect Streets stood the John Hay Library of Brown University. Located directly in front of the site of H. P. Lovecraft's last home at No. 66, its Lovecraftiana collection held the major works of the horror fantasist. And Lovecraft for her also meant *him*.

Deborah Lane went home.

Still numbed by her decision to have Mr Nibs put to sleep, she picked up her mail from the downstairs box without glancing through it.

When she opened her apartment door a wave of depression hit her on seeing that empty spot where every day the cat used to wait for her return.

She looked at the mail.

The first piece was an Exxon bill.

The second was a letter from a New York publisher.

Just a letter! Deborah thought. Not the manuscript. That must mean they want to publish it!

Quickly she tore the envelope open to find disappointment.

Dear Ms Lane:

*Re:* TRADE WINDS BLOWING

Regretfully we will not be making an offer for your novel.

I could not relate to your central character. The male/female relationships are stilted and I got the feeling that Corinne Grey was afraid of men. That is not what today's woman wants in a romance.

Thanks for letting us see it.

*Jackie Sim*
Assistant Editor

p.s. I am returning the manuscript under separate cover.

Deborah's shoulders slumped. This was her thirteenth rejection. She was rapidly running out of major publishers. Then her stomach lurched to her throat as she noticed the third envelope.

God, please. Not him again, she thought in despair.

The envelope was postmarked in London, England, six days earlier. The sheet of paper it contained was dark grey with black typed lettering. The note inside read:

Deb—

I dreamt about your snatch last night, you juicy little slit.

You don't know me, but I know you. And before we're finished I'll know every inch of your cunt.

One day when you least expect it, sugar, I'll come gunning for you.

I'm going to hang you muff-bare by your wrists from a ceiling beam and lick your pussy till you scream and come all over my face.

But what I'll do after that, you're not going to like.

Snuff time, baby.

Your Master,
SID

Disgusted, Deborah's stomach convulsed and she fought down the urge to be physically sick.

She went to the front door and engaged all three locks.

As she then turned around her eyes caught the small white buckled circle near one corner of the hall table.

Deborah picked up the flea collar she had removed from her cat just before the trip to the vet's.

"Oh, Nibs!" she choked as her dam of emotion broke. Then she sat down on the floor to cry it out.

# Heavy Metal

## Vancouver, British Columbia
### *Friday January 10, 8:15 p.m.*

Zinc was sitting propped up on the bed with two pillows behind him when the telephone rang. He picked up the receiver. "Chandler," he said.

"It's Caradon, Special O. What ya doing?"

"Reading."

"Anything good?"

"Germaine Greer. *Sex And Destiny.*"

"Jeez, I'm sorry I asked. Know the enemy, huh?"

That was not the reason, but Chandler let it go.

"Well, if you can tear yourself away from Ms Greer I might have something important."

"Shoot," Zinc said.

"Since the day he made bail we've been following Mohawk all over town. He hasn't gone near or made contact with Hengler but a couple of non-cops have been tailing him too."

"Hengler's boys?"

"That could be."

"Did *they* connect with Mohawk?"

"Not that we can tell. But half an hour ago we followed the biker to a rock club on Hastings. He's in there now."

"What's the connection? Why the call?"

"Cause in addition to drugs, fuck-films, and outcall hookers, it seems Ray Hengler is moving in on the music scene. Rock videos and band promotion, that sort of thing. He brought in the act that's playing the club tonight."

Chandler fished pen and paper out of a drawer in the hotel bedside table.

"What's the name of the club?" he asked.
"It's called The Id."
"Address?"
He wrote down the answer.
"What's the name of the group Hengler's promoting?"
"Ghoul," Caradon said.

## 10:22 p.m.

Death was the latest fad in the world of rock 'n' roll.

The Id was fashioned from the mould of the Zero and the Fetish Clubs in L.A. Situated on the main floor of a rundown skid row building, it was squeezed between a skin-book emporium and an outlet for second-hand clothes. There was no sign to mark its presence for those not in the know, for The Id was a club of creep chic and fuck-the-rest-of-the-world. Chandler felt totally out of place.

Zinc wandered in wearing black jeans, a black leather jacket, white socks, and black boots. His wallet hung on a chain. His hair, sprayed black and dangling over his forehead in greasy curls, was swept back at the sides into a duck tail. Dark aviator shades masked his eyes.

The club, however, had been designed for those awaiting the drop of The Bomb. A video screen along one wall pulsed silently with black and white images of exploding mushroom clouds. The main room was an oblong box in the shape of a coffin. A bar was entombed at one end; a stage curtained off and hidden at the other.

In a dusty glass case in one corner was a human skeleton, and beside that a painting of a naked woman kissing a throbbing heart she had just torn out of her chest. A large photograph of the Sex Pistols was framed on the same wall, next to an old movie poster of The Thing. Written across the ceiling in lipstick and lit by the hard cold glare of green spotlights were the words *Only Women Bleed*. Figures moved through the murk below as if they were walking on the ocean floor.

The music from the speakers was mostly Doom and Gloom-rock—the Cramps, Marc Bolan and T. Rex, Siouxsie and the Banshees, Prince doing "1999" and Bauhaus performing "Bela Lugosi's Dead". The cut playing at the moment was Frankie Goes To Hollywood's single "Relax".

A lot of the women were underage, dressed in a strange assortment of peek-a-boo slips, old leather miniskirts, and moth-eaten furs. Their garments might have been chosen by a coven of smacked-out junkies gone wild in a second-hand clothing store. Most of the men were either ball-hefters verging on homoeroticism or dressed up to look like zombies of indeterminate gender.

Standing near Zinc was a woman with skull rings on each finger and a skull tattoo on her back. Around her waist a belt heavy with upside-down crucifixes appeared to have permanently altered her posture.

A man in a black monk's robe sat empty-eyed at the next table over. His eerie face was whiter than pale and half his bumpy head had been shaved clean of hair. The opposite half of his moustache and beard had also been shaved away, making him look to Zinc like an animated chess board.

The guy slouched beside him could have been Little-Orphan-Annie-on-steroids. Red ringlets cascaded down to his chest which was wrapped in a lacy purple corset. His eyebrows were plucked out and all his attention was centred on an emaciated platinum blonde sitting across the table. Maroon streaks had been sprayed in her hair which was combed forward over her face like a ratted waterfall. Around her neck she wore a surgical collar simply for its style, the front of which had been painted to look as if her throat were cut.

Emerging from the buzzing crowd and approaching Chandler's table was a figure leopard above the waist and female below. This woman's upper body and face were painted a tawny brown with large black spots. Yellow toreador pants clung tight to her shapely hips and legs. Her eyes were ringed with black circles; her lips the colour of moonless night; her hair a fright-wig of wild tangled spikes. When she reached Chandler's table she stopped, put one stiletto-heeled pump up on the tabletop and removed the cigarette dangling from her lips.

"I'm public property," she said. "How'd you like a fuck?"

Zinc turned away.

The Leopard Woman, however, did not take the hint.

"There's nothing quite like the closeness of death to really get you off. If The Bomb explodes tonight let's beat it to the bang."

She was overheard by the Antichrist at the table next to them. He wore a crown of black thorns on his head and his eyebrows were arched with black paint. Blood of the same colour ran down the side of his face while black mock nail holes pocked his palms and the backs of his hands. "I'm game," he said.

The Leopard Woman turned to him and blew out a halo of grey smoke that swirled about her head.

"Then go stick your cock in a blender set at high speed."

"Cunt," the religious mutant sneered as he gave her the finger.

"Take him up on his offer," Chandler said. "You're not my type."

"Who cares?" the Leopard Woman purred. "I think you're mine."

She turned the chair opposite him around and sat down with her arms on its back and her breasts bulging overtop.

Chandler took off his shades and gave her a baleful stare.

Biting her tongue with her teeth in reply, she leaned closer to him and whispered, "Hengler's the one beside the stage with the chains around his neck."

Surprised, Zinc turned from the Special O undercover and looked toward the wide end of the coffin-shaped room.

The fact he had thought she was bare-breasted had really sucked him in. That was not something you would expect from a female cop. On closer examination, however, he discerned the body stocking beneath the cake of paint.

Change perspective, Chandler thought, and you pull off a sleight of hand. People are mentally designed to fool themselves.

Ray Hengler was leaning against the curtained stage talking with two other men. The door beside them, Zinc supposed, led to a dressing room.

Hengler was a fat, oily slob with a skinhead's haircut and the nose of a hawk. He was flashing a lot of jewellery, all of it gold: the Rolex on his pudgy wrist, the diamond-encrusted pinkie rings on his stubby fingers, the chunky chains around his neck. An embroidered cowboy shirt stretched across his girth and designer jeans hung low beneath his belly. One armpit of his suede bomber jacket was stained by salty sweat, the other saved by a bulge that Chandler knew would be a semi-automatic pistol in a shoulder holster. Guys like Ray Hengler you could read a mile away.

"Note the rattlesnake boots," said the Leopard Woman softly. "He's got fallen arches and he grunts when he walks. He curls his upper lip to speak and he's wearing expensive cologne. He pays for his drinks with a fat wad of $100 bills. You'll also note he's continually hefting his genitals. The guy's a human pig."

Chandler smiled.

"Impress me some more," he said loud enough to be overheard by those who were sitting nearby, "and I just might take you up on that fuck."

"Ooooh," the Leopard Woman teased. "You do talk my language."

Then she lowered her voice and said, "The name of the creep with the codpiece is Axel Crypt. They call him "The Axe" because he plays bass guitar with Ghoul."

Chandler studied the young man to Ray Hengler's right. He was tall and bony and naked except for a black leather jockstrap worn beneath three layered belts. Miniature skulls and shrunken heads dangled from his waist. One hand was buried in a fingerless black leather glove, while the other gripped a bass guitar shaped like an executioner's axe. His face was made up to look like a skull with Day-Glo paint. It shone ghostly pale in the light of an ultraviolet strip on the wall above the door. His blond hair was cut short at the sides but left full at the crown.

"The third guy's a mystery," the Leopard Woman said. "No one seems to know him so I can't get an ID. But he and Hengler have been tête-à-têteing all night."

The third man—dressed in a black shirt, white tie, and double-breasted suit—looked like a gangster off the set of a thirties B-film. A grey fedora was cocked on his head and a trenchcoat was draped on his arm. Like Chandler, he too was wearing shades.

"What a zoo," Zinc muttered, and whistled under his breath.

Ray Hengler and his cohorts abruptly stopped talking as a roadie came out from behind the curtain and spoke

to the promoter. Hengler nodded his bowling ball head
and the roadie went backstage. Then the three men disappeared through the door beneath the ultraviolet strip.

"Where's Mohawk?" Chandler asked the Leopard
Woman.

"Don't know," she answered. "I'm not his tail. Hengler's
the one I've been assigned."

"You think he might be in the room beyond that
door?"

She shrugged her shoulders as they settled down to
wait.

The vamp sitting at the dressing room table swivelled her
chair around as Hengler and the other two men came in.

Her stage name was Erika Zann, and she was twenty-
eight years old. There was not an ounce of fat on her tall,
slender, well-defined frame. She was naked above the
waist, dressed in nothing but a pair of black bikini panties. In movement and bearing she had the look of a
sensual reptile. Her real name was Rika Hyde.

Outside the door to the dressing room, Hengler was
the person being observed. Inside he was the one doing
the watching. Leering, he now ran his eyes over the
woman from foot to head.

As Rika slithered into fishnet stockings and a black
garter belt, he noticed that she had small toes with a hint
of webbing between them. She walked on the balls of her
feet when she stood up to retrieve a pair of stiletto heels
while Hengler ogled her long slim legs, her narrow hips,
and the S-curve of her spine. A silver pendant on a
serpent chain hung around her neck, its square frame
imprisoning a black and white enamel picture of the
Hanged Man from the Tarot deck. As Hengler watched
her take a black dress down from a hook near the table
and stretch her arms above her head to slip into the
garment, he thought, Too bad, no tits. This babe's as flat
as a board. Then the dress fell like a curtain to hide her
body from his view, so Ray Hengler strip-searched her
face instead.

Hengler's taste in sex ran to pre-pubescent boys and
dark outré women. Rika Hyde—"Erika Zann"—fit the
latter bill.

Her face was sleek but chiselled sharp in the same
strange way as her body, with a tongue that constantly

flicked to her lips like a snake's. A rats-nest of blue-black spikes framed her long jaw and intense brown eyes. Her nose was aquiline and her canine teeth were large. A Swastika with counter-clockwise arms hung from her left ear.

Hengler scratched his balls and turned back to the other two men.

Several minutes later, the bone-rack with the jockstrap broke away from the group of men and crossed to the dressing room table where Rika was seated, applying her make-up. Codpiece pulled up another chair and began to chalk his body white. The words he now whispered tip-toed to her ear.

"Hengler's hiding something. He's not coming clean."

"How so, Axel?" Rika replied.

"First, the guy has no experience in video rock."

"Yeah, but he's got money. He did fly us out and he's picking up the tab."

"He's a rock virgin, Erika. The guy's into porn. He's up before the courts for peddling twat on film. Rumour is he did a snuff flick a year ago."

"All the better," Rika said, a cool smile on her lips. "We need all the trash publicity we can get."

Her face and exposed limbs were now caked white with base make-up that made her living flesh look dead. The low-cut gown she wore was full length and slit to the waist to reveal her underwear. Black circles ringed her eyes and the only colour about her was her scarlet lips and the red she now trickled down her chin below her canine teeth.

"The guy's a cunt-hound, Erika. He wants into your pants."

"That only shows he's got good taste."

"Hengler's a thug. He's no rock promoter. He's using us to launder money from his other crimes. The guy is dangerous."

"So am I," Rika said, pulling on a pair of black elbow-length gloves. "Predatory females run in my family."

As they talked the door burst open and a drunk in a white blood-spattered lab smock staggered in. His eyes were hidden behind thick-lensed psychedelic-spiral glasses that made him look like a crazed scientist who had spent the last few hours inhaling mercury fumes.

"Get the fuck outa here," Ray Hengler snarled. He pushed the man by the face to shove him out the door.

At that same moment Rika Hyde glanced at the pseudo-gangster in the black shirt, white tie, and double-breasted suit. Her eyes locked on his glasses as they exchanged cold smiles.

"What's going on here?" Chandler asked.

He was still watching the dressing room door beside the stage. Some guy in a white lab coat had just gone in—but as Zinc asked the question the same man came flying back out.

"What you see and hear is post-punk rock," the Leopard Woman said. Her real name was Constable Sandra Maas.

"Around us is the whimper that comes before the bang. The Zero Generation. The Children of the Bomb. They're Sex Ghouls, my friend, filled with nuclear hopelessness."

"Looks like you've attracted yet another admirer," Chandler said.

The drunk in the lab coat was approaching their table. Two feet away he stopped, cupped his hands to his face and leaned over the surface to vomit a half-eaten rat from his mouth.

Zinc recoiled in disgust as flecks of spittle hit his face and he pushed back his seat. Those at the tables around him began to laugh. Chandler stared at the rotting rodent in its pink and yellow puddle, then at the jerk in the lab coat who was pulling up a chair.

"I got it at Krak-A-Joke," Caradon said. "Realistic, eh?"

Chandler frowned, then grinned, then replied, "Still eating junk food, are you, Bill?"

Caradon picked up the plastic vomit pad, wiped it on his sleeve and stuffed it in his pocket. Then he lowered his voice and whispered, "Mohawk's disappeared."

"What do you mean disappeared? Surely you covered all the doors once you followed him in?"

"Of course," Caradon replied. "But with all the weirdos here we lost him in the crowd. We've checked the entire club on the sly, including the dressing room from which I just got booted out on my ass."

"What about the basement?"

"Access to it's boarded up. Fire regulations."

"Upstairs?"

"Negative. Zinc, I know my job. Playing the drunk I also barged into the manager's office. Mohawk's not there either."

"Then he's got to be here somewhe—"

Suddenly the lights were killed and the club went dark. A ghostly pale grey glow seeped out from beneath the curtain hiding the stage. As the curtain began to rise, billows of mist from dry ice blocks immersed in water swirled out from the wings to hover above the mock graveyard set. Luminous stalagmite tombstones like crooked fangs protruding from a giant lower jaw jutted up out of a layer of dirt covering the stage. A papier-mâché vault rose near the back of the set, its false stone ceiling mounted by a grinning skull. On a flat grave slab at centre stage, a couple sat necking.

A power chord boom from a bass guitar of at least a hundred decibels shook the club. Several people watching recoiled from the wave of subsonic sound. But the couple went on necking.

When the bass rumbled a second time the ground of the graveyard set began to heave. One by one, three zombie-like guitarists crawled out of the earth. Axel Crypt was among them, and as he hit the bass again a speaker exploded in a flash of smoking cones.

"Aw right!" someone shouted at the table next to Zinc.

A low moan erupted from one of the yawning grave pits. Axel Crypt crept up behind the necking couple onstage. To a roar of approval from the crowd, he took a swipe at them with his axe-shaped guitar. The man's head ripped from his body in a fountain spray of blood. It bashed the strings of the guitar before it spun off into the crowd. The sound blasting from the speakers rattled Zinc's front teeth.

The guy's a dummy, Chandler thought as the grave slab swivelled open and the woman with the mannequin dropped out of sight.

A drummer on a platform rose up out of the same pit. When he pounded his skins it sounded like howitzers being fired. The other two undead zombies launched a flash-and-burn attack with their twin lead guitars, laying down thick and vicious clots of heavy metal fuzztone.

The moan that was coming out of the pit rose to a wail as the tomb at the rear of the stage burst its door.

Erika Zann sprang from the black maw beyond screaming like a banshee with burning bamboo splinters rammed beneath its fingernails.

She landed in a fencer's lunge of raw and seething power, snarling at the crowd as if lusting for its blood.

While other men in the club were fantasizing about driving their stakes toward her heart, Chandler stared at the pit onstage and thought, So that's how Mohawk got out.

Ray Hengler stood in full view of the crowd and watched the show with a knowing smirk on his face.

# London, England
## *Saturday January 11, 6:44 a.m.*

At that very moment eight hours ahead and 4707 statute miles away by the Great Circle Route, a man sat at the kitchen table of a flat in the East End.

The surface of the table was spread with newspaper clippings divided into three separate piles. On top of the pile about the bombing at The Roman Steambath lay a remote-control explosive device serving as a paperweight. The clipping on top of the second pile blared "SEWER KILLER STRIKES".

Picking two of the articles at random, he scanned the print.

From the *Sun:*

> *Vampire Killer! Sewer Killer!*
> *Jack The Bomber!*

> ### BLOODBATH

> There is fear in London. Total fear of strangers. Fear of the monster in the sewers. Fear of being blown to bits. Fear for children's safety.

From the *Star:*

> ### THEY DIDN'T HAVE TO DIE

"The grief is gone now and it's replaced by anger. I hate this bloke badly. I'm no longer living in fear, I'm living for revenge."

So said Christopher Hickson yesterday, summing up the anguish of the parents of eight young girls murdered last summer who do not believe the police are doing enough to catch the killer. Hickson showed the *Star* a poster that read: OUR CHILDREN ARE DEAD! YOURS MIGHT BE NEXT!

"Nine months," he told reporters, "without an arrest. Now someone is phoning the friends of the victims and threatening, 'You will be next!' The police are too busy with the Sewer Killer and Bomber cases to think about us."

The man put the clippings back, then finished carving the wooden handle of a 12-inch icepick into the shape of a monster.

# Raw Meat

## Vancouver, British Columbia
*12:07 a.m.*

While Zinc sat eyeing Hengler who was watching Ghoul perform, several miles away a Ford Mustang drove into an alley behind a meat packing plant. The driver cut the motor, killed the lights, and both occupants got out.

The alley, dark and deserted, was in the city's industrial section near the waterfront. Although it was a clear night with a moon high above, a raft of cloud now scudded across the lunar surface hiding it from sight. Wind whipped down the alley and whistled in the wires, blowing the trenchcoat flaps around the legs of the man in the double-breasted suit. He clamped the fedora to his head and clutched the coat lapels shut over his black shirt and white tie.

"What's this dump?" Mohawk asked.

"A recent acquisition, mate," Sid Jinks replied. "Wind's a bitch tonight. Let's go inside."

Mohawk watched as the man took two plastic litre bottles of Watney's Pale Ale and a briefcase from the rear seat of the car, then crossed over to unlock the plant's alley door. Jinks looked up and down the lane which was devoid of movement except for the stealth of a grey tomcat.

"After you, mate," he said. "We'll have a bevy or two while we wait for Hengler."

Mohawk didn't know what the hell to make of this limey asshole. To start with he could barely understand the fuckin guy. For Jinks spoke in a Brit tongue so thick you'd need a chainsaw to cut off a piece. Mohawk was born and raised in East Vancouver. Lots of chinks and ragheads there, but fuckin few limeys. His life was his bike club, hard dick, and ridin hog. Now here he was saddled with some guy he'd never met before who mouthed on and on about shit that made no fuckin sense. You'd think the fuckin limeys would learn to speak English like everybody else.

The guy'd started with the crap before they split the club. He'd first grabbed Mohawk by the arm as he was makin his way through the Id crowd to Hengler, deflectin him toward the stage before he could connect.

"Not here, mate," was the first thing the tea bag said. "You're *fuck*in bein followed. Have a bit of nous."

Was that how all limeys yapped when they said "fuckin"? No one else talked like that—hittin the front half of the word so hard.

Then friggin Jinks had shoved him down that pit in the stage.

"Wait in the cellar corner, mate. Hengler's comin down."

Forty fuckin minutes he'd spent down there jerkin off, wonderin what the fuck they thought . . . that he was fuckin dumb? Fuck he didn't know that he was fuckin bein followed. Why the fuck did they think he hadn't been around? Cause that fuckin lawyer said, "Stay cool, friend. You will be called for once the heat's chilled down?"

Yeah, well fuck em. He'd ditched the tail himself. They think he'd come near Hengler with fuzz on his ass? Give'm a break.

But when, just before the gig, the fuckin platform came back down on its hydraulic lift, who the fuck do you think had come down to see him? Hengler? Fuck you. Fuckin Sid Jinks.

Mohawk wondered more than once if Sid Jinks liked to take it in the ass.

"Hengler says to tell you, mate, you're goin to Barbados. Then a fortnight later to his beef spread in Montana. You'll come back a new bloke with new ID. Sod the *fuck*in trial. Hard enough havin it off to get you out of nick. That cost a wedge of notes.

"Hengler needs a bit of time to put the trip together. You'll be leavin on the first flight out of town this mornin. But here is not the place he wants to talk to you. Let's get a *fuck*in edge on, eh, before we both get tumbled?"

Fuckin Sid Jinks with his candy gangster clothes. Talkin

about "wide boys" and "lags" becomin "milers". Yakkin
about "hoisters" and "workin the tweedle", and playin
"Kalooki in the spielers, eatin bacon butties."

Where the fuck had Hengler latched onto this prick?
Was this the sort of asshole he thought he could use to
reconstruct a gang? Mouthin on about these two guys
called the Krays, as he led him down the tunnel from The
Id club cellar to the basement next door. With his "*Fuck*in
Ronnie" this, and his "*Fuck*in Reggie" that, and who the
fuck were the fuckin Krays anyway? A minute with
the 'hunters and Jinks'd be dork meat.

Shit, all he talked about once they were on their way—
first in the Mazda—then into the garage—then a quick
change to the Corvette and out another door—then finally the Mustang that was parked beneath the bridge—
was how the Krays had enforced the rule "not to grass on
your mates".

"Grass", my ass, Mohawk thought. Next to fuckin
"*fuck*in" that was Jinks' favourite word.

The biker had told him that he'd shook the tail himself
. . . but on and on Jinks went about how "a bit of savvy
gave the Krays the edge". So that was why—with Mohawk at the wheel and Jinks readin a fuckin map—they'd
driven around for an hour makin sure the pigs were lost.
Never mind the fact that Mohawk knew this town like he
knew his own cock, there was Jinks ridin shotgun in his
candy black shirt and friggin white tie sayin, "Turn here,
mate" and, "Cambie Street comin up."

Well thank fuckin Christ, at last they had arrived.

Mohawk was aware that what had really ticked him off
was the fact that Jinks had frisked him as they moved
toward the stage pit back at The Id. This fuckin jaw
queen was lookin for a wire in case he'd body-rolled.
What a maggot hugger. Suck his gopher tits.

Here in the hallway just inside the alley door it was
dark and narrow like a coal mine shaft. Up ahead in the
main room of the meat packing plant a single 100-watt
bulb cast dull light.

Walking behind Mohawk, Sid Jinks now said, "You
see, the thing about the Krays was it was all the way with
them. That's why Ronnie and Reggie were the royal wide
boys of the *fuck*in London scene. Ronnie was a villain,
eh, a *fuck*in callous man. When Ronnie did a job, the
*whole* job got done.

"I heard about this one bloke grassed on his mates. He was a mug, eh, a Jekyll in the pack. Ronnie dealt with grasses by the use of deep interrogation with acute humiliation and distress, my friend."

As they moved along the corridor, Sid Jinks chuckled at the euphemism.

"Ronnie did him properly. He didn't like a mate who tried somethin on. Ronnie broke his arms and legs, then his shoulder blades. Next he did the bloke's jaw, teeth, and eyes. Then Ronnie cut him . . . *phoooooo*. He did.

"Ronnie was the geezer taught me how to deal with grasses. If Ronnie was around today, not in and out of Broadmoor, he'd be the scourge of the modern supergrass.

"But then he's not, mate. So that leaves me."

"Grass", my fuckin sweet ass, the biker thought again. This limey peg boy can blo—

The bullet slammed into the back of Mohawk's head and blew out his face in splinters. The force of the muzzle velocity hurled the 'hunter to the hall floor and smeared him along its surface. Nice piece, Jinks thought, hefting the gun in his hand.

Back at The Id while Mohawk had been waiting in the cellar, Jinks had asked Hengler for a piece that was clean with no paper on it. The chunk he'd been given was an Ingram MAC-10 .45 with a 12-inch silencer. The .45 was a heavy slug that would retain full energy when it struck the target, yet one with a velocity less than the speed of sound. There would, therefore, be no supersonic boom. The silencer was a baffle with a 2¼-inch diameter 4 inches out from the muzzle, narrowing down to 1¾ for the final 8. This was covered with a canvas heat jacket. The net result was that the noise of the shot through Mohawk's head was no more than the *phhht* of wind whispering through grass.

Done ya, mate, Sid Jinks thought.

For a minute Jinks just stood there to savour the thrill of the hit, then he stepped over Mohawk's corpse and walked down the corridor to the main room of the plant.

He took off his double-breasted suit, white tie, black shirt, and hung them on a hook. He removed a heavy rubber butcher's apron from the coat rack, put it on and tied the straps. He opened the briefcase he had brought in with him and took out a pair of rubber boots and a pair of rubber gloves. Then he looked around.

The packing plant was a large room two hundred feet square. Jinks' eyes took in the brutal hooks where carcasses would hang, the large refrigerated locker with heavy wooden doors, the giant stainless-steel machines to process raw meat. Chopping blocks and cutting tables were scattered about the place as grisly stations for the butchers who worked here during the day. The odour of death and dead flesh was soothing to his lungs.

Jinks walked back to the hallway where Mohawk was sprawled on the floor. Grunting in effort, he dragged the corpse into the plant and hauled it up onto one of the chopping blocks. A wide smear of thick blood trailed the cadaver like slime from a slug.

For several minutes Jinks examined Mohawk's shattered face.

Yes, he thought clinically. An Ingram does the job.

He poked with one finger at the gaping hole where the bikers nose had been, touching the bone fragments that were sticking out like spikes. From now on, he decided, he would use a .45.

Next he removed Mohawk's clothes and set them to one side. He put the briefcase on the block, took out all his gleaming tools and instruments, then restuffed the case with the bikers leathers.

Jinks returned to the coat rack and from a shelf above it took down a Plexiglas helmet like a welder's face shield. Normally he liked the feel of blood and gore spattering his face as he worked, revelling in the closeness of death and the fact that he controlled it. But the name of the game tonight was not to leave a trace and there wasn't going to be time to take a shower later.

Ah well, Jinks thought. Save that for London.

He used a straight razor to slice the genitals away. He always did that first—removed the cock and balls. Sid Jinks thought of these appendages as trophies.

Then he picked up a cleaver and chopped off Mohawk's head, plucking out the eyes next and setting them down beside the severed sex organs. With the penis as a nose, he rearranged the body parts to look like a face.

Reaching for a scalpel, he slit a midline incision down Mohawk's chest and abdomen from neck to pubic bone. With a pair of bone cutters and tenaculum forceps, he opened up the torso to get at the organs inside.

To the right of the chopping block was the stainless

steel hopper-mouth of an industrial grinder. Jinks now cut away Mohawk's meat with a surgeon's precision, placing each organ and hunk of muscle into the machine. When he was finished he could see white bones in among the remaining strands of salmon-coloured tissue and peeled-back skin.

He picked up an autopsy saw from among the tools and instruments that he had carried in, one of the portable type that plugs into the wall. Stringing an extension cord to the nearest socket, he gave the saw a test. The saw was the length of a mugger's sap with a fine-toothed, crescent-shaped blade the size of a child's fist. Turned on, the blade vibrated rapidly back and forth.

Jinks set to work dismembering Mohawk's skeleton. The blade hummed shrilly in his ears and his nose filled with the acidic stink of burnt human bone.

Done, he carried each skeletal piece over to another grinder designed to powder up bone meal for household pets.

Make doggie grow up big and strong with a built-in taste for postmen, Sid Jinks thought with a smile.

He returned to the chopping block and went to work on the head.

Attached to one end of the cutting surface was a swing-up wooden flap fitted with a vise. Jinks locked the table addition in place, then secured Mohawk's skull by tightening the vise plates against both ears. Using first the razor, he peeled the skin away from each side of the dead man's Iroquois scalplock. He placed the swath of hair above the other severed trophies to complete his Frankenstein's Monster jigsaw face.

For a moment the sight of the swath of hair made Jinks think of Deborah Lane and the cunt between her legs. But soon he pushed this image aside with the thought, A time for work, and a time for play. You must eat the cake before you lick the icing.

Jinks positioned the humming saw just above the empty eye sockets with their dangling cranial and optic nerves. He lowered the blade onto the skull at an angle slanted toward him. The teeth bit deep into Mohawk's frontal bone. Then Jinks placed the vibrating blade against the parietal bone at the back of the bikers head and lowered the saw again. Similar cuts were made through the temporal and sphenoid bones on each side of the head just

above the vise plates. This cut out a square piece of loose
skull that looked like a trap door to Mohawk's cranial
vault. With the point of a scalpel Sid Jinks flipped the
skullcap away.

Now exposed before his eyes were the glistening me-
ninges that encased the bikers damaged brain. Jinks carefully peeled away this opaque sac.

He next cut Mohawk's brain free from the skull, lifting
it gently at the front to sever the nerves underneath. He
cut the brain stem just below the bullet-torn medulla
oblongata where the man's spinal cord entered his cranial
vault. Then he raised the gore-spattered Plexiglas shield.

Jinks picked up the piece of flesh and brought it to
within a foot of his face. Once again he marvelled at the
convoluted grey and white humps of soft tissue and those
mysterious crevices. For here was the centre of all Man's
mental and physical actions. The core of Man's *being*.

He gave the brain a gentle squeeze, shivering as its
warmth seeped through his rubber glove. He opened his
hand slowly and watched how the clinging, sticky tissue
adhered to his fingers as if it were a part of him and
under *his* control. Sid Jinks' penis hardened in his pants.

Several exquisite minutes later, Jinks returned to the
meat hopper and tossed in Mohawk's brain. He picked
up all his severed trophies and stuffed them into the
biker's now empty cranial vault. He flopped the peeled-
back head-skin over like a lid, then removed the cranium
from the vise and carried it across to the bone-grinder's
yawning mouth. He dropped in the head.

When he flipped the power switch on each of the
machines, the grating sound of meshing gears and crunch-
ing bone filled the packing plant.

For the next half hour Jinks steam-cleaned the area
where he had done his work. Then he removed the trays
of powdered bone and ground human flesh from the base
of each machine. These he carried over and set down just
outside the refrigerated locker doors.

Returning to the chopping block he cleaned the butcher's instruments and packed them away. He washed both
grinders with strong soap and gave each a steam-cleaning.
He wiped down his rubber clothes and the Plexiglas face
shield, putting the meat cutter's garb back where he had
found it. Then he dressed in his black shirt, white tie,

double-breasted suit, and trenchcoat. He put on the fedora and the dark sunshades.

To finish, he crossed to the freezer and pulled open one of the doors. A blast of cold air jumped him, chilling his breath to fog. Careful not to soil his fashionable threads, he carried the tray of ground bone meal into the refrigerated locker and placed it on a shelf beside the other pet food trays.

Then he went back outside to retrieve the hopper containing what had once been flesh surrounding Mohawk's skeleton. This he took in and buried among similar trays of frozen sausage-stuffing meat.

Come Monday, Jinks thought, Vancouver shoppers'll have a bit of extra protein in the hot dogs they buy.

# Tunnel of Love

London, England
*9:01 a.m.*

The Fleet River flows underground from Hampstead Heath and Highgate Ponds in the northern heights of London through Camden Town and King's Cross before it joins the Thames at Blackfriars Bridge. It was there that Edwin Chalmers QC lost both his eyes and his life.

West of the Fleet the Tyburn flows underground from Hampstead south to cross the Grand Union Canal at Regent's Park by means of a cast-iron pipe built into a brick footbridge. From Little Venice on the Canal you can boat eastward to the London Zoo.

The upper reaches of both rivers, which are now part of the London sewer system, were meadows until the middle of the nineteenth century when a sudden housing boom swallowed up Hampstead village. Today the Heath is undoubtedly one of the city's finest parks—790 acres to lure 100,000 Londoners north on a sunny summer weekend.

The funfair south of Hampstead Heath had seen much better days. It flanked the open waterway near where the underground river was trapped in the sewer tunnel.

During season the first thing you'd notice as you came through the gates was the smell of fried onions, fish and chips, popcorn and candy floss. Bright colours and dazzling lights would assail your eyes as your ears filled with the screams of people spun around on the rides. Any fair at its heart is really a theatre of machines—The Whip, Roller Coaster, Ferris wheel, Tip-Top, Tilt-A-Whirl, and Loop-O-Plane; the Paratrooper, Octopus, Dodgems, and Trabant. And here was no exception.

"Try your luck," a fairground hustler would call, "Come in! Come in!", while around him the shots and bells and wooden concussions from the shooting galleries, the bass organ rumbling at the hub of the merry-go-round, the drone of Bingo numbers being yelled out, the clamour of sirens in pinball machines and the dangerous grinding of metal on metal would all combine into one cacophonous noise.

At first you'd see all the glitter and glamour and the not-quite-honest cheap and tawdry sleaze.

Then you'd look again and this time see the punks.

Rape in the House of Fun is not a funny affair.

Besides, it's bad for business, Lennie Coke thought.

Coke was the ultimate hustler, one of a dying breed. He had the squat look of a bull terrier about him—medium short, broad-shouldered and stocky with thick bow legs.

Coke's clothes were fairground-snappy though frayed a bit at the edges. A fake diamond stickpin was jabbed through his tie and he carried a cane the knob of which was shaped like Punch. Behind eyes that oozed larceny, Coke's philosophy of life was "What you think you see is not what you're going to get". And as a result his red-veined nose had been broken in several places.

Coke used to work the Roller Coaster before he hit the bottle. Then a few years back he'd had an inspiration, and that season made lots of money selling balloons blown up with nitrous oxide laughing gas to the kids.

By the time he was released from jail twelve months later, herpes and rock fashion had wounded the Sexual Revolution and helped resurrect romance. Girls were wearing skirts again so air jets in a House of Fun would lift them for a peek at their knickers. Boys could use a Tunnel of Love to aid a quick grope, so Lennie—always tuned to what would currently turn a penny—had built both a House of Fun *and* a Tunnel of Love.

The weirdos and creeps and nutters had always loved the fairground, but something had changed in their make-up while Lennie was in jail. For deep in the housing estates that spread around Camden Town, a generation of alienated glue-sniffing kids had been spawned, a sub-human horde that now haunted the fair, armed with imbecilic grins and switchblade knives.

It had started with two or three skinheads pissing on the kiddies as they galloped by on the merry-go-round.

Soon a handful of hoodlums were regularly crowding around the pinball machines in the arcade. An unseen lout at the centre would then break open the cashbox with an iron bar and fill his pockets.

Later the punks had taken to knocking off the fairground concessions. Two thugs would start a fight to distract the attendant while a third vaulted the counter and cleaned out the till. Or they would simply rush a popcorn stand and smash it to pieces to retrieve whatever money could be found in the debris.

But last year the situation went from bad to worse.

The punks would now trash anything and everything in sight. Gangs of Chelsea and Millwall supporters stood under the skyrides and bombarded the passengers with rocks and bottles and cans. A Ferris wheel patron had been struck by a slingshot ball-bearing as he passed by like a wooden duck in a target gallery. Then last season two teenage girls had been raped in the House of Fun. Ticket sales had dwindled and now the fair was closing down.

Welcome to bloody *Clockwork Orange*, Lennie Coke thought.

Coke could not decide whether to dismantle the House of Fun or the Tunnel of Love first. In the end he flipped a ten pence coin.

The morning was overcast with the sky threatening rain, but that had not kept the onlookers away. They milled around the workmen as they took apart the fair, breaking up the metal rides into several hundred pieces, rolling up cables, taking down lights, and packing the power generators into crates.

The Tunnel of Love had been a good stand for Coke the last few years. It was built next to the open waterway and channelled some of the canal stream through two sluice gates, front and back, to float the gondola boats. Since the close of the fair last season the treadle-pit had been dry. It was now clogged with twigs, leaves, old gum wrappers, and cigarette butts.

Coke walked back to the rear sluice gate and cranked it up. He watched as water ran into the metal gondola channel, first as a muddy trickle, then a dark brown jet, then a gushing frothy stream. It surged into the hole in the wall that fed the Tunnel of Love, seconds later spewing out like a haemorrhage through the exit in the front façade of the building.

The water surface was now rainbow-veined with oil and grease from the treadmill mechanism that powered the boats. It flowed churning up all the debris and dirt that had gathered since late last year, sweeping back into the entrance mouth to complete the circuit. The stream in the channel rose until it had reached its normal depth of four feet as marked on the side of the treadle-pit.

Leaving the back sluice open, Coke moved to the front gate and also cranked it up. He spent the next few minutes guiding the debris bobbing in the water toward the main canal stream with the flat of a coal shovel. That done, he cranked down the front sluice gate.

Coke next dismantled the ticket booth and packed it away for shipment to Scotland. As he laboured a tall ugly guy kept pestering him to launch his boats once more for old time's sake.

When Coke glanced up to tell this geezer he'd drown him in the treadle-pit if he wasn't left alone, Lennie couldn't help noticing the glum look on the faces of other passersby. Was that because a major part of their misspent youth was being shipped away?

This got the old hustler thinking, for he instinctively recognized an opportunity to make thirty or forty quid when he saw one.

So once the ticket booth was dismantled and packed away, Lennie circled to the shed behind the Tunnel building and dragged out four of his ten flat-bottomed gondolas. Launching one in the water he locked it with a boat hook to the Tunnel entrance dock and switched on the motor drive.

Beneath the water the treadmill groaned as soft waves rose to the surface from the circular action of the submerged treadle-struts. The boat rocked gently and bumped against the wooden dock.

The entrance to the Tunnel was painted so it resembled a sexy woman's mouth, her pouting Cupid's bow lips surrounding the yawning darkness beyond with a circle of vivid red.

As Coke plugged in the electric cord that turned on the exhibit lights, a sarcastic voice behind him said, "Paint it to look like her fanny, mate, and you'd do a lot more trade."

A teenage girl giggled.

Coke turned to observe the couple watching him. A boy with fuzz on his face had his arm around a fat-arsed girl in a tight sweater. They were openly smoking a joint.

"I'll give you fifty pence, guv, to let us go around. Give me a chance to slip me hand under 'er top."

"Dickie!" the girl giggled, pushing him away.

Coke smirked at the kid with the fuzz on his face. "Don't be so cheap," he said.

"Aw right, a quid. Be a sport."

Coke shrugged, paused, then cracked a larcenous smile. He could never resist a con job.

Lennie helped them into the craft, holding the gondola steady with the gaff hook. Then he cast off as the boat bumped the sides of the channel and moved toward the yawning throat of the tunnel. It swayed as the boy and girl adjusted their balance.

Coke watched as the rocking gondola was slowly swallowed by the mouth.

Deep inside the tunnel a second pair of eyes watched the boat come in.

"Leave off! Your hands are cold!" the teenager giggled.

"C'mon, Mandy. It's the middle of winter, luv. Give it a go."

"Piss off. Don't touch me tits."

"What a waste of a quid."

It was black in the tunnel and darkness poured over them as the boat bumped along steadily, treadle groaning and water gurgling. Further along, red and blue lights glimmered behind moisture-laden windows to reveal busts of long-departed matinée idols—Valentino, Harlow, Dietrich, and Bow. A papier-mâché Mae West leaned out over the channel, her chest grimy from years of exploring fingers. Hazy purple images of David Niven and Cary Grant, of Tracy, Hepburn, Gable, and Leigh glowed with ultraviolet light.

"Who are all these fossils, Dickie?" Mandy asked.

"Dunno, luv. Couldn't give a toss."

They had just passed one of the murky exhibit windows when a deafening explosion rumbled outside. Startled, the girl jumped, making the gondola lurch as the magnified sound pulsed through the tunnel.

"What you doing?" the boy shouted, grabbing for the gunnel.

Mandy began screaming uncontrollably as she saw the slimy figure now rising up out of the water just in front of the boat.

Then Dickie gasped and jerked back from the looming monster.

The remote-control diversion bomb set off from inside the Tunnel of Love was packed with incendiaries—a cake of paraffin sawdust, a box of aluminium flake, thermite, and kerosene. Its detonator cap was rigged up to be blown by radio frequency. The deadly device had been dumped in a black rubbish bag behind the Hall of Mirrors. When it exploded flames leaped twenty feet in the air, spewing glass and causing pandemonium.

The screams coming from the Tunnel went unnoticed.

The monster rising up out of the water had skin that was slimy black and insect-like eyes too large for its head. Its breath frothed and hissed with a gargling sound akin to that of a freshly-cut throat. Then its right arm came plunging down.

Dickie screamed in pain as the steel stabbed through his thigh at an angle, jerking back in reflex so the weapon tore the artery and gaped the wound. Blood fountained up from his leg in a spurt that rained all over the girl.

Mandy stood up in the boat, again rocking the gondola sharply as she kicked at the dripping monster's face.

Glass splintered and water splashed as whatever it was fell tumbling back in the stream.

"I'm bleeding! I'm bleeding!" Dickie shrieked again and again, each pump of his heart spewing blood from the punctured artery in his leg to splatter the tunnel walls.

The gondola bumped and lurched as it hit something in the water.

Mandy threw herself over the screaming boy's lap and smashed with her fist at the thing submerged in the stream, freeing the boat which now moved toward the tunnel exit.

Outside, people ran in all directions away from a wooden building engulfed in smoky flames.

As they emerged Dickie passed out and crashed back in the boat.

Mandy glanced down at his spurting leg and was shocked to see it pinned to the seat of the gondola by an icepick rammed through the flesh of his thigh.

The icepick handle was carved to depict the Creature from the Black Lagoon.

# Mother/Myself

## Vancouver, British Columbia
### 1:03 a.m.

Today we celebrate your First Coming on January 11. Is that why your blissful brilliance is so blinding tonight, Mom? I know Heaven waits for me in our ultimate reunion.

I promised your niece would suffer the Fate for what she's done to you. *Babylon the great, mother of harlots and of earth's abominations . . . The woman was arrayed in purple and scarlet, and bedecked with gold and jewels and pearls, holding in her hand a golden cup full of the filthiness of her fornication.*

*I will tell you the mystery of the woman, and of the beast with seven heads and ten horns that carries her . . . They will make her desolate and naked, and devour her flesh and burn her up with fire.*

So, Mom, what do you think of your son now that you see all? See what I mean? *Give up worshipping demons and idols . . . which cannot either see or hear or walk . . . We who have understanding reckon the number of the beast . . . Its number is 666.*

I forgive you not loving me then as you love me today.

Happy birthday, Mom.

# Warped

"Ever see *Forbidden Planet*?" Caradon asked.

"No," Zinc replied.

"Well, this spaceship lands on Altair Four to see what happened to a previous mission, eh? This is AD 2200 give or take a year. What they find is Walter Pidgeon as the resident mad scientist and a monster on the loose that starts making chopped meat out of the crew. This monster is invisible, huh? Can't see it. Can't feel it. Can't catch it either.

"Anyway, the ending is that Walter Pidgeon finally comes to realize that the killer is a monster from the id. *His* id, see? It is a manifestation of his darkest desires, and since he wants the intruders gone, when he falls asleep it escapes from his subconscious to make mincemeat of the crew. Nice concept, eh? The monster of the id. And that's how I see all the geeks in that club."

Chandler laughed. "Bill, you're quite the philosopher."

"No," Caradon replied. "I'm actually a voyeur. And that's a damn good kink for a cop to have."

They were sitting in an unmarked car parked on the other side of Hastings Street half a block down from The Id. Alley shadows hid them from view by the patrons trickling out of the club. Caradon—in the driver's seat—reached back into the rear of the car to retrieve an athletic bag. From it he removed a coffee thermos and two Styrofoam cups, passing one to Chandler.

The more Zinc learned of Caradon, the more he was intrigued. For here was a man who lived alone with a 40-inch rear projection TV screen, a Zenith VCR, and

9000 videotapes. His work with the RCMP was to peek at others' lives, then he went home and turned on the tube and spent his time off doing the same thing. *Miami Vice, Dallas, Benny Hill, Daffy Duck*— they all went through his brain. Ask a trivia question: Bill would have the answer.

"Hey," Caradon said. "Take a look."

Chandler picked up a pair of binoculars and focused them on the club. Rika Hyde, aka Erika Zann, the singer with Ghoul, and Axel Crypt, the bass player, had just come out. They stood for a minute talking on the north side of Hastings, then parted company and went in opposite directions.

Chandler put the binoculars down as a group of young club patrons walked in front of the car. One of them was a girl no more than fourteen years old. When she spotted the two men sitting in the vehicle, she opened her winter coat and flashed them a glimpse of the whalebone corset she wore underneath. Then she stuck out her tongue and ran off laughing to rejoin the others.

Caradon shook his head and licked his lips in mock lust. "There ought to be a law," the Special O cop said.

Chandler nudged him in the ribs. "There is," he replied.

"You like horror stories?" Caradon asked.

"Not much," Zinc replied. "I see too much horror in my work."

"I do," the Special O man said, sipping his coffee.

The two cops sat in silence staring at the club, waiting the long wait for Hengler to come out. The Id crowd had now disappeared into the night that skulked around the neon lights along Hastings Street.

"Think they rot the brain?" Caradon asked.

"Think *what* rots the brain?" Chandler replied.

"Horror stories. Films. Records. You know what I mean."

Chandler shrugged. "In some ways, yes."

"Like what ways?"

"The club tonight."

"You mean the monsters of The Id?"

"Not exactly. But some of them have problems."

"You sound like a critic," Caradon said. "You know why so many critics get their knickers in a twist over horror fantasy?"

"No. But I'm sure you'll tell me."

"Cause horror fiction isn't written as a means of escape. It's meant to be a genre of personal confrontation and they fuckin don't understand that. I always think the more a critic wrings his or her hands in disgust, the deeper and more serious that person's own psychiatric problems."

Chandler grinned. "Look, Bill," he said. "How many jean-clad kids with an anti-social attitude have you encountered since you became a cop? You know the type I'm referring to—the ones with severe problems of anger who are deeply immersed in the sub-culture and fantasies of violent rock. You can't tell me those fantasies aren't affecting their way of thinking and their behaviour in an anti-social direction, cause I know they are. I've seen the results. So in one way horror stories do rot the brain. In that they supply fuel for the flame."

"Some senators' wives in Washington would love to meet you," Caradon said. "The ones with the campaign against 'porn rock'."

"No, they wouldn't," Chandler replied. "Cause I think they're more dangerous than the issue they debate."

"Keep going," Caradon said, spinning his hand like a wheel.

"Bill, you and I both know that what the horror novel, movie, or comic book is trying to do is search out that place in the subconscious mind where each of us lives at his most primitive level."

"I'm with you so far," Caradon said.

"The normal human mind," Zinc continued, "is always at work on two different levels—the conscious and the subconscious. The drive in our lives is to somehow reconcile both of these levels in order to obtain a sense of psychic harmony. The most potent horror stories do just that for us."

"I'm still with you," Caradon said. "Go on."

"The danger in horror fiction, however, is that it might trigger off someone who adopts the horror fantasy as his own insane delusion then seeks to act it out in the real world. For what about the person who—because of mental illness—has suffered a break with reality? Such a person lives in the land of his subconscious mind cut loose and isolated from his conscious state. You still with me, Bill?"

Caradon nodded his head.

"Therefore, the only harmony a madman can obtain between his conscious and subconscious minds is to force reality to conform to his delusion. In other words, to seek to create a parallel experience for the horror fantasy in the real world."

"What's the punchline?" Caradon asked.

"Simply that in such a case horror fantasy leads to horror fact as the madman tries to bring the fictional act alive in everyday life. That's how he derives a sense of psychic harmony. Instead of art reflecting reality, reality is made to reflect art."

"Now who's the philosopher?" Caradon asked.

## North Vancouver, British Columbia
### 1:45 a.m.

Rosanna Keate was dressed in a white silk negligée, the lacy bodice cut low to show off her full breasts. Her hair was piled up on her head with the occasional wild strand falling loose. Her skin was still pale from her bout of glandular fever.

She had just finished sketching her own face onto one of the nudes, but as yet the other outline on the canvas was featureless. Looking at her watch, she thought, He'll be here in fifteen minutes.

Rosanna believed that young men, old men, ugly men should have a ring circling their cock and balls by which to lead them around. Such men had always been easy prey for her. But recently Rosanna's taste in fulfilling sex had veered in other directions. Unlimited money opened many new doors.

Rosanna enjoyed only sex that was totally on her terms. She liked to be the one in absolute control. She enjoyed saying, "Do this, do that," with an instant response. But most she liked beautiful people who could be convinced to sell her their humiliation. Like the man from the escort service who was coming tonight?

Rosanna adored pretty boys with movie star faces who were hung like stallions. Boys with a taste for fine clothes and sleek cars, cocaine and champagne and exotic for-

eign places. Boys who had all the visions, but not the
money in their pockets.

Rosanna could offer that money so long as she got her
money's worth. Plus she paid a bonus for every minute a
stud could fight himself to keep from getting the erection
she was out to induce.

As she was removing her toys from the floor of the
wardrobe closet—the saddle strap to separate the buttocks for spanking, the slave sandals, locking bib, anti-
sitting harness, posture collar, anal probe, phallic corset,
nipple caps, and the deadly tubed and valved controlled-
inhalation submission helmet—the door bell rang.

Looking at her watch, she thought, He's thirteen minutes early.

Rosanna rose to her feet and pinched her nipples sharply
to ensure they'd be erect.

She crossed to the door.

But as she opened it a sudden unexpected frown creased
her beautiful face.

"You!" she said, surprised.


# Vancouver, British Columbia
*1:46 a.m.*


"It's a very old issue," Bill Caradon said. "The morality
of horror fantasy has been called into question for more
than a hundred years. The recent controversy is but a
new tentacle on an old octopus."

Chandler poured another coffee from the thermos.

"I don't suppose you ever read the reprints of *Weird
Tales* or *Tales From The Crypt*?" Caradon asked.

"No," Zinc said.

"During the thirties there were accusations that the
'shudder pulps' like *Weird Tales* and *Horror Stories* were
polluting the minds of the youth of America.

"Then in the 1950s, the U.S. comics industry strangled
*Tales From The Crypt*, *Vault Of Horror*, *Haunt Of Fear*,
and other publications before the muscle of a Senate
sub-committee did it for them. In Britain, Churchill actually passed legislation to kill the horror comics.

"So what's now going on down south is nothing but the
cycle coming round again."

"You don't sound like a conservative cop," Chandler said.

"Being a cop doesn't mean I have to check my common sense at the door."

"True," Zinc replied.

"You don't kill the messenger for the message," Caradon said. "If a madman finds inspiration for a crime in a book or film, or if he uses a rock song to soundtrack a killing, insanity is the problem, not the authors or directors or musician's fantasy. If the psycho hadn't used that source he would have used another. Zodiac found inspiration in astrology. Son of Sam spoke to his neighbour's talking dog. You wanta know what I think?"

"I'm all ears," Chandler replied.

Usually stakeout was the most boring part of a cop's job. But not tonight. Caradon was no dummy and he certainly spoke his mind, right or wrong. Most people were so concerned about public image that they were afraid to be frank for fear they might not be seen to conform to the present norm. Such people to Zinc's mind were homogenized bores.

"I got no use for dolts who are blind to reality," Caradon said. "And I don't like powerful people trying to impose their artificial concept of the world on me. You know why people like horror stories?"

"Yes," Chandler said, grinning. "Because supernatural events symbolize neurotic personal problems."

"Wrong. Because ancient ideas survive in modern minds And the reason some people reject horror stories is either because they find them too terrifying or because they find the entertainment crude and degrading. I suspect the latter snobbery hides the former sort of qualm."

"I don't think that's all of it," Chandler said. "The attack of a monster is horrifying in itself. And the human monster is the most unsettling of all. You ever see *The Fly*?"

"Sure. H-e-l-p m-e-e-e!" Caradon said, his voice becoming a squeak.

Chandler laughed.

"I'll bet you didn't know the screenplay for that film was written by James Clavell," Caradon said. "The guy who wrote *Shogun* and just sold his latest book for 5 million bucks."

Chandler blinked.

Amazing! he thought. Where does Bill store all these esoteric facts?

"Anyway, you were saying . . ." Caradon prompted.

"When I was a boy on the prairies *The Fly* scared the shit out of me. During the summer the flies in the room I shared with my brother—"

"Whoa!" Caradon said. "Hengler just came out."

## 3:33 a.m.

"In the time of the Black Death," Chandler said, "European churches were decorated with bones. Think about that in the context of what you were saying."

He and Caradon were now parked outside Ray Hengler's home in Shaughnessy. It was a modest dwelling with a 2000–bottle wine cellar, a breakfast room complete with a secret panel, and spacious grounds including three gardens, squash and tennis courts, and a very large pool.

They had followed Hengler from The Id to an after-hours gambling club, then tailed him here. Both cops were now ready to call it a night.

"Concerning your story about *The Fly*," Caradon said, "if it's any consolation, most people consider the latex mask worn in that film to be Ben Nye's finest make-up creation. David Cronenberg's doing a remake."

"I'm still hurt," Zinc said. "You called me a chicken-shit."

"I just said if you want to see a *real* horror flick try Romero's *Dawn Of The* . . . Hey, something's up."

Ray Hengler was coming down the driveway of his mansion. Thirty feet away from the ghost car parked out on the street, he turned and walked along Angus Drive to a phone booth on the corner. There, pacing back and forth, he waited impatiently.

Seven minutes later Hengler picked up the receiver quickly on what both cops assumed to be its first ring.

"I want that phone wired too," Chandler said.

The Mounties were parked too far away to overhear any of this conversation:

"It's done."

"Completely?"

"The man is no more. As they say, life's a grind."

Hengler laughed. "You want another job?"

"Same price as the last one?"

"More. This guy's a cop."

"That's a whole lot more. Danger pay."

"His name's Zinc Chandler."

"Where do I find him?"

"He's staying at the Westin Bayshore. Eighth floor."

"I know the place."

"Good. I want him skinned alive . . . literally. Bring me Chandler's face in a bag, I'll give you five grand more."

Back in the ghost car Caradon said, "I wonder who he's talking to? And what they're talking about?"

# Black Museum

London, England
*12:15 p.m.*

London—*her* London—was falling apart, but Rand was unable to pinpoint just when the decay began.

As a child in the years before the war, she well remembered walking in Regent's Park with her mother and being told that she lived in the most civilized city in the world. "Your father helps to make that so," her mother used to say.

Hilary had always been proud of the traditional image of the unarmed British bobby. The Metropolitan Police—*her* police—were a sterling example for others of patient tolerance. She had once asked her father why he didn't carry a gun. He'd replied, "Gunfire is contagious. More villains will carry guns if the police do. And they'll use them."

Now ten per cent of the British police were licensed to carry firearms, and they'd shot five innocent people in recent incidents. An officer had been shot to death outside the Libyan Embassy, another hacked to death in the streets of north London, and yet another stabbed in the grounds of a millionaire's home. They'd found bomb factories in Tottenham and gasoline-filled garages rigged to be ignited in order to booby trap police. Plastic bullets and tear gas were ready for use in the next urban riot, while marksmen from Dll squad patrolled Heathrow Airport in full view of the public with Heckler and Koch submachine guns.

Rand could not help worrying, Where will it all end?

If pressed to give a date for when the real decay set in, she'd pick the late sixties during the reign of the Krays. Hilary had been a WPC then and only played a minor

part in the Yard's effort to secure charges against the
twins. But she'd known instinctively that the Krays had
forever changed the face of crime in Britain. Ronnie, the
dominant one in the pair, had studied Al Capone and the
Chicago gangsters of the early thirties. The Krays had
used this knowledge to structure their own "firm", and
thus brought American-style organized crime to the East
End of London. And that meant guns.

Today the police were like an armed camp.

You're letting the work get you down, Hilary Rand
thought.

She turned from her office window to face the six men
sitting on the chairs lined in front of her desk.

"Gentlemen," Rand said. "Meet Basil Plimpton. Now
let's discuss the sewers."

The first sewer workers were the rakers or gong-fermers
of 800 years ago. Their job—at the rate of two pounds a
clean by the fourteenth century!—was to scrape out
Britain's stinking medieval cess-pits. This could be dangerous work. In 1326 a gong-fermer named Richard the
Raker tumbled into his own cess-pit and drowned "mon-
strously in his own excrement".

The water closet was invented by Sir John Harington
in about 1596. Sir John made one for himself and one for
his cousin, Queen Elizabeth I. Unfortunately for London, the invention did not catch on. So by 1810 the city's
one million suffocating citizens were themselves drowning in the overflow and stench from 200,000 cess-pits
which polluted the underground rivers and all emptied
into the Thames.

Even walking down the street in those early days could
be a hazardous pastime. British in-house facilities then
consisted of a chamber pot the contents of which were
tossed out the window to a cry of "Gardy-Loo!" This
came from the French term *Gardez l'eau*— and God help
the Englishman who wasn't bilingual. The term is still in
use in "going to the loo".

By the middle of the nineteenth century something *had*
to be done. During the 1840s there were major cholera
outbreaks. 1858 was the year of the Great Stink when the
smell in London got so bad that the windows of the
House of Commons were hung with curtains soaked in

chloride of lime and there was talk of moving the government upstream to Hampton Court.

The man who solved the problem was Sir Joseph Bazalgette, an engineer with the Metropolitan Board of Works. Between 1859 and 1865 Bazalgette built a series of "interceptory sewers" which are still in use today. Three of these sewers were constructed running west to east parallel to the Thames north of the river, with three similar ones to the south. The interceptory sewers connect with the main sewers flowing north and south to divert their contents east before they reach the Thames.

The sewer system of present-day London is more than 100 years old. It works by the principle of gravity. Waste from 13,000 miles of small local sewers threaded beneath the city's streets is fed into 700 miles of main sewer pipes running north and south. Some of these main sewers contain the bricked-over underground rivers that once flowed openly through London.

More than 100 miles of interceptory sewers start in the west of the city with tunnels no more than four feet high. They are egg-shaped so the lower the water level, the faster the flow. As they move east to draw off the contents of the main north-south sewers, they increase in size to eleven feet. Far downstream they empty this sewage into the Beckton treatment plant north of the river and the Plumstead plant to the south. Half a million gallons of waste flow through the bowels of London every day.

Basil Plimpton was an engineer with the Thames Water Authority. He was a middle-aged man who talked with both his mouth and hands and when the subject was the sewers could never talk long enough. While delivering these dramatic lectures he chain-smoked cigarettes. By the time Rand introduced him to Braithwaite and the four Yard detectives, her office was clouded with a swirling grey haze of smoke.

"Let me give you some idea of the problem you face," Plimpton said with a flourish.

"For more than two thousand years London has been a city both above *and* below ground. The Romans built a sewer network which is still down there. Tunnels and crypts were constructed during the Middle Ages but we have no idea of their whereabouts today. Sewer construction before the mid-nineteenth century was by private endeavour. No central records were kept. Even the network that we know is such a mystery that we will not have explored and videotaped all of it by remote-control miniature hovercraft until the mid 1990s.

"The ground exposed by German bombing during the Second World War showed us all sorts of things the presence of which was completely unfathomed before.

"There are 1500 miles of neo-gothic *main* sewers in our system. You can travel all over London using them. There is a manhole cover leading to these tunnels every hundred yards or so on every street in London. Then there are thousands of miles of local authority sewers which connect to ours. Travel through them is difficult because they are so small, but it can be done.

"In addition there are eighty-two miles of tube tunnels, twelve miles of government tunnels, and hundreds of thousands of miles of cables and pipes carrying fresh water, gas, hydraulic power, electricity, telecommunications, cable television, the Underground and other trains, channels under the Thames, baseworks for the canals, 'deep shelter' fortifications for defence of the city in past and possible future wars, abandoned cave warehouses and cold storage rooms, old deserted safe deposit vaults—plus all the hidden oddities that collect beneath a city dug up and redug up for two millennia.

"Then all these systems that honeycomb the ground beneath our feet either interconnect or overlap or twist around each other."

"In other words," Rand said, "we'd need a force several thousand times the size of the Yard to police that labyrinth?"

"Yes. And you would be doing so completely in the dark. Except for the odd location where light filters down from above."

There was silence in the office as this information sank in. What if it didn't just concern the manhunt they had launched to catch the Sewer Killer? What if the Vampire Killer and Jack The Bomber with their separate hidden threats were using the sewers as well? Three maniacs loose at once and preying on the city.

"Let's take the problems one by one," Rand said. "First, whatever happened beneath Blackfriars Bridge."

"That's where the Fleet Storm Sewer outfall opens on the Thames," Plimpton said, one arm T-connecting with the other to illustrate his point.

"Let's begin with the facts we have," the DC Supt suggested. "The Yard received a 999 call from a man with an American accent. He reported an emergency at the foot of the Embankment wall. When the Thames Police arrived they found blood on the riverbed rocks, several small ceramic birds, and a pair of eye-spike binoculars like those we have downstairs in the Yard's Black Museum.

"No body was found at the scene, nor later recovered from the Thames. However, a trapped wheelbarrow had wedged open the giant doors of the sewer outfall nearby and there were signs a body had been dragged into the outfall opening. What does that mean to you so far as it should concern us?"

"Well," Plimpton said, moving to the sewer map tacked to the wall and pinpointing the location under discussion. "First you must understand how the outfalls work.

"Bazalgette, who built our system, constructed a number of dams across the main north-south sewer channels. These dams block the water flow and allow the west-east interceptory sewers to take the sewage away before it reaches the Thames.

"But if there's a major rainfall so the main sewer waters swell beyond the capacity of the interceptors, then excess water flows over the dams and into storm relief sewers that carry it off to the outfalls on the Thames.

"There are forty outfalls north of the river, and thirty to the south. There are no sewers that cross the Thames," Plimpton stated.

"Since all our present investigations are connected to sewers *north* of the river," Rand said, "would we be safe to concentrate there and cut our job in half?"

"Well, there are other tunnels under the Thames, and if he's using the manholes he could walk across any bridge."

"But not if he's carrying bodies to some location near or connected with the system?"

"No. Then he'd have real problems if he crossed the river.,"

"Go on," she said.

"Since the system works on gravity all the interceptory sewers are built at levels lower than the main north-south channels. That means if the river water were allowed to flow in, the entire sewer system would be flooded and its workings sabotaged. Therefore, the outfalls on the Thames all have heavy metal flaps which only open outward to let the sewer water exit when pushed by the flow, but won't swing the other way to let river water in.

"All rain water goes directly into the sewers. When the flow in the system is higher than that of the river at low tide, the flaps swing open and let the sewer empty. When the river is higher than the level in the sewers, the flaps stay closed and the flow remains trapped in the system or surges down other storm reliefs."

"So," Rand said, "the Blackfriars Bridge outfall would only open at low tide."

"Yes."

"Normally it would swing shut once the water had flowed out."

"Yes."

"In this case, however, a wheelbarrow came down with the flow, got trapped when the door swung shut before the barrow had completely left the sewer mouth, and wedged the outfall open. So that gave someone access to the sewers from the river."

"Perhaps. But what a fluke. Did you find a boat abandoned outside?"

"No."

"Then unless your killer was either swimming in the Thames, or just happened to climb down the ladder from the Embankment walk—and remember he couldn't see the outfall doors from above—the only other possibility is he came out from within the sewer system, then went back inside. What time are we talking about?"

"Approximately 7:30 a.m."

Plimpton shrugged his shoulders. "From what you've said there was an assault on the river-bottom rocks. The body was then dragged into the wedged-open outfall. So where did the victim materialize from? Out of the sewer system along with the killer?"

"No, that doesn't fit the spiked binoculars or the fact the body was then dragged away. I believe a trap was set to ambush a random victim. Either someone on the river or walking up above. The location of this particular crime was determined by the coincidence of the wheelbarrow getting caught. If the door had not been wedged open, he'd have struck somewhere else."

"Whoever your criminal is," Plimpton said, "he's ei-

ther very lucky or he knows the system well. All flaps on
the outfalls are double-doored, with one flap on the river
and the other in the sewer tunnel to back the first one
up. If both are left open alarms go off. The flaps themselves are so heavy that we have to use a block and tackle
to get them open. The only way he could have gone into
the sewer and escaped up the tunnel was to carry the
body up the gang ladder that's beside the inner flap, then
over the top and down the other side. It can be done,
however. Didn't the Black Panther also use the sewers?"

"Yes," Rand replied. "Once he's in there, what's it
like moving around?"

"It's easy to move north and south within the main
sewers. They will take you all over London. You can
only move west to east in the interceptory sewers because
they have a constant flow. And to move within them
you'd need a rubber raft. But again, it can be done.

"Moving, however, is just part of the problem. There
are the additional dangers of surprise surges in the water
flow; of gases from rotting waste, like hydrogen sulphide,
which is toxic, or methane, which is flammable, collecting in the tunnels; and of lack of oxygen in certain
locations.

"Nor is the environment down there pleasant. It's a
world teeming with rats, fungi, eels, mice, frogs and a
hundred other forms of creeping life. In 1963—4,650,000
brown rats were killed in London's sewers. There are
estimated to be ten million more down there today. It
takes a certain type of mentality to love the sewer system."

"Then we're looking for a sewer worker?" Hilary Rand
said.

Plimpton shook his head. "I wish it were that simple.
But it's not. Do all of you know about digital maps? No?
Well, this is how they work.

"We put an Ordnance Survey map on a drawing board
with a grid of tens of thousands of tiny crosswires on top.
The crosswires mark points horizontally. Then each point
is plotted vertically by depth. This is computer enhanced
and stored in forty 'layers' or 'views'. When we call up
this digital map, what we get on the screen is a three-
dimensional survey. At the touch of a computer button
we can have any cross-section or longitudinal spread.
Perspective can be programmed at the turn of a dial.
Anyone with such a map of the London sewers can then

weave a route or pattern of routes from any point in the system to any other by giving the computer certain instructions."

Plimpton paused.

"Last May, the Thames Water office at Drayton Park was broken into," he said, indicating a point on the map tacked to the wall. "Stolen in the burglary was software containing digital maps plotted by the North Thames Gas Board, the London Electricity Board, the London Tele-communications Region, the Public Health Department of the Greater London Council, and us.

"Whoever stole those maps—if he is able to use a computer—can plot his way anywhere in London by a million different routes entirely underground."

"Jesus!" Detective Inspector Derick Hone whispered.

The others had now left. Remaining in the Murder Squad office were Detective Chief Superintendent Hilary Rand, Home Office psychiatrist Dr Winston Braithwaite, and DI Derick Hone, the DC Supt's bagman. Hone was not wearing a hat so he had combed several strands of hair across his shiny balding pate. All three were drinking tea.

"My nose tells me," Hone said, "of all the missing persons we have considered, the barrister Chalmers is the one most likely to have been attacked beneath Blackfriars Bridge. His life was going far to well for him to have walked out, and the Middle Temple is just down the Embankment walk."

"I agree," Rand said. "I also think our Sewer Killer—from the voice recorded on the 999 call tape—is an American from the East Coast of the States."

"Home Office is checking that," Derick Hone said. "But with the present exchange rate, there's been a veri-table flood of Yanks through the city. As far as we know, the Sewer Killer first surfaced eight days ago. He might have been here just a fortnight, or a very long time."

"Winston, what do you make of the Sewer Killer leaving these objects behind?" Rand asked. "A top hat and broken mirror at the scene of the Stonegate Cemetery disappearance. A pair of bloody spiked binoculars and several small ceramic birds beneath Blackfriars Bridge. Both crimes do have a similar MO."

The doctor contemplated the question a moment before he said, "Attention-seeking of this type—leaving cryptic clues to taunt the police—is common to both psychotic and psychopathic killers.

"Such a person believes that he is superior to and better than everybody else. He doesn't make mistakes and if one should occur it is blamed on others. In effect such a killer is saying, 'I can do no wrong. You've not been able to catch me yet, so see what you can make of this.'

"We are talking here," Braithwaite said, "about self-assertion. Such random killings cause shock waves in a city the size of London, and that's exactly what this murderer wants. There's then a double satisfaction in sending obscure messages that make the police struggle to puzzle out the killer's motive. It's all a game in which the killer is the one in complete control. He's saying, 'I'm sending a message you'd better decipher and listen to—or else!'"

"In the 1880s Jack the Ripper sent taunting letters to the London police. Recently Zodiac did the same thing in San Francisco, signing his notes in cypher with an astrological cross superimposed on a circle. When finally decoded, one of these said, 'I will be reborn in Paradise and all I have killed will be my slaves.'

"Zodiac also sent a piece of a victim's shirt to the American police just as Jack the Ripper sent the Yard part of one victim's kidney. Neville Heath, Charles Manson, the Boston Strangler, Peter Kürten, Son of Sam, the Headhunter, all behaved the same. So did your Jack The Bomber with his flowers last week.

"In the end, however, this sort of game is self-defeating for the killer. What he really craves is publicity. But anonymous publicity is ultimately frustrating. He reaches a point where he cannot advance any further into the limelight without getting caught. And without further murders his celebrity wanes. So soon he's trapped in a vicious circle that leads to more and more killings.

"Eventually a copy cat may jump on the bandwaggon either with crimes of his own or claims that cash in psychologically on the real killer's fame. Such a response happened with the Yorkshire Ripper hoax letters and tape. Then the real killer's only way to denounce the phony is to kill again so as to take back centre stage. The psychological need for personal publicity almost guarantees that response.

"Alternatively," Braithwaite said, "perhaps the true reason for these particular taunts is to call you out personally and thus identify the killer's police adversary. Every Moriarty wants to outwit Sherlock Holmes."

"What do you make of the Sewer Killer's clues?" Rand asked.

Braithwaite shook his head. "That's difficult, Hilary. Their connection to each crime is the product of an insane mind."

"We've got to try," the detective said. "It's our only lead."

"Okay. Let's begin with the spiked binoculars. You said you have a similar pair in the Yard's Black Museum?"

"Yes. In 1945 a girl in Southampton received a pair in the post as a nineteenth birthday present. The enclosed card told her that if she took a look she would be surprised 'how closely it brings things'. Her father, however, sprung the knives by mistake. We never did find the person who sent them."

"You've checked your list of all those who have toured the Black Museum, of course?"

"Yes. But the killer could just as easily have read about our binoculars in a book."

"All right," Braithwaite said. "Now the ceramic birds. They're less specific in meaning so our response should be a looser one. Use free association and give me the first thought through your head. Of what do they make you think?"

" 'A Nightingale Sang In Berkeley Square'," Hilary replied. "Bluebirds over 'The White Cliffs of Dover'."

"Alfred Hitchcock," Hone cut in.

" 'When The Red, Red Robin Comes—' "

"Stop!" Braithwaite said, snapping his fingers. "I saw that film. Hitchcock's *The Birds*."

"Remember the farmer sprawled in the bedroom with his eyes pecked out?" Hone asked.

The three of them looked at each other in puzzled silence. After a lengthy pause Rand said, "Let's slowly think this through."

"The Sewer Killer uses a bizarre weapon to do someone in," Braithwaite prompted.

"He leaves the weapon behind for us to find," Hone added. "He later calls the Yard to ensure the tide doesn't wash the binoculars away."

"He also drops a handful of ceramic birds at the site of the killing so we'll connect his putting out the eyes of the victim with a certain horror film. Where does that take us?" Rand asked, perplexed.

"Let's turn to the Stonegate articles," Braithwaite suggested. "What do the mirror and top hat conjure up?"

"The Mad Hatter," Hilary said. "*Alice In Wonderland* and *Through The Looking-Glass.*"

"Fred Astaire," Hone said. "W. C. Fields. The Piccadilly Masher. The Phantom of the—"

A sharp knock at the door interrupted the detective. A Murder Squad cop poked his head into the room.

"Looks like we've got another, Chief. Up at a funfair near Hampstead Heath."

# The Hit

It was early in the morning—or very late at night, depending upon your perspective—by the time Chandler
returned to the Westin Bayshore hotel. He was now
running on second wind and his mind was still spinning
from his conversation with Caradon. His body, however,
ached with cramps from having sat in the car for hours,
first outside The Id, then outside the gambling club, then
outside Hengler's mansion. He knew he'd have a restless
sleep if he didn't walk the knots in his muscles out.

Chandler went up to his room to get a warmer jacket
and a pair of fleece-lined gloves. Then he left the hotel
by its back door and walked around Coal Harbour on the
Seawall into Stanley Park.

He didn't notice the man who followed him.

Though he still wore his black shirt and white tie, Sid
Jinks had changed his suit and overcoat for a sheepskin
bomber jacket. The fedora and the sunglasses were gone
too.

He had waited in the parking lot until the narc returned. His original plan was to follow the Horseman up
to his room then take him with a knife as he was opening
his door. Not to kill him outright, of course—not until
after he had shed his skin—just put the blade to the small
of his back till they were both inside. Then he would tie
the narc up, gag him and get down to work.

But the couple in the corridor had spoiled all that.

As Chandler had stood in the hotel lobby waiting for
the elevator to come down, Jinks had raced up the firestairs

to the eighth floor where he had lurked in ambush outside the door to the hall. Just his luck that a man and woman out for a night on the town would choose that moment to return to their own room across from the Horseman's suite.

So Jinks had returned to the lobby to formulate another plan. Yet no sooner had he sat down to think matters through, than who should come out of the elevator and leave the hotel but the narc he had been sent to skin alive.

Now, as Jinks followed Chandler around the curve of the Seawall into Stanley Park, he felt in his left pocket for his skinning knife. Then he hefted the bag gripped in his right fist that contained the Taser electric stun gun.

Zinc walked briskly into the park, breathing deep lungfuls of cold sea air that came gusting across the Pacific Ocean. He passed the rowing and yacht clubs silhouetted to his right against a million neon lights blazing in the office towers at the city's financial core. The tide was out and the mud at the base of the Seawall glistened silver in the moonlight. Off in the zoo to his left an Arctic wolf howled.

Chandler was too good a cop not to sense that Ray Hengler had managed to slip through the net. Even though the RCMP and the Department of Justice knew the rock promoter was a kingpin of drugs, where was the proof? The Headhunters Motorcycle Club to which Mohawk belonged had been caught red-handed with the stuff; but until Ray Hengler was tied to the gang there was a crucial missing link.

After the slaughterhouse shootout and Mohawk's subsequent arrest, Burke Hood and Cal Waechter had arranged to have the biker released on bail even though his charges—trafficking in heroin, assault, possession of a restricted weapon and use thereof—would warrant detention. Fortuitously, at about the same time, the prosecutor on the case had been subtly approached with a bribe by a minion in the office of Glen Troy, the lawyer involved. He was told to accept it by his legal superiors, both as a coverup now and as grounds for possible additional charges later. The bribe would make what they had already independently decided to do look less suspicious in the eyes of the power behind the biker.

Chandler *knew* that power was ultimately Ray Hengler. But still there was no proven link.

Passing the gate to Deadman's Island on his right, the Mountie stopped to light a cigarette. Here whitecaps crashed against the isthmus leading out to the harbour island, exploding in heavy spray. Zinc continued walking.

With Mohawk gone, their only solid lead to Hengler had evaporated as well. Sure, both men used the same lawyer, but what did that prove? So did hundreds of other thugs in this city. True, Hengler had been at The Id tonight when Mohawk disappeared, and as promoter he had access to the stage. Mohawk, therefore, could have gone behind the curtain and down to the basement by means of the hydraulic lift used in the show. There was probably a common cellar with the property next door or some sort of passage that led to the street. But again, so what? Unless Hengler had met Mohawk face to face none of that was evidence of the crucial missing link.

Now Mohawk had vanished and Hengler would go free.

Zinc stepped on the butt of the cigarette as he closed on Hallelujah Point and the Nine O'Clock Gun ahead. He abandoned the Seawall promenade and branched left toward the Indian totem poles at Brockton Point.

Fifty feet behind him, Jinks did the same.

The Taser electric stun gun is marketed by Quality Creations of Youngstown, Ohio. It works on the principle that the human body's nervous system is a giant electrical grid that can be short circuited. The weapon is nine inches long and weighs one-and-a-half pounds. It has the stopping power of a .38 pistol—like the one Zinc had left behind in his hotel room when he changed his clothes.

The Taser shoots two tiny darts connected to a power source in the belly of the gun. Strike a human with the darts and as long as the trigger is depressed an incapacitating current will spark through his flesh. It will assume control of his nervous system and produce an immobilizing series of muscle contractions, twitches, and spasms.

One blast from the Taser and Zinc would be out long enough for Jinks to tie him up and stuff a rubber ball held with a gag into his mouth. Then he could drag the Horseman into the woods that bordered Brockton Oval, there to skin him alive. Genitals first.

The deeper the narc went into the dark that covered the park, the better for Jinks.

At that moment half a mile away in the Stanley Park service yard, John Delaney was lusting for "a nice piece of tail". His girlfriend, Holly Calderwood, was thinking about "a long hard rod".

The Nine O'Clock Gun is a Vancouver institution. At one time fired each night at nine to mark the close of the fishing day, it is now usually discharged by a timeclock located in the Old Boathouse down near the sea. It used to be shot by telephone circuit from Lions Gate Bridge. The Indian totems—some of them dating from the last century—are usually lit by an astronomical timeclock with a 240-volt system and trippers fifty feet away. But neither usual procedure was in use this month.

For this was the year of the Expo 86 Fair when Vancouver hosted the world. To ensure that millions of visitors saw the city in all its electrical splendour, lights had been strung from Lions Gate Bridge, and the totems and Nine O'Clock Gun were being rewired. Until the rewiring was complete, all automatic-circuit functions were being operated manually through radio control from the park service yard.

It was John Delaney who turned the totem lights on at dusk and off at 2:00 a.m., and who fired the cannon each night at nine o'clock.

Chandler was thinking of Mohawk as he approached the totem poles.

Vancouver is one of the world's foremost heroin centres. It is the junk capital of the whole West Coast. Since the turn of the century, heroin has been shipped from the opium fields of the Golden Triangle and the Golden Crescent by way of the Hong Kong Chinese to Vancouver. From here it flows east or down to the States.

Vancouver, of course, has an underworld to service this trade. And if someone should play the game foolishly, Stanley Park is a favourite body-dumping ground.

For all Zinc knew, Mohawk might be sprawled dead in the woods thirty feet from him.

In fact it was Sid Jinks who was thirty feet away.

He aimed the Taser for Chandler's neck just above the

collar because he was afraid the darts might not pierce the jacket.

Then he closed the gap silentiy.

The totem poles were aglow in the dark, each Thunderbird and Killer Whale sheened with silver moonlight. Zinc stood with his back to the open playing field of Brockton Oval, facing the woods of the Point that backdropped the Haida and Kwakiutl carvings. His mind was lost in the mystical feeling such mythic art creates.

Eight feet behind Chandler, Sid Jinks pulled the trigger of the Taser gun.

Half a mile away at the park service yard, Holly Calderwood's skirt was hiked up around her waist. Her head was thrown back in orgasm and her legs were wrapped tightly around John Delaney's butt. He had her backed up against a Parks Board desk as he humped toward completion, unaware that Holly's flailing arm had just hit the manual switch that turned on the totem lights and the one that fired the Nine O'Clock Gun.

Elsewhere the hit on the buttons was having sudden repercussions, but right now John Delaney couldn't have cared less.

The totem lights flashed in a seering burst as the Nine O'Clock Gun fired.

With a start Zinc Chandler whirled toward the deafening sound.

The Taser darts missed his neck and hit his right shoulder. They didn't pierce the sheepskin hide of his heavy winter jacket but the dew on the leather surface completed the Taser circuit. Chandler lit up like Electric Man and his hair stood on end.

Jinks jumped back in shock as the totem lights exploded to expose him totally. It could have been twelve noon on the longest day of the year. He turned and ran.

Zinc chased him for two steps until his legs got tangled up in the Taser wires and he fell flat on his face. By the time he was free again, cursing the mess of wires looped about his feet, the hitman had disappeared into the surrounding woods.

Chandler fished a cigarette from his coat pocket. Death

had been walking too close to him lately, which always helped bring life into clearer focus.

As he lit the smoke, he promised himself, This cigarette is definitely the last one.

Half a mile away, John Delaney came like a cannon.

## Newport, Rhode Island
*Sunday January 12, 9:17 p.m.*

Ronald Fletcher was in his den at home reading a case in the *U.S. Supreme Court Reports* when the telephone rang. The precedent was a tax decision which had the lawyer worried. Fletcher feared that his past was catching up with him.

He picked up the receiver. "Hello," he said.

"Hello, Ronald." A female voice.

Fletcher sighed.

"What now?" he asked.

# Monsters

**New York, New York**
*Tuesday January 14, 4:50 p.m.*

Deborah Lane, her manuscript beside her, was waiting at
Kennedy Airport for Delta Air to announce her flight
back to Providence. She had spent the last two days
lugging her novel around to various New York publishers
and agents, trying to talk her way through the door.
Discouraged and exhausted she now closed her eyes and
sank back in the chair. From behind her came the sudden
smash of someone dropping several bottles of duty-free
liquor. "Hugh Lamb," an angry woman snapped, "you
are the world's biggest klutz!" A memory sparked back.

**Providence, Rhode Island**
*Wednesday July 23, 1969, 3:45 p.m.*

*The door to Saxon's bedroom was ajar.*

*As the nine-year-old walked by she could see him sitting
on the floor with his back toward her, chanting over and
over, "Hugh Lane, Hugh Lane, Hugh Lane." Though
Debbie could not see what Saxon held in his hands, each
time he whispered the name his elbows moved.*

*The walls of the bedroom were papered with movie
posters and stills: Christopher Lee as Dracula, Morlocks
from* The Time Machine, *Chaney, the Mummy, Lugosi,
the Wolf Man, Karloff as Frankenstein. When his mother
had once asked him how he could sleep in such a place,
Deborah had heard Saxon reply, "They're my friends.
They protect me from harm."*

147

On a shelf above the bed several Aurora plastic models stood guard: *The Creature from the Black Lagoon, The Phantom of the Opera, The Forgotten Prisoner, Dr Jekyll as Mr Hyde.* At one end of the shelf, praying mantises in a jar scurried beneath breathing holes punched through the lid. The floor of the room was a mess of horror comics and terror magazines, among them sheets of paper on which the boy had graphically drawn his own bloody stories.

On a small desk just inside the door Saxon had constructed a cardboard Roman Colosseum, its sand pit strewn with the bodies of slain plasticine gladiators. A bottle of red nail polish had been dribbled over them for gory effect.

The bookshelf beside the desk was crammed with *Popular Mechanics* and other scientific periodicals, along with a chemistry set and a microscope.

A piranha-filled aquarium bubbled beneath the windowsill, next to which Saxon had his carnivorous plants on display—sundews, Venus flytraps, cobra and pitcher plants.

His hidden hands working feverishly, Saxon continued to chant, "Hugh Lane, Hugh Lane, Hugh Lane." Then as Debbie walked away from his door toward the bathroom at the end of the hall, she saw him put something into a cigar box on the floor.

The next day when Saxon was out somewhere she snuck into his room and found the stashed-away box. Inside were seven head-tear-aparts.

The boy had folded each strip of paper like this:

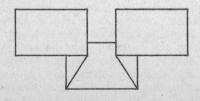

He had then drawn half a face on each of the wings:

*When she pulled the tabs apart this is what she saw:*

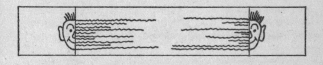

*All seven faces resembled her father, Hugh Lane.*

# Hacker

Elaine Teeze had ordered Jack Ohm to steal the access code to Scotland Yard's Police National Computer and the C + C.

So tonight he had wandered the streets which surrounded more than a dozen police stations scattered throughout the city. What he was searching for was a window that looked in on one of the Met's computer rooms. Finally, when he found such a window with a building across the street to provide the right viewing angle, Ohm climbed to the roof and set up his video equipment. Then using a camera with a telephoto lens he videotaped the operator inside the station working her PNC keyboard and screen.

Later, when he was back home in his lab and sitting mentally at that desk in the steel room that was his mind, Ohm went through the videotape frame by frame. From this he was able to reconstruct the access code the operator had typed in.

The Scotland Yard computer system is based on the principle of wide access from all over Britain. Because it handles thousands of requests a day, the PNC does not have the usual built-in fences that protect confidential data: dedicated lines, shielding of any equipment that emits measurable impulses, automatic cutoff for random password assaults by outside hackers, call-back devices, secret codes, and that sort of thing. Any one of these fences would destroy efficiency.

So now that Jack Ohm had Scotland Yard's computer

access code he could worm his way through their data banks any time he pleased. Which meant that he and Elaine Teeze could know every move the Yard planned before it was put into action. Not a bad night's work, Jack Ohm thought.

The walls of his lab in reality were sheeted with metal as were the imaginary walls of his mind. Below the shelf upon which were displayed the eight small hacked-out hearts floating in glass jars was a freezer used for storing his supply of young girls' blood. In front of the freezer stood a Plexiglas-domed slab ringed with grooved collecting troughs. This had been used by Ohm to watch his eight young victims, locked inside with their throats surgically slit, bleed to death. Balanced on top of the Plexiglas dome was a book entitled *The Language Of Flowers*.

As Ohm now began to leaf through the volume to search out his next two bouquets, he thought, Our second statement must be much more emphatic.

# Acid Bath

Vancouver, British Columbia
*Friday January 17, 8:15 a.m.*

*H-e-e-l-p m-e-e-e!* the tinny voice shrieks high above his head.

Zinc jerks his eyes up to isolate the source. To his amazement he sees that the spider's web is more than sixty feet across. It spans the entire flower garden and hangs from the towering Douglas firs that make up Stanley Park. A man is hanging from several spirals twenty-five feet in the air—if a man is still defined as a man when he has the head of a fly. The adhesive gunk of the drooling web has fouled his scarlet tunic.

*No, Ed!* Zinc cries out, grabbing hold of the nearest silk strand and desperateiy trying to climb. But his hands and legs instantly stick to the web as if they've been Crazy Glued, and try though he might he cannot yank his eyes away from the horrible sight unfolding above.

The fly-man gibbers and struggles as the giant spider closes in. Chandler can make out the spurs on his boots and the corporal's stripes on his arms. Out one sleeve pokes a hand, out the other an insect's claw. The hairy face is black with two bulging compound eyes. Its proboscis twitches in terror as if it were a tongue.

Then the spider attacks.

Its fangs bite the fly-man in the neck as its jaws clamp his head, pumping him full of poison that cause his body to convulse. The spider uses its hind legs to rotate the prey, wrapping him up like a mummy in a shroud of smothering silk. Its maxillae go to work.

The serrated edges of the jaws crunch up the fly-man's head as the spider pours digestive fluid over the mangled *flesh. As its sucking-stomach mechanism begins to slurp at the mess, the threads of the web are a-hum with sound like telephone wires.*

*H-e-l-p m-e! H-e-l-p m-e! H-e-l-p m-e! the lines throb over and over again, a fly with Jennie Copp's head now buzzing across the dream, while that horrid, unnerving sucking-slurp goes on and on and on until*

Chandler awoke with a start to feel something crouched high on his chest up near his throat. He lashed out blindly with one fist to fling it away from him, his other hand groping and fumbling in the dark for the lamp beside the bed.

Recoiling from its sudden brilliance, Chandler gasped as the light burned his eyes. Then his vision focused slowly on the hardcover novel he had just cast across the room. Still sweating profusely from the aftermath of the dream, he realized he had fallen asleep reading in bed.

Get a grip on yourself, man, he thought sheepishly.

Zinc swung out of the covers and made for the bathroom to rub a cold cloth over his face. He knew that the logic of a dream is determined solely by the demands of the subconscious mind. A guilt-ridden, nicotine-starved face stared glumly back at him from the bathroom mirror. He would have laughed at his foolishness were it not quite so serious.

When the bedside telephone jangled, he walked back into the other room. After his brush with death in the park six days ago, Chandler had moved from the Westin Bayshore to the Sylvia Hotel overlooking English Bay. As he picked up the receiver on its fifth ring he could hear rain pounding the window behind the closed curtains.

"Chandler," he said.

"Did I wake you up?"

"I only wish you had. Ten minutes ago."

"Bad dreams, huh?" Caradon said. "Quit eating junk food before you go to bed."

Chandler grinned. "What's up?" he asked.

"Get your ass in gear, Zinc. We just might have Ray Hengler on a murder charge."

# North Vancouver, British Columbia
*9:17 a.m.*

Caradon met Chandler downstairs in the lobby of the Horizon View Apartments.

As Zinc was let in the security door that opened by intercom, he took note of several Ident men working the ground outside. As usual they were looking for tyre prints, footprints, abandoned vehicles, weapons or clothing disposed of on purpose or dropped by mistake, tool or jemmy marks on the doors that led into the fourteen-storey building. Driving rain from an overcast sky hampered their work.

"A waste of time," Caradon said. "Killing's about a week old. Been a lot of traffic outside since then."

Chandler could faintly smell fresh paint in the lobby beyond the door.

"Place was redecorated last weekend," Caradon said. "Works both for us, and to our detriment. Either we got a clean surface ripe for relevant prints, or they're buried under two coats of paint."

"Any signs of forced entry on the doors?" Zinc asked.

"No need to. The front door was wedged open from early last Friday morning till Monday afternoon to let in fresh air and take away the fumes. Painters worked around the clock except for coffee breaks."

"All the time in the lobby?"

"Nope. Sometimes the manager's suite. It was painted too."

"So anyone could have slipped in unnoticed?" Chandler said.

"Looks that way."

Both the lobby and the elevator had been vacuumed by Sergeant Bob George then worked by the fingerprint crew. There was powder everywhere. Although fingerprints are usually the most important evidence to find in any case, fingerprinting has to wait until later on in the scientific process. The powders and chemicals used for it could contaminate other hair, dust, and stray fibre finds.

"Nothing of interest was found outside the penthouse," Caradon said.

As they rode up in the elevator Chandler asked, "Bill, why were you called to the scene?"

Caradon winked. "The day we saw Mohawk leaving court I had the force computer flagged to notify me if any other officers made inquiries about Ray Hengler, his lawyer Glen Troy, George 'Mohawk' Geddes, or Fantasy Escort Service. I included addresses and telephone numbers. This morning our GIS members found a phone number in the penthouse upstairs and requested a computer check. My flag was activated, so I got called. Then I raised you."

The elevator opened and both cops entered the hall.

At the door to the penthouse they presented their regimental shields, then were issued clip-on tags and plastic gloves so as not to leave personal prints or sweat contamination in the suite. The cop at the door reminded them, "No smoking. No lighting matches. And on pain of death don't lay *anything* down."

The fact the exhibit officer had set up his station in the living room meant that here was not where the action was. As other cops brought him their finds he sealed them in bottles or plastic bags or "E" exhibit envelopes, ordering comparison samples if he thought that necessary. He labelled each item distinctly and marked where it had come from on a sketch map of the scene.

The south wall of the living room was a solid sheet of glass that looked out on the city. The Horizon View Apartments stood where the North Shore mountains slip gently into the sea. Zinc glanced across the harbour mouth at Stanley Park and Brockton Oval where someone had tried to kill him six days ago. Beyond that was the Westin Bayshore hotel and his original room. Cold rain savagely pounded the window-wall as westerly winds swept in, wave upon wave, from the Pacific Ocean. Out here on the Coast, either you get used to rain or you get out of town.

The first thing Chandler noticed on entering the bedroom was four noosed ropes tied to knobs screwed into the frame of the bed, one at each corner. Charcoal pictures of nudes covered the wall above while various sadomasochistic submission devices were scattered about the floor. Constable Neil Turner was standing over Sergeant Bob George who was working the sheets on the waterbed. Chandler and Caradon crossed the room to join them.

"Bob, Neil," Caradon said. "Meet Zinc Chandler."

Both cops nodded.

Turner was in his mid thirties. He was wearing civilian clothes and had the boyish blond good looks of a California surfer.

He and his partner, Gaetan Dubois, both of the Serious Crimes Squad, General Investigation Section (GIS), were in charge of the case. As is common with police throughout the world, RCMP homicide cops work in pairs. No matter how many members are ultimately involved in any particular manhunt, final responsibility rests with a two-man team. What is unusual, however, is the fact that the initial training of a Mountie at Regina, Saskatchewan is so complete that it is common for low-ranking constables to be in practical charge of murder investigations. It has been that way for 116 years.

"Looks like sex games gone astray," Chandler said.

"Kink time for the idle rich," Caradon added.

Turner held up a plastic pouch inside of which was a wallet.

"We found this on the floor near the far edge of the bed. It could have been dropped in a struggle to tie someone down. The ID inside is that of Raymond Hengler."

He held up another bag that contained a glass eyedropper and a bottle.

"This was on the floor beside the bed near where I'm standing. It's strychnine."

"What an ugly way to go," Chandler said.

"That's for sure," Turner replied.

Strychnine is extracted from the seeds of the *nux vomica* tree. Once administered it is absorbed rapidly by the stomach then passes on to the central nervous system. At first the victim feels excited, restless, and suffocated. Then, as the nervous system degenerates further, the slightest vibration or noise will trigger a violent spasm that locks the chest and bends the spine until both the head and heels touch the floor. In this case the rocking motion of the waterbed would have caused someone perpetual torture. During each spasm the victim's breathing stops, but the mind remains perfectly clear. The face contorts into a horrible grimace known as *risus sardonicus*. Fully conscious, the victim then suffers convulsion after convulsion until death is caused either by exhaustion or suffocation.

"It may be something, maybe not, but the electric clock on the night table's stopped at 1:51," Turner said.

"The plug could've been jiggled loose during a struggle near the bed."

"All the drawers and closets have been tossed," Caradon said. "Either someone packed in a hurry or was doing a thorough search."

Sergeant Bob George was known within the force as both the Human Vacuum Cleaner and the Tracker. A full-blooded Plains Cree from Duck Lake, Saskatchewan, he was the cop in charge of Hairs and Fibres Section. His hair was black and cut short, his cheekbones wide. His eyes were as sharp as knife points and his skin burnished bronze. When George was through with a crime scene, it was *all* "in the bag".

The Sergeant scanned the black satin bed-sheets with a large optic glass, lifting any finds with a piece of Scotch tape. The hair or fibre would then be transferred to a labelled microscope slide from a box on the floor. In a second carton nearby were several glassine envelopes containing slides that he had already prepared.

"My initial impression," the Cree said, "is that two people have used this bed. Each left behind several head and pubic hairs. Both sets of pubic hair appear to be female: they're coarse and short. One has black head hair, recently cut. The other black head hair with streaks of blue dye. Also, whoever was tied down suffered extreme pain."

"How do you know that?" Turner asked.

"The ropes," George said. "The fibres of a rope are round, not flat. Here each cord was cinched around a wrist or ankle then tied to one of the knobs at the corners of the bed. In the process each rope was stretched tight over the upper edge of the wooden frame. The fibres are flattened for several inches away from the point of each rope's initial contact with that edge *toward* what would have been the position of the victim. That in itself is a telltale direction, but in addition some of the fibres have actually snapped. What occurred here was more than someone struggling to be free of the bonds. I see a body contracting in the throes of extreme pain."

"Like the convulsions that come with strychnine poisoning," Chandler said.

"Could be," George replied.

As the scientist crossed to the dressing table and began to remove hairs from the brush on its surface, Turner pointed to a notepad near the telephone on the small night stand next to the bed.

"When we arrived that pad was blank," the Constable said. "Our Ident man was able to raise the impression of a telephone number written on the last sheet torn from the pad. It turned out to be the listing for Fantasy Escort Service."

"We've got a tap on that phone," Caradon said. "It's Hengler's hooker front. I've got Behnes of Special I checking our tapes for the call."

As he spoke, the telephone rang. Turner picked it up and waited for the party on the other end to speak first.

"It's for you," he said, handing the receiver to Caradon.

Chandler walked over to the door that led to the bathroom *en suite*. Two men were crouched near the bathtub, each wearing a gas mask, a rubber apron, and rubber gloves. One was Turner's partner, Constable Gaetan Dubois; the other was Nick White, a forensic pathologist from Lions Gate Hospital.

The bathtub was filled with acid on top of which floated a greasy yellow sludge. Tipped up against the wall at the tap end of the bath was a plastic mesh screen with weights around the edges. The screen had been cut to the shape of the tub. From the yellow slime that hung dripping off the plastic strands, Chandler knew the mesh had been used to ensure a body stayed beneath the surface of the corrosive until it finished its work.

On the floor next to the bathtub sat several empty carboys marked *Concentrated* $H_2SO_4$ and a pump. A rubber sheet beside the men held two cherry-sized stones with polished facets. These were wet and had obviously been removed from the tub. The pathologist was stirring the mess in the bath to see what else could be found, but he wasn't having much luck.

When Caradon got off the phone he called Zinc back to the bedroom.

"That was Behnes of Special I," he said. "They've checked the index log for calls in and out of Fantasy Escort Service and have played the relevant tapes. On Tuesday January 7 at 1:49 p.m. a woman who gave her name as Rosanna Keate called from this number. She asked that a specific male escort picked from a book be sent here to her suite on January 11 at 2:00 a.m."

"January 11, huh? Early last Saturday morning. That's

when we were tailing Hengler from The Id to the gambling club," Chandler said.

"Right after she phoned on the seventh a call was made from the escort service to a guy named Reid Driver setting up the date. Driver said he would attend at the appointed time."

"So," Chandler said, "we now have Hengler's company tied to this suite in which someone has most likely been poison-tortured and killed for a sadistic sexual motive. We also have his wallet found near the bed."

"It gets even better," Caradon said. "For later on in the afternoon at 12:02 p.m. that same Saturday, Ray Hengler *himself* phoned this telephone number from his office. A female answered the call and Hengler asked her if Rika Hyde was there."

Chandler's eyebrows rose. "The singer with the rock band Ghoul that played The Id?"

"Yep. Hengler was told to come on over, that Rika Hyde was waiting. He closed off the call by saying, 'I'll be right there.' "

"Did your boys on stakeout follow him here?" Zinc asked.

"No such luck," Caradon replied. "Before Hengler came out of his office and they could pick up his tail, a call came over the radio that a member was down. With a possible cop-kill nearby, of course they responded immediately. We didn't pick Hengler up again till he returned home that night."

Chandler shook his head. "Isn't that always the way? If Keate's escort date arrived here at two in the morning, I wonder if he was *still* here when Hengler came calling ten hours later? Probably not."

"One way to find out," Caradon said. "Behnes traced his address through B.C. Tel from the number the escort service called to set up the date."

Zinc glanced at Turner, who was listening and taking notes.

"It's your squeal," Chandler said. "Mind if we speak to some people?"

"Not as long as you file a report and keep me informed."

"Done," Zinc replied.

# The Cellar

Deborah Lane was at home eating lunch while marking a student's paper entitled "Ernest Hemingway—An Overgrown Boy Scout?" when the telephone rang. She picked up the receiver.

"Hello."

Nothing.

"Hello."

Just breathing.

"Hello. Who is this?"

Very heavy breathing.

As she hung up she thought of Sid and all his obscene letters.

Sid . . . Was he the same Sid who Saxon used to talk about years ago when he was first hanging out with The Ghouls?

Then thinking of Saxon brought a distant memory creeping back.

## Providence, Rhode Island
*Thursday August 13, 1970, 4:15 p.m.*

*A complete collection of H. P. Lovecraft's stories lined the shelf above Saxon's bed where his monster models had been. Most of the books were paperbacks, one a hard-cover from Arkham House.*

*Saxon and Rika had spent the entire morning in his room. Deborah could hear them beyond her bedroom* wall growling and groaning and speaking a gibberish language of their own. Words like "YogSothoth", "Cthulhu", "Necronomicon", "Erich Zann", and "Abdul Alhazred" came through. She knew they were playing their private fantasy game "The Great Old Ones", each taking a role from Lovecraft's Cthulhu Mythos. Deborah was always excluded from the twins' theatre of the macabre.

In the early afternoon Rika went down to the record store. That meant she would spend the rest of the day mimicking hard rock vocalists on the Seabreeze record player in her room. Saxon spent the hours after lunch rereading a Lovecraft story for the hundredth time, or else using the jolt from a battery to make a dead frog twitch.

From her window later on that same afternoon, Deborah watched Saxon sneak next door. The neighbours were away on vacation for two months, and behind their old house was a slanted trap door which led to a disused root cellar. Saxon pulled it open and disappeared down the stairs.

After a while he came back out and Debbie watched him walk off in the direction of the comic store where he bought most of his magazines. Because she thought she heard a tiny scream as Saxon opened the root cellar door which died away as he eased the cover shut, Deborah's curiosity got the better of her.

So once Saxon was out of sight, the ten-year-old crept next door, pulled the trap door open and stared down into the murk. Shafts of light like brilliant knives stabbed through cracks in the wood. Spider webs and slug trails were everywhere. And something was squeaking in terrified pain near the bottom of the stairs.

As Deborah descended the root cellar steps a mouse scampered across the dirt floor below. Then to the sound of another heart-tearing squeal from across the room, the young girl's eyes froze to the far wall.

The barrier of old wooden boards which sealed the root cellar off from the neighbours' house stood in shadow opposite the foot of the stairs. Nailed to it by long thin spikes were dozens of mummified rats and mice arranged in a circle, the most recent victim still convulsing on its spear. She could see from the scratches on the wood surrounding the other remains that they had all been impaled alive.

Drawn in crayon at the centre of this circle of pain was Lovecraft's monster Great Cthulhu.

# Forensics

North Vancouver, British Columbia
*Friday January 17, 1986, 10:37 .m.*

Police work benefits from the fact that man used to swing
from tree to tree. For as Charles Darwin pointed out, the
palms of our hands and the soles of our feet are covered
with "friction skin". Unlike the skin that sheaths the rest
of the human body, friction skin has patterned ridges that
provide good gripping surface—and leave prints.

A fingerprint is produced because each ridge on a
fingertip has minute pores through which the skin both
breathes and secretes sweat. Each ridge also collects a
layer of grease every time a person touches either his
forehead or chin, which contain sebaceous glands. Touch
a smooth surface later and these ridges will leave their
pattern behind in a sweat and oil mark that can remain
for years.

The first cop to reach the penthouse that morning
when the nurse phoned in the squeal at 7:07 a.m. was
Constable Patricia McKay of the North Vancouver Detachment of the RCMP. She had sealed off the suite and
stood on guard outside the door after sending the nurse
down to the lobby to wait for the members from GIS.
The nurse was told to lead the detectives up by the exact
route she had taken when she'd arrived earlier that
morning.

The first cop *into* the penthouse was Corporal Sam
Hickok of North Van Ident Section. A tall easygoing man
with a waxed walrus moustache and alert grey eyes, he
was the RCMP crime scene photographer. Before anything could be touched or evidence collected it was Hickok's job to make a complete photographic record of the

location as found. To do this he donned a protective non-fibrous clothing cover, plastic gloves, and anti-static footware. This precaution was to ensure that in his search for fingerprint areas, stray hair and fibres, bloodstains, bullet holes and spent shells, signs of forced entry, possible footprints on the floor or impressions in the carpets, he did not remove or contaminate minute evidence particles that might be in the rooms.

After he had finished photographing the scene and the Hair and Fibre crew had done their work Hickok retraced the most probable routes taken by the killer through the penthouse suite. He was now looking for any smooth surfaces that might have picked up prints. These he first examined by angled light from an electric torch, then dusted with powder. Black graphite was used for light-coloured surfaces; white lead or aluminium to contrast with those that were dark. The powder adhered to a number of latent sweat impressions in Rosanna Keate's apartment which Hickok at once circled and marked with grease pencil for evidence continuity. The developed prints were then photographed with a fingerprint camera and lifted with transparent tape. Each piece of tape was then stuck to a fingerprint transfer card.

Since pulp is an absorbent material, powders will not uncover prints on paper. So any and all documents found in the suite that might prove relevant in the case were sealed in plastic and taken back to the North Van Ident office. Early that same afternoon, Hickok developed the prints on these papers by using a combination of the chemical reagent ninhydrin and iodine fume technique.

The wallet found near the bed, however, presented special problems.

Leather is a porous surface thought until recently to be impossible to work. But not any more. Most of us come in contact with chemical traces in our everyday lives—newspaper ink, make-up, various types of oil, paint ions, and a thousand others. When exposed to laser light these chemicals fluoresce. The result is that any fingerprints will appear as glowing images which can be photographed.

At 2:15 p.m., Hickok dropped the billfold off at the RCMP Crime Laboratory on Heather Street. Because the wallet leather was smooth and therefore did not break up most of the ridge lines, an Ident Service technician was able to laser-develop six fingerprint impressions plus a glove smear. These prints she then blew up for the purpose of poroscopy. This involves examining the sweat pores of the skin, for like the ridge patterns that make up our fingerprints, the size, shape, and position of the pore openings on each ridge differ uniquely from one person to another.

While this was going on at the lab, Corporal Hickok was laying the groundwork for print identification. He determined that the woman who had rented the penthouse suite was an American named Rosanna Keate. Keate had taken up residence in the Horizon View Apartments in early September of last year, just after the penthouse had been redecorated. Shortly thereafter she had come down with infectious mononucleosis. From that point on the only people to visit her regularly were a housekeeper and a registered nurse who both came once a week. They arrived on Friday and each had her own key. Hickok therefore took a set of elimination prints from both women.

The Corporal knew that Ray Hengler's prints would already be on file from the porno bust that presently had him before the courts. After a computer check and several telephone calls, he discovered that Rosanna Keate had been fingerprinted last August pursuant to Section 27 (1) of the Immigration Act. After obtaining her prints from the Feds, he drove back to the RCMP Crime Lab to pick up the laser impressions developed by the technician. Then he went next door to Ident Services in the Operations Building.

The RCMP Automated Fingerprint System is state-of-the-art. Each print in the Ottawa files has been videotaped and then broken down electronically into sixteen shades of grey so that a computer can scan it and plot the minutiae of its ridge patterns against an XY coordinate. All this information is stored in the memory banks as an array of binary digits.

Late that afternoon at E Division Headquarters, Corporal Hickok watched as Ident Service scientists plotted the ridge pattern details of each print found at the Keate apartment on a fingerprint latent terminal. After they set aside those which matched the elimination prints of Keate, the nurse, and the housekeeper, the remaining unknown wild prints were transmitted electronically to the main computer in the Fingerprint Division at RCMP Headquarters in Ottawa.

There, using its Image Storage Retrieval System, the computer laser-searched its data base and called up all prints matching or similar to the wild ones found in the suite. Within minutes these were transmitted back to Vancouver where Hickok and the fingerprint specialists found themselves staring at several matches on a screen.

The net effect of all this was that the only prints found in the suite that did not belong to either Rosanna Keate or the other two women were those of Ray Hengler.

Hengler's prints, however, were only found on the wallet retrieved near the bed.


## Vancouver, British Columbia
## *12:15 p.m.*

The basement suite was in a house three streets up the hill from Kitsilano Beach. Chandler had to knock on the door seven times before it was opened by a man who was soaking wet and wearing a towel around his waist. "Police," Caradon said, flashing the tin.

"Shit," the man replied.

Reid Driver was rich in good looks and poor in material possessions. He was a well-developed man in his late twenties with brown hair, brown eyes, and an artificial tan. The sparse furnishings behind him showed that he had yet to arrive.

"Mind if we ask you some questions?" Chandler said.

"About what?"

"Your work. And last Friday night, Saturday morning."

"What if I say no?"

"Then you're a suspect in a homicide and we all go downtown."

"And if I say yes?"

"Then that might be avoided. Depending on the answers."

"Come on in," Driver said. "Let me get dressed."

The living room had movie posters all over the walls. A model's portfolio full of Reid Driver pictures lay spread out on the coffee table. The bass of a stereo pounded through the ceiling from the suite upstairs.

When Driver rejoined them he was wearing a pair of pleated blue slacks and a white open-throated shirt. "So what do you want to know?" he asked, sitting down opposite them.

"You work for Fantasy Escort Service," Caradon said.

"Yeah, part time. It helps pay the rent."

"What else do you do?"

"Modelling. Acting. Dancing. Anything creative."

"What does being an escort involve?"

"Depends on the client."

"What about your client early last Saturday morning?"

"Miss Keate?"

"That's the one."

"I don't know. She wasn't home. Which pissed me off considering the time I was told to arrive. 2:00 a.m."

"Expand on that," Chandler said.

Reid Driver shrugged.

"The escort service keeps a book of all our photographs. Clients can shop through it and choose the date they want. They pay the service which keeps a percentage and contacts us. Fantasy tells us where to be and when, and what's required. After the date they send a cheque less their percentage. It's as simple as that."

"So what could this woman want of you at 2:00 a.m.?"

"To sketch me as a model. According to Fantasy, she's an artist."

"At 2:00 a.m.?" Chandler said.

Driver shrugged again.

"Ever meet Miss Keate before?"

"No," the man replied.

"So what happened when you got there?"

"I pushed the security intercom and got no answer. The lobby door was wedged open but there was no one around. I took the elevator up and knocked on the penthouse door. This was precisely at 2:00 a.m. I'm paid to be punctual. Again I got no answer, so after a few minutes I left to try and salvage the evening."

"Where'd you go then?"

"Down to a club on Richards."

"Anyone see you there?"

"Only a thousand people. I'm a regular."

"Where had you been before you arrived for the date?"

"Down at the same club," Driver said. "All in all I was gone about thirty minutes."

"Hear anything inside the penthouse while you were at the door?"

"No."

"One last question," Chandler said, "before you give us the names of other patrons at the club that night. How much did Miss Keate pay Fantasy Escort Service to have you fuck her?"

Reid Driver smiled. "No way, José. I'm an escort. Being a gigolo hook's against the law."

"Sure," Caradon said. "And I'm Donald Duck."

### 2:22 p.m.

Sergeant Bob George was both a natural and a trained observer.

Down at the RCMP Crime Lab that same afternoon, George concentrated on the hairs from the bed which he had taped to microscope slides at the scene. He had retrieved comparison hairs from the brush on Rosanna Keate's dressing table. At Chandler's suggestion the Sergeant had later stopped by The Id where he determined that live bands played only on the weekend. Since no one else had performed at the club since Ghoul last Friday night, he had taken comparison hairs from the make-up table in the room beside the stage.

Human hair is divided into six types: head, eyebrow/eyelash, beard/moustache, body, pubic, and axillary underarm. Head hairs are circular in section and if they have been neglected, split at the ends. A freshly-cut hair is square at the tip. Pubic hairs are oval or triangular and tend to curl. They are less deeply rooted than those of the head. Female pubic hair is shorter and coarser than that of the male.

Viewing them longitudinally through a comparison microscope, George analysed his specimens for length, colour, and texture. He confirmed his initial opinion formed at the scene that the head and pubic hairs found on the bed were from two different sources. Both sources corresponded visually with the control hairs taken from the penthouse brush and The Id make-up table.

Next he removed each hair from its individual slide and imbedded it in a block of wax before shaving off a cross-section. Hair has three parts when viewed transversely: the core or medulla containing air; the cortex surrounding this which is composed of a horny protein substance called keratin, plus pigmentation; and the outer layer or cuticle made of tiny overlapping scales of epidermis.

There is a striking difference between the cuticle layers of human hair and those of an animal. By making an impression of these scales on cellulose acetate, George was able to study them and prove that all the hairs he'd found were of human origin.

Caucasian hair in cross-section tends to be oval while Mongolian hair is circular in shape. All the hairs seized were from Caucasians.

Finally he determined that the blue-black head hairs from the sheets which matched those taken from The Id had been dyed recently and contained traces of theatrical make-up.

Later that same afternoon, the Sergeant drove out to the University of British Columbia to use their equipment for one further test.

At the University of Toronto, Dr Robert J. Jervis pioneered a method for the neutron activation analysis of hair. This highly sensitive technique involves bombarding a sample with high-density neutrons in a nuclear reactor. The process causes the hair's chemical atoms to irradiate. Hair naturally contains such elements as iron, zinc, antimony, arsenic, and copper. Hair dye contains other chemicals. By measuring the irradiation cast off in the UBC reactor, the Sergeant was able to identify both the types and amounts of chemicals in his various samples of hair.

Forensic science cannot yet conclusively say that this hair came from that individual. But by the time he was finished late in the day, Bob George knew in his heart that the two people who had stretched out on the waterbed in the penthouse suite were Rosanna Keate and Rika Hyde.


## North Vancouver, British Columbia
## 2:55 p.m.


The house was near the Mission Reserve of the Squamish Indian Band. It was small, with a white picket fence, and the trim was creatively painted. A five-year-old boy in a yellow raincoat sat on the wet front steps playing with his Transformers.

As the cops approached the door he looked up at

Chandler and asked, "Hey, Mister, what's up your nose and goes 200 miles an hour?"

Zinc shook his head.

"A Lamborgreenie," the kid replied.

Caradon knocked on the door.

"It ain't locked," someone shouted from inside.

Chandler opened the door on a cosy living room. The TV was showing a Canucks hockey game. The man who sat in front of the set was in his late forties. He had freckles, red hair, and a cast on his leg. A bowl of Cheezies was within reach and a can of Moosehead beer was gripped in his hand. From the kitchen behind him came the sounds of a mother coaxing her baby to eat something he definitely didn't like.

"RCMP," Chandler said, displaying the regimental shield. "May we ask you a few questions?"

"Do I need a lawyer?" the man replied.

"Not unless you've done something wrong you want to tell us about."

Caradon smiled. "What happened to the leg?"

"I finished a round-the-clock job early this week and took a day off skiing. Christ knows what that's gonna end up costing me."

"You paint the lobby of the Horizon View?" Chandler asked.

"Yeah. That was the job. What's this about?"

"We're investigating a homicide," Caradon said. "You might have seen something to help us out."

He handed the painter a folder of eight different mugshots from police files.

"Know any of these?" the Mountie asked.

Just then there was a shot on goal on the TV screen. It missed by a mile.

"That guy's a bum," the painter said, turning in disgust from the set to leaf through the photographs.

A minute later he passed one of the snaps to Caradon. "I seen this one," he said.

The photograph was Ray Hengler's mugshot from his porno bust.

"Where and when?" Chandler asked.

"Lemme think. It would have been last Saturday, about 1:00 p.m. The second day of the job. Guy came into the lobby and almost knocked me off the ladder. He coulda busted my leg too."

"The lobby of the Horizon View Apartments on Marine Drive?"

"Sure. Same place."

"How do you remember the time?"

"Cause I was just gettin ready to call it quits."

"Know what floor he went to?"

"I didn't look."

Out in the kitchen the baby let out a full-scale howl.

"Keep it down, honey," the painter shouted. "We're talkin business here."

"Did you see the guy come back out?" Chandler asked.

"No. But then I left right after that."

"What hours did you work?" Caradon asked.

"Sixteen on, eight off, till it was completed. Job's a bonus contract. I started Friday at 9:00 p.m."

"What's a bonus contract?"

"The sooner the job was done right, the more it paid. Lemme explain. The manager had us quote on painting the lobby and his suite. But he's got posh tenants, eh, so he wants it done quick and us to keep out of their way as much as possible. That meant working two people twenty-four hours a day. Four's too many bodies cramped in that small a space. I got a partner and we've each got a helper. My partner worked Friday from 5:00 a.m. to 9:00 p.m. I finished another job that morning, then slept the afternoon. Me and my apprentice took over that night. We worked from 9:00 p.m. Friday till 1:00 p.m. Saturday afternoon."

"Then your partner picked up the job again at 1:00 p.m.?"

"Yep. That's the way it was done."

"When did you complete the work?"

"Late Monday afternoon."

"There's a woman lived in the penthouse suite. You see her at all?"

"Yeah. Early Saturday morning. She came down at 2:30 a.m. just as we were startin our coffee break. That's how I know the time."

"You see her just the once?"

"Uh huh. But I wish it was a million more."

The painter leaned forward in his chair and glanced at the kitchen door to see if his wife were listening. Then he whispered, "Built like a brick shithouse, she was. Blouse unbuttoned down to here, showin a valley 'tween her tits put the Grand Canyon to shame."

He winked at the cops.

"See her go back up?" Caradon asked.

"Nope. Went right out the front door, then we left for coffee ourselves a minute later."

"Was the door left open?"

"Sure, all the time. We were usin oil-based paint."

"See where she went once she left the building?"

"Just walked up the street."

"How long was your coffee break?"

"Half an hour."

"How do you know who she was?"

"I saw the elevator lights come down from the penthouse floor. There's only one suite up there."

"At any time did you see anyone else go up to or come down from that suite?"

"Yeah. A pretty-boy did the up and down about 2:00 a.m. We had just come out of the manager's suite after a two-hour argument over price cause he wanted to change colours part way through the job. Some guys, huh? But he backed down."

"How long was this pretty-boy up there?"

"No more than a coupla minutes."

"See anyone else connected to the suite?"

"Nope. Just the babe with the cans come down and that guy in your picture go up."

"We'll need your partner's name, address, and telephone number. Perhaps he saw something when he took over Saturday afternoon."

The painter grinned. "Poor old Arn," he said. "I asked him about the babe with the tits, if he got an eyeful. Said he was paintin the manager's suite from 1:00 p.m. Saturday on. But he did come out once about an hour later just in time to see a black-haired broad with two suitcases climbin into a cab. Thought it might have been her, but only saw her back. Didn't see them boobs."

"Don't suppose he mentioned the taxi company?"

"No," the painter said.

"When you saw her that morning, how was this woman dressed?"

"Classy. Open black overcoat showin her chest, black hat and sunglasses."

"At 2:30 a.m.?"

The painter shrugged.

Caradon passed him another folder of female photographs. Among them was an Immigration Act picture of Rosanna Keate. "Recognize the woman?" he asked.

The painter looked through them and shook his head.

"You mean she's not among them?" Chandler said.

"Oh, she could be one of 'em, all right. I just can't place her features."

"Sunglasses the problem?"

"Nope," the man replied.

He leaned forward again to check on his wife in the kitchen. Satisfied she was occupied, he smiled at the cops and winked a second time. "A set of jugs like that goes by, who looks at the face?"

As the Mounties were leaving the house, the kid on the front steps looked up at Zinc and asked, "Hey, Mister, know how you make a Kleenex dance?"

Chandler waited.

"Put a little boogie in it," the boy replied.

When the two men reached the car Bill Caradon said, "Now that's what I call a snotty little kid."

## 5:05 p.m.

Sulphuric acid will completely destroy a human body.

Though flesh is composed of fats, proteins, and minerals, its single major component is water. In concentrated form sulphuric acid is a highly corrosive liquid which acts by extracting water from body tissues. This process generates terrific heat. $H_2SO_4$, however, also dissolves the mineral and protein components of humans into watersoluble elements, thus completely destroying hair, muscle, bone, and skin. The parts of a corpse left exposed to air will be charred as if burned, but a body completely immersed in corrosive will be totally digested, bones and all, within a couple of days.

Fats however—though altered—are not rendered watersoluble by the action of the acid. Therefore they remain behind as a greasy sludge.

All that Nick White, the forensic pathologist from Lions Gate Hospital, recovered that day from the bathtub in the penthouse suite was four pounds of yellow melted grease left to float as scum on the surface of the acid and two multifaceted, cherry-sized stones.

Later, examined chemically at the pathology lab, the yellow grease proved to be body fat. But since sludge is sludge, the altered lipid residue of a human is qualitatively similar to that of a cat or dog. The sophisticated immunochemistry involved in establishing species identity from blood, tissue, or bodily fluids rests on the recognition of specific plasma proteins. Unfortunately, there are no plasma proteins left to be found in sludge.

The cherry-sized stones, however, were a definite bonus. When analysed, they proved to be compacted bile-sand coated with cholesterol, which is a type of fat. Because of this coating they were not dissolved by the acid but remained behind at the bottom of the tub.

White had encountered such stones many times before. A body with a single stone always has a round one, or one that is tear-drop shaped, as is the organ of origin. A body with several stones, however, will produce multi-faceted ones since they rub against each other constantly.

Because a cholesterol coating is like a protective cocoon of fat, it preserves traces of a dissolved body's proteins inside. These immunochemical fingerprints therefore remain unharmed, and from them Nick White was able to positively establish the species identity of the residue in the tub.

All that remained of the person who had taken the acid bath was a little slimy fat and two human gallstones.


## Vancouver, British Columbia
### 6:10 p.m.

Ray Hengler drove his XKE up the driveway to his home and shut off the engine.

He was locking the car door when he saw a shadow move nearby.

As his hand closed around the butt of his semi-automatic pistol the muzzle of a .38 was pressed against his temple.

"You're either dead," Chandler said, "or under arrest."

# Jack Be Nimble

**London, England**
*Tuesday January 21, 1:40 a.m.*

"Midnight Rambler" by the Stones was on the stereo, from their LP *Let It Bleed*.

The open Poe mirror/door reflected a litter of rock album jackets scattered about the cellar floor—Alice Cooper, Iron Maiden, Twisted Sister, Grim Reaper, Mötley Crüe. . . .

Beyond the door was a secret tunnel that ultimately joined the London sewers. Off this tunnel thirty feet in was an old, partly bricked-up vault abandoned for centuries.

Ten deer-skinning frames were ringed in a circle around the centre of the crypt. The bodies of all The Ghoul's victims to date were hanging naked upside down from several of the frames.

At the centre of this circle stood a clay statuette sculpted to depict the pagan image of a monster. It had an octopus-like head and its pulpy face was a mass of feelers.

Eyes glowing, mesmerized, The Ghoul was now crouched near this idol chanting a gibberish ritual.

*"Ph'nglui mglw'nafh Cthulhu R'lyeh wgah'nagl fhtagn."*

### 3:21 a.m.

Fifty pence was the going price, at least for a peek.

Wardour Street, Rupert Street, Tisbury Court. That was the place.

Sex was the commodity.

During the day Soho was abustle with shoppers, office workers, and market stalls. Vendors in leather aprons tempted passersby with an array of fresh fruit and vegetables stacked on well-stocked carts. The smells of fish and well-hung game wafted from the shops tucked away behind the stalls. Sellers called out continually, "Help yourself here," as derelicts picked through dustbin scraps to put together a meal. Beefburgers, hot dogs, and kebabs greased the air.

During the day Soho sleaze was also on sale, but it was not till sundown that sex truly prevailed. Ask a bobby at six p.m. the way to Wardour Street, he was apt to reply, "You want Soho, sir? You may keep it."

For at night "Hot Love" by T. Rex pulsed from one of the live sex joints. The Raymond Revue Bar called itself "The World Centre Of Erotic Entertainment" in garish neon light, three shows nightly, but not Sundays. The store in which Edwin Chalmers QC had shopped for his mistress Molly sold French chantelles, mitzi bras, saucy crotchless coquette briefs, and nurses' outfits complete with enema bags. Books in the bookshops had little black squares stuck over crotches on the covers and the din from the slot arcades nearby was deafening.

By 10:00 p.m. the hookers were out in full force. The usual London standstill traffic moved even slower here, for tight jeans and cleavages were on display to catch the driver's eye. Whores hung out in the alleys or vamped from recessed doorways. Bright red lips mouthed the words, "I'm a *very* naughty girl. Do you want to go?" You could take your choice of the blonde with the ponytail, the black girl who winked as she sucked her thumb, the redhead with the leather shorts, fishnet stockings, and stiletto heels. Ten pounds bought thirty minutes. Twenty got an hour.

But it was now after 3:00 a.m., and Soho was shutting down.

The alley behind the strip club had a T-cross lane at one end and a *cul-de-sac* at the other. The strippers who came out of the club's rear door were both congenital mutes. One was a woman, the other a man. They were Danish cousins, honey blond, blue-eyed, tall in stature. Three times a night, six days a week, they writhed in simulated sex on a twelve-foot stage.

The night was overcast, the alley dark except for a single bulb which burned beside the club's rear door. It cast a pale half-circle for fifteen feet, but not far enough to light the open manhole cover hidden in the shadows just beyond its glow.

The mutes paused beneath the bulb and briefly spoke to each other with their hands. The sound of a car on Wardour Street echoed down the alley, then died away. The strippers began walking.

The open sewer manhole was halfway between the T-cross lane and the club's rear door. Neither stripper noticed the pit nor the razor-sharp knife sticking up like a Vietcong punji stake just below street-level.

A sudden shock jolted the man as his left leg disappeared into the sewer well, his right foot sliding along the pavement until his pelvis slammed the ground and his body sprawled flat. He opened his mouth wide to scream in pain, but only a soft mewl escaped from his throat as the woman crouched to help him. She was not aware that a knife was jabbed between his legs, slicing his intestines and piercing his stomach. Now skewered on the blade, he was thrashing about like a fish fresh out of water.

Struggling, the woman dragged him clear of the pit, then kneeled over his convulsing body in the darkness. She didn't see the figure climbing out of the sewer hole until a voice whispered inches from her ear, "Last night I saw your show, that's why I chose you. No screams, baby. Shall we play The Game?"

The woman whirled around as life drained from her cousin and blood pooled at her knees.

The black-caped figure grinned at her, candlestick in one hand and 10-inch double-bladed knife in the other. His heartless, predatory eyes glared out from under the rim of a bowler hat. As she gained her feet he leaped in front of her, blocking access to the lane that led to Wardour Street.

Backing away, the woman bolted for the rear door of the Soho club. Then remembering the exit was locked from inside to prevent non-paying sneak-ins, she raced down the alley to find herself trapped in the *cul-de-sac*. Her back hugging the wall, she turned to face the threat.

Stalking her, the figure was just eight feet away.

"Who am I, you wonder? I see it in your eyes."

Six feet and closing, knife in the air.

"I'm not a butcher, I'm not a Yid, Nor yet a foreign skipper . . ."

Four feet.

"But I'm your own lighthearted friend, Yours truly . . ."

Three feet.

" . . . Jack the Ripper."

The terrified woman threw back her head and let out a squeal as the figure laughed aloud, and with a brutal stab, stuck the knife right down her throat.

# The Package

As the package arrived downstairs at the Yard and was being processed, upstairs in the Murder Room, Rand, Hone, and Braithwaite were looking over a constable's shoulder at a computer screen. A digital map of the sewer system glowed green on green.

Yesterday, after work, Hone had secretly attended a Piccadilly Circus hair transplant salon. One section of his baldness was now pierced with little hooks, and it was driving him crazy just trying to keep his fingers from ripping them out of his skin.

Rand's dragnet of the London sewers was an almost impossible task. Still, something had to be done and maybe they'd get lucky.

First she'd met the gangers, or leaders, of each five-man team of sewer flushers who spend their working hours cleaning the bowels of London. They told her they'd keep an eye peeled for anything suspicious.

High-tech equipment was of little help. With millions of rats down there moving through the pipes, motion sensors like LEA Manikins and microphones placed at key locations would be a joke. However, Rand knew the Sewer Killer could not move around in the dark, so using a pattern of Robot RSK IIs and Zenith Video Sentinels deployed as light detectors seemed to be one good plan. So did employing a system of cameras that used their own infra-red light source to see in the dark.

The Central Integrated Traffic Control of the Metropolitan Police uses closed circuit cameras to keep watch on certain intersections where problems occur. Some of these were now in place in the sewers surveying key pipe junctions in the main north-south lines. Pye Lynx zoom control cameras are used by the Yard to watch for developing trouble at London political demonstrations. Some of these were now down there too.

Ten feet in front of these cameras, electric eye sensors were positioned at waist height to detect movement. A sudden break in the beam would trigger an alarm in the Yard's C + C computer and activate the camera at that location. Hopefully as a result they would have not only the Sewer Killer cornered, but also a picture of the murderer's face.

The location of all this equipment had been fed into the PNC. It was now up on the screen that Rand and the two men were viewing, showing as a digital enhancement of the map.

"If we had more equipment," Hilary said, "and fewer miles of sewer, I might not consider our effort a hunt for a needle in a haystack."

"The Sewer Killer is too active over too great a distance not to show up eventually," Braithwaite said.

"I'd like to believe that, Winston, but my copper's nose tells me something else is going on that we don't know about."

"You'll see," the doctor said.

The three of them left the Murder Room and returned to Rand's office. The icepick carved as a monster and the Soho candlestick were lying on her desk. As the package was making its way upstairs to the Murder Squad, the Detective Chief Superintendent sat down in her chair and stared intently at the two cryptic, taunting objects.

A call had come in from the *Daily Mail* twenty minutes ago to report that a typed letter had been received in the morning post concerning both The Roman Steambath bombing and the funfair case. The letter was signed "Jack".

The documents section of the Yard had analysed the typeface on the note sent to Rand along with the flowers on the night of the steambath explosion. The typewriter carriage misaligned the first letter of each word on the left-hand margin of the page. The note sent to the *Mail* was on its way over to the Yard for comparison.

Rand was bothered most, however, by the funfair crime near Hampstead Heath.

As far as the Murder Squad could tell the killer had

entered the Tunnel of Love by means of the rear sluice gate that opened on the canal. The canal also intersected with the sewer system and the underground river it contained. Pieces of a frogman's shattered goggles were retrieved from the treadle pit near where the ambush occurred, so no doubt the "monster" described by the victims had used scuba equipment to set up the attack. Finally, the icepick carved to resemble the Creature from the Black Lagoon had the eerie aura of the Sewer Killer about it.

The incendiary device, however, smacked of Jack The Bomber.

Judging from fragments found by the Yard, the remote-control explosive gadget had been sophisticated. The device had certainly distracted those outside away from the scene of the attempted murders so the killer could escape. The attack fit Jack's MO.

Or was it that one of the killers was now incorporating the other's MO into his own crimes to baffle the police and act as a blind?

These were Hilary Rand's concerns as the package arrived upstairs in the hands of a constable who, in disgust, held it as far away from her body as possible.

"This came by special delivery," the PC said, placing it on the desk and quickly leaving the office.

The piece of flesh in the box had lost its usual shininess and was now a dull, dark reddish-brown in colour. It was 4 inches long, by 2½ inches wide, by 1½ inches thick. At the centre of its concave side were three tubular structures severed one inch from the organ and surrounded by a little fat. At the upper end was a streak of yellowy orange-gold that had been the adrenal gland. It looked similar to, but was smaller than, a kidney you might find in any butcher's shop window.

A note stained with blood was tucked down one side of the package that held the organ. Hand-written, the note read:

From Hell, Legrasse
  I send you half the Kidne I took from one woman prasarved it for you tother piece I fried and ate it was very nise I may send you the bloody knif that took it out if you only wate a whil longer.

Catch me when you can, Legrasse.

I

As the three of them considered the message scrawled on the paper, the Detective Chief Superintendent muttered, *"Déjà vu."*

For she knew the note was a mimic of a similar letter sent to the Whitechapel Vigilance Committee on October 16, 1888. The original Jack the Ripper had also included a human kidney.

For a minute Rand stared at the organ and message, lost deep in thought. Then she turned her attention to the list chalked on her blackboard:

Ceramic birds plus binoculars = Hitchcock film?
Top hat plus mirror = Mad Hatter in *Alice Through the Looking Glass?*
Icepick = Creature from the Black Lagoon?
Candlestick = ?

Again she stared at the candlestick found in a pool of blood in a Soho alley beside an open manhole.

Jack be nimble/Jack be quick/The Ripper jumps over the candlestick? Am I catching on to the Sewer Killer's game? Rand thought. For if I am it belongs more to an Agatha Christie novel than it does real life.

"Who's Legrasse?" asked Braithwaite.

"I've no idea," she said.

"And what does the 'I' at the end of the note indicate?" Hone asked.

"Perhaps it's not meant to be a letter of the alphabet," Braithwaite replied. "It might represent the Roman numeral."

"An old one?" Hone said.

"Yes," the doctor agreed.

# Gallstones

**Vancouver, British Columbia**
*10:17 a.m.*

TROY and INKERSALL
barristers and solicitors
Glen Troy
Thomas Inkersall

No 1 Burrard Circle
Vancouver, BC
(604) 555–8541

January 21, 1986

Royal Canadian Mounted Police
North Vancouver Detachment
160 East 13th Street
North Vancouver, BC

Attention: Constable Neil Turner, GIS.

Dear Sir:

*Re: Raymond Hengler*
*First Degree Murder*

Further to our discussion this morning I confirm the following information is provided pursuant to your undertaking that it will be investigated both for Mr Hengler's benefit as well as your own purposes. The wording is mine, not his.

My client does not know Rosanna Keate, nor as far as he is aware has he ever met her. He has never been inside her penthouse suite at the Horizon View Apartments. He did, however, knock on her door on Saturday January 11, 1986 at shortly after 1:00 p.m.

Here are the relevant facts.

My client is a rock music promoter and video film producer. He also operates a well-known Vancouver escort service.

In early October of last year, Mr Hengler was offered the opportunity to bring a rock group named Ghoul from London, England to perform in our city. A deal to produce an album and video was discussed. On January 8 the group was flown to Vancouver at Mr Hengler's expense. They subsequently performed one of two concerts contracted for a club called The Id on Hastings Street.

Mr Hengler took a fancy to the lead singer of Ghoul, known as Rika Hyde. Her stage name is Erika Zann. After the show he asked her to spend the night at his Shaughnessy home. Miss Hyde declined, stating that she was to meet someone else that evening, but gave him a telephone number to call the following day at noon.

Mr Hengler went from The Id to a social club in town where on attempting to purchase refreshment he found his wallet missing.

On Saturday January 11 at about noon, he called the telephone number provided by Miss Hyde. A female voice answered and told him to come right over. This my client did.

The front door of the Horizon View was wedged open by painters when Mr Hengler arrived. He walked into the lobby in plain view of the workmen and took the elevator up to the penthouse suite where he knocked on the door. Finding no one home, he left the building for the hotel where the band was accommodated. To his amazement the group had checked out that morning and left Vancouver. Ghoul did not perform at The Id that second night as required by the contract.

My client states without reservation that he is being framed. If he were planning to kill someone he would not walk through the Horizon View lobby in full view of several painters who could then identify him. Nor would he take his wallet and identification which might be lost at the scene of the crime. Nor would he phone the location of the proposed murder when in light of other legal problems his phones could be tapped. These are the actions of an innocent man.

There is no legal obligation for my client to provide this information. We do so because he has nothing to hide and you have promised him a hope of benefit. Consider dropping the charge before you look like a fool in court.

Yours truly,
TROY and INKERSALL

*Glen Troy*

Chandler put down the letter.

His counsel's sharp, he thought.

A statement by an accused to police is only admissible in court if it is in the words of the accused himself and given without fear of prejudice or hope of advantage. This letter was in the lawyer's words and given expressly so that it could be checked out to Hengler's benefit. Therefore, not only was it inadmissible to help prove their case, but it set the police up for a possible lawsuit against them later on.

Chandler felt depressed.

It was another dull morning of West Coast winter rain. He was working in a small GIS office at the North Vancouver Detachment of the Mounted Police. The room smelled of burnt coffee and an overworked Xerox machine. Zinc had just reviewed the case to date and now his stomach churned with the uneasy feeling that Hengler would slip loose again. In addition he was dying for a cigarette.

The darkest spot in the investigation was the fact that they had yet to ID the victim.

Rosanna Keate was an American from Newport, Rhode Island. She had been in Vancouver since early August of last year, staying first at a swank hotel, then moving on September 15 to the Horizon View Apartments. Because of an illness contracted just before she switched homes, Keate had lived in virtual quarantine until January 11.

Arnie Powell, the other lobby painter, had added little to what his partner had told them. He'd not seen the woman's face when he came out of the manager's suite at 2:00 p.m. on Saturday, just her back as she was climbing into the cab. The driver stored two suitcases in the trunk and they pulled away. He did remember, however, that it was a North Shore Taxi.

Through the cab company they had traced the fare, pickup time, and the driver. A woman who said she was Rosanna Keate had called for a taxi at 1:37 to arrive at 2:00 p.m. The driver was an East Indian who had shrugged his shoulders when they showed him a picture of Keate. The woman had been wearing sunglasses, he said.

The cab had gone directly to Vancouver International Airport. That same Saturday a woman giving the name of Rosanna Keate had purchased a ticket to Seattle connecting to New York. From there, half an hour later, she'd picked up a flight to Providence, Rhode Island, then a shuttle to Newport. All the tickets were purchased with cash.

Keate had recently had a complete physical examination in North Vancouver. The police found her doctor's name written inside the telephone book. Four days before she had left the city he'd pronounced her cured of glandular fever, and X-rays taken during the illness showed no sign of gallstones.

Because of Keate's long bout with the infectious disease, few people in Vancouver had actually seen the woman. Those who had all gave a similar description: that of a voluptuous vamp, cool and sophisticated, with stylish short black hair.

Keate's bank records had revealed that each month she received a cheque from Newport, Rhode Island, for $25,000 US drawn on a lawyer's trust account. The attorney's name was Ronald Fletcher.

At the request of the RCMP, Fletcher had been questioned by the FBI. He confirmed that Rosanna Keate had come to his office on Monday, January 13 to discuss estate business, and that she was sole heir to the Keate family fortune which she had inherited early the year before. Fletcher was the executor of the estate. Where Keate was at the moment, however, the lawyer had no idea. He had only seen her that one time in recent months.

Rosanna's alive, Chandler thought, so the sludge isn't her. It must be Rika Hyde.

A check of the various airlines had shown the rock group Ghoul left Vancouver on Saturday morning, the day following their Friday gig at The Id. As stated in Hengler's lawyer's letter, the band was also supposed to play the club that Saturday night. But most interesting was the fact that when the group flew out it was minus Rika Hyde.

Special X is the Special External Section of the Royal Canadian Mounted Police. Chandler was presently on loan to the Hengler investigation from the Special X liaison unit stationed in Britain. He'd telexed his London office and asked them to check out the rock band Ghoul and its lead singer Rika Hyde, stage name Erika Zann. He had yet to hear anything back.

Okay, Zinc thought. Assume the sludge in the bathtub is Rika Hyde. Where does that take us?

Chandler's mind assessed their case against Ray Hengler for the penthouse crime as follows:

1. There was some unknown connection between Rosanna Keate and Rika Hyde. The police had Hengler on tape phoning Keate's suite at about noon on Saturday January 11, and being told by a woman that Rika was there and to come on over.

2. Hengler arrived at 1:00 p.m. that same afternoon, and was seen by the painters going up in the elevator to the penthouse suite. Hengler himself admitted this in his lawyer's letter. None of the painters, however, had seen Hengler come back down. Perhaps that was not surprising since they were redecorating the manager's apartment from 1:00 p.m. on. But Arnie Powell and the cab driver said that a woman who gave the name Rosanna Keate came down from the penthouse at 2:00 p.m. and went to the airport. So was Hengler up there for just a few minutes as he stated, or up there much longer?

3. The staff at the hotel where Ghoul was staying did not remember the promoter inquiring about the band having checked out as written in his lawyer's letter. Was that because of the hubbub caused by a Japanese tour group checking in at the same time, or because Hengler had not left the Horizon View when he said?

4. Hengler's wallet with only his fingerprints and a glove smudge on the leather was found near one side of

the waterbed. Rosanna Keate and Rika Hyde—at least as near as science can tell—had both left head and pubic hairs on the bed's satin sheets. Yet no other prints of Henglers and none of Rika Hyde's were found anywhere else in the suite.

5. Rosanna Keate had ordered a male model, Reid Driver, from Fantasy Escort Service. Driver was told to arrive at 2:00 a.m. Saturday morning and was seen by the painters going up to and coming down from the penthouse suite. Prior to that the workmen had been in the manager's apartment having an argument, so anyone else could have slipped in unseen before Reid Driver. The model's alibi at the club on Richards had checked out. He was only gone for about half an hour as he'd said. Rosanna Keate, however, had not answered the door when he knocked.

6. Rika Hyde had left The Id just after 1:00 a.m. that Saturday. He and Caradon had seen her with Axel Crypt, the bass player, as they were waiting in the car for Hengler to leave the club. If something was going on in Keate's suite when Driver arrived at 2:00, Ray Hengler could not have been directly involved. For he was under Chandler's surveillance till 5:00 a.m. that morning.

Pretty damn weak, Zinc thought, if that's our entire case. Any lawyer worth his salt should make mincemeat out of it. Had Rika Hyde gone to visit Rosanna directly from The Id, and entered the lobby unseen while the painters were in the manager's suite? Maybe Keate killed Rika Hyde and dissolved her body, then packed her bags and fled back to Rhode Island. But if that were so, why the acid bath? To stop the police identifying Hyde because the connection between them was Rosanna's motive?

Zinc was going through the file yet another time when Constable Neil Turner entered the GIS room.

"Try some of this," Turner said, placing a cup of coffee down on the desk. "North Van's notorious for the quality of its brew."

"Thanks," Chandler said. "How long till the cup dissolves?"

"About as long as it'll take our present case against Hengler to fall apart."

"Yeah. We got troubles."

"Crown counsel says we might have to cut him loose.

Without a positive time of death and ID of the victim we can't prove the charge."

"No way," Chandler said. "His ass stays in the can. If our case falls apart, it unravels at the prelim. Maybe we'll come up with something more concrete by then."

"Like what?" Turner asked.

"Ray Hengler has led us to Rika Hyde and Rosanna Keate," Zinc said. "There's been a murder in Keate's suite and we know the victim's not her. She was seen recently in Newport, Rhode Island. So let's assume for a moment the victim is Rika Hyde.

"Hengler says he doesn't know Keate, but I think he's lying. She bought studs from his flesh farm and he phoned her apartment and went over there on the 11th. From the sketches on the walls and the sado-masochistic paraphernalia in her suite with her fingerprints on it, I'd bet Rosanna's a pretty kinky lady. We know Hengler makes porno flicks and might have shot a snuff film. The whole concept of the rock band Ghoul fits right into that. So let's assume Hengler, Hyde, and Keate are somehow mixed up together.

"Now let's hypothesize something went wrong. Rika was poison-tortured and murdered by Rosanna and Hengler in combination, Hengler alone, or Rosanna on Hengler's orders. Then Keate flew the coop and ran for the States.

"Rosanna, therefore, is the key to the case. I plan to find her, break her down and make her tell me Hengler's role, or search out evidence through her to nail that bastard."

Turner said nothing in reply. Instead, he picked up the lawyer's letter and read it once again.

Thinking back on what he'd just said, Chandler was concerned. He'd put forth so many assumptions with such vehement conviction that any trained cop would ask himself, What the hell's driving this guy? And to that question, Zinc knew the answer.

During the past week he had done a little reading on nightmares. This was motivated by two more dreams he'd suffered after "The Fly", both of which were also about Ed Jarvis and Jennie Copp. Zinc was ready to grasp at straws if that would make them stop.

He'd read that nightmares are like fissures in the earth, canyons which show us the strata layers of the dark pit below. Nightmares are commonly related to mental stress in that psychological pressure increases their frequency. In extreme cases they can literally scare a person to death.

The worst nightmares, Zinc had learned, are like a mental illness. They are distorted reflections of real life traumas to which we have not adequately reacted or adjusted. The most potent of these arise from guilt.

Sometimes the objective experience is upsetting to the mind because of what it does to our self-image. For this reason it may be repressed and locked away by dissociation in our subconscious well. The mind, however, cannot leave such problems unresolved, so they persist in returning at night when our mental inhibiting forces are not at work.

Chandler was angry with himself for naively thinking he could solve his own problems by convicting Hengler of murder in revenge for Jennie Copp's death. Yet that's both what he wanted to do and what was driving him.

Your guilt is yours, Zinc thought. It's not Ray Hengler's. So how will—

He was interrupted by a knock on the door.

"Come in," Turner said, putting down the lawyer's letter.

A uniformed cop poked his head into the room and said, "Inspector, you just received a telex from London."

Turner took the print-out and handed it to Chandler. The telex read:

> RIKA HYDE'S DOCTOR IN LONDON TRACED THROUGH
> AMERICAN EMBASSY. IN JULY 1985 HYDE DIAGNOSED
> AS HAVING TWO GALLSTONES. NO OPERATION. BOTH
> HYDE AND GROUP GHOUL CAME TO BRITAIN LAST
> APRIL FROM PROVIDENCE, RHODE ISLAND.

## Providence, Rhode Island
### 9:11 p.m.

Deborah sank down in the bubble bath and languished in its warmth, scooping a handful of scented suds and blowing them away. How Nibs used to love to watch her do that, eyeing the multi-coloured soap balloons that hovered in the air, pawing at the ones which floated near to him. The drip of the tap on the water, he loved that too, cocking his head to one side awaiting the next splash. Oh God, how she missed him, these lonely days alone.

The telephone rang.

For a moment she contemplated just letting it ring, a little apprehensive about whom it might be, but in the end curiosity got the better of her. Wrapping a towel like a sarong around her dripping body, she trailed a puddle behind her all the way to the phone.

"Hello."

No answer.

Oh no, she thought.

"Hello." A lot weaker.

Then the breathing began.

Him again, Deborah thought, slamming down the phone.

She waited a few seconds for the connection to break, then picked up the receiver and dialled the police.

# Lust

The walls of the windowless room were painted black and the total lack of light left him lost in a dark void.

Sid Jinks was stripped down to his Jockey shorts and sweating profusely as he did pushups, all the while imagining that he was going down between Debbie Lane's legs.

The door opened abruptly and a flash of light stabbed into the room, glinting off the cutlery hanging like art on the walls.

Squinting, Jinks turned his head to see the silhouette of a woman framed in the doorway.

"I'll have another job for you soon," she said, and then was gone.

Alone again in his room with the pitch-black walls, Jinks lit a candle and systematically removed all his cutlery from its hooks, lining the butcher's instruments up in four neat rows on the floor beside the grinder. Then he got to work.

Sparks flew out like metallic spray from the blade of the skinning knife as he ran it across the spinning stone. While he sharpened the steel he thought once more about Debbie Lane. Jinks had not made contact with her since his letter early this month. Should he send her another note to soften her up, or had the time finally arrived to plan a personal call? Lately just the thought of her pussy was driving him mad.

One day soon he would cut off her tits, stuff those beauties and mount them beside the door.

Then he could give each mound a squeeze whenever he left the room.

# Grim Reaper

London, England
*Friday January 24, 7:17 p.m.*

Hilary Rand was caught in a vise and the plates were moving together.

On the one hand she had been reprieved by the crimes of both the Sewer Killer and Jack The Bomber. For just as she was about to be sacked as head of the Murder Squad working the Vampire killings, personal contact by Jack The Bomber in sending her flowers the night of the steambath explosion provided a link to the new killer which the Yard could not afford to sever immediately. Then when the Sewer Killer—who initially seemed connected to the Vampire Killer crimes—mailed a human kidney to "The Head of the Murder Squad", Rand's stock with the men on the eighth floor had jumped again. For these tenuous links with her *personally* were the only real leads the Yard presently had in both cases.

On the other hand she knew the same acts would soon be her undoing. For Hilary sensed the two killers were now taking each other on, trying to compete with each other in the press, with the police, and no doubt before long, in the audacity of their crimes. The resulting public reaction was getting out of hand, so once again there were rumblings upstairs about giving Rand the sack.

It's all a deadly game, she thought, slumping back in her chair.

The Detective Chief Superintendent was now alone in her office. Out beyond the windows, black night smothered London. Earlier she had gone out to buy the tabloids, taking the papers back to the Yard's in-house pub to read over a much-needed beer.

The Tank, as always, had been filled with the usual

Friday crowd, tired cops closing the week off with a couple of pints after work. Rand was really not a beer drinker by preference, but long ago she'd learned that a few jars with the boys helped to make them accept her as part of the team. And that helped her work.

Tonight, however, as she had walked into the Tank, the usual level of noise had abruptly hushed to a whisper. Hilary knew they were all talking about her imminent fall, so she had pretended to search the crowd for some-one specific, then, not finding him or her, had left. Behind her the level of noise had risen louder than before.

The newspapers were now spread across her desk. Rand's eyes skipped from sheet to sheet, picking out paragraphs.

From the *Daily Mail:*

"I'll strike soon . . . I'll kill em all"

## LETTER FROM THE BOMBER

Scotland Yard experts confirmed today that a letter received by the *Mail* in yesterday's post was typed by the same person who is suspected in the January 4 bombing of a London steambath. That attack resulted in twenty-seven deaths.

The letter, addressed To the Editor of the *Daily Mail,* read: "The cops are bloody fools. That funfair mess wasn't me. When I do a job, the whole job gets done. You'll see cause I'll strike again soon. Before I'm finished, I'll kill em all." The letter was signed "Jack".

Commenting yesterday afternoon, Detective Inspector Derick Hone, a spokesman for the Yard squad investigating the bombing, told the *Mail:* "We do not believe the funfair crime to be the work of The Bomber. It is more likely connected to the recent sewer attacks."

From the *Daily Express:*

## GAY ANGELS ON GUARD

Gay groups in London are forming patrols to

protect themselves from the threat of Jack The Bomber.

From the *Mirror:*

## THAT SINKING FEELING

With no arrests and the murders coming faster and faster, Detective Chief Superintendent Hilary Rand, head of the Murder Squad investigating the Vampire Killer, the Sewer Killer, and Jack The Bomber crimes, is under pressure that few police colleagues around the world will ever know.

Each time a mother goes to pieces at a funeral, each time vigilantes arm themselves, each time the House of Commons appeals for faith in the Yard and declares that London is "not about to crack", the pressure builds. And no one feels it quite so much as the quiet, reserved woman who spearheads the hunt.

For such is Hilary Rand's job, and her crucible. She directs the search. She approves the strategies, right or wrong, as history will show. And ultimately she alone is responsible. But is enough being done?

A reliable source close to the investigation informed the *Mirror* that changes are forthcoming. A special team of detectives is to take over the Murder Squad hunt. This new team will bring together five specialists who . . .

Hilary pushed the papers aside and closed her eyes. In her mind she saw her father looking down at her, the buttons on his uniform shining in the sun as he removed his policeman's helmet and placed it on her head. The sound of laughter in her ears was that of a happy, excited little girl.

"You look tired, Hilary," she thought she heard him say, but when she opened her eyes she found Derick Hone standing at the door.

"Long day," Rand said. "I thought you'd gone."

'Just about to," Hone replied. "Went downstairs to see if they'd traced the special delivery order that sent the kidney."

"And?"

"Nothing," he said. He paused, then added, "I see you've read the papers."

"Yes."

Hone smiled weakly. "Don't let them get you down."

"I'm trying not to."

"Well . . . Good night."

"Good night, Derick. See you in the morning."

Hone turned to leave, but then turned back. "Hilary, you know I'll not abandon ship no matter what."

"Thank you, Derick," she said, managing a smile herself. "You're the only friend I feel I have left at the Yard."

## *10:54 p.m.*

The Ghoul grabbed the edge of the mirror/door and, hinges squealing, pulled it open. The movement of the glass reflected pictures on the walls.

There was Mr Gristle in *Tales From The Crypt* displayed as tainted meat; the opening panel of Osborne's "Kid Kill" in *Thrilling Murder Comics,* the picture all black and white except for copious red ink the artist had used for his concept of "Bloodarama"; the notorious panel from "Foul Play" in EC's *Haunt Of Fear,* the one where the home team carves up Herbie Satten to use in a baseball game, the home plate Herbie's heart and the baseball bat his leg, the base path his intestines and the ball his mangled head, one of Herbie's eyeballs dangling on its stalk.

When the Poe mirror ceased to move, its murky glass revealed a cluttered actor's make-up table backed by a second mirror. Pinned around the lights that ringed the edge of this looking glass were clippings from the magazines *Cinefantastique* and *Fangoria*. Step by step the clippings showed the special effect make-up techniques of Hollywood's best: Dick Smith, Rick Baker, Bob Bottin, and Tom Savini.

Scattered across the make-up table were chips of human bone.

## *10:55 p.m.*

After he brushed his teeth and prepared for bed, Detec-

tive Inspector Derick Hone examined his thinning hair. It
was going quickly, no doubt about that.

Hone had read that a possible cure for baldness was to
be shot full of massive doses of female estrogen. A tug-of-
war raged inside his head over whether or not it was
worth the chance. What if he developed breasts, or something worse than that?

Hone went into his bedroom and crawled between the
sheets, switching on the telly by remote control, and
there he was on the BBC repeating the comments he had
made to the tabloids yesterday. The DI winced at how
the lights accentuated his baldness.

When the cameras moved to other news, Hone switched
the channel and came upon a rock video programme.
Some zombie dressed up in tails and top hat was creeping
about like a ghoul. The announcer came on to tell him it
was Alice Cooper in "a blast from the past", his video
"Welcome To My Nightmare". Hone shook his head and
frowned. Could that be the meaning of the top hat and
the mirror? Maybe tomorrow he should chalk it up on
the board.

Yawning and stretching, he punched off the telly and
switched out the light.

## Saturday January 25, 3:02 a.m.

Hone awoke with a violent start as something stabbed his
arm. For a second he thought he was in the grip of a
nightmare from watching that rock video. Then the pain
began to radiate out from his elbow crease and when he
tried to climb out of bed his body would not respond to
the order from his brain.

It was dark in the bedroom, yet there were colours in
front of his eyes. Strangely, he had the feeling that these
spots were once removed, as if they were dancing beneath the rippling waters of a stream. Their movement
made him nauseous but still he could not get up. He was
shocked when involuntarily all his muscles began to twitch.

Now a voice cut through his growing anxiety like a
black-edged lick of flame rumbling up toward him from
the fires of hell. The words slowed, sped up, slurred,
then shrilled in his ears. Vomit bubbled to his throat and
he thought he was going to choke.

"The drug is succinylcholine chloride," the voice growled

ominously. "All your muscles are paralysed except those of your diaphragm. It won't affect your mind, and it won't calm your fears. No doubt you're feeling anxious now, as you have cause to be."

Hone was unable to move his head or shift his eyes. Individual muscle fibres were jumping and twitching spasmodically all over his body. Lying on his back and sweating, he stared up at the ceiling as tears ran down his cheeks.

Abruptly a match ignited and light seared his eyes; then it dimmed to a knot that cast off a chilling aura. A figure was moving around the walls at the corner of Hone's vision, a point-headed demon that appeared to drag the shadows with him. In one hand he held a flickering candle taper. Whatever was in his other fist was shiny and very sharp. Hone wet the bed.

"I didn't like your comment in the papers," the figure said. His voice was muffled as if it were coming from another world.

"I didn't fuck up whatever went down in that Tunnel of Love. That wasn't me. It was too poorly planned. But now, thanks to your flapping lips, London thinks I did. Plus you've got this asshole Jack making fun of me. You're going to pay for that."

Hone's lacerated psyche cowered down inside his brain as the figure, dressed in a grey monk's cloak with a pointed cowl, bent over his bed. The detective's emotions felt shredded with jagged glass and bleeding out of control. Candlelight shimmered off the face, the mask, whatever it was that was sunk deep back in the hood. For fractured pieces of human skull were stuck to the skin of his face and moved each time this grisly demon grinned. Then by the light of the candle moving toward the head of the bed, Hone saw a scythe gripped in the monster's hand.

The Detective Inspector's eyes began to flutter.

As the figure dripped wax onto the table beside the bed, sticking the base of the candle into the hardening tallow pool, he hummed the rock song "Highway To Hell" by Grim Reaper. Then he was gone from the detective's line of vision.

Ghastly images born of Hone's mind now slinked into view. Shadows shaped like pointing ghouls marked off parts of his body as if claiming that particular piece.

Black tar oozed down the surface of the closing walls, while his ears perceived a malignant chorus of macabre voices laughing at his plight.

Now the bone-mask was back, suddenly hovering once again above his face. He could hear the skull pieces rub together as the mouth behind them spoke.

"You have lost control of all voluntary movement," the Reaper said. "The drug, however, will not impair your breathing and other autonomic functions. I want you to lie nice and still while I set up this contraption. One size fits all, Detective Inspector."

Hone watched with mounting terror as the skull-face fitted a homemade guillotine around his neck. A piece went under the back of his head and slotted into knife guides that ran up like fence posts from both sides of his face. From the effort it took the figure to then lift the razor-sharp blade and slide it into the top of the guides five feet above Hone's eyes, the Scotland Yard detective knew the cutting wedge was heavy. Bone-Mask snapped a bar on top to complete the rectangular run down which the knife would drop. He ran a rope attached to the blade up over a pulley hanging from the top bar, then temporarily tied it to one leg of the bed. Candlelight glinted off the guillotine's cutting edge.

"Almost finished," the Reaper said as he ripped the policeman's pyjamas.

A cold object was being taped to Hone's chest but he couldn't see what it was. The figure then attached a horizontal rod to the edges of the knife runs facing Hone's feet, joining them together just above his collarbone. The guillotine jiggled as Skull-Face untied the rope from the leg of the bed and passed it under the rod, stretching the cord overtop of whatever was taped to the Yard cop's chest, then stringing it around his crotch and pulling it back up between his buttocks to follow his spine. Finally the rope was fastened to the headboard of the bed.

The Grim Reaper sat down next to Hone's now spastic face. The bone fragments clinked and scraped as words came from his lips.

"You told the London papers it was only a matter of time until the Yard brought me to bay. Reassuring the citizens, were you, Detective Inspector?

"Now why do you think I have been leaving those puzzling clues behind? Because I must know the identity

Inspector Legrasse has taken to stop us this time. We can't have Louisiana all over again. This time the Great Old Ones must break through. And the pressure of the press concern over my cryptic trail has forced Legrasse to show himself in his present female form. You limey fools have played directly into my hands. And Hilary Rand, like you, will be dead long before the stars are right."

Abruptly the bone fragments clattered and clinked as the Reaper's mouth twisted into a horrible grimace. The stink of acidic sweat assailed Hone's nostrils. The monster clutched his head.

After a minute, however, the leering grin returned.

"Just the worms," the Reaper said, as if that explained all.

"I think it only fitting that your death undo the harm you've done. It should let people know I'm too clever to have bungled that Tunnel of Love affair. But enough of these distractions. Such thoughts spoil the fun.

"I've taped a very sharp scalpel blade to the bare skin of your chest. The rope holding the guillotine knife up passes over it. Each time you breathe your rising chest will cause a small strand of hemp to be sliced away. When enough are gone and the rope snaps, the steel will descend to chop off your head.

"How much self-control do you have, Detective Inspector? How long can you keep from taking a breath?

"Now, you watch the guillotine and I'll watch you.

"What say, my British friend? Shall we play The Game?"

## Part Two

# THE
# GAME

Are they blighted, failed and faded,
    Are they mouldered back to clay?
For life is darkly shaded,
    And its joys fleet fast away!

              —*Charlotte Brontë*
              RETROSPECTION

# Twisted Sister

United Airlines Flight 242 from Chicago had to race a storm into T.F. Green Airport. Out the window off toward the state line with Connecticut, Chandler looked down on the Western Hills of Rhode Island as the lights of Providence slipped beneath the plane. Across the aisle to the east, angry black clouds were sweeping in from the Atlantic. His would be the last flight to make it in tonight.

The woman who met him at the baggage claim was Special Agent Carol Tate of the FBI. Born and raised in Texas, Tate was six feet tall. She had blue eyes, straight teeth, strawberry blonde hair and those Kellogg's Corn Flakes freckled good looks that come from living a healthy life outdoors. Here in Rhode Island in winter she sported an artificial tan.

Zinc put the woman's age at about thirty-five. As she had removed her fur coat and draped it over one arm, he could see that her figure was muscular and strong. He concluded that she was a born athlete and worked out with weights. From her handshake he sensed she could take care of herself in any situation, and from her movements deduced that she was trained in karate.

Reaching out with her other hand to peek inside his coat, Tate broke the ice by saying, "Where's the scarlet tunic?"

"Back home in the closet," Zinc replied. "Packed in mothballs."

By the time they left the terminal, the storm had hit full force. Snow came flying at them so thick and fine it felt like sand as it bit their faces. Zinc's clothes billowed about him like a boat under sail while his hair turned

203

white and was plastered to his head. A northeast wind was howling at fifty miles an hour, rubbing out their footprints as fast as they could make them. Already two inches of snow had collected on the ground.

"You can drive in this?" Chandler yelled above the wind.

"I didn't choose the flight, my friend. You did," Tate shouted back. "I've an important call I've got to catch in town tonight. We'll have to give it a try. They're forecasting two feet."

Interstate 95 was closed because a longbed truck had jackknifed and overturned. U.S. 1 was moving at twenty miles an hour due to the murderous wind, the strongest gusts of which rocked Tate's car on its shock absorbers. Ice crystals ground against the glass of the windshield. The headlights reflected off the snow to blind Carol as well as block her view of the road. Then they came upon a six-car pile-up which blocked U.S. 1 as well.

"It's no use," Tate said. "The blizzard's a whiteout. Is that an off-ramp out your side?"

"I can't see a bloody thing," Chandler replied.

"What say we try it before we get rear-ended?"

"Agreed," the Canadian said.

But it was not an exit ramp and the car slipped off the road to nose-dive into a snowbank. The sound of metal scrunching on ice came from the rear undercarriage. "Oh, oh," Zinc said.

Carol Tate grinned. "Thank God it's a government car."

Chandler laughed. "Yeah. And that I don't pay the taxes."

When the vehicle then began to fill with carbon monoxide fumes, the two cops knew their troubles had just begun. As Tate opened the driver's door to go take a look, the screeching northeaster almost ripped it off its hinges. Snow spilled into the car.

Zinc glanced back through the rear window, and by the red glow of the taillights could just make out the woman shaking her head. It was now freezing cold inside the vehicle.

"The exhaust pipe's crushed flat," Carol Tate said, climbing back in and switching off the engine.

"If we don't keep the heater on we'll freeze to death."

"And if we do we'll both be poisoned," the American replied.

"Is this the standard welcome you have for tourists?"

"No. Usually we take them on a walking tour of the state, as I'm about to do."

As they vacated the car the wind grabbed them brutally and flung snow in their faces. Each time Chandler blinked the swirling vortex of minuscule flakes transmogrified into a different weird shape. Snow ghosts, he thought as the windchill froze his face. All the hate in the whole world seemed to be packed into this storm.

"Come on," Tate yelled. "If I've got my bearings right there's a motel up ahead."

"I can't see my hand in front of my face."

"Then trust my intuition."

By the time they stumbled across the motel beside the pond, the snow was blowing fiercely in heavy drifts. With zero visibility, if Tate hadn't walked into its sign they might have missed it completely. A snowplough sat abandoned in the parking lot. Insanely, the wind laughed at them from the eaves as Carol yanked open the office door.

"You folks spooks or people?" the man behind the registration desk asked. Both cops were pure white from head to foot.

"We'd like two rooms," Chandler said, stamping his feet.

"'Fraid you're out of luck, chum. A lot here before you in the same predicament. Got one room left."

"Twin beds?" Tate asked.

"Nope. A double. Ain't queen either."

"I've seen this scene on the late show," Carol said. *"It Happened One Night."*

"Do I look like Clark Gable?" Chandler asked.

"Yep. You both got big ears." Tate fished a coin from her overcoat pocket. "You call," she said. "Loser takes the floor."

The room was small but cosy, and had a fireplace. The floor was pegged together rather than nailed. The pictures on the walls were of New England rural scenes ablaze with the colours of autumn. Outside, the furious wind threw itself against the windows.

While Tate got the fire going, Chandler went back to

the office and bought a bottle of wine. As he left the manager winked and flashed him a knowing grin.

Returning to the room he found Carol stretched out across the floor in front of a cheerful blaze. She was lying on her right side with one arm propping up her chin. Tate wore a checked flannel shirt and a pair of jeans. Her waist dipped into a valley before swelling to form the curve of her hip.

Easy, boy, Chandler thought. This trip's strictly business.

"So," Tate said as the Canadian uncorked the wine. "Who do we talk about first? Rosanna Keate or Rika Hyde?"

"Keate," Zinc replied, filling a Pyrex tumbler from the bathroom and passing it to her.

"Skoal!" Carol said before she took a sip. "Where shall I begin?"

"Her background," Chandler said as he joined her by the fire. Its warmth made him relax.

"Rosanna comes from old Rhode Island stock. There was a Keate in Roger Williams' group that fled Salem, Massachusetts, in 1636 to found a colony at Providence. The Keate family fortune is very old money indeed."

"Her father and mother, what about them?"

"Enoch Keate, her father, was born in 1924, if I remember correctly. My notes are in the car.

"He was heir to the family wealth which was amassed in Newport, a few miles south of here. That's where the Keate Mansion presently stands. After the old man died in 1984, the house was taken over by The Preservation Society.

"Enoch had a sister two years younger than him. Her name was Elena, and I'll come back to her.

"Enoch's father held interests in vaudeville, New York and London theatres, and early Hollywood films. As a young man Enoch worked around the New York stage. There in 1950—again if my memory's right—Enoch met and married an actress by whom he subsequently had a child. This girl was Rosanna, born in 1953. Enoch's wife died of cancer in 1955."

"Was Rosanna his only child?" Chandler asked.

"Maybe. Maybe not, according to the testimony at last year's trial."

"What trial's that?"

"There was a probate challenge to Enoch Keate's will."

Zinc refilled their glasses.

"It's common gossip," Tate said, "that for generations the mental and physical health of the Keate family's not been good. They've suffered inherited latent schizophrenia in both sexes. In addition, genetic haemophilia was passed on by Keate mothers to some of their sons. Genetic haemophilia, I'm sure you know, only occurs in males."

"Yes," Chandler said. "Queen Victoria's family was the same."

"Well, the Keates' health has been cursed for centuries," Tate said. "Some in Newport call them 'The New House of Usher'."

Carol stoked the fire as Zinc again refilled her glass. The colour that licked the walls of the room went from red to brilliant orange. The glow of the Mouton Cadet made Chandler once more crave a cigarette. He fought the desire down.

"Thanks," Tate said, placing the tumbler of wine on the floor and rolling up her sleeves. She had strong wrists and beautiful hands with long, tapered fingers.

"According to evidence at the trial, Enoch Keate must have really loved his wife. On her death he suffered a complete nervous breakdown and became a total recluse at the Newport Mansion.

"Elena, his sister, had been disinherited when she eloped to marry a sailor. The union, however, was ill-fated and the man had run off with the little money she'd spirited away. In a manic-depressive state, she too had then returned home to the Keate Mansion."

It was getting hot in the room so Zinc took off his sweater. Carol loosened the top button of her shirt.

"Okay," she continued, "here's where it gets murky. Some of the following is no more than rumour or hearsay which bubbled around the trial. My major source was a catty, old rich-bitch from Newport.

"According to her, it was almost inevitable—given both Enoch and Elena's fragile state of mind and the fact they were locked away together with a mutual need for immediate comfort—that incest should result between the brother and sister. The rumour is that on finding out she was pregnant not long after she had returned home, Elena ran away once more, fearing that Enoch would make her destroy the child on the chance that it might be his and not her absconding sailor husband's."

"Was there a birth?" Chandler asked.

"Yes. But the family name registered with the state bureau of vital statistics is that of Elena's long-gone nautical husband."

"Boy or girl?" Zinc asked.

"Both," Tate replied. "Twins were born to Elena Keate in 1957. They were named Saxon and Rika Hyde."

## 9:51 p.m.

"There, Daffy," Deborah said, filling the new litter box and setting the kitten down in it. "That's where you do your business, and nowhere else. Understand?"

Daffodil looked up at her as if to say, But the living room carpet is so much softer on my ass.

"Don't you stare at me that way. *I* make the rules here, Cat. I'll break you in, not you me."

We'll see, Daffodil seemed to say—as the telephone rang.

The Breather, Deborah thought, scared. He must be watching me. I only just got in.

She crossed to the phone, hesitated, reached for the receiver, paused, then lifted it and listened.

She hung up quickly.

For as before The Breather's call made Deborah think of Sid—which in turn brought back memories of Saxon Hyde.

Ugly memories.

## Saturday September 11, 1971, 1:00 p.m.

*Debbie was playing with Mr Nibs when she saw movement outside her door. At first she thought it was her father, but he was passed out dead-drunk on the living room couch. Rika, as always, was down at the record store. Her mother was still in Butler Hospital, so it had to be Saxon.*

*Debbie smoothed Mr Nibs' fur and put him down.*

*"Who's there?" she asked.*

*The eleven-year-old's eyes grew wide with fear as Saxon stepped into the open doorway. He had taken off all his clothes and caked his body with black mud. Silver light-*

ning bolts were painted on top of the dirt to radiate out from his groin and his growing erection. His eyes were pinpoints that drilled into hers and his teeth shone white within the gunk that caked his face. Red poster paint had been dumped on his head to flow down his body like blood from a hatchet blow.

"You're my slave," Saxon said. "Lemme see your cunt."

Deborah got off the bed slowly and backed toward the open window. Mr Nibs had already jumped up on the sill. The young girl never once took her eyes off the youth. "You're ill, Saxon," she whispered.

He laughed at her and stepped into the room. "Cthulhu lives, witch. Wanna play a game?"

As he lunged at her, Deborah cried for help. But Saxon grabbed her arm before she could get out the window. "Lemme have it bare," he snarled, tearing at her skirt.

Deborah punched him in the face and Saxon slapped her back. Powdered mud and poster paint cracked off one cheek in chunks. When she dropped to the bedroom floor he grasped her by one leg and yanked her upside down in the air. "Gimme it," he ordered as he reached up under Debbie's skirt for the waistband of her panties—but then there was a sharp snap from outside in the hall.

Saxon whirled to find Rika standing in the doorway. She'd snapped her fingers with one hand while the other gripped several records. She snapped them a second time, then pointed at him and said, "You. Put her down."

Saxon dropped Deborah's leg.

"Now get into my room and wait there for me. You want to play games, brother? I'll show you how to play."

Debbie scrambled to her feet and moved toward the window.

"You," Rika said, snapping her fingers again. "Stay here and don't you dare think of ratting on him. One peep and I'll rip off your cat's head and stuff it down your throat."

Then she turned and was gone.

For the next hour, crying alone, Debbie listened to sounds of moans and squeaking bedsprings coming from Rika's room.

## Saturday January 25, 1986, 10:02 p.m.

Outside, a foot of snow had already fallen from the

black, howling storm. The wind was blowing hard and
heavy and showed no sign of letting up. Beyond the
window was a crystalline miasma.

Chandler went back to the office for a second bottle of
wine. Again the manager winked and said, "You better
take two. You don't wanna have to get dressed to come
back for a third."

When he returned to the room Zinc found Carol standing at the window. She turned and smiled at him and
said, "My eight-year-old niece would be scandalized by
this situation. She once warned me not to fool around
with strange men. She'd heard on TV that's how you get
rabies."

"Did you set her right?" Chandler asked.

"Yeah. I told her 'You mean herpes?' To which she
replied, 'Rabies. That's what I said.' "

Chandler sighed. "Kids, eh?"

"Yeah," Tate said, and she looked back out the window.

"Carol, I'm going to need certified copies of both
Rosanna Keate's and Rika Hyde's birth records. They're
either cousins or half-sisters, which will provide an evi-
dential link we need for our case. It sure would help if I
could show Enoch Keate fathered both girls. Any ideas?"

"I doubt it can be done, Zinc. That's what the Hyde
twins alleged at the probate trial and it failed. Any proof
would long ago have been covered up. There was a
rumour scandal in Newport at the time of the twins' birth
in '57. It was even suggested that wrong birth dates for
Saxon and Rika were recorded in the official state documents. That money changed hands.

"Then both to keep face and as a gossip diversion, a
servant in the Keate Mansion was fired for allegedly
taking advantage of his mistress in her mental distress.
The Keates, of course, maintained publicly that the twins
were fathered by Elena's husband Hyde. Rumours were
all there ever was to substantiate suspicion. But we can
take a look at the records early Monday morning if you
want."

"I do," Chandler said. "I'll also need a copy of Enoch's
will and the court proceedings concerning his estate."

He uncorked the second bottle of wine and once more
they sat on the floor. Tate sipped from her glass and
stared at the dancing flames a while, then she turned to
Zinc and said, "I envy you."

"Envy me what, Carol?"

"You know. The colourful pageantry. The whole Mountie image and the fun you guys must have. At least your tradition gives you the chance every now and then to wash the dirt of this job away and cover up the cracks."

Chandler smiled. "Carol, the grass is always greener . . . Walk a mile in my shoes."

Tate sighed.

"A few years ago I was in Detroit," she said. "I got asked by these two Motor City cops to go for a beer. We ended up eventually at this 'knock-knock' club."

"What's that?" the Canadian asked.

"A private hangout for cops. Your knuckles go knock-knock on the door and some guy opens this little window to check out your badge. If you pass muster, he lets you in."

"Sounds exclusive," Chandler said.

"Inside it was dark and smoky and filled with nothing but cops. Except for the strippers up on the stage. They all had big breasts and were performing lewd acts with plastic guns. Then I heard this out-of-place sound: *click . . . click . . . click*. Some of the clicks were rhythmic, others overlapped."

Chandler arched an eyebrow. "Go on," he said.

"At first I couldn't make it out," Carol explained. "Then *click-click-click*, things fell into place. All these guys were drinking and sitting around half cut, watching the strippers fuck those guns while under the tables they were cocking and uncocking their own service revolvers.

"Rarely, Zinc, have I felt as depressed as I did that night. I thought, Is this how we all end up in this job? Is this what lies ahead? At least you Horsemen can don your scarlet and go for a musical ride."

"Carol," Chandler said, casting her a mischievous smile to lighten the darkening mood. "Take a little credit yourself. You Yanks are the reason we Canucks formed the Mounted."

"Gimme some more booze, honey, and tell me why." A playful hint of her Texas roots had crept into her voice.

He filled her glass.

"Back in the 1870s, the Canadian government was afraid you southerners would sweep up in the west and

seize our unsettled land. The Mounted Police were literally formed to cut you off at the pass. And the reason the
scarlet tunic was used was because the Plains Cree and
Blackfoot through whose land we had to travel had long
held respect for the British soldiers of Queen Victoria,
their Great White Mother. A Montana newspaper coined
the phrase, 'The Mounties always get their man.' So
when you blow away the chaff, the force in actual fact is
an American creation."

Carol Tate laughed and punched him on the shoulder.
"I don't know if that's a compliment or a not-so-subtle
dig, but hell, I'll take credit for creating the RCMP. I
look great in red."

I'll bet you do, Zinc Chandler thought.

## Sunday January 26, 1:15 a.m.

Chandler had never before made love with a woman like
Carol Tate. In the first place it was rare for him to look a
female straight in the eye while they were fucking. Carol
Tate's height made that possible. Even more rare to
encounter, however, was a woman with a body as rock-
hard as his own. Carol Tate was without a doubt one of
the strongest human beings he had ever wrestled. At one
point she brought both arms up behind his shoulder
blades to lock over his collarbone before driving herself
down on his cock as hard as she could. Zinc thought for a
moment she might have sprained his back in the process
and could see the look on the manager's face as they
carried him out on a stretcher in the morning. Then when
Carol Tate climaxed she let out a scream that could be
heard three rooms down while her nails tore valleys in his
back as deep as the Rocky Mountain Trench. Never
before had he seen a woman put quite so much raw
animalistic power into her orgasm. By the time they were
finished, Chandler's muscles ached as much as if he'd
worked out several hours in a gym. And that felt good.

But now as he lay awake in the dark with Tate asleep
in his arms, it bothered Zinc that he didn't feel something more. How many one- or two-night stands had he
had in his life? Fifty? A hundred? Two hundred? What
did it matter? That was a young man's game and he was
young no more. The important point was how empty
such loveless acts now made him feel inside.

What used to fascinate Zinc about women in his younger days—and, he supposed, fascinated women about men
too—was how hard it was to know what an individual
would be like sexually from the image she projected.
One of the poorest lovers he had ever had came across
like a nuclear reactor at meltdown point. And one of the
best, who looked like the stereotypical Miss Librarian,
had started out as a charity-fuck.

Was it because he came of age in the late sixties that
he could not, or would not, equate sex with love? Why
did he feel so much like a refugee lost in the dead
morality of the past? Even when he was inside, he felt
like an outsider. Erotic distancing. That wasn't right.

More and more lately he was frightening himself with
the content of his thoughts. It was so easy to let the best
of yourself slip away.

Alone in the dark with Carol now cuddled up next to
him, he wondered if perhaps she felt much the same way.
So independent, self-assured, confident and in control
when she was awake, Tate was snuggled up and clinging
to him in her sleep. Two strangers seeking comfort from
the cosmic wind.

Such a fine woman, Zinc thought. Why don't you feel
more?

Outside, the storm howled mournfully across the frozen pond.

## London, England
### *3:16 a.m.*

Hilary Rand was angry. Her right hand clenched and
unclenched, the knuckles white.

Early yesterday afternoon they had found Detective
Inspector Derick Hone's decapitated body. His naked
corpse was sprawled across his blood-soaked bed, the
guillotine having tumbled to the floor. A scythe had been
rammed full-force through his heart after he was dead,
pinning a piece of paper to his chest. The note read,
"Legrasse, beware the stars!" The Yard had searched the
flat from top to bottom but Hone's head had not been
found.

Now this.

The hospital near King's Cross was small and old and had no sign outside. Beyond the barred windows spread the lights of north London. Rand was standing in a stuffy second-floor room, looking down at the body of a nurse who'd been hacked to death. The hatchet that had split her skull still protruded hideously from her head.

The hospital matron and a female constable approached Rand. "We've searched the entire building. They're gone," the PC said.

"Anything amiss or out of place?"

"A door to the boiler room which is usually kept locked has been prised open. We found one of their shoes in the corridor outside."

"From where was the door forced?"

"Inside the boiler room."

"Does the boiler room have another exit?" Rand asked.

"Yes. It joins an air-raid tunnel built during the war."

"And does that tunnel connect with the sewers?"

"Yes," the matron said.

How does he do it? the DC Supt wondered. There are more than a hundred cameras and light detectors down there at key points in the system, yet none of them was tripped. Including the three close to here. Who in hell is he? The Invisible Man?

"Examine every inch of excavation beneath the local streets," Rand ordered the PC.

Hilary turned to the matron. "Is it possible they could have done this?" she asked, glancing at the corpse.

"Certainly not! Really, detective!" the woman replied.

"Can they survive by themselves without hospital support?"

"Barely," she said. "Neither has an IQ above eighty-five. Both are severely handicapped."

"Why were they never separated?" Rand inquired.

"It couldn't be done medically. They share too many organs."

"Have you got a picture?"

"Yes," the matron said. She opened the folder in her hands and passed over a photograph.

What in God's name is going on here? Hilary thought. Why kidnap them? This case is a horror film script.

She stared at the picture with pity in her heart: two Siamese twins joined together down one side of their bodies. Both had enlarged heads and dull, vacant eyes.

One had two legs but was missing arms. Her sister, however, had four twisted arms, each upper limb ending with five hooked claws.

## 3:22 a.m.

The Poe mirror/door squeaked open as The Ghoul returned from the sewers.

He crossed the cellar room to study his picture collage on the wall beyond the TV screen, searching out one of his movie stills.

The photograph showed a group of circus side-show geeks: the armless, legless human torso Randian; Olga the bearded lady; Pete the living skeleton; Josephine/Joseph, half-woman, half-man; Daisy and Violet the Siamese twins; plus four pinheads: Schlitzie, Zip, Pip, and Jennie Lee.

The film, from 1932, was Tod Browning's *Freaks*.

You're dead meat, Rand, The Ghoul thought.

# Motley Crew

## Providence, Rhode Island
*8:15 a.m.*

Zinc Chandler desperately wanted to buy some cigarettes. For one thing a smoke would kill the lousy taste in his mouth. His toothbrush was still in his bag in the car abandoned down the road. For another he didn't know what to do with the empty hand that didn't hold his coffee cup. And finally, since he and Carol had fucked again before going to breakfast, a stupid joke from his teens would not leave his head. "Do you smoke after?" "Don't know. I've never looked." Quit when the investigation's over, he told himself. Which, of course, is every smoker's rationalization for having no backbone.

The restaurant was a Ma 'n' Pa affair beside the motel overlooking the pond. Two and a half feet of snow had fallen during the night. Patchy thick cloud still clung to the sky, but now and then it would break and the sunshine that poured through was blinding to the eyes. It bounced blue supernovas off snow crystals on the ground.

"I wouldn't mind doing that," Carol Tate said. She was watching four bundled-up children toboggan down the slope of a hill on the other side of the pond, a barking dog in fast pursuit.

"Neither would I," Chandler replied.

"So what shall we do instead?"

"Trace Rosanna Keate, if we can. And talk to Ronald Fletcher."

They both ordered the ranch breakfast: bacon, sausage, two poached eggs, and a small stack of pancakes. As they ate, a blue jay landed in a tree just outside the window and took a peck from a hanging plastic bag of fat.

"What else do you know about Rosanna?" Chandler asked.

"Bits and pieces. She looks just like her mother, and her father idolized her. Rosanna lived at the Newport Mansion until she was eighteen, then went off to study at an art school in Europe. Paris, I believe.

"They say she was a wild one, with money coming out her ears, and threw terrific parties. To belong to her social set your attitude had to be completely devil-may-care. She arranged a party once where a couple ended up having sex and no one, including the participants, knew who was screwing whom."

"How did she do that?"

"I didn't get the details."

"What happened to her father, Enoch Keate?"

"After his wife died of cancer in '55 and he had his nervous breakdown, everyone I talked to said he never completely recovered. Subsequently he produced some plays but all of them flopped. More and more he turned in on himself, locked away in The Mansion pining for his beloved wife. He died a year ago last summer. In 1984."

"How?"

"He drowned. Fell near the swimming pool when no one was around, hit his head on the concrete and slipped into the water. Evidently the old man walked with a cane. The verdict was that what occurred was an accident. It was the servants' day off and his body wasn't discovered till late that evening."

"Rosanna still in Europe at the time of his death?"

"No, she'd returned home about a year before and was also living at the Keate Mansion. During the probate trial last spring to settle Enoch's will, the twins alleged that Rosanna'd killed her father. But it was never proved."

"Where was Rosanna on the day Enoch died?"

"Shopping, she said. But that was only partly confirmed."

Chandler signalled the waitress for another cup of coffee. Again he thought how good a cigarette would be. But having come this far, quitting was now a question of principle with him. You either are or you aren't, Hemingway said. You either do or you don't. Zinc would never give in.

"Tell me about this probate trial," he said.

"It was the legal *cause célèbre* of the year, the Rhode Island scandal of the decade. The twins—Rika and Saxon

Hyde—challenged the will by alleging that Enoch Keate
was their natural father. Therefore, they deserved an
equal part of his estate. The gossipmongers loved it.
Money, power, incest, murder, dirt, dirt, dirt."

"Is that why Rosanna left Newport for Canada last
summer?"

"I wouldn't think so, from what we know of her. She's
the type who'd thrive on clucking tongues. They say
Vancouver is the most beautiful city in North America."

"No doubt about that."

"Then moving there would be a change to fit Rosanna's
style. She won the probate case and it was time to move
on."

"The twins got nothing?"

"Not a cent."

"Why would they have tried a lawsuit in the first
place? What was the evidence they advanced as giving
them legal status to sue?"

"Enoch's *previous* will. They had a piece of that. Plus
they once spent a week at the Keate Mansion while their
mother was hospitalized."

"Where had they been raised?"

"I told you Elena'd left The Mansion by the time she
gave birth to the twins in '57. She married again a year or
two after that, so Saxon and Rika were brought up in
that new home. They were not well off, according to
testimony at the trial. Their new stepfather drank a lot
and their mother was in and out of hospital due to her
mental disorder. She was manic-depressive.

"By the early 1980s Enoch Keate was in very sorry
shape. He was living as a total recluse in The Mansion.
Except for the servants, the only people he ever saw
were his doctor, his lawyer Ronald Fletcher, and his
daughter Rosanna. Evidently he longed for the only happy
days he'd ever had—those with his dead wife, the New
York actress. He decided to leave his estate, which was
worth millions, in a trust with part to go toward building
a theatre in his late wife's name, and the other part to be
divided sixty per cent to Rosanna and twenty per cent to
each of his sister's twins. The rumour mill in Newport
concluded that Enoch viewed this last bequest as a settling of accounts and expiation of guilt for how he had
shunned his sister over the years."

"In other words," Zinc said, "he *knew* he was their father?"

"That's what the twins alleged at the probate trial."

"You said they once stayed with Enoch for a week. When was that?"

"The early seventies when Elena'd flipped out."

"Why just a week?"

"Rosanna hated them. She thought they were garbage and Rosanna was Daddy's girl. So Saxon and Rika were sent home to their drunken stepfather."

Chandler motioned to the waitress to bring him the check. Outside the window, the sun passed under a cloud.

Tate continued. "Less than a month before he accidentally drowned on the family estate, Enoch changed his will and left everything to his legitimate heir, Rosanna. The twins were disinherited completely."

"Why?" Chandler asked.

"Because of their outré behaviour with the rock band Ghoul. Or at least that was the reason Fletcher gave in his testimony at trial."

"I've seen the group perform," Zinc said. "The violence in their act would certainly upset more cultivated tastes."

"Which is what Judge Herbert Jackman has, I am told. He's an authority on Beethoven, Handel, and Bach."

"I see," Chandler replied.

"In court the twins alleged: 1. that Enoch Keate, a most prominent Newport citizen, had conceived them through incest with his sister while they were both mentally ill; 2. that he had changed the original will under pressure from his daughter, Rosanna, who was having sex with her father while he pretended she was her mother, his beloved dead wife; 3. that Rosanna was also screwing Ronald Fletcher, Enoch Keate's lawyer, who handled the estate; and 4. that after she'd manipulated all of this and Fletcher had drafted a new will and had Enoch sign it, though he knew his client was mentally and legally incompetent to do so, Rosanna then killed her father and made his murder look like an accident."

Chandler whistled. "Who witnessed the will?"

"Two servants who the twins said were paid off, and who hoped Rosanna would keep them on if she inherited."

"Where did the twins get their information about Enoch's incompetent state of mind?"

"Rika said she got it from a receptionist who liked Ghoul's music and worked in Enoch's doctor's office. The doc, however, had died of a stroke by the time of the trial. When his office was searched, Enoch's medical file was gone."

"Who do you see as the thieves? Rosanna and Fletcher? Or the twins?"

"If it were the twins they'd have used the file at trial."

"Rosanna's chief witness was Fletcher, right?"

"Yes. Who's also known to play golf now and then with Judge Herbert Jackman."

"What was Jackman's judgment like in throwing out the case?"

"He was apoplectic. Ghoul was already the bane of Newport's ritzy image. They *were* the local punk scene, playing sleazy clubs for dirt wages. Jackman called them 'disgusting', 'vile', and 'the Devil's spawn'. He said the suit was a slimy attempt to slander the good name of some of Rhode Island's most outstanding citizens. That it was an attempt to extort money which he would crush with all the majestic power of the law. Or something like that."

"You've seen too many judges in action," Chandler said. "We're talking about the spring of 1985, huh?"

"Yeah. Ten months ago."

"I know Rika sings lead for Ghoul under the stage name of Erika Zann. What's her brother Saxon's connection to the group?"

"He writes the lyrics, stages the shows, and plays bass guitar. His stage name is Axel Crypt."

## 1:11 p.m.

It took them several hours to get the car to a local garage for repairs, then press on into the city. As they drove down the ploughed streets of Providence into Kennedy Plaza, Chandler took in the Biltmore Hotel, City Hall which boasted it was designed in the manner of the Louvre, the Railroad Station where Amtrak moved 'em in and out, and a building topped with a huge green lantern 400 feet in the air.

"That's the old Fleet Bank Building," Carol said. "But it's known locally as the Superman Building because it looks like *The Daily Planet*."

The FBI office on Kennedy Plaza was in Room 210 on the second floor of the red brick U.S. Post Office and Federal Building. The reception room was carpeted and had the FBI seal, posters of the Ten Most Wanted felons in the States, and pictures of J. Edgar Hoover and Judge William Webster on the walls. The one set of windows in the little office beyond looked out over the grey Courthouse on the Plaza. All the most important work was handled out of Boston.

Carol Tate spent half an hour on the phone near the computer. Shortly after she hung up, a teleprinter in the office began to clatter. When it stopped she ripped off the top sheet and sat down across a desk from Chandler.

"Boston's done some checking," the Special Agent said. "Interpol helped chart the movements. Who do you want first?"

"Rosanna," Zinc replied.

Carol studied the print-out.

"Rosanna Keate flew from Vancouver to Seattle to New York on Saturday, January 11. The next day she travelled to Newport, Rhode Island. Ronald Fletcher said when we first spoke to him at your request that she came to his office on Monday, January 13 to discuss estate business. He's the sole executor of Enoch Keate's will."

"Fletcher sent Rosanna a monthly cheque for $25,000 U.S. while she was in Vancouver," Chandler said.

"Did I tell you that Fletcher has tax and legal problems of his own?" Tate asked.

"No."

"Well, he has. All his affairs are being investigated by the IRS and Treasury for possible tax evasion and breach of trust indictments. The guy lives like a king. One of the allegations is that he launders and hides money for clients. Usually it's moved through Bahamian and Cayman Island banks. Sometimes he uses numbered accounts in Switzerland. The tax authorities are having trouble tracing his schemes because so many of them run into the roadblock of attorney-client privilege. But we do know from *his* bank records, to which we have access, that after the probate challenge to Enoch's will was dismissed, most of the money from the estate went down south and out of the country. It's from the cash that stayed behind that he sent Rosanna her monthly cheques."

"Any idea where the main part of the estate ended up?" Zinc asked.

"I can make an educated guess. On Wednesday, January 15, two days after Fletcher said he saw her in his office, Rosanna flew from Providence to Zurich."

Chandler nodded in thought, then said, "So Rosanna came here from Vancouver to see Fletcher so she could get access to the estate money in Switzerland. Any way to check that through official channels?"

Tate shook her head. "If the money is in a Swiss numbered account we've lost track of it. The Swiss only recently started giving us information from their banks, and only in rare cases. This transaction wouldn't be one of those. Rosanna Keate is legally entitled to the money."

"Is she still in Switzerland?" Chandler asked.

"No. Three days later she flew to London."

"Hmmm. Which is where Rika Hyde and Ghoul moved last spring after the trial."

"Y'all got that right, honey," Carol Tate said.

Zinc laughed. "I wish you'd drawl like that more often. Pure sex appeal."

"Ha! Any idea how long it took me to break the habit?"

"Your gain, my loss," Chandler said. "Run down Rika."

The FBI Agent checked the print-out again. "The rock band Ghoul—including both Rika and Saxon Hyde—left Providence for London in April of 1985 and have been there ever since. On November 23 last year, Rika flew to Mexico City by herself. On January 10, 1986, she travelled from Puerto Vallarta to Vancouver."

"That was the day before I saw her perform at a club in the city," Chandler said. "Long holiday."

"Ghoul, including Saxon Hyde, flew from London to Vancouver on January 8. They flew out again on the 11th, without Rika Hyde."

"By then," Zinc said, "she was sludge floating in a bathtub. Is that the lot?"

"Yes, except for the fact that Saxon Hyde travelled to Vancouver for the last two weeks of September '85."

"Thank God for immigration computers," Chandler said.

A picture suddenly flashed before his mind's eye. He and Caradon were sitting in the car on Hastings Street waiting for Hengler to leave the club. Out of The Id came Rika and the bassist Axel Crypt. Crypt, Tate had told him, was the stage name of Saxon Hyde. The two of them talked for a moment then walked in opposite directions.

"A penny for your thoughts," Carol said.

"Just wondering where Saxon Hyde comes into all of this."

"What shall we do now?"

"Let's check me into the Biltmore Hotel, get some lunch, then drive down to Newport and talk to Ronald Fletcher."

## Newport, Rhode Island
## 6:02 p.m.

Ronald Fletcher's Gothic Revival home was none too shabby for a lawyer. Built one year after Queen Victoria came to the throne in 1837, it was a grandiose structure on Bellevue Avenue. During the day sunlight would stream through its windows to reflect off the gold walls and marble columns. The furniture, crafted by the Goddard-Townsend artisans of Newport, was accented by accoutrements from La Belle Epoque: antique tapestries, massive chandeliers, stained glass, ornate fireplaces, and a Grand Hall that soared to a ceiling fifty feet high.

Chandler and Tate were let in by a French maid dressed entirely in black and white. Carol identified herself as a Special Agent with the FBI and advised the woman they wished to speak to Mr Fletcher.

The maid said she was sorry but the attorney wouldn't see them. She handed Tate the business card of Ronald Fletcher's counsel, the best criminal lawyer in Rhode Island. The maid then turned to usher them out the door.

"Tell Mr Fletcher," Chandler said, "this has nothing to do with his legal practice problems. Tell him we're here about a murder and his relationship with Rosanna Keate. Tell him we know everything, and he had better see us."

Both the maid and Carol Tate frowned. Hesitating a moment, the servant asked them to wait while she crossed to a door off the hall. As she entered the room beyond, Zinc caught a glimpse of a roly-poly man sitting at a carved table surrounded by leather-bound books.

"That was brazen," Carol whispered as the door clicked shut. "Don't you have a Bill of Rights in Canada?"

"Nothing ventured, nothing gained," Chandler replied. "The most he can do is still refuse to see us. Then we'll leave him with a worry that will grow and grow."

The door to the study opened and the maid returned. "He'll see you in a moment," she said, her voice gone cold. She walked off down the hall and disappeared into an ornate, gilt-encrusted room.

"Do you really get away with stuff like that back where you come from?" Tate asked.

"Of course not," Chandler replied with a grin. "That's why I'm glad I'm not back where I come from at the moment."

His words were cut short by a single gunshot from behind the library door.

## Burnaby, British Columbia
## 7:31 p.m.

Oakalla Prison Farm—known officially as the Lower Mainland Regional Correctional Centre—stands atop a hill in this suburb of Vancouver. Built of red brick back in 1912, the jail is surrounded by over 275 beautiful acres of land. Between 1919 and 1959 the government dropped 44 prisoners down the elevator shaft on the end of a rope. Canada ceased such fun and games in 1962, so today Oakalla is mainly a maximum security holding centre for those awaiting trial.

Ray Hengler stood in the West Wing shower tunnel soaping his genitals and thinking about the boy. The kid had a pretty face and a nice white ass. He was not quite as young as Hengler usually liked his chicken, but what the hell, eh? Oakalla wasn't a borstal home and beggars can't be choosers.

The kid was a fish-face in for several burglaries and no doubt new to the joint. Hengler had received no response when he gave him the wolf's handshake twice yesterday afternoon in the yard. So last night he hadn't stopped to ask many questions, just yanked the peach fuzz into his cell as he was walking down the tier, then told him he'd rip his balls off if he didn't get done right there.

The kid's roundeye was nice and tight, but then Ray Hengler was a big, big jocker. All today that gash would have walked bowlegged.

Tonight Hengler had decided to leave the boy's bronco-busted bullhead and buns alone. Let him recuperate. The kid could either polish the knob or give him a thigh sandwich instead. At least those were Hengler's thoughts until the three men appeared in the mist.

Steam was swirling through the shower tunnel like dank October fog when Hengler first noticed the ghost approaching him. Then before he knew what was happening two more forms had grabbed him, pinning his arms from behind and ramming a towel in his mouth.

All three men were rip-cord muscled and covered with tattoos. Emblazoned over the heart of the big guy to Hengler's left was the red-tongue trademark of the Rolling Stones. Above that a carnivorous griffin was eating his shoulder flesh. Four screaming skulls with streaming hair and flaming breath were strung down one pop-veined arm of the man on his right. The con facing him had so many ink punctures in his chest that they all ran together. And he had no teeth.

"Hey, Fat Boy," Black Gums sneered, spitting out the F. "What ya done to Tom's gonna make tonight's party a drag. Yer shovel hurt him so bad his cherry ain't no use to us."

Then Hengler noticed the workshop blade jutting from his fist, the handle wrapped with electrical tape.

"You a real tusk, huh, Fat Boy?" Black Gums said. "Think every spread in here's fruit for the monkey?"

He handed the workshop hawk to Rolling Stone.

"Gonna get us some hide tonight—you spoiled that."

"Gang-splash ruined," Screaming Skulls hissed in Hengler's ear.

"Big John gonna be lonely," Black Gums said, glancing down at what was hanging between his legs and starting to rise.

"Big John don't like to be lonely. Needs another hole to pork."

Hengler swallowed hard.

"Either blood on the blade or shit on the dick," Screaming Skulls whispered as he hammerlocked Hengler's head and bent him over.

"If he squeals, shank him," Black Gums said to Rolling Stone.

# Watts, Volts, and Ohms

London, England
*Monday January 27, 1:05 p.m.*

*Get that rump in the air, kid, cause you're gonna get stuffed like a Christmas turkey.*

*It felt like a hot iron poker being jammed in his ass as with a grunt and then a sigh the man behind the boy plunged forward with his hips.*

*In pain the lad's spine arched up from the floor as one smelly hand was clamped over his mouth and another forced his face back down in the mud until*

Jack Ohm awoke in a sweat to find himself curled up in a foetal ball over in one corner of that metal-walled control room which was his mind.

## 3:42 p.m.

Fuckers, Ohm thought. I'll show you.

He now sat at that desk in his mental room opposite the large computer screen which—except for the door—took up most of one imaginary, stainless-steel wall. The image cast by the cathode-ray tube was of a dark and forbidding tunnel, its arched ceiling six feet high, its brickwork oozing and dripping down both sides of the screen.

The darkness was broken ten feet from him by a shaft of grey light that filtered down from a pavement grating above. Through speakers that fed the sound outside into his mental room, the tunnel echoed with the noise of footsteps and traffic on the rain-slicked streets above, and the gurgle of water in the pipes that ran along the passage.

There are over 8000 miles of water mains in London, the major ones snaking beneath the streets in a series of service tunnels built to also carry hydraulic power and gas. There are eleven and a half miles of such subways under the City, Docklands, and the West End. Jack Ohm was presently down in one of these service tunnels.

The centre of this underground network lies buried beneath Piccadilly Circus. From there the tunnels octopus out under Regent Street, Shaftesbury Avenue, Trafalgar Square, Holborn, and Charing Cross Road. The ones just under pavement level can be identified from the street by long rectangular grids set into the road through which replacement pipes are periodically lowered.

Jack now imagined he was sitting at that desk in his steel-walled mind while his body crouched down in the subway passage. He punched a button on the computer console in front of him to magnify the power of the video cameras that were his eyes. The camera lenses zeroed in on his gloved fingers as they worked with frenzied dedication wiring up the radio-controlled explosive device.

Fuckers, he thought again.

## 3:58 p.m.

They were moving in around her; soon she would be moving out.

Rand knew there was conflict on the eighth floor in the office of the Commissioner of Police. One faction wanted her sacked right now and replaced by the hard men immediately. Their argument was that she had been slated for removal since early January because of lack of progress on the Vampire Killer case. If that alone was enough to kick her off the Squad, what were they doing keeping her in place with the added volatility of the Sewer Killer and Jack The Bomber cases whirling around her office? That didn't make sense.

The more cautious faction, however, said that was just the point. Within the past day alone there had been two more killings—Hone and the hospital nurse—and two, well one really since they were Siamese twins, kidnappings. It would take the hard men they'd pulled from

Special Branch and brought back from retirement at least a few days to familiarize themselves with the investigations so far. If her replacements took control right now the pressure of those killings would immediately fall upon their heads and tarnish them before they could get their feet on the ground. So why not let Rand take the heat a day or two more, then move her out when the new boys were ready to fully respond?

Besides, the cautious faction said, what led to Rand's reprieve earlier was the fact that both The Bomber and the Sewer Killer had made personal contact with *her*. So far those were the Yard's only leads which might have potential, and what if both links were severed when Rand got the sack? Better to wait a few days to see if yet another message arrived in the mail. It might be the one that would break the case.

So far she was still here, so the cautious faction must be the force in control.

But for how long?

Hilary sat in her office with the door ajar while outside in the Murder Room the hard men milked the computers and planned their strategy. Every so often someone would be sent to retrieve a report or document from her. It was all very civilly done—like offering a condemned prisoner a choice of final meal.

Rand picked up a report analysing the tape of the 999 call to the Yard informing them of the crime under Blackfriars Bridge. Attached to it were a voiceprint and a Psychological Stress Evaluator projection of character. A number set up that people could call to listen to the tape had provided hundreds of tips, none of which had worked out.

She picked up another report written by a behavioural scientist. Part of it read: "There is no doubt the Sewer Killer goes home bloodstained. Blood may not be dripping from his hands but his clothes will be marked. This implies he lives alone or with an aged parent and can slip in unseen."

Yet another document listed all those in Britain who were imprisoned on or after the date the last of the eight young girls disappeared. Rand wondered once more if that was why the Vampire Killer had not struck since late last summer. The list contained 17,500 names and the date when each was jailed.

Hilary went to pick up another report, then dropped it back on her desk. Letting out a deep sigh, she stood up and walked to the window. Outside it was pouring rain and the sky was dark, dark grey. For a long time she stared at the Yard sign below turning round and round.

It wasn't worth it, Rand thought. You've thrown your life away. Where was the happiness in all those years? Did your job ever compensate you for that?

She tried to shake off such inhibiting thoughts by again considering the list chalked up on the blackboard.

## SEWER KILLER TAUNTS

Ceramic birds plus binoculars = Hitchcock film?
Top hat plus mirror = Mad Hatter in *Alice Through the Looking Glass?*
Icepick = Creature from the Black Lagoon?
Candlestick = Jack the Ripper?
Scythe = The Grim Reaper?

Like Manson and Zodiac, Hilary thought, is the Sewer Killer writing his own horror script in blood? All except one of these connections read like a personal pantheon of the macabre. The Mad Hatter, however, is somehow out of place.

Rand opened the telephone book on her desk and found a listing under "horror"—*"The horror! The horror!" Heart Of Darkness*— which she dialled.

A telephone was answered on the first ring.

"Heart Of Darkness," a male voice said.

"I'd like the manager, please."

"Speaking," the man replied.

"My name is Hilary Rand. I'm a detective with Scotland Yard. To whom am I speaking?"

"Richard Grant."

"Mr Grant, what is the nature of your business?"

"We sell books, videos, posters, comics, and golden age collectables concerned with the realm of the weird."

"Good. I know little about your field of expertise and wonder if you'd help me?"

"I'll try," Grant said.

"What does Jack the Ripper mean to you?"

"The Whitechapel killer, of course. And there's a classic story by Robert Bloch titled "Yours Truly, Jack the

Ripper". Plus another by Harlan Ellison. And then there's *The Lodger* and a host of non-fiction books and films."

"How about the Grim Reaper?" Rand asked.

"The heavy metal rock group by that name. And then if my memory serves me well, he was a comic book character in the forties. Let me check that."

The detective heard pages rustling, then Grant came back on.

"I can't find it here in the price guide so he must not have had a comic of his own. He was probably an adversary for a superhero."

"Next, the Mad Hatter?"

"*Alice In Wonderland,* wasn't he? Children's stories are not my field. And there's a John Dickson Carr novel, *The Mad Hatter Mystery.*"

"What about a looking glass or a mirror?"

"I don't understand."

"I don't either," Hilary said. "I'd hoped you'd jump to an instant connection. All it means to me is *Alice* again."

"Alice, to my mind," Grant said, "just means the king of nasty rock."

"Who's that?" Rand asked. "You've lost me."

"Alice. Alice Cooper," the man replied. "Do you not remember him? He caused quite a fuss in the early seventies by chopping up dolls representing babies on stage. The friend of Salvador Dali. Rumour is he'll be making a comeback later this year."

"Is there a top hat connection?"

"He wears one in his video, *Welcome To My Nightmare,* and also on stage. He puts on a rivetting show."

For a moment Rand said nothing as her mind slipped off in thought, then came back to ask, "Does the name Legrasse, L-e-g-r-a-s-s-e, mean anything to you?"

"It rings a bell," Grant said, "though I can't remember why. Would you like me to look into that along with the Grim Reaper comic character?"

"Yes," Hilary replied. "That would be a help." She gave him her telephone number and rang off.

Rand got up from her desk and crossed to the blackboard list. She rubbed out "The Mad Hatter" and substituted "Alice Cooper". Then she wrote down "Siamese Twins (shoe?) = . . ." and stood back.

The shoe, Rand thought. There's another headache.

For if the hospital killing and double kidnapping at

King's Cross was a Sewer Killer crime—and who else could it be when the facts were that weird?—what did one discarded shoe mean? The shoe found outside the boiler room had a broken lace, so was it left on purpose or by accident? And if left by accident, why had the killer not taunted them with his usual cryptic message? Had he simply forgotten this time, or was his precarious state of mind now breaking down and losing its mad internal cohesion?

As Rand stared at the list on the blackboard she thought, That's the irony of a case involving the insane. It sucks you from reality into an eerie fantasy. The game must then be played according to some madman's rules.

A sudden weariness hit her and she collapsed in her chair.

I'm too old for this job, Hilary thought. It's no use. I'm exhausted halfway through the race.

She closed her eyes and was resting when there was a knock at the door. Rand looked up to find Braithwaite contemplating her. "Mind if I come in?"

"No, but close the door."

The doctor stepped into her office. "Why didn't I hear from you about Derick's death?"

"Too much happening. I'm sorry," Rand said.

"Who are those new fellows in the room outside?"

"My replacements," she replied, paused, then added, "Winston, I'm finished."

"So long as you sit in this room, Hilary, you're still on the playing field."

"Two, three days at most. As soon as they're ready."

"A lot can happen in two or three days."

"Winston, thank you. But we both know it's over."

"The game is never over until the last ball is bowled."

"That's not reality," she replied.

Braithwaite shrugged. "Who's your new bagman, now that Derick's gone?"

"No one," Rand said. "I'm alone. Hundreds of detectives work for me, but none with me. I might as well have no squad; they might as well have no leader."

"Every governor has a bagman. Isn't that the way of the Yard?"

"Winston, the power-to-be is just outside that door and everyone in the building knows it. No one wants to work with me. I'm stale history on whom the book is about to be closed."

"You can order them."

"Oh, come on!"

Braithwaite moved Rand's note-pad over in front of him. He took a pen out of his jacket pocket and wrote down a name. He handed the pad back to her and said, "How about him?"

The Detective Chief Superintendent read what was written on the paper. *Sergeant Scot McAllaster.*

Shaking her head in disbelief, Hilary tossed the pad onto the desk and went to look out the window. She felt like an animal goaded in its cage.

"You British and your supposed sense of fair play," Braithwaite said.

Rand turned sharply, a sheet of grey rain running down the glass behind her. "What happened to your use of 'we', Winston?" she asked dryly.

"Today quitters don't hold stock with me," he replied.

Rand's eyes hardened. "McAllaster," she said with contempt in her voice. "What do you know about him?"

"Just the rumours. Same as everyone else."

"For me that's enough. He stands for everything I despise about the modern Yard."

The doctor stared at her. "In May of 1980," Braithwaite said, "when those seven men seized the Iranian Embassy and took twenty-four hostages, before the Special Air Services counterattacked, killing four of the terrorists and capturing the others, what would you have done with the three who surrendered?"

"Try them," Rand said.

"And give their organization just exactly what it wanted? A full-blown British courtroom drama complete with the media world-wide as a platform for their cause?"

"Do *you* endorse what the rumours say McAllaster did?"

"To date I'd say it's kept this country relatively free of other hostage-takings. The price here isn't worth what's to be gained."

"One after the other," Rand said tightly, raising her voice, "he placed his pistol against the heads of three unarmed men and blew out their brains!"

"Yes," Braithwaite said, looking her straight in the eye. "But what does a civilized man do when faced with the tactics of a barbarian? That's the great philosophical question, isn't it?"

"He also struck an officer. Do you admire that?"

"Lucky for you," the psychiatrist said. "That's why the Yard now has him and the army doesn't."

"Politics," Rand scoffed. "And I want none of his kind."

"Maybe those on the eighth floor are correct," Braithwaite said. "Perhaps a case this tough does require a man."

A muscle along Rand's jaw jumped as the telephone rang.

"Yes," she snapped on picking it up, frowning as she listened. When she replaced the receiver she said, "That was downstairs. An East End florist just phoned to say a book on a clearance stand outside her shop was stolen this morning. In its place was left a note, 'Thanks, Elaine Teeze'. That's the same name the person used who ordered the bouquets for the night of the steambath bombing. We circulated it and asked all florists to watch for any such future orders."

"Hilary, it's coming."

"I know, Winston," she sighed.

"And either you fight back with all you've got and maintain your self-respect, or you go down with a whimper in an ugly way."

He pushed the note pad across the desk toward-her.

"Trust me," the psychiatrist said. "I've worked with him."

## 4:04 p.m.

The National Grid supplies London with power. Electricity enters the city at a dozen different points as alternating current. It is then fed into substations where it is transformed to a lower voltage and conducted through 17,000 miles of cable to its ultimate destinations. These cables run through the London Electricity Board's or British Telecom's own tunnels, or by way of the Underground along with London Transport's wires. Finally these transmission lines move up shafts through shallow ducts to distribution boxes, then into businesses and homes.

Jack Ohm was presently underground, crouched in one of these tunnels.

He had climbed down the steel ladder fixed to the side

of the shaft, then moved into the wide brick-faced passage parallel to the street. The tunnel contained not only electric cables and the water main, but also a disused six-inch high-pressure pipe from the days when London's hydraulic lifts and hoists were kept running by pneumatic force. He could hear the feet of pedestrians passing along the street above, and when he glanced up through the dripping grate could see parapet-like buildings looming against the sombre, overbearing sky.

Ohm now stopped to study the London Electricity Board map glowing on the screen of his portable computer. The map showed the locations of all the substations in this part of the city, plus the high-voltage cables called feeders which led into each building from the transmission network of the London Grid. The location of the clinic was marked with a black Germanic ✠ like those favoured by North American newspapers to indicate on diagrams where dead bodies are found. Ohm had programmed the clinic into the software himself.

Jack punched in a computer code to shift to another map. The second chart outlined the system ties. It was a detailed enlargement of the feeder cables supplying each substation with high-voltage power from the London Grid. The substation nearest the clinic was designated "Whittington 3". On this map Jack Ohm was able to spot feeder "17 W.L. 9" which passed beside the clinic before continuing on to the substation.

Ohm punched in another computer code. The third map was labelled "17 W.L. 9" and subtitled "Whittington 3". It was a long narrow diagram running vertically which Jack had to scroll up and down on the screen. In minute detail this chart showed the route travelled by this particular high-voltage substation feeder beneath the West End streets. It also outlined the manhole covers that gave access to the cable. The manhole nearest the clinic was twenty-seven feet away. The cable switch that Ohm was searching for was designated "B–926718".

He shone his flashlight up toward the cable switch protection box screwed to the tunnel wall just above his head. Stencilled in white on its metal surface was the designation "B–926718".

Eureka! Jack thought.

Though Ohm would never admit it to himself, following the Sewer Killer's exploits in the papers had given him good ideas. London's weakness was definitely the city's underbelly—and the maps provided by Elaine Teeze gave him access to that weakness.

Earlier today Ohm's mind had boiled over with bad blood and virulence toward his rival. The man's crimes were so petty and juvenile you would think his brain was frozen in an adolescent state. Yet those ridiculous attacks and disappearances had stolen the prophetic thunder from his own Roman Steambath bombing retribution.

Well, Ohm thought, that will now change.

And just thinking about his planned, soon-to-be double-header calmed his mind.

It had taken Jack three weeks to get the supplies together. A few he had purchased himself while the others were obtained somehow by Elaine Teeze. That woman could be remarkably resourceful.

Imagining he was now sitting at the computer console within that metal-walled room which was his mind, Ohm watched his gloved hands at work up on the giant screen. The cable he had already attached to the clinic pipes dangled from a vertical shaft above his head. Ohm could just make it out at the top of the screen, for the cameras that were his eyes were now focused in the direction of what he held in his hands.

The box was a remote-control switching device. A high-voltage input and output were located on opposite sides of the gadget. Current would travel this route when the switch was closed. A second high-voltage output exited from the top of the device. Current would travel that route when the switch was open. Jack Ohm made sure the switch was closed, then attached the wire dangling from the clinic pipes to the output on top of the device.

It was as he was opening the protective cover around the tunnel cable switch stencilled "B–926718" that Ohm froze, alarmed. What was that noise? From where he imagined he was sitting at the console in his mind watching the giant screen, the sound seemed to come from behind the sheetmetal wall to his right. It scratched and fuzzed like a wire short-circuit.

Ohm reached out quickly and punched a button to cut off the speakers that let in the sounds from the tunnel and the street above.

*Scrrrt! Scrrrt! Kchhht!* The noise *was* behind the wall.

Ohm sat up and cocked an ear.

Silence fell. Nothing more.

Only after several minutes did he begin to relax. God, Jack Ohm thought, that's all I'd need. A glitch in the electronics at a crucial time like this.

He looked back at the screen.

The cable switch inside the protective box buried in the tunnel had a lever that was painted brilliant red. Ohm's gloved hand reached out on the screen and pulled this lever, opening the feeder cable switch and causing the lights in the street above to go out. Quickly Ohm spliced in his own device, then pushed back the lever. The wires began to hum. Current now ran not only through the London Electricity Board's feeder circuit, but also in through the cable input and out the opposite exit terminal on his own device. Up in the street the lights had come back on.

Satisfied, Ohm thought, I wonder if the flowers have arrived yet?

## 4:39 p.m.

Rand looked up from her office desk and saw him standing in the doorway. McAllaster was just over six feet but his frame made him look much taller. His shoulders were thick and his chest a barrel, his hands massive and held loosely at his sides. The Scotsman was thirty, maybe thirty-two. His hair was blond and cropped. His face was round, stern, and his eyes were intense.

"Close the door," Rand said. The hard men outside were beginning to make her feel like a prisoner in her own office.

McAllaster shut it softly.

"Have a seat," the woman said, watching the man cross the room. There was an explosive tenseness beneath the Highlander's precise and fluid movements. He sat.

Rand looked the Sergeant in the eye and he looked straight back. Neither one wavered. He's a long way from Derick Hone, she thought.

"Coffee? Tea?"

The man shook his head.

"Well then, I'll be blunt. You know who I am and you'll have heard the rumours. I've got two, maybe three days left at most."

The Scotsman watched her stonily.

"No one wants to work with me and board a sinking ship. They're lining up with the new men outside that door. I don't blame them, but I can't do the job alone."

She wished the man would blink, or at least say something.

"I don't know your background, except for more rumours. I do know you've had problems and are starting back near the bottom."

McAllaster was rigid. Not a muscle moved. He showed no reaction.

"I also know from experience," Hilary said, "that it will take a long, long time for you to move up the ranks. I am willing, therefore, to offer you a deal. The odds are astronomical, but then you've been trained to work with odds like that. Be my backup till the end, and if I get the sack you can say I gave you an order while still in command and you were forced to obey. On the other hand, McAllaster, if something breaks and somehow I survive, your career advances at warp speed."

The Highlander didn't pause one second to think it over.

"I'm your man," he said.

## 5:20 p.m.

The clinic in the West End was in the cellar of a two-storey Victorian building with grills on the windows and soot on the bricks. It was a self-contained unit with only two exits, a front and rear door. Hissing steam could be heard in the pipes of the boiler beyond one wall. Here at the clinic each Monday afternoon at 5:00 p.m., the support group met regularly.

The twelve men sat in a circle on wooden straight-back chairs. Some of them looked worried, others physically ill. A thin man with a silver stud in one ear was speaking now.

"What frightens me the most is fear of losing my mind. I read in the papers last month that researchers in Boston believe the AIDS virus hides and spreads in the brain. That it can drive you insane. I couldn't bear that."

"AIDS anxiety is a common reaction among the worried well, Don," the psychologist said—as outside in the alley beyond the rear door Jack Ohm applied epoxy cement to a wooden wedge. "Sometimes people without the disease or even AIDS-related complex get so terrified they can no longer function normally in everyday life."

"I had a friend with AIDS who contracted a common parasite from being scratched by a cat," a second young man said. "In anyone else the problem would have stayed benign. In him, with no immune system, it caused cerebral toxoplasmosis. He started suffering seizures so bad they had to anesthetize him to prevent his limbs from jerking completely out of control. The drug calmed his body but his brain inside never stopped convulsing. Tell me a worse way to go than that?"

There was subtle agitation in the room. All of the men shifted a little in their seats—as out back in the alley Jack Ohm eased the epoxy-coated wedge under the rear door and with a wooden mallet tapped it gently into place.

"God," a third man said. "It's so unfair. I spent years being called sissy, queer, pansy, homo, queen, pantywaist, and even being beaten. I was a freak to everyone because I was gay. Then finally when I can accept it and be proud of whom I am, AIDS comes along and I'm a freak again. It adds fear on fear until I think I'm going to snap!"

"How do we cope with the witch-hunt?" a fourth man asked. "The homophobia? To straights, being gay now equates with AIDS. And that means being gay also equates with death. We're now feared, shunned, and despised. I feel like a leper waiting for the backlash."

"That's already come," a fifth man said—as Jack Ohm knocked the second epoxy-coated wedge in under the front door and pinned a picture to the wood.

"I lost my job and was thrown out of my flat," the third man said. "You talk about us developing AIDS anxiety. The straights are now exhibiting AIDS psychosis."

"It's like a state of siege. My lover left me as soon as he found out."

"Morticians refuse to embalm us if we die, for God's sake!"

"My dentist refused to work on my teeth."

"I heard a chat show in which people were asking this doctor about the safety of toilet seats, swimming pools, and sitting on a bus."

"It's like the Black Plague."

"Next there will be lynch mobs with ropes and stones. Or quarantine."

"Calm down," the psychologist said. "It's good that we can express our fe—"

"Fuck you and your calm down! I'm afraid and I have reason to be. The world's going creepy. There's craziness happening!"

"It will pass," the psychologist said reasonably. "Right now it is in the interests of the press and scientists to feed the fear. Fear sells papers and provides research grants. Fear fuels the election rhetoric of politicians. The business opportunities in AIDS are now spreading far quicker than the disease itself. But it's only a matter of time before AIDS affects heterosexuals as much as gays. Then the 'gay plague' tag will be outmoded," he said—as three blocks away Jack Ohm pressed remote-control button Number One.

Under the boiler room next to the cellar in which the AIDS support clinic was meeting, a charge of Frangex explosive went off suddenly. Packed around the water main that fed the building, it blew the pipe and ruptured the boiler. Steam and water surged into the cellar like a tide, covering the floor to a depth of six inches, sweating in rivulets down the walls and misting the air.

"The back door won't open!" someone shouted through the instant fog.

"Neither will the front!" another cried.

The sound of the window grills being rattled filled the room as several streets away Jack Ohm pushed remote-control button Number Two.

Down in the tunnel beside the building through which high-voltage feeder cable 17 W.L. 9 ran toward Whittington substation, the device Ohm had spliced into cable switch B-926718 flipped open. The current which had up until then flowed through both the switching box circuit and the closed path of Ohm's device was now diverted up the wire attached to the top of the spliced-in gadget. That wire was attached to metal pipes which entered the cellar where the AIDS support clinic was meeting.

The resulting screams were deafening.

One hundred and fifty thousand volts of electricity surged into the cellar as a blue fireball. The *crackkk!* as the power arced from object to object and danced across the surface of the water covering the floor sounded like a tree being split by lightning. Several of the men burst into flames as their contorting bodies jerked like puppets and bounced off the walls. The flesh on the hands of one victim who was touching the metal window grills melted as he was viciously fried alive. His chest burst out in a violent heave and saliva gushed from his mouth. Puffs of smoke and silver sparks streamed from his head.

Three streets away the pitiful shrieks could still be heard. Jack Ohm ignored them, however, as he did the dimming streetlights. He was far more concerned about the scratching and fuzzing that once again was coming from beyond the metal wall of his mind.

# Iron Maiden

Providence, Rhode Island
*9:00 a.m.*

Vital Statistics is part of the Health Department in the State Offices at 75 Davis Street. Room 101 on the first floor had a counter stretched in front of rows of files containing birth and death records since 1853. The woman who checked the files for them reminded Chandler of his maternal grandmother. White hair, wire rim glasses, mole on her chin. When Zinc asked for a certified extract confirming Rosanna's birth to Enoch Keate she looked overtop of her spectacles and snorted, "Hmmmph. Her."

As Chandler examined the document the woman then dug out, she folded her arms across her chest and asked, "Anything else?"

"Yes, I need the same thing for the children of Elena Hyde, née Keate."

Again granny snorted, "Hmmmph. Her."

"Popular family," Chandler said to Tate.

Ten minutes later the woman was back to lay three birth certificates on the counter below Zinc's eyes.

*12:01 p.m.*

Deborah Lane had dismissed the class and was alone in the well of the lecture theatre packing up her notes when she heard footsteps on the stairs. She looked up to find a stranger—a dangerous-looking stranger—rapidly descending the centre aisle toward her. The man was over six feet tall and powerfully built. He moved like a jungle cat, ready for anything. His hair was grey, not old-grey but gun-metal grey, as were his eyes. There was a scar along the right side of his chin. Sid, she thought.

241

"Who are you?" Deborah snapped, glancing toward the door twenty feet away. Her worst fear was that she was finally going to meet the unknown tormentor who had been sending her obscene letters for so many years.

The man stopped short and held up both hands. "No need to be jumpy. My name's Zinc Chandler. I'm an Inspector with the Royal Canadian Mounted Police."

"Then let's see your badge."

He reached into his jacket pocket and removed the regimental shield.

Deborah relaxed. A wry smile touched her lips as she said, "Surely it wasn't necessary to call you fellows down here for a few dirty phone calls. The FBI would do."

"You've got that problem, eh?"

"Not any more. I took care of it myself."

"How'd you do that?"

"You really want to know?"

"I like stories about amateur sleuths."

Deborah's smile straightened. It wasn't a full smile yet, but it was getting there. Chandler sat down on a desk in the front row to put her more at ease.

"I received several calls," she said, "in which the person placing them did nothing but breathe heavily over the phone. After the second call I informed the police. For years I've been getting these dirty letters from some guy named Sid whom I'm sure I've never met. I feared it might be him finally looking me up. I was afraid you were Sid too."

"What did the police do?"

"Nothing," Deborah said. "They told me the same fellow had been telephoning other women on the staff here. If he called again they said they would set up equipment to trace the calls."

"Is there a staff telephone directory?"

"Yes. That's what I thought too."

"Did he call another time?"

"Yes. And I got mad. Cause here was this jerk coming into my life and playing upon a fear I've had for years."

"Again just breathing?"

"Yes. The Breather. That's what I called him. I was about to hang up, but then, as I said, I got angry so I shouted into the phone."

Suddenly Deborah averted her eyes and dropped her voice. At first Zinc thought it was shyness, telling a stranger a story with sexual overtones. The more he looked at her, however, the more he realized it was something else. Something deeper.

Deborah Lane—it then struck him—was doing her best to look as plain and physically unattractive as she could. Her blonde hair was pulled back and tied in a bun. Her deep blue eyes were washed out by her clear complexion rather than emphasized by a judicious hint of make-up, of which she used none at all. Her clothing was so baggy it destroyed any figure she might have underneath.

What a waste, Chandler thought, vaguely aware that she reminded him of some actress. "Don't leave me hanging in suspense," he said, smiling. "You've got to finish the story."

Deborah actually blushed—and no one did that these days.

"I shouted into the phone, 'What sort of wimp are you? A real man wouldn't be afraid to speak.' "

"So he hung up?" Chandler prompted.

"No. There was this long pause, then a whispery voice says, 'Baby, I've got the phone in one hand. Guess what I've got in the other?' "

"What did you say to that?" Zinc asked, his grin cracking wider.

"I told him, 'If you can hold it in one hand, I'm not interested.' "

Chandler broke into laughter.

"Then I hung up and he hasn't called back."

For a moment there was silence, then Deborah smiled too. "If you didn't come about the calls, what are you here to discuss?"

"Your half-sister, Rika Hyde," Chandler said.

## London, England
### 6:03 p.m.

Good cops are trained.

Great cops come to the job naturally.

Every mystery has a centre, an eye of the hurricane. For a mystery is like a wheel, the hub of which gives it both shape and motion. The problem is that when the wheel is either coming toward you or going away, all you can see is the rim or tread and not the central hub.

Hilary Rand sat alone in her office and stared at the note which had just arrived along with the picture of the flowers. The photograph of the plant had been clipped from a book and was labelled *Hydrangea*. Hydrangea was also what had been ordered by "Elaine Teeze" to be sent to the Yard on the night of The Roman Steambath bombing. As far as the police could tell, there was no such person as "Elaine Teeze" on record as residing anywhere in Britain. The note in her hand read:

What's the matter, Hilary?
Don't you speak the language of flowers?

Jack

Rand had a sudden memory from a long, long time ago. She was a young girl walking across a field with her aunt. Spring flowers were in bloom and the view was marvellous. Her aunt was speaking from high above her head. "Hilary, do you realize that each of these flowers has a different meaning? When your grandmother was a girl, bouquets were made up to convey particular sentiments. They were exchanged between lovers and friends as if they were notes. I think that an enchanting custom, don't you—speaking the language of flowers instead of words?"

I wonder? Rand thought. The case is mad enough.

She was about to pick up the phone when it rang. "Yes?" she said, answering the call.

"It's McAllaster."

The hard men had responded to the 999 that had come in twenty-five minutes ago on the AIDS clinic disaster. Rand had dispatched the Highlander to fill her in on the scene. The envelope from Jack had just arrived downstairs and was being fingerprinted. Hilary had stayed behind to see its contents.

"What happened, Scot?"

"Pipe burst with explosives to fill the building with water and steam. Electricity then diverted by remote—control from power cables underground. We have the device. Twelve people inside were fried alive."

"Any flowers found?"

"Wooden wedges knocked in under both doors so no one could escape. Epoxy-glued in place. Pinned to one of the wedges was a picture of a plant snipped from a book. The flower is Wild Tansy."

"Keep me informed."

"Aye," the man said, then hung up.

Without putting down the receiver, Rand dialled a number in the village of Meeth. The call was answered on the third ring.

"Hello," a shaky, elderly voice said.

"Hello, Auntie. This is Hilary."

"My dear, what a pleasant surprise. Where are you?"

"London, Auntie. I need your help and I'm sorry I can't talk for long." She saw the eighty-year-old woman in her mind's eye. Liver spots. Thin white hair. Laugh wrinkles by the hundreds. Sparkling eyes.

"Yes?" her aunt said.

"The language of flowers. Do you still speak it?"

The old woman wheezed with what passed for a laugh. "No," she said softly. "But I do have a book."

"Auntie, it's important. Would you get it, please."

There was a long pause before she came back on. "Had to find my spectacles. Sorry dear."

"What does Trefoil mean?" Hilary asked. That was the plant Elaine Teeze had asked the florist by letter to send to The Roman Steambath.

A minute later the old woman replied, "Birdsfoot Trefoil is Revenge."

"How about Wild Tansy?"

Another long pause, the sound of pages being turned. "Wild Tansy is I declare war against you."

"And finally Hydrangea?" Hilary asked. That was the flower Teeze had tried to send her at the time of the steambath bombing, and the picture that had arrived tonight.

After a while her aunt replied, "Hydrangea Heartlessness."

Heartlessness = No heart, the Yard detective thought. And she knew right then, by sixth sense, by intuition, by copper's nose, by call it what you may, that Jack The Bomber and the Vampire Killer were one.

That's why Jack sent the bouquet of flowers specifically to *me* on the night of The Roman Steambath blast. That bombing wasn't his first crime like we thought. I was already assigned to his case in its Vampire Killer form.

But *why* murder the eight young girls? Rand wondered. Then she saw the hub.

## 6:00 p.m.

A distance away from New Scotland Yard a man sat at the kitchen table of an East End flat. Propped up on the table surface was a mirror he was using to examine his face. When the scuba mask had shattered during the Tunnel of Love fiasco, his forehead and cheeks, his nose and chin had been slashed by shards. It was a miracle he hadn't lost his eyes, though he would be severely scarred for the rest of his life.

Couldn't risk a doctor, he thought, as he now got up from his chair. The Yard might have traced me if I'd tried that.

Leaving the kitchen he walked down the hall to the bedroom of his flat. One bedroom wall was plastered with newspaper clippings concerning the Vampire Killer crimes. The adjoining surface was devoted to the Sewer Killer case. Jack The Bomber's exploits dominated the third.

For a while the man stared at the blank fourth wall behind the headboard of his bed.

He glanced at the clippings spread out on the floor reporting the botched Tunnel of Love attack.

His eyes returned to the blank wall as he sighed and shook his head.

Then he sat down to study the pictures in *The Monster Book*.

## Providence, Rhode Island
## 1:04 p.m.

"Tell me about Rika," Chandler said.

"I didn't like her," Lane replied.

"I gathered that. You didn't even flinch when I told you she was dead."

"They were very cruel to me. Both of them, Inspector. I'm a Christian so I try to forgive and forget. But, believe me, with the twins that's not easy."

Outside the sun was shining and it was a cheerful day. As they stood on the steps of the private girls' school where Deborah taught, the cruddy slush turned up by the cars sliding along Angell Street already beginning to freeze, Lane turned to Chandler and said, "Is this your first trip to Providence?"

"It is," he replied.

"Do you know that you're at the very heart of America's terror country?"

"I thought that was up in Maine," Zinc said.

Deborah smiled. "King's popular and very good, but he's a Johnnie-come-lately. See that building across the street? On that lot used to stand 454 Angell Street, Lovecraft's birthplace and first home. You have read H. P. Lovecraft somewhere along the way?"

Chandler nodded. "By coincidence I had a discussion—well, more an argument—with another cop while on stakeout recently. He later gave me a book of stories to prove his point. One of them was 'The Rats In The Walls' which I read on the plane."

"Over there," Deborah said, pointing west, "is No. 88 Benefit Street where Sarah Whitman lived. It's right across the road from my apartment. In 1848, the last year of his life, Edgar Allan Poe came to Providence to court her. She agreed to marry him if he gave up his drinking. He didn't so she spurned him, and the following year Poe died.

"Let's walk," Deborah said.

They strolled along Angell Street toward the Providence River ("The original home lots were laid out in the seventeenth century"), passing a forty-acre tract surrounded by a high stone wall ("That used to be Dexter Asylum," Lane said. "A name Lovecraft picked up for 'The case of Charles Dexter Ward' "), turning right at Prospect Street and walking north toward the vast dome and Ionic columns of the Christian Science Church ("The house this side of Meeting Street, that square Georgian one with the monitor roof, was Lovecraft's last home when it was located at 66 College Street"), branching left into Cushing Street where a cannon was buried muzzle down to once use as a hitching post, then crossing Congdon Street into Prospect Terrace.

"What a view," Chandler said, gazing out across the city at the white Georgia-marble dome and flanking cupolas of Rhode Island State House.

"That," Deborah said, pointing over the railing toward

the foot of College Hill, "is Benefit Street. At No. 133 stands The Shunned House from another Lovecraft story, one about a horror buried deep beneath its basement. Over there once stood the Golden Ball Inn, where Poe is supposed to have stayed. And there, just down the steps from No. 66 near my home, is Saint John's Graveyard. Some of the headstones go right back to colonial times. Both Poe and Lovecraft used to sit there in the moonlight thinking up stories."

"You certainly give a spooky tour," Chandler said.

"You asked me what Rika was like, Inspector. I'm showing you that Providence is a horror-lover's Mecca because Rika and Saxon Hyde were the *ultimate* horror fans. The twins ate, drank, and breathed the stuff."

Zinc looked up at the statue of Roger Williams, Rhode Island's founder, which crowned the terrace park. Then he glanced down at his grave.

"There's a good horror story," Deborah said. "When Roger Williams died in 1683 he was buried out back of his home beneath an apple tree. In 1860 the grave was opened to move his remains to the North Burial Ground. It was found the apple tree root had gone where the eating was good, worming its way down the trunk of his corpse, then forking along both legs. The root's now in the collection of the Rhode Island Historical Society."

Chandler grinned. "This city grows on you the longer you're here."

"Ouch!" Deborah winced, then she chuckled.

A silence fell between them for a minute. Lane broke it by saying, "Aren't you going to ask me about the probate trial? You've heard about that, I'm sure."

"I've heard," Zinc said.

"You're wondering about the twins' allegation that my mother conceived them incestuously?"

"Am I that obvious?"

"In some ways, yes."

"Is the allegation true?"

"No," Deborah replied.

Chandler said nothing; he gave her room to breathe. Lane searched his face, sizing him up. Then she said, "My mother converted to Catholicism after the twins were born. She was a good woman who liked nothing better than to spend a day in her garden. She did everything she could to convert the twins. In the end she came to the opinion that Saxon was an Antichrist, but she never gave up. My mother was devoted to her only son."

"Did he love her?"

"Their relationship was strange. A mutual obsession."

Chandler sensed Deborah was uncomfortable with this discussion so he backed off.

"Were the twins slow-witted?"

"Back to incest, are we?"

"No," he replied. "I've seen Ghoul perform and they put on quite a show. Just wondering about the brain behind such weird ideas."

A hint of an ironic smile touched Lane's lips. "Quite the opposite," she said. "Both were of superior intelligence, with Saxon the most gifted. That, plus the fact that they *were* twins always made them different and separate unto themselves."

"In what way different?" Chandler asked.

"They had creepy personalities. That may have been because they were not full members by birth in the Lane family and rebelled against the fact by adopting outrageous and vicious behaviour. It may also have been because my father was not a nice man."

"I'm sorry to dredge all this up," Zinc said, "but it's important."

"You told me Rika was murdered. That's why I'm telling you."

"Do you think your half-sister was mentally ill?"

"No," Deborah replied. "Rika was cunning and always knew exactly what she wanted. She protected Saxon and used him by playing his games. She was great at dominating and manipulating people. Whenever she wanted to keep me under control, she would threaten Mr Nibs' life."

"Mr Nibs?" Zinc said.

"He was my cat. He died recently."

Chandler could see that Deborah Lane had had a rough life. She seemed a lonely, compassionate person who had chosen to retreat from the world. What a waste, he thought for the second time.

"How about Saxon? Did *he* have mental problems?"

"Yes," Lane said without hesitation.

"Schizophrenic?"

"Back to incest?"

"Deborah, your mother was a Keate. Incest or no incest, Saxon has her genes."

"He could be schizophrenic. He was that disturbed."

"A haemophiliac?"

"No," she replied. "That Keate genetic curse he managed to escape. But he couldn't escape my father, Hugh Lane. For that I pity him."

"Tell me about it," Chandler said, lowering his voice.

Deborah sighed and pointed across Congdon Street. "See that two-storey, clapboard house painted yellow? That's where we lived and the twins were raised.

"My father married my mother for the little money she had. My mother married my father out of desperation. After she left Newport she had nowhere else to go. The home in which we kids grew up was not a happy place. That was not my mother's fault, she was just unlucky with men.

"My father never held down a real job. He sponged off my mother and all he did was drink. From the time of my earliest memories they slept in separate bedrooms. I once heard my father beat her for having 'cut him off'. Those were the words he used. The rest of that day my mother had her rosary in her hands. I was four at the time."

Zinc felt uncomfortable listening to Deborah Lane. He knew the first man in a woman's life will determine to a great extent the way she relates to all others. That man in most cases will be her father. How he reacts to his daughter will seriously affect her future self-image. That's why many women have a deep-down fear of, and difficulty with, men. Their fathers are to blame.

"How did you survive, Deborah?" Chandler asked.

"You'd think the answer silly."

"Try me," he said.

"I had a good friend who saw me through. Nibs. My cat."

Zinc smiled. He wanted to touch her hand, but his mind stepped back.

"It wasn't as bad as it could have been," Deborah said. "My father never hurt me. He loved me . . . I think. Saxon was the one he hated."

Lane glanced at her watch. "I must get back. I've a class to teach."

As they walked towards Angell Street, Chandler asked, "What did your father do to Saxon?"

"Around other people my dad would keep it to verbal abuse, but when they were alone I know he used to strike him. Once from my bedroom window on the second floor of the house, I saw my father whip off Saxon's pants and lay into him with a leather belt out back in the yard. Then he pushed him into the garage and must have gone at him again. The screams were unnerving."

They turned up Angell Street.

"The net result," Deborah said, "was Saxon took his seething anger out on me. After all, I was Hugh Lane's beloved daughter. For years I could feel this growing animosity. It took the pattern of what Saxon called The Game. I overheard him use the term while talking with Rika. That was always his excuse to my mother. 'We were only playing a game when Debbie fell from the tree.' 'Debbie tripped and hurt herself in a game of hide-and-seek.' Rika, of course, backed him up."

"You must have been strong to survive intact," Zinc said.

"That's what Rika used to sneer when I stood up to them. 'My Debs, aren't we the iron maiden.' The worst part, however, was after he joined the club."

"You mean Saxon?" Chandler said.

"Yes. When he was fourteen he met this creepy group of guys. They used to wear leather jackets and call themselves The Ghouls. Shortly after joining he tried to rape me," Deborah said.

Tate was parked outside the school in an unmarked car.

"I must go," Lane said. "I'm late for class."

"Can I meet you after that? I need the rest of the story."

"Sorry," Deborah said. "Faculty meeting."

She looked away from his eyes.

"But if it's that important you . . . you may come to my place for dinner if . . . if you'd like."

"Yes," Zinc said, "I'd like that very much."

Deborah wrote down her address, then disappeared into the building.

As Chandler was climbing into the passenger seat of Carol's car, Tate looked at him and said, "She's got nice skin and facial bones, but man does she need help. What a frump."

## London, England
### 6:06 p.m.


The aerial photograph captured the regal beauty of Hampton Court, the extensive gardens of which were laid out by King William of Orange, incorporating elements from the time of Henry VIII. In the extreme north corner of a large meadow known as The Wilderness, William had planted his famous maze made out of hedges of shrubs.

So much of Hilary's life these days seemed to consist of memories. She had been a happy child, and never as happy as when her father would take her to Hampton Court and let her loose in the maze. What fun it had been to spend hours using trial and error to find her way back out. Her father had bought her the photograph now propped up on her desk.

Often when Hilary encountered a difficult problem with twists and turns and sudden dead ends, she would place the large yellowed picture before her and follow the maze through as she worked at the present puzzle. It was a mental game she played with herself, for joining the problems together and knowing the maze by heart meant she was already halfway toward the solution.

Jack The Bomber and the Vampire Killer are one, she thought.

Jack is either psychotic or a psychopath.

Jack is also a homophobe, afraid of homosexuals and harbouring hate for them. As a result he has bombed a gay steam bath and an AIDS support clinic.

Why? she wondered.

Her eyes ran along one of the routes in the maze.

Answer Number One: paranoid schizophrenia. Jack believes that all gays are connected in a conspiracy to persecute, deceive, cheat, or kill him. His crimes are an attempt to fight back or get revenge.

Answer Number Two: he has AIDS. The mass murders are in retribution for the disease. Did he contract it through consensual sex or being raped? Most likely the latter since his hate has exploded out not in.

Stop, Rand thought. That doesn't make sense. Why would he have killed the young girls before going after the gays?

Her eyes struck a dead end in the maze.

Rand knew that at the heart of most murder mysteries lies the identity of the victim or victims. *Who* was killed will often reveal why the crime took place. Here the first eight victims were prepubescent girls from upper middle-class families. All drained of blood.

Why? Rand asked a second time.

Purity, her intuition replied.

Jack needs blood free from AIDS. He's afraid the public blood banks are tainted, so he kills to obtain his own supply. Adults are sexually polluted from the mates they've had. Make love and you make love with every partner that person has had for years. Young boys may have been victimized by gay pederasts. Girls from families living at the poverty line are statistically more likely to have suffered incest. So prepubescent upper class girls are as safe from sexual contamination as you can get. Their blood is free from the virus causing AIDS.

No, Rand thought, there's another dead end.

What would Jack need blood for if he already has the disease? Also it wouldn't keep this long.

Her eyes retraced the maze path back to the last fork.

But then, she thought, let's not forget that Jack is insane. A mad delusion by definition is divorced from reality. What if he doesn't have the disease but is afraid he'll get it? What if he has Type O blood like five of his victims, and killed the girls hit-and-miss until he had built up a compatible reserve supply?

Rand's eyes ran down the maze path and jumped over the shrub barrier at the end.

What if what we have here is a combination of reasons?

Jack was once sexually attacked and suffers homophobia.

He is also a paranoid schizophrenic with haematomania overtones.

He is obsessed with both the blood of others and his own.

He is convinced that gays are in a conspiracy to kill him by means of the disease.

He is also afraid that he might need a transfusion soon.

So he kills the young girls to build up a pure blood supply as a hedge against his fear and to insulate himself.

He drains the blood dramatically by cutting the artery, not the vein, and subsequently removes the heart because his haematomania overrides everything else.

Blood fascination is the genesis of his fear.

He then launches a campaign of revenge to kill off the ultimate source of the contamination.

For he has now become a self-righteous vigilante.

Rand knew that she was on a roll so her eyes locked instinctively on the exit from the maze. She recalled what Braithwaite had said about the need such a killer has for

attention. That's why Jack had twice sent her the "heartlessness" message. He *wanted* her to connect the Vampire Killer murders with the crimes of Jack The Bomber,
yet subconsciously at the same time was afraid to expose
himself completely for fear of being traced. Still, because
his was a rampage of purification, self-righteousness demanded he somehow alert the world. Zodiac used astrology; Jack the language of flowers.

   *I declare war against you*, Rand thought. He's planning
something bigger.

## 6:09 p.m.

Sid Jinks had made up his mind—it was time to seek out
Deborah. A cunt as sweet as hers could not be ignored.

   He had drawn a picture of her sex, of how he imagined
that two-inch strip between her legs to be. The picture
was now pinned to one black wall of his room. Jinks
stood ten feet away with four throwing knives in his
hands. As he thought of Deborah he heaved a blade to
*thunk* into her pussy.

   Abruptly the door opened and a flash of light stabbed
into the shadowed room. It glinted off the other cutlery
hanging on the walls, drowning the glow of the candles
positioned around the floor.

   Jinks turned his head, squinting to make out the black
silhouette of the woman standing in the doorway.

   "I have another job for you," she said.

# Sharp Teeth

Deborah Lane answered the door casually attired in a Bill the Cat sweatshirt and a pair of jeans. She was licking something sweet from one of her fingers. "Maple sugar pie," she said, "to make you feel at home. I picked up the recipe when I was in Quebec."

"Great," Chandler said, handing her a bottle of wine. He had never tasted maple sugar pie in his life.

Suddenly a flash of movement streaked across the hall. A tiny ball of fluff sprang at him and swiped his leg.

"Inspector Chandler," Deborah said, "meet Daffodil."

As Zinc bent down toward the feisty kitten, she hissed at him and scooted back into the bedroom.

"Daffy's very protective of me, as you can see."

Lane led him to the kitchen which was a mess of pots and pans, passing him a corkscrew while she got out two glasses. "Something smells good," Chandler said.

"You are about to taste Cannelloni à la Deborah. Lucky man."

"Anything I can do?" Zinc asked as he popped the cork. He wished she would look at him as she spoke; it made him feel frightening the way she kept avoiding his eyes. Shy, he thought.

"You cook?" Debbie asked, preparing the garlic bread.

"Of course," Zinc replied. "My mother used to say, a man who needs a woman to feed him starts out at a disadvantage."

"Good," Deborah said. "You may feed the cat."

## London, England
## *10:37 p.m.*

Charlene Willcox took a moment to straighten her dress before she knocked on the door of the posh flat. She was dressed exactly as the agency had instructed, conservative dark blue skirt, high-necked white blouse, hair drawn back from her face and held with a blue bow. Why her employer had insisted she wear the mask she had no idea, but then artists were a strange lot and as a model she was accustomed to their idiosyncrasies. Knocking on the door, Charlene wondered what this Mr Hazard would be like.

Mayfair has long been regarded as one of the classiest addresses in London. Around the turn of the century the aristocrat's townhouse in which Charlene now found herself had been sold and converted to expensive flats. This suite was on the second floor of the building.

The woman who answered the door also wore a mask, her face framed by stylish short black hair. Her dress had a spider's web pattern traversing the chest, while around her neck she wore a cross with a ruby at its nexus.

"Hello. I'm Charlene Willcox," the model said. "Mr Hazard, please."

"It's *Miss* Hazard," the woman replied. "Miss Rosanna Hazard." She stood aside so Charlene could enter the suite. "Pass me your coat and umbrella. They're soaking wet."

The tastefully decorated flat was dimly lit around a harsh red spotlight focused on a dais in front of an artist's easel. Its canvas was orange from the glow of a candelabrum burning on a nearby table. Charlene heard Miss Hazard close and lock the door.

"Well, well," the artist said, "don't you look fine."

From her accent she must be American or Canadian, Willcox thought.

"Stand on the dais and let me examine you."

Charlene crossed to the platform where she was bathed by the bright red light.

"Now turn around slowly," the spider woman said.

Willcox gracefully swivelled in a circle several times as Miss Hazard looked her up and down. Then the artist walked over and tucked five £100 notes into the waistband of Charlene's skirt.

"You have a magnificent figure," Hazard said appreciatively. "I think we should get started. Let me study your muscle tone as you slowly remove your clothes."

"What's all the money for?" Charlene asked.

"We'll discuss that once you're stripped."

Down in the rain-soaked mews beyond the front windows, Sid Jinks stared up at their silhouettes as he put in the teeth.


## Providence, Rhode Island
### 6:07 p.m.

As Deborah tossed the salad Zinc questioned her about the relationship between Rosanna Keate and the twins.

"Except for a week they once spent in Newport when my mother was ill, there wasn't a relationship until the trial last year. We never saw Rosanna while we were growing up. Enoch Keate lived like a recluse in his Mansion, shunning my mother while his daughter was away at finishing schools in Europe. The twins, however, hated Rosanna with a jealous vengeance, for she was living in luxury while they suffered with my father."

"How would you describe Rosanna Keate?"

"Born with a silver spoon in her mouth and determined to keep it. No matter how."

"What if someone were to threaten her financial position?"

"Who knows?" Deborah said. "Now would you please shoo out of here and let me put this feast on the table. You're under my feet."

Chandler was pleased that Lane was relaxing more and more the longer she was around him. He could still feel a tenseness beneath her attempts at banter, but it was dissipating as time went on. He took his glass of wine into the living room which was warmly decorated in creams and chocolate brown. Whenever alone in someone's home, Zinc made straight for the bookcase to take a peek at his or her mind. Deborah Lane's library was diverse. On one side there were such classics as Faulkner, Proust, Greene, Camus, Dostoyevsky, and Woolf. On the other just as many novels by Rosemary Rogers, Laurie McBain, Kathleen Woodiwiss, and other romantics.

She likes bodice-rippers, Chandler thought.

He went to find the bathroom to take a leak. Three doors opened off the entrance hall. Daffodil poked her fuzzy head through the crack of the only door ajar, Deborah's bedroom. The lady or the tiger, Zinc thought, choosing one of the other two. Beyond was a spare room cluttered with junk heaved here and there to keep the rest of the apartment neat. We all have secrets, Chandler thought.

On returning to the living room he noticed a computer set up on a desk in front of the window overlooking Saint John's Graveyard. Pencil-scrawled chapter print-outs were stacked beside it. A small mirror propped up on the desk had a picture of a woman taped to one side.

"Do you write novels?" Zinc asked, calling out to the kitchen.

"Ones that don't sell," Deborah answered back.

"Who's the woman in the picture taped to the mirror?"

"Corinne Grey." Then quieter. "She's my alter ego."

## London, England
### *11:19 p.m.*

Charlene Willcox had locked herself in the bathroom, naked and crying. Her make-up was smeared all over her face and her genitals hurt. She was now afraid of the woman beyond the door.

I should've known better, Charlene thought, the way she looked at me. But all that money, how it would've helped my mother. All that money, to let her do that!

Suddenly there was a crash of glass breaking beyond the door and a violent thump as something hit the floor. A voice cried out, "Oh please God no . . . Somebody help!" Then silence.

Charlene Willcox was too scared to move. She looked around the bathroom for another way out, but there was none. Only a vent in the ceiling covered by a grill.

Now conflicting thoughts began to flood her mind.

What if Rosanna were out there either hurt badly or dying of . . . dying of what? An epileptic seizure? A fall and crack on the head?

What if the woman expired while she sat bawling in

here naked and let her die? Charlene could see the headlines now, "Lesbian Sex Fling Leads to Death!"

"Oh, God," Willcox moaned as she slowly unlocked the door and opened it a crack.

One of the windows that led to the balcony above the mews was smashed. Glass lay scattered on the floor inside the suite, while rain blew in through the hole and drenched the curtains. Muddy footprints walked across the carpet toward the bathroom door.

Charlene was staring down wide-eyed at the body sprawled unconscious five feet away when abruptly the door swung open and slammed her back into the bathroom. A hand reached in and grabbed the model by the hair, dragging her out into the hall where it yanked back her head as fangs sank into her throat.

Charlene wrenched away, flesh tearing from her neck.

In utter shock she now found herself face-to-face with Dracula. The man was tall and sinister in a flowing red-lined cape, his hair sprayed black and swept back from his forehead in a widow's peak. Bloodshot eyes burned red from his chalk-white face, two razor-sharp canine teeth jutting down from the roof of his mouth. The fangs dripped blood and shreds of skin.

Charlene stumbled across the room as in close pursuit the Count clawed at her with gloved hands. In the reflection of the windowpane beside the broken balcony door she could see him reaching out to grab her by the hair. To escape she hurled herself crashing through the sheet of glass and tumbled from the second storey to the garden below.

Lights went on in the mews.

## Providence, Rhode Island
### 6:29 p.m.

After they had eaten, Deborah showed Zinc Sid's letters. For a while he sat silently reading the obscene threats. Then he looked up and asked, "How long have these been coming?"

"Since I was sixteen."

"And you've never met this guy?"

"Not that I remember."

"He writes as if he knows you intimately."

Deborah's face reddened. "Creepy, isn't it? Almost like he's been spying on me for ten years."

"Why did you not take them to the police until the phone calls started?"

"Because they read like a fantasy, like all their other stuff."

Chandler frowned. "I don't get what you mean."

"Inspector, I . . ."

"Drop the Inspector, huh. My name is Zinc."

Deborah glanced at him, then looked away. "Zinc," she said, "I'm sure I know who Sid is. I once overheard Saxon talking to Rika about a Sid at the time he joined the club."

"You mean that eerie group of friends your half-brother had?"

"Yes. The Ghouls."

Chandler turned to the stereo and the records lined beside it. "You like music, eh?" he said, scanning the album spines. "These are all classical. Where's the rock and roll?"

"Don't have any," Deborah said. "Rock was always a nightmare for me."

"Nothing wrong with feeding your mind and heart with Brahms. But other parts of the body often need loosening up. Lets go get a drink, then find some Devil's music. I want to hear all about Rika and Saxon Hyde."


# London, England
*11:53 p.m.*


Hilary Rand was discussing her theory about Jack The Bomber and the Vampire Killer with Scot McAllaster when her office phone rang. "Rand," she said, picking it up.

The Sergeant noticed a sudden tenseness fill her eyes.

She was already rising from her desk as she replaced the phone.

"We've got the Sewer Killer trapped in Mayfair. Let's move."

# The Man Who Read
# H.P. Lovecraft

**London, England**
*Tuesday January 28, 12:11 a.m.*

Jumping from the still-moving car, McAllaster ran toward a group of PCs standing around an open sewer manhole. As the vehicle screeched to a halt, one of the hard men approached Rand's rolled-down window through the rain.

"We have it all under control, Hilary," he said. No need for you here, he might have added.

"I'm still in charge," Rand said tightly. "Now what's going on?"

The man gave her a baleful look, then stepped back from the brink of confrontation. Time, after all, was on his side.

"A woman crashed naked through that second-storey window. She's still alive but badly broken up. Her throat's lacerated. We're checking the flat now."

"Can she describe the man?"

"Yes. It was Dracula."

If he expected a startled response he didn't get one. All the DC Supt said was, "That fits."

"The neighbours report seeing a man in a cape on that balcony next to the window from which the woman fell. They saw him throw a rope down, then rappel the side of the building mountaineer-style with a body over his shoulder. Once in the mews he vanished down that open sewer manhole. The first PCs arrived about four minutes later."

"Where's the man now?"

"In the sewers beneath where I'm standing."

"Have you found the body down there yet?"

"No."

"If he's still lugging it, he can't be moving fast. So long as you have the sewers completely cordoned off we should get him soon."

"There are forty officers underground converging from all directions. We've got the mobile computer directing the hunt. He'll not get away."

Lord, I hope not, Hilary thought.

McAllaster grabbed the sides of the ladder loosely in his hands and jumped. Twenty-five feet below he struck the sewer bottom with a jolt, his body recoiling like a spring to absorb the shock. For a moment he crouched in the pitch dark and listened intently. From all around him came the sound of moving water, sweating and dripping from the brickwork of the well, swirling about his feet and legs up to his thighs, rushing and pounding and cascading through other tunnels nearby. He detected faint voices shouting then dying away. Turning in their direction, he switched on his torch.

Ten feet in front of him the sewer tunnel forked. Both passages were dark oval veins of slimy green brick. McAllaster stopped to calculate which route to take. The carcass of a dog, its eyes gnawed out, came floating toward him in a stream of shit and street debris down the channel to his right. That meant this tunnel sloped up and away from the river, an impossible route for someone carrying a body. McAllaster turned left.

As he waded down the sewer the stench was nauseating. Waves of mist billowed about him like breath expelled from hell. Eerie shadows clawed at the walls and rats squealed from chinks in the masonry. The light of his electric torch followed the geometric lines of the shrinking bricks as they converged ahead, claustrophobically closing the tunnel in on him.

A sharp scream suddenly roared down the canyons of the sewers, followed almost immediately by echoes. Above the steady rush of the stream, a waterfall hissed. Once the shriek had subsided, voices, confused and alarmed, hummed through the fetid, murky bowels of the earth.

McAllaster switched off his electric torch and squinted through the haze of mist at a faint yellow gleam before him. Using his senses instead of the flashlight to guide his course, he sloshed through the muck and waste, advancing down the tunnel.

"In here," someone shouted to his left.

A beam of light knifed through the darkness. Small hunched figures were crossing the sewer pipe thirty feet ahead. The waterfall's hoarse roar increased in volume. An eel slithered along his leg and the smell of rotten eggs assailed his nose. Sixty seconds later he waded into an underground cavern.

McAllaster now found himself in what looked like a medieval tomb. Pillars and arches and buttresses supported a vaulted stone ceiling twenty feet high. Along this side of the chamber a series of angled tunnels brought in the flow of the main north–south and local sewer systems. These waters tumbled into a channel moving right to left in front of him, and flowed out through a yawning portal in the east wall. This channel was one of Bazalgette's interceptory sewers. An overpass crossed it to the other side.

The opposite bank of the stream was also a dam. When the level of the interceptory sewer rose beyond its capacity, the excess flow cascaded over the dam to tumble into a chamber on the other side. This occurred when the rains came as they had tonight. The lower chamber beyond the dam emptied into a storm relief sewer that surged toward an outfall on the River Thames.

As fingers of fog in the vast vault grasped at him, McAllaster's mind knew intuitively where the Sewer Killer had gone. He would at this moment be using some sort of rubber raft to escape east down the interceptory sewer or along the storm relief tunnel flooding toward the Thames.

Without similar equipment the Yard could not follow him.

And the killer could get off anywhere he desired along the way.

## 12:22 a.m.

Hilary Rand was standing in the mews looking up at the broken window when a uniformed Sergeant came out of the building and approached her.

"The flat was leased four days ago," he said. "The

lessee gave the name Rosanna Hazard. All the papers in the flat, however, identify her as one Rosanna Keate. Her driver's licence was issued in Newport, Rhode Island."

"Did you find her passport?" Rand asked.

"No," the Sergeant replied.

The Detective Chief Superintendent looked back up at the window.

Something is not right here, she thought. The Sewer Killer's original MO was to attack on the streets, then escape underground. Why did he then convert to cat burglary to murder Derick Hone, kidnap the Siamese twins, and perpetrate this crime? There's a hidden motive.

"Sergeant, have HQ contact the FBI in Rhode Island immediately. Mark the request highest priority. I want everything they can provide on Rosanna Keate."

## 12:37 a.m.

A PC lay sprawled dead at the far end of the crosswalk over the flowing channel of the interceptory sewer. Five feet beyond his corpse on the other side of the dam was the waterfall chamber that fed the storm relief sewer. The roar of the churning cascade was deafening here. A green glow spread up the sides of the PC's torso from beneath his chest. He was lying face down, the blade of a throwing knife sticking out of the back of his neck.

McAllaster manoeuvred along the gangway above the flowing channel to approach the four men standing at the dead constable's feet.

"Who is it?" a voice shouted over the din of the waterfall.

"PC Orris," another yelled back. "Right through the neck."

Water sprayed up from the cascade pit, drenching them.

"Pick him up," McAllaster ordered. "Someone radio above, the Sewer Killer appears to be in the storm relief tunnel."

"Already done," the first cop shouted back. Then because he was at the front of the line of men strung along the narrow walkway, he bent down to grip the body beneath the shoulders and lift.

"What the bloody hell's that?" the second officer yelled. "There, beneath his chest?"

He reached around the first PC's legs and under the rising corpse. When he pulled back his hand it held a waterproof, portable IBM computer, the screen of which still glowed green to show a digital map of the Mayfair section of the London sewer system.

## Providence, Rhode Island
*Monday January 27, 8:25 p.m.*

The Hot Club is one of the most popular bars in Providence. It used to be the firebox and steam boiler for Narragansett Electric across the Providence River, the plant now lit up and reflecting in the water. Deborah found a table looking out on the Fox Point Hurricane Barrier while Zinc went to the bar to buy a couple of beers. The barmaid served him two Rolling Rock Extra Pale.

Deborah poured hers into a glass as Chandler drank from the bottle.

"Is the beer you drink in the Great White North that much stronger than ours? The McKenzie Brothers portray you Canucks as a nation of drunks."

"Our brew gets you where you're going faster," Zinc replied.

"You know, I really wouldn't mind living in Vancouver."

"You've been there?" he asked.

"No, but I've seen pictures and the Expo brochures."

"Canada's not as lively as the States."

"That's what I'd like about it," she replied.

Chandler wondered what Deborah Lane did for a social life. Whatever it was he had the feeling she did it alone. Maybe sitting by herself at a Mozart concert or just watching the seasons change.

"So, where shall I begin?" she asked.

"You said that Saxon once tried to rape you. When was that?"

"1971. Just after he joined The Ghouls."

"How old was he?"

"Fourteen."

"How old were you?"

"Eleven."

"How did it happen?"

"That's a complicated question. How long have you got?"

"All night," Chandler replied.

Deborah took a deep breath and let out a heavy sigh. 'That summer was the weirdest one of my life. My mother had been readmitted to Butler Hospital and—"

"Readmitted for what, Deborah?"

A pause. "Mental problems," she said.

Chandler waited, sipping his beer.

"My mother suffered bipolar bouts of manic-depression," Lane said. "That August she'd become obsessed with the idea that Saxon had inherited Keate genetic haemophilia through her. Just before she was admitted to the hospital she was going to him five times a day and ordering him to strip off his clothes so she could check his body for cuts and signs of bleeding. Meanwhile my dad was really hitting the bottle."

"You told me Saxon in fact wasn't a haemophiliac."

"Correct. That was just my mother's delusion."

"Was it while she was in hospital that Saxon joined The Ghouls?"

"Yes. He was initiated that same month."

"What was the initiation?"

"I have no idea. You know how boys are with their secret clubs."

"Tell me about them."

"They were a Providence gang of punks that was like a horror cult. My half-brother by then was completely gone on Lovecraft. Alice Cooper was big that year and Rika's favourite song was 'Halo Of Flies' off the album *Killer*. I once overheard Saxon tell her there were hidden messages in some of her other records. She replied, 'Yes, I know.' "

Chandler's mind flashed back to his stakeout conversation with Bill Caradon. Back to their discussion of how the line between fiction and fact, between fantasy and reality can eventually cease to exist for certain people. Like the insane.

"Zinc," Deborah said, slowly shaking her head, "you can't understand what happened with Saxon unless you know more about H.P. Lovecraft. Saxon was such a fanatic fan and disciple of his, that to discuss the writer is also to reveal the mind of my half-brother."

"I'm listening, Teach."

"In some ways Lovecraft was as strange as his fiction. He was born here in Providence in 1890 of old New England stock. His father and mother both died insane, which no doubt had a dramatic influence on his writing."

"When did he die?" Chandler asked.

"1937."

"Twenty years before Saxon was born."

"Right. Lovecraft was eight the year his father succumbed to syphilis in a mental institution. His mother then visited all the resentment she felt against her husband unwittingly on her son. She relentlessly convinced him he was an ugly-looking boy, and to cure him of a fear of the dark he was led about an unlighted house at night. For the rest of his life Lovecraft preferred to be up and about after sundown. He used to wander the streets of Providence at night and sit in Saint John's Graveyard in the moonlight. During the day he would draw the blinds and write by candlelight. For a time as a child he imagined his ears were growing points and that horns were sprouting from his head."

Chandler motioned to the barmaid to bring him another beer. Deborah Lane had barely touched hers.

"In his youth Lovecraft was often sick and of weak disposition. As a man he lived like a recluse and wrote voluminous letters. During his lifetime his stories were mainly published in the pulps and he lived at the poverty line. He had such a prissy view of sex that when the magazines containing his stories arrived with half-naked woman in jeopardy on the covers, he would tear the pictures off and just keep the stories.

"The face of Great Cthulhu, his Freudian monster, resembles a woman's sexual parts. His Cthulhu Mythos is perhaps the most influential force in modern horror fiction. Lovecraft is the horror writer's horror writer. Stephen King, Robert Bloch, Ramsey Campbell, Colin Wilson and dozens of others have written Cthulhu Mythos stories in homage to him. His literary cult is now worldwide. Saxon not only identified with, but idolized him."

"The story I read on the plane, 'The Rats In The Walls', is that about the Mythos?"

"No, that's an early work. The Mythos came later. 'The Call Of Cthulhu' is its central core."

"Give me the theme in a nutshell?"

"Easy," Deborah said. "The Cthulhu Mythos represents the primal struggle between good and evil. It parallels Satan's expulsion from Eden and his desire to regain control over the world of Man.

"The Earth was once ruled by hideous monsters called the Great Old Ones who originally came from space. Because they practised Black Magic they were eventually expelled from here by cosmic forces to live on in other dimensions and other worlds. The remnants of their cities are hidden in inaccessible parts of the globe, under the Antarctic ice-cap, in subterranean caves, places like that. Great Cthulhu himself now lies sleeping in Atlantis-like R'lyeh deep beneath the sea. The others exist in dormant form on various stars and planets from Pluto to the farthest galaxies.

"The Great Old Ones, however, still have telepathic influence and their legend lives on. They are worshipped by certain primitive people as well as sophisticated cults dedicated to bringing about their return. When the stars are right the Old Ones can plunge from world to world through the skies or rise from their deathless sleep. There exists a book called *The Necronomicon* written by the mad Arab Abdul Alhazred which provides the key to the monsters' return. Lovecraft describes this volume as the ghastly soul symbol of a forbidden corpse-eating cult. In both *The Necronomicon* and Lovecraft's work there are rituals and incantations which, when combined with blood sacrifice, will draw the Great Old Ones from their present exile back into our world. 'The Call of Cthulhu' is about earthly attempts to help them break on through."

"Do you read a lot of horror fantasy?" Chandler asked.

"No," she replied. "But you can't live in Providence without knowing about Lovecraft. The World Fantasy Convention is often held here, and he's its patron saint."

"Debbie, what do you think of the recent controversy in Washington over the influence of horror fantasy?"

She smiled ironically. "In a democracy you can't stop people from thinking and expressing their ideas. Still, I have suffered because of terror fiction. One need only witness a weird fantasy convention to know that some people take it *very* seriously."

"Who exactly are the Great Old Ones?" Chandler asked.

"There are lots of them," Deborah said. "One is Azathoth, the blind idiot god. He is depicted as an amorphous blight of confusion which bubbles and blasphemes at the centre of infinity. Yog-Sothoth shares Azathoth's domain. He is the 'all-in-one and one-in-all' who is not subject to laws of time and space. Great Cthulhu—the creature of Lovecraft's repressed sexuality—is, as I said, imprisoned in R'lyeh beneath the sea. His release will herald the coming of the others. Hastur The Unspeakable dwells in the air and interstellar spaces. Shub-Niggurath, the fertility god of the Cthulhu Mythos, is 'the black goat of the woods with a thousand young'. And then, of course," Deborah said sarcastically, "there was the Great Old One who came to my room that day."

In a low voice, she told Chandler about Saxon's attempted rape of her.

"See what I mean when I say that to know about Lovecraft is to know my half-brother?"

The Canadian nodded.

"Saxon was always a total social misfit. His only real friend until '71 was my half-sister Rika. They used to play these fantasy games much like kids play Dungeons and Dragons today. One was called 'The Great Old Ones' in which they would act out roles from the Cthulhu Mythos. Another was 'Stop Legrasse.' In Lovecraft's story 'The Call of Cthulhu', Inspector Legrasse was a New Orleans policeman who interrupted a voodoo rite deep in the Louisiana swamps just in time to stop the cultists' incantations from helping the Great Old Ones break through. If Legrasse had been known to the cultists and killed before the stars were right, Great Cthulhu would now be ruling the earth. The twins' game of 'Stop Legrasse' always ended with him tied down while they cut out his still-beating heart."

Zinc frowned. The conversation had reached the point where an act that took place in objective reality could not even be described, let alone understood, without resorting to the realm of fiction. Reality and illusion were mixed in a dizzying whirl. He thought again of his conversation with Caradon.

"Saxon and Rika had been playing these fantasy games for quite some time, right?"

"Yes."

"Up until the summer of 1971, you personally were also tormented indirectly by what Saxon called The Game. In other words setting you up to be hurt like a cat playing with a mouse?"

"Correct," she said.

"Then Saxon joined The Ghouls and The Game turned deadlier. Soon after initiation he attacked you in an attempted rape?"

Deborah nodded her head.

"Any other indications things had changed?"

"The day of the attack—later, after I'd heard the twins making love in Rika's room—Saxon told my half-sister he was not Saxon Hyde, but that he had broken through to earth from another dimension and now couldn't get back. He said he wanted the other Great Old Ones to join him. I could hear them speaking through the wall."

"What did Rika say?"

"She always humoured him. Her reply was, 'So Lovecraft's right. But first you must stop Legrasse.' Then a week or two weeks after that the police came around."

"What for?"

"To question Saxon about the disappearance of Freddie Sterling. He was the gang leader of The Ghouls. But nothing came of that."

"This was September of 1971?"

"Yes. The day before my mom returned from the hospital. I remember that night our neighbour found a dog in his yard with its heart cut out."

"Saxon and Rika?"

Deborah shrugged.

"After your mother came home did you tell her about the attempted rape?"

"No. I couldn't burden her, Zinc. She was already convinced that Saxon, her only son, was an Antichrist. What he had done to her mind so far was what made her sick."

Plus Keate genes, Chandler thought.

"Tell your father?"

Lane shook her head. "He'd have beaten Saxon, who would then have killed Mr Nibs."

Zinc reached out and briefly touched Deborah's hand. "What happened next?"

"A week after my mother came home she was dead."

Chandler said nothing.

"Yes, it was suicide. Sleeping pills. The next day my father shot himself out in the garage."

The same place he used to beat Saxon, Chandler thought.

"We kids were put in a foster home, but the twins ran away. I never saw either one again until the probate trial."

"Providence isn't that big."

"I don't go out much, Insp . . . Zinc. Reading is my life."

"Did the twins say at the trial what they'd been doing all those years?"

"Yes. Living in rock communes and putting together Ghoul."

"Do you have a picture I could keep of Saxon and Rika?"

"Zinc, I burnt those long ago."

"What happened to The Ghouls? The club Saxon joined?"

"I really don't know. Disbanded, I guess. Why do you ask?"

"My instinct as a cop tells me that something happened during his initiation. Like a fraternity hazing getting out of hand. That's the reason why he changed, became more violent."

"I see," Deborah said.

"Did Saxon ever mention anyone else in the club? Other than Freddie Sterling whom the police were asking about?"

"That summer he talked about a lot of people I never met."

"Like who?"

"Like Sid and some other guy named Jack, but that was early on. Then he seemed to forget about them, and only talked about Freddie, Peter, and Reuben. After he joined The Ghouls I don't remember him mentioning Sid and Jack again."

Chandler fell silent.

"What are you thinking, Zinc?"

"I'm wondering, did any other boys in The Ghouls club also later go on to become part of the rock band Ghoul?"

## 11:42 p.m.

From the Hot Club they had moved on to Lupo's Heart-break Hotel near Westminster Mall. Pictures of dead rock stars covered the wall outside: a two-headed Elvis Presley (pre-and post-decline), Janis, Jimi, Buddy, Hank, Sam, and Jim Morrison. The music inside was loud. Zinc taught Deborah to shimmy-and-shake and put on her boogie shoes. It was good to see her loosen up to "Jail-house Rock" and "Twistin' The Night Away".

After he'd dropped Lane at her place he returned to the Biltmore Hotel. Walking through the lobby now, past three dragons in a fountain near the reception desk, Chandler hoped his nightmares had ceased. There'd not been a recurrence for the last few days. He wondered why.

The desk clerk gave him a note from Tate as he picked up his key.

A glass-enclosed elevator ran up the outside of the hotel, facing east toward the train station and State House. Zinc glanced right at College Hill and was struck by how many church spires stood on guard above Lovecraft's domain.

He read Tate's note in his room.

> Zinc
>
>    1. The Bureau received a telex from Scotland Yard this evening. Rosanna Keate was killed and/or abducted in London early tonight. They want all the background information we can sup-ply on her.
>    2. It appears that Ronald Fletcher obtained a new passport for Rosanna when she was in Newport this month. It was a rush request. We'll have a copy of the application by tomorrow.
>    3. You are to call Superintendent Burke Hood at home in Vancouver no matter what time you get in. (604) 702 4041.
>
> *Carol*

Zinc picked up the phone and dialled the Vancouver number.

"Hello," Hood said.

"Burke, it's Zinc. You called?"

"Last night Hengler was gang-raped at Oakalla and stabbed eight times. He's still alive but probably won't make it."

The tone of the Superintendent's voice told Chandler there was more. He waited.

"Hengler's lawyer, Glen Troy, has filed a habeas corpus in Supreme Court returnable this Thursday. We've all been subpoenaed, including you. He's alleging Hengler was imprisoned without legal evidence to support the murder charge. He says it's false imprisonment and malicious prosecution. I've looked at the file, Zinc, and we don't have a case. Troy's talking a massive lawsuit and private prosecution. If you're not here on Thursday with evidence to support the charge, be warned, Inspector . . . heads will roll."

Burke Hood hung up.

A moment later, Zinc dialled Tate.

## 11:59 p.m.

Once Carol Tate rang off from talking with Chandler, she made a cup of cocoa and reviewed her notes concerning his request. The Mountie had asked her to check up on all the information he'd gathered tonight from Deborah Lane, and Tate herself was intrigued with why Ronald Fletcher had blown his brains out rather than speak with her and Zinc. What exactly had been the relationship between the lawyer and Rosanna Keate? Was his suicide in fact linked to the Canadian case, or did the FBI have a fresh investigation of its own? She'd start checking tomorrow.

But right now Carol was more than just a little pissed off with Zinc Chandler. For had she not given him right from the start the very best of herself—plus fucked his ever-lovin' socks off in the process—and were they not really two of a kind in background and profession? So how could he turn his back on her and all she had to offer to concentrate his attention on some frumpy young thing so unsure of herself.

Men! Carol thought. I'm just a woman who loves too much.

"Save The Last Dance For Me" by The Drifters was playing on her clock radio as she climbed into bed. Tate stretched out on her back in the dark to drift away with the tune.

You Mounties aren't the only ones who get your man, she thought. Zinc Chandler, don't think you get rid of this girl that easily. A Texan never gives up without a helluva fight.

# Revenge Is a Dish Best Served Cold

London, England
*Tuesday January 28, 3:02 a.m.*

He sat in a chair made of human bones and dreamed about R'lyeh.

There was the monolith-crowned citadel within which Great Cthulhu slept waiting, his city of unbelievable size built from stone blocks in the measureless aeons before history began, its colossal statues and hieroglyph-scarred bas-reliefs now dripping green slime and weeds and ooze countless fathoms beneath the sea. A voice not a voice but more a mental calling rumbled up from underground, *"Cthulhu fhtagn."*

Then the worms were at his mind again, so The Ghoul opened his eyes.

He could hear and feel and sense them sucking and chewing inside his skull at the grey cells of his brain. Just his luck to have possessed *this* particular body when he broke through from the Other World. Now all he had left were little islands of memory, each isolated and cut off from the others by the spiral tunnels the grave worms left behind, tunnels that ran right out of his head and into the Great Beyond. Tunnels down which soon the Old Ones would arrive.

The Ghoul glanced across The Well to where he'd hung his star chart when he moved in yesterday. Or was that the day before? Time seemed to disappear. Not that it really mattered, for in less than two days the stars would be right, perfectly aligned for the Old Ones to break through. And this time nothing would go wrong so long as he stopped Legrasse.

Beneath the chart and flanking it around the brick cylinder that was The Well, the clay face of his Cthulhu idol and all the empty eyes of the others stared vacantly back at him.

As he savoured the stench of death and decay and subterranean rot, his stereo blaring "Break On Through (To The Other Side)" by The Doors, The Ghoul thought, You'll not fool me, Legrasse, by taking female form. Rand's heart will be ripped from her chest and fed to my friends. Her blood sacrifice will help the Old Ones to break through.

For The Ghoul knew how to deal with those who did him wrong.

## The Great Swamp, Rhode Island
### Saturday September 18, 1971, 3:46 p.m.

*"I'm gettin cold," the Grave Worm said. "How much further is it?"*

*"Not far," The Ghoul replied as Saxon pressed on ahead. He and Freddie Sterling were now deep in the swamp. "Fuckin Legrasse'd not have stopped us if this'd bin the bog."*

*It had started out a bright autumn day when they had left Providence. Freddie had obtained his driver's licence a week ago so the two boys had taken the 1949 Chevy for a spin. It had spewed blue oil fumes all the way down Route 2 from the city to South Kingstown. There the weather had suddenly changed for the worse as clouds and a cold wind swept west from the far-off Atlantic. The sky now threatened rain.*

*The Great Swamp is a 3000 acre morass, virtually untouched by man, in the southern part of the state. It was carved out by a glacier 100 centuries ago. Here on December 19, 1675, British Colonials had attacked the winter camp of the Narragansett Indians for the Great Swamp Fight during King Philip's War. The Indians had thought themselves secure surrounded by natural moats of water in the wilds of the marsh. But that frigid day the swamp had turned to ice and a thousand New England Colonials took them by surprise, burning their teepees and massacring the people. Today, however, the Great Swamp was in its usual stagnant state, a soggy peat bog of tangled vegetation where carnivorous sundews and pitcher plants and thirty kinds of orchid and poison sumac thrive, where furtive creatures walk, crawl, fly, swim, and glide.*

*They had turned off Route 2 onto Liberty Lane, then driven further in by Great Neck Road. The Chevy was now parked in a picnic grove cut from the most civilized part of the swamp. From there the two boys had walked to the western section of the bog, lifting the cable across the road to get in. They were now standing on top of the dyke.*

"Where in hell's yer secret?" the Grave Worm asked.

"Not much further," The Ghoul replied. "Over in those trees."

*They left the dyke for a path that both did and did not exist, for here the demarcation line between what was liquid and what was earth was vague and ever-changing.*

"Shit!" *Freddie cursed as his right foot was sucked into mud.* "Saxon, ya dickhead, I'm goin back."

"Hey, we're here," The Ghoul replied, pointing straight ahead.

*The Grave Worm followed Saxon's arm and could just make out what appeared to be a dilapidated vehicle parked at a slant in the trees.*

"Come on, ya gotta see this," *the younger boy said.*

*The truck was hidden in a grove of oak and holly trees. It was an old farm pickup with a canopy shaped like an upside-down V built onto the back. The canopy was made of horizontal planks with a salvaged ship's porthole cover set into one sloping side like a window. Each plank was painted a different colour then wood-burned with a slogan of salvation from the Bible.* "Repent sinners! The end is near!" *was the overall effect. The truck had a bumper sticker on the back:* "Richard Nixon Is Rosemary's Baby".

"Jeez," *Freddie Sterling said.* "What the fuck is that? How'd ya find this thing?"

"I drove it here," The Ghoul replied, "the day I was initiated into the club." *He squashed a fly that had landed on his cheek.*

"Ya came all the way down here after we dug ya up? Man, ya ran off cryin like a baby soon as we gotcha outa the ground. Freak out city. Where'd ya go?"

*"Down this road near the reservoir,"* The Ghoul replied. *"I came upon a hippie camp in the middle of a bust. There were state cops everywhere, searching for pot and taking the longhairs away in a van."*

*"Jesus freaks, huh?"* Freddie grinned that grin as he watched Saxon nod his head.

*"The hippies' cars were left behind,"* The Ghoul continued, *"so I hotwired this one and drove it away."*

*"Yer lucky ya didn't get stopped, Hyde. Yer only fourteen."*

*"I'm tall for my age."*

Freddie now noticed there was a door built into the back of the canopy. It had an open padlock hooked through the latch.

*"Ya bring it straight down here from Scituate?"* he asked.

*"I drove through farm country, then came down at dusk. I hid it here and hitchhiked back."*

*"How'd ya get it through the gate?"*

*"The pin was out. Fish And Wildlife musta bin doin some work with trucks in the swamp."*

*"Ya take a look inside this thing?"* the Grave Worm asked.

*"Uh, uh,"* The Ghoul replied.

Suddenly there was a lightning flash and it began to rain. Thunder growled down at them from dirty, churning clouds.

*"Come on,"* Freddie said. *"Let's climb inside."*

He walked to the canopy door, unhooked the padlock and pulled out the latch. On yanking open the door he immediately turned his head away.

*"Holy shit, what a stink! Smells like a fuckin pigsty!"*

He watched Saxon poke his head in the door.

*"What's that?"* the younger boy asked, reeling back himself while pointing at the canopy wall that backed on the cab of the truck.

*"Looks like a big crate,"* the Grave Worm said.

*"Let's get outa here, Freddie. I don't like this."*

The sixteen-year-old turned to him and flashed that famous grin. *"Y'ain't chicken, are ya, Hyde? Fraid of a whiff o' smell?"*

*"Freddie, I think I just heard somethin move inside that box."*

*The Grave Worm pushed him out of the way and peered into the dark. A shaft of dull grey light pierced the interior through the porthole cover. "Yer right," he said.*

*"Come on. Let's scram."*

*"Mama's boy," Freddie sneered, and with that he put one foot up on the truck's bumper and hoisted himself inside.*

*The Ghoul slammed the door and snapped on the padlock.*

*"Hey!" Freddie yelled, his voice echoing from within. "What the fuck ya doin?"*

*The Ghoul darted around to the running board beneath the driver's door and jumped up on it. Two holes had been drilled through the front wall of the canopy backing on the cab just below the peak of the roof. A pipe ran into one of these holes through which The Ghoul over the past month had periodically fed in water, but no food. A rope tied to a two-foot bar pulled flat against the outside of the canopy disappeared through the second hole. Inside it was cinched to an eye-bolt that held the hinged front of the crate shut. The Ghoul now quickly cut this cord with a linoleum knife.*

*From within the canopy came a crash as the front of the crate fell away. A frenzied grunting and squealing followed immediately as the animal stolen from the farm the month before broke loose.*

*Freddie's scream was nerve-shredding as the ravenous hog bit deep into its horrified meal. The truck rocked on its suspension springs to the frantic clawing of fingernails splintering wood inside. The starving hog sucked and chewed and ripped Freddie's flesh incessantly. A spray of red splattered across the porthole window as the Grave Worm gibbered, yammered, and shrieked within. All these sounds were music to The Ghoul's attentive ears.*

*Soon the boy climbed into the cab of the truck and crosswired the ignition. The motor choked and sputtered then caught as blue smoke hazed the air. The Ghoul drove the truck out of the woods and up onto the dyke, heading south toward Worden Pond. When it reached a predetermined point the vehicle came to a halt.*

*Here, alongside the dyke, ran a deep and stagnant canal. Beyond the canal rose Holly Hill, its hump traversed by a catwalk and several power poles, one pole topped by* an osprey nest. Wood ducks and Canada geese paddled along its surface, the water so cloudy that anything more than a few feet down would never see light.

Wedging the accelerator down with a stick, The Ghoul now popped the clutch and leaped from the cab as the vehicle lurched straight into the swamp.

For a moment the truck appeared to float, then it listed to one side. After a few minutes it sank beneath the surface of the murky, rain-pocked water.

The last sight The Ghoul had as he waved goodbye was Freddie's fingers feebly clawing at the bloody smear across the inside surface of the porthole.

*Part Three*

# THE GATES
# OF HELL

They worshipped, so they said, the Great
Old Ones who lived ages before there
were any men, and who came to the young
world out of the sky. These Old Ones
were gone now, inside the earth and under
the sea; but their dead bodies had told
their secrets in dreams to the first man,
who formed a cult which had never died.
This was that cult . . .

—*H. P. Lovecraft*
THE CALL OF CTHULHU

# Vamp

Chandler boarded the Concorde, British Airways Flight 192, and searched for his seat. He was out of money, tired, and craving a cigarette. Without his American Express Card he would not have been able to finance this last-minute do-or-die trip. Thank God, as Karl Malden says, he had not left home without it.

Zinc was shocked to find Deborah Lane sitting in the window seat beside his. "Good morning," she said cheerfully as he sat down.

"Right. And what the hell may I ask are you doing here?"

"Flying to London, of course."

"I'll repeat that. What the hell are you doing here?"

"Well . . . uh . . . let's see. Last night when you called to say you were leaving unexpectedly, I got to thinking and turning matters over in my mind."

"Uh, huh."

"I mean, you can't just drop into my life and stir up all these unresolved issues then blow away on the wind."

"Yes I can. I do it all the time."

"And how will you recognize Rosanna and Saxon if you find them?"

Chandler said nothing.

"Zinc, I can't go on being tormented by my past. I want to know who Sid is and stop his obscene letters. Only Saxon can put me onto him. I've had enough of this adolescent crap. I want to resolve my feelings once and for all toward the twins. Besides, you told me a mystery with the last chapter missing. I've got to know the answer."

"Don't stop now. You're on a roll."

"I plan to flog my novel to some British publishers. And . . . uh . . . well . . . uh . . . I had a great time last night and might never . . . well . . . see you again."

"Is that all of it?"

"No. I've never been to London. This should be fun."

## London, England
## *2:13 p.m.*

Sid Jinks knew there would be trouble with Elaine Teeze over loss of the computer. Sure, he had made the crime look as if it had been committed by the Sewer Killer. And he had spirited the woman away from the Mayfair suite just as he had been ordered. Plus he had made good his escape with her down the storm relief sewer on the rubber raft. But in spite of all his success he knew Elaine would still be choked. She would say he'd botched the job and probably punish him by denying him time.

Bitch, Jinks thought. I'm the one who stole the software from Thames Water. Where do you get the right to tell *me* what to do? Just once I'd like to drink *your* blood and turn the tables around. You and your precious body. Its mine as much as yours.

Sid was alone in his room with the pitch-black walls. Any minute now he expected Elaine's silhouette to appear at the door. If she kept distracting him with all these urgent jobs, how was he going to find the time to go after Deborah?

Just get my hands on you, Debs, he thought staring at his knives. I'll skin your twat and mount it with your stuffed tits, there beside the door.

## *2:15 p.m.*

Fame was part of it—but fame wasn't all. For it was Nietzsche who had inspired him, just as it was Nietzsche who showed Hitler the way.

The Will To Power, he thought as he put down the book, staring up at the blank wall above the headboard of the bed in his East End flat.

According to Nietzsche, he had read, history is made

by individuals too strong for their social environment. All men can be rated on a scale from one to ten, the highest-raters in a society forming its elite. This dominant five per cent is heir to The Will To Power, that blind and groping force in life which has no purpose but to endlessly renew itself, that striving in elite man to become a god.

In a healthy society the elite man—be he Gandhi or Jack the Ripper—may realize his inherent right to dominate the weaker members.

In a decadent system like Britain today, where a man with elite potential can't even find a job, was it not his biological right to smash and kill his way to domination?

The Will To Power, he thought again as he rose from the bed where he had been reading and crossed the floor to pick up the paper bag near the door.

Peering inside, he reached in and removed one of the tools from the sack.

Then he returned to the bed and opened *The Monster Book* at the page he had marked earlier.

*My* Will To Power, he thought as he grabbed his carving knife.

## 2:16 p.m.

The London papers on her desk were screaming hysterically that something must be done. The AIDS clinic bombing and Mayfair crimes of yesterday had pushed them right over the top.

The memo that Hilary held in her hand was the death knell of her career:

> You are required to attend a meeting in the office of the Commissioner of Police tonight at 21:00 to discuss transfer of command. A press conference announcing the fact is scheduled for one hour later.

## New York, New York
## 9:17 a.m.

There was something about the Canadian that attracted Deborah Lane. His rough good looks were no doubt part

of it, but even more alluring was the sense of danger
that she felt in his presence. Not sexual danger as if he
might ravage her in the white heat of a sudden overpow-
ering passion— Ha, she thought. No way. Not like my
characters—but adventurous danger, stuff to write about.
Corinne Grey would be here, no doubt about that. And
maybe, finally, it was time to live her alter ego. To *be*
Corinne Grey.

"Don't you feel guilty playing hooky from school?"
Chandler asked.

"Are you scolding me?"

"I'll be spanking you in a minute."

"Oooh, such terrifying talk. I phoned my boss at home
and said I had an urgent family problem. Which is close
to the truth."

"Is it? And just how do you come to be sitting beside
me? Coincidence?"

"You said you were leaving quickly for London so I
guessed you might take the Concorde."

"Quite the detective, aren't you?"

"I phoned British Airways to check and told them I
was your sister. Then I asked to be seated with you."

"How did you get here from Providence? Charter a
plane? Drive through the night?"

"No. I asked my Fairy Godmother to wave her magic
wand. You really *would* give me a spanking wouldn't—"

"Excuse me," a voice said from above the two of
them. Zinc and Deborah glanced up.

The woman standing in the aisle was about twenty-
five. Her hair was black and as casually wild as only
constant attention could make it. Multi-variants of purple
shaded her dark eyes, her full lips rose-coloured over
perfect teeth. She was fashionably clothed to show off
her hourglass figure, her clinging fuchsia dress sheer enough
to reveal her nipples and the curve of her hips. The scent
of Giorgio, subtle and expensive, wafted on the air. In
her left hand she carried a large tackle box.

"Going fishing?" Chandler asked as the woman stretched
up to store her coat and spent a little too long showing
off her body.

"In a manner of speaking," she replied, lifting the lid
of the box with perfect hands and giving him a peek.
Inside were compartmentalized at least three hundred
different kinds of make-up.

She stored the tackle kit beneath the seat in front of her and sat down beside Chandler as Deborah Lane's face went suddenly wooden.

## London, England
## *2:28 p.m.*

Hilary Rand stood at her office window and looked out over London. She wondered how many other police detectives also had their careers on the line. What a thankless job, she thought, then took a deep breath and returned to her cluttered desk. Last night Hilary had slept for all of forty-five minutes.

The reports stacked before her were rapidly piling up.

Braithwaite had expressed an opinion on Rand's theory that the Vampire Killer and Jack The Bomber were one. Both showed signs of haematomania, he wrote, which often leads to ritual murder and human sacrifice, or any other crime concerned with a fascination over human blood.

The storing of blood was common in Black Magic and Satanic cults, Haitian voodoo, Mau Mau, and Oriental medicine. With the advent of hysteria over the possibility the AIDS virus had polluted national blood banks, even "sane" people had taken to storing their own blood. Such autologous donations, he wrote, were particularly high in America. Add the element of insanity and Rand's theory was psychologically plausible.

Braithwaite had also noted in a postscript that the maximum time blood can be stored without freezing is thirty-five days.

The Yard's initial attempt to investigate AIDS hysteria within particular individuals in the hope that might provide a possible lead to the killer had—as she anticipated—run into a roadblock. The British Medical Association had informed the Murder Squad that any request for confidential files would be denied. The BMA had pointed out: "If a patient did not see his doctor because he felt he could not trust him and that patient had a serious disease, the consequences for the community would be potentially far worse than the threat of any murderer."

Rand did not have enough time left to concentrate on

her Jack The Bomber/Vampire Killer theory. So that left the Mayfair crime as her Last Hurrah.

The Mayfair case bothered her.

It bothered her a lot.

On Rand's desk was a serology report from the Forensic Science Laboratory which raised the first problem. For in the Mayfair suite of Rosanna Keate, splatters and pools of Charlene Willcox's blood had been found but not one drop from anyone else. In other words, not only had the Sewer Killer again changed his original MO by attacking within doors, but for the first time he had not injured the victim whom he had then carried away. That didn't mesh with the previous crimes, except for the Siamese twins.

Rand wondered if the Mayfair kidnapping might be a blind. Were they hunting for a Peter Sutcliffe-type of random serial killer who changed his technique by going indoors when he sought out *particular* victims? Obviously Derick Hone was not a random kill. Neither were Willcox and Keate, the detective's instinct told her. And if the women were chosen selectively that raised the question, *Why?*

Rand reread the FBI report from Carol Tate, then studied the list of Sewer Killer taunt connections written on the blackboard. She closed her eyes.

Is the Mayfair case separate from the previous Sewer Killer crimes? she wondered.

Is Mayfair the work of a copy cat killer who has a specific personal motive concerning Rosanna Keate and is using the Sewer Killer's crimes as a smokescreen?

If so, the FBI report points a finger at this fellow Saxon Hyde.

Something tells me the Vancouver murder is also tied in somehow.

I must speak to this Zinc Chandler when he arrives.

She was still lost deep in thought when Scot McAllaster walked in with the laboratory report on the computer discs found beneath the policeman's body in the Mayfair sewers.


# New York, New York
## 9:35 a.m.


"How fast is the take-off?" the Cover Girl asked.

"Fast enough," Chandler replied.

"I'll bet," the woman said, smiling suggestively at Zinc, then giving him a perfect Brigitte Bardot pout.

Are you two talking about the plane or her clothes? Deborah thought.

The Concorde was out on the runway cranking up for takeoff. Debbie watched the Cover Girl lean across Chandler to look out of the window. As she did so she pushed her breast against his arm.

"Cruising speed is Mach 2 or 2150 kph," Zinc said.

"Yours or the plane's?" the Cover Girl teased, laughing lightly.

How corny, Deborah thought, glancing at Chandler. I'd be scorned for writing such junk, but you'll fall for it, won't you, Zinc?

"He's a Mountie," Deborah said, her voice sarcastic and dripping sugar.

"Really," the Cover Girl said. "How exciting. Is this your girlfriend?"

"No. My sister," Chandler replied.


# London, England
*3:56 p.m.*


McAllaster removed his jacket and rolled up his sleeves. The sinews of his wrists were taut as he flexed and unflexed his hands. Hilary Rand had switched from tea to her first cup of coffee in years to help stay alert. Together they went over the two reports yet again.

"God," Hilary said, tapping the lab analysis of the computer discs found in the sewer. "This does change the picture. I *knew* there was something eluding us."

"He must have our access code," the Scotsman said.

"Yes, or else he's spliced into the cables. Is that technologically possible? They run through the sewer tunnels, don't they?"

McAllaster nodded. "The CIA recently did the same thing in Berlin. They tunnelled under the Wall and tapped into the East German telephone trunk lines. For a while they listened to everything the Russians had to say."

"But you don't think that's what has happened here?"

"No. We've checked under the Yard and nothing is amiss. The further you go from the source, the harder it gets."

"Do you think he's one of us?"

"A policeman would have access."

"Or someone who knows one of us?"

"Maybe carelessness."

"Damn," Rand said as she spread out the photographs.

They stared at the blown-up pictures taken of the recovered computer's screen once its software had been accessed. Each showed a different portion of a digital map of the London sewer system similar to that stolen from the Thames Water Authority last May. The digital maps, however, had been reworked since then. For each now contained the exact location of every one of the Yard's tunnel detection devices—light sensors, camera monitors, the works.

"You see what he's done?" McAllaster said.

"Yes. He's reprogrammed the digital maps to feed in all the dangers inherent in our manhunt. So each time he down-loads the programme to plot a particular route through the system to the scene of his next crime, he works around any spot we will detect him."

"However," McAllaster said, "I'll bet he goes further than that. My guess is that he travels with *two* portable computers. The one we recovered that plots his route, and another by which he can tap the PNC by radio-control. That way he knows exactly what we're doing as we do it. Every local inquiry and command goes directly to him. He could even feed in misdirections if he wanted."

Hilary Rand shook her head. "Brilliant," she said. "But he's made a major mistake."

"The routes?" McAllaster asked.

"Exactly," she replied.

The mistake the Mayfair abductor had made was unavoidable. For what he had done—as Hilary had said—was down-load the enhanced digital map and plot his route upon it. A route that would take him both to the scene of his crime and allow him to escape. A route that had both a destination and a source. The destination was close to Rosanna Keate's suite. The source, still plotted on the map, was perhaps near where he lived.

In addition there was also a "wild route" on the map. It had a different origin and a different destination, although it was impossible to tell which was which. Rand took the photographs of the two routes and tacked them up on the corkboard wall. Then she looked at her watch.

"Where do we go from here?" McAllaster asked. He was drinking a bottle of mineral water.

The Detective Chief Superintendent was silent for several minutes. She paced from her desk to the window and back again, her muscles twitchy from lack of sleep. Her mind ran through all the options, weighing and comparing them. Finally she picked up the FBI report telexed to London by Carol Tate.

"We go with this," she said.

## Approaching London, England
## 5:50 p.m.

Chandler spent most of the flight across the Atlantic reading papers and magazines. At Kennedy Airport before departure he had purchased every British publication available. The tabloid headlines shrieked about the AIDS clinic electrocution and Mayfair fiasco of the day before, but he skipped over them. Most of his time was devoted to the entertainment sections, or reading *Melody Maker, NME, The Face* and other music periodicals.

Now, as the Concorde made its final descent into Heathrow Airport, Chandler tore a page from one of the London papers.

The Cover Girl had just returned from the toilet with her tackle box. Deborah winced at how perfect she appeared: perfect make-up, perfect hair, perfect clothes and accessories. Lane felt dowdy enough to be Chandler's grandma.

"Here," the model said, passing Zinc a note. "London can be a lonely town without a port in the storm. Call me tomorrow."

Deborah was convinced that Zinc was right now dreaming of sailing his ship into her warm, snug cove. In actual fact, however, Chandler took one look at the model's long, sharp, immaculate claws and thought, Uh, uh, lady. For Carol Tate had ravaged his back again yesterday afternoon before Lane made him supper.

"What did you find?" Deborah asked, glancing at the torn sheet of paper in his hand.

"This," Chandler said, passing it to her.

Tonight at 10:00 p.m.
*A Taste Of American Gothic At The Gates Of Hell!*
*In Concert Dead Or Live*
*The Return Of*
GHOUL

## London, England
*6:01 p.m.*

Cosmic winds from beyond the stars blew through the tunnels burrowed in his mind.

Relentlessly, the grave worms slurped at what was left of his brain.

The Ghoul's naked body was streaked with blood and gore.

The Soho stripper lay on the marble slab in death with her legs spread.

*"Cthulhu fhtagn,"* he whispered as he caressed her cold, cold skin. "Tonight, Legrasse, when the stars are right, Rand will lie here instead."

All the empty eyes watched him as he climbed up on the altar slab.

# In From Outside

Jack Ohm was computing the odds for success when the trouble began again.

He sat at the console within the steel-walled room that was his mind, punching the keyboard before him and analysing the figures that appeared on the screen. The procedure he was using had taken several months of hard and dedicated work to develop. He had begun by studying bloody video-movie scenes, reducing the murder techniques to a series of binary numbers based on time-motion movement sequences. From the resulting complex mathematical formulae he could figure the odds of getting away with any crime. The computer now told him that what he had planned for later tonight was risky in the extreme. It set the odds at five in ten that he would escape undetected. There was a fifty per cent chance that he would spend the rest of his natural life in jail.

Too high, Ohm thought.

The trouble started when a warning light flashed to inform him that someone was outside the door that led to his mental room. Jack punched a console button to activate the security cameras out in the hall. Instantly Elaine Teeze appeared on the screen.

"Let me in," she ordered.

Ohm pressed the release button to slide back the steel-plate partition. As it moved he heard a scratching fuzz beyond the wall to his right and the door jammed halfway open. Ohm's heart missed a beat.

"I said let me in," Elaine snapped. Her black silhouette was half-framed in the entrance as if her body had been split by an axe.

Ohm punched the back-up system and the steel plate slid open. The fuzzing scratch beyond the wall, however, continued unabated.

"What sort of game do you think you're playing, Jack?"

"Jesus, we've got problems. It can't go down tonight."

"What sort of problems? Have you got cold feet?"

"Elaine, something's wrong with the electrical system built into the walls. I can't isolate the glitch to analyse it. I'm going to have to cut through the steel to find the fault."

"There isn't time. You've got to leave right now."

"Dammit, I *can't* leave! Don't you understand!"

"Jack, your flowers are already on the way. We'll never get another chance like tonight. It's too big to abort. It must go through."

"Elaine, the odds are fifty-fifty even without the glitch."

"If you don't go through with it, everything will be set up with no body count. We'll lose momentum with the cops, the press, and the people. And there goes The Cause."

"Elaine, I can't—"

"I'll cut you off, Jack. Permanently."

For a moment there was silence in the room except for the constant scraping beyond the wall. Ohm stared at the black silhouette standing in the doorway. Then he sighed and said, "What am I to do?"

"First put the Yard PNC on line."

Ohm cleared the screen and punched in the access code. As the memory banks of Scotland Yard opened up for them, Elaine Teeze whispered, "Very good, Jack. Now put the security system at the Hall up on the screen."

Ohm punched the keyboard as a different image came alive.

"Do you see any alterations since you moved in the stuff?"

"No."

"We're not using explosives so the dogs are no good, right?"

"Yes."

"You've already got past them once just as you will tonight."

"I guess."

"Not 'I guess'. Yes or no."

"Yes."

"Good. Then get going," she said—and the silhouette was gone.

Now Jack Ohm was left alone in the steel-walled room of his mind, listening with growing apprehension to the scratching that went on and on and on.

## 8:33 p.m.

Deborah hiked her dress up and straightened her panty hose. The woman who stared back at her from the mirror could have been a stranger she'd met on the street. Well, not with a lifted skirt, she thought, dropping the dress.

Lane was about to turn away when an impulse overcame her. Reaching up with both hands, she pinched her nipples sharply. She'd seen Rosanna do that in the courthouse restroom during the probate trial. The rigid tips of her breasts now poked visibly at the front of her dress.

Resist that, Zinc, she thought with a reckless smile that set her libido tingling, an erotic sensation she savoured until an even more thrilling desire rose unbidden from her subconscious mind: the hope that Chandler would nail Saxon for what he'd done to her.

## 8:35 p.m.

When Zinc rang Deborah's room from the lobby of the Strand Palace Hotel she told him to come on up. Once again Chandler was dressed in his all-black party clothes, concerned that if he stuck out at The Id in the backwater of Vancouver, what would happen here in London at The Gates Of Hell?

Zinc had been tired before the flight but now he felt wasted. All he wanted was to sleep for a year. He asked himself for the hundredth time what he was doing in Britain. How in hell could he hope to make a case against Ray Hengler in less than half a day, then catch a flight back to Vancouver to be in Supreme Court on Thursday morning for the hearing on the habeas corpus writ?

The cab from the airport had dropped Zinc at the Special X flat he called home in London, then taken Deborah Lane to her hotel. Chandler was kicking himself for suggesting they grab a light bite to eat before hitting the club at ten, but then Debbie was new to this city and it didn't seem right to abandon her. He knew he was totally out of it when he knocked on her door and a strange woman answered.

"Sorry. Wrong room," Chandler said, stepping back and rechecking the numbers on the wood, surprised to find they were the same ones he had just rung from the lobby, then flabbergasted when he realized who this magnificent creature was.

"Deborah?" Zinc asked, shock etched all over his face.

The heavenly apparition smiled—and didn't avert her eyes.

"No. I'm Corinne Grey," Deborah said.

The paradox of acting is, of course, that you reveal so much of who you really are at precisely the same time as you are disguising yourself.

Deborah Lane was wearing a turquoise silk dress that plunged low in front and clung provocatively to her body. Her hair, cut shorter than on the flight, was swept up and back from her face to reveal her ears. All attention was focused on her now-mysterious eyes, the eyelids shaded smoke with a hint of plum, the lashes thick and dark. Her lips glared sensually, a soft silver-pink.

"My God," Chandler said. "Why the transformation?"

"I thought you liked your women war painted for battle?"

"How? You've been gone no more than an hour and a half."

"The American dollar, my boy, goes a long way in this town. I checked in, went downstairs and told the beauty salon to completely do me over. One girl did the make-up while another did my hair, the boutique owner running back and forth with dresses. And *voilà*!"

"Yeah, well, that dress is a little out of place for where we're going tonight."

"No problem," Corinne/Deborah said, grabbing Chandler by the lapels and pulling him into the room. "I don't plan to be wearing it very long."

Naked, she was even more beautiful than he imagined she would be, with her elegant throat and ivory skin sloping down toward her full young breasts, the nipples pink and erect with erotic expectation. Her waist was narrower than it seemed when she was clothed, her hips flaring then tapering into long, shapely legs. Chandler's throat went suddenly dry as she walked toward him gracefully and cupped his chin with one of her hungry hands.

"I've been saving a lot of love," she said, "for someone just like you."

She kissed him with a ferocity that sparked along his nerves and made him quiver with its jolt.

Then she pulled away abruptly.

"Take me," she said.

Exhausted, Chandler lay on the bed with Deborah in his arms, just as he had done with Carol the night before last. The more he got to know this woman, the more he was intrigued. She had spent her life hiding from the experiences of the world, and yet she was without a doubt the finest lover he had ever had, one minute so totally innocent that he felt guilty fucking her, the next devouring his body as if she had bought him on a slave auction block. Deborah kept him coming and going so fast just trying to keep up with her, snowballing lust upon lust in him until he was sure both his mind and body would explode. When he finally came, the decibel level of his orgasm must have rivalled that of Carol Tate.

But Deborah Lane was so much more than that.

Intelligent, tender, a lover of cats and similar joys in this world. Witty, humorous, vulnerable. Cool yet passionate. The list went on and on.

As he lay with one arm around her and ran through her virtues in his head, Zinc knew he would fall in love with her and probably already had.

How difficult it is, he thought, to really judge people. Who they are. What they want. You don't even know yourself.

A memory came back.

*It's your father, Mom wrote. Son, I think he's dying.*

*No need to say more, you knew the rest. The old man had his dreams too, and he had his pride.*

*Dull, flat Saskatchewan. The land of your birth. All you ever wanted was the fastest ticket out. The West Coast, the Rockies, anywhere but home. Your brother too, of course, but he came back. Didn't have the arrogance to kill the old man. Not like you.*

*A hot, listless summer day; Rosetown just the same. Golden wheat fields left and right as you stepped down*

*from the train. Old MacKinnon there to meet you, he
hadn't changed a bit.*

*How is he? you asked.*

*Bad, MacKinnon replied, looking you over carefully
with those eighty-year-old eyes. Not accusing, just curious.
Wondering if you'd ever found what you were searching
for. Hoping you were old enough to see that it was here.*

*Man leaves the land, MacKinnon said, his life turns to
shit.*

*Dust outside the pickup; dead bugs on the windshield;
the farm up ahead.*

*Hello, Pop.*

*Nothing in response. Just lying there on the bed: white
hair, white skin, already dead. Didn't even turn to acknowledge you were there. Two, three, four fans going
round and round. Chintz curtains blowing in the artificial
breeze.*

*Tuesday, Wednesday, Thursday, visiting that room, will-
ing Friday on, when you'd make your escape. Ritual
completed, the old man laid to rest, wait at a distance for
the news that he was dead.*

*What's wrong with him, Mom? I don't understand. It's
like somebody pulled the plug and drained his life away.
Stole his will to live.*

*You're both in the kitchen, working on a meal. Pop's in
the bedroom staring at the wall.*

*Zinc, check the drive, Mom said. I think your brother's
here.*

*Then finally Friday morning, come at last. Tom could
take over the vigil while you made your great escape.*

*So long, Pop. Got to catch a train.*

*Just the two of you alone, sunlight at the windows and
streaming in the door. You near the dresser, him on the
bed. Tom and your Mom talking outside as you said your
last farewells.*

*Then suddenly there was a long shadow right across the
floor. Tom, your kid brother, standing in the doorway.*

*Dad, we got a farm to work. That was all he said. But
damn if an hour later the old man wasn't out in the fields,
working the land with his one son who turned out to be a
man, the family farm passing on to yet another generation.
While you, his other son, the cop, left to catch your train.*

*Was it anger that blinded you to the old man's desperate
need, to the fact that he had two sons because he had the*

farm? Worked his entire life to leave them a legacy, only to have both turn their backs and walk away.

But then the moral son returned—while the other didn't. God, did Pop hate cops!

Zinc.

Yes, Mom.

Is this what you really want?

What, to be a member? To join up with the force?

Umm, hmm, she said.

Why? Has Dad been grousing, bending your ear? The problem lies with him, Mom, not with me. Yes, it's what I want.

You know how he feels?

That's too bad. It's not his life. The Dirty Thirties are no more, and neither are the riots. Why does he have to live in the past and blame today's police?

The memories of an aging man are the deeds of a man in his prime.

Right. And I'm in my prime, so I'll choose my own deeds. They won't be determined by his choice when he was a younger man. Now belongs to me.

A man leaves the land, Zinc now thought, his life turns to shit. Seventeen years with The Mounted, and what the hell have you got? A habeas corpus writ in Vancouver waiting to take your job. You've spent too long outside. It's time to come back in.

Zinc pulled Deborah close to him and clung to the warmth of her body. Strange, how that one simple act made him feel as if the world were a perfect place, a place where so long as she was at his side nothing could go wrong.

But before tonight was over, all that would change.

# Poison Ivy

*8:40 p.m.*

Hilary Rand was in the Tank having a gin and tonic. The drink was one for the road before her meeting with the Commissioner of Police. She had only twenty minutes left in her career.

Scot McAllaster had been told to hunt down anything he could find on Saxon Hyde. "You've got a free rein," she had said. The Highlander had left New Scotland Yard hours ago.

The others in the Tank left her alone. Everyone knew what was going on upstairs, and Rand, like an old elephant, was given room to die. She sat alone at a table and sipped her gin, reading Carol Tate's report yet another time.

Chance, they say, is the fool's word for fate. The consequences of every act, Orwell had written, are implicit in the act itself. Free will is only a fantasy confined within the skull.

These were Hilary's thoughts as she now mentally closed out her part in the Yard investigations.

Was it chance or fate that the car she had sent to pick Chandler up at the airport had suffered a collision before it arrived? By the time she'd then searched out his address in London by contacting Special X, the RCMP Inspector had left his flat.

Was it chance or fate that the computer had been found in the sewers just as the final curtain was coming down on her? The discovery opened up so many avenues. At the end of one route was Rosanna Keate's flat in Mayfair. At the other end must be the starting point

300

for the attack. A house to house search of that area could turn up the final lead. The "wild route", on the other hand, did not interlock with any crime that she knew of to date. Was it the path to be used for a *future* offence? With time enough for analysis she might have been waiting for the killer to arrive.

Hilary put Tate's report down and glanced at the note they'd found pinned by a scythe to Derick Hone's chest. "Legrasse", she read, "beware the stars!" Had the stars also sealed her fate?

Time, Hilary thought wearily. Not enough time.

She looked at her watch.

Seconds ticked away.

The more she considered Saxon Hyde and the rock band Ghoul, the more she was convinced that he was connected to the Sewer Killer case in some way.

The Sewer Killer obviously had a bent for the macabre. From what they knew he also had an actor's drive to live different and changing roles. He enjoyed the notoriety that came from the taunts he left, all of which seemed to be connected to the realm of horror fantasy. But then with his last few crimes the taunts had stopped. Why? Rand asked herself. Were they actually left for some other reason, now satisfied?

Saxon Hyde, according to Tate's report, came from a background connected with the stage. His maternal grandfather—his father too if Enoch Keate had sired him—was an American theatre promoter. Had his mother instilled a love of theatrics in her son?

Hyde had an all-consuming obsession with the weird that appeared to have possessed him all his life. In addition, the FBI report indicated that he was in London when all the crimes attributed to the Sewer Killer took place, except for the funfair attack. On that day he was in Vancouver with the band, during which time his twin sister was killed in a local penthouse suite. A suite owned, incidentally, by the same Rosanna Keate who was subsequently abducted by the Sewer Killer.

Did that mean the funfair ambush was really the work of Jack The Bomber, or that Saxon Hyde appearing to fit the Sewer Killer's mould was just one of those strange and inexplicable coincidences in life?

No, Rand thought. The odds are too great.

All of the Sewer Killer's early crimes were random attacks perpetrated in the streets. Then came the killing of Derick Hone, the Siamese twins kidnapping, and the Keate/Willcox affair. Why the change in pattern? Hone was easy to explain as a break in the usual method; his murder was the ultimate arrogant taunt to the Yard irrespective of anything that the killer might leave behind. But the abduction of the twins and the attack indoors on Willcox and Keate were more difficult to place. The twins fit in with the Sewer Killer's macabre psychology. Willcox was probably a random victim in that she just happened to be there. So that left Rosanna Keate as the real unexplained change in the Sewer Killer's MO.

Yet Keate was personally tied to Saxon Hyde.

According to the FBI report from Carol Tate, Rosanna was at the centre of an RCMP investigation in Vancouver. It was thought that she was involved in the murder of her possible half-sister Rika Hyde. Rika was Saxon's twin, which gave him a motive of revenge for killing the heiress. In addition Rika was the singer for the rock band Ghoul, so her death economically injured Hyde as Axel Crypt in his vocation. Also, Rosanna had seized in probate court what he probably thought was his rightful portion of the Keate estate. The man had motive upon motive for doing the woman in.

Now Keate had disappeared in a kidnapping that broke the previous pattern of a psycho-maniac. Saxon Hyde came from a family run through with mental illness. If he were the offspring of incest between a Keate brother and sister, he could have the mutated genes of insanity concentrated in him. The motif of Ghoul and Hyde himself dovetailed perfectly with the Sewer Killer's madness.

As the Detective Chief Superintendent saw it, Saxon Hyde might be involved in one of three ways:

1. He could be fascinated by the Sewer Killer's crimes and have decided to use them as a cover for abducting and killing Rosanna Keate to settle any one or more of his possible motives. Or perhaps he wanted to hide his own part in the Vancouver death of his sister Rika. In other words, kill the only witness.

2. He and Keate *together* might have planned *her* disappearance to put the police off Rosanna as a suspect in Rika Hyde's murder by making them think she had

become a victim of the Sewer Killer. Thats why none of her blood was found in the Mayfair flat.

3. Best of all from Rand's point of view, Saxon might be using the Sewer Killer as a blind to eliminate Rosanna and therefore tie up the loose ends of his involvement in the death of Rika—and at the same time be the actual Sewer Killer as well.

She glanced at her watch and realized that time had just run out.

As the detective left the Tank to go upstairs to her beheading, she wondered, Will Scot be resourceful enough to think of checking the music papers for a lead on the rock band Ghoul as a road to Saxon Hyde?

## 8:51 p.m.

Jack Ohm first got the idea from a Teflon pan. The pan came with a sticker that warned: *Do not place in an electric oven set at clean cycle.* Ohm's inquisitive mind had wondered, Why?

Teflon is a trademark for polytetrafluoroethylene. It is a polyethylene plastic in which all the hydrogens have been replaced with fluorine. $CnF_2n^{+2}$ is a solid and usually inert.

If Teflon, however, is heated to between 600 and 800 degrees Centigrade, it depolymerizes into perfluoro-iso-butylene, a highly toxic gas. A Teflon-based paint used to be manufactured until one day a doctor was coating his boat and a tiny spatter hit the end of his cigarette. He dropped dead instantly.

Jack Ohm had 150 grams of Teflon in the Hall.

100 grams would be enough to kill the people gathered here tonight.

All 7000 of them.

## 8:53 p.m.

Hilary Rand stopped at her office briefly as she went from the Tank to see the Commissioner on the eighth floor.

If I'm accompanied to the lift when the meeting's over, she thought wryly, I must make sure the lift is there when the shaft doors open.

Two telephone messages had been left on her desk.

One call was from the man who worked at Heart Of Darkness, the horror shop. He had rung up to say that the Grim Reaper was a character in *Wonder Comics,* Nos. 1–18, 1944–47, by Better Publications. A different Grim Reaper appeared throughout the seventies in *Avengers,* by Marvel Comics. He was Wonder Man's brother and his secret identity was Eric Williams.

Legrasse, he added, was the name of a New Orleans policeman who stopped a voodoo ritual and blood sacrifice designed to help a race of monsters break through to our world from another dimension.

Rand sighed, then almost choked when she read the final line: "Legrasse appears in 'The Call Of Cthulhu', a story by H. P. Lovecraft."

Tate's report said Saxon Hyde was a Lovecraft fanatic.

The second call was from Inspector Zinc Chandler of the Royal Canadian Mounted Police. He'd left two telephone numbers and a message saying it concerned Rosanna Keate.

Rand dialled the first number which was the Special X flat in London, and let the phone ring ten times before she hung up.

The DC Supt glanced at her watch. There was time for one more call before her execution. The second telephone number was for a room at the Strand Palace Hotel.

When Rand picked up the receiver she couldn't get a dial tone.

"Hello," someone said.

"The lines must be crossed," Hilary replied.

"I'm calling Detective Chief Superintendent Rand."

"That's me. Who is this?"

"Mr McGregor at McGregor's East End Florist. Do you remember me?"

"Of course. The flowers sent to The Roman Steambath and New Scotland Yard the night of the bombing were ordered from you." Rand glanced at her watch. She had to get upstairs. "I'm sorry, sir, but I have very little time to talk. What is this about?"

"We sent a bouquet out early tonight that was ordered by cash in an envelope pushed through the letter box. I was just doing the accounts and noticed the signature at the bottom of the order. It's signed T.Z."

Rand gripped the phone tighter.

"My assistant is an American studying in London. I read the signature initials as 'Tee Zed'. But then she asked, 'Who's "Tee Zee"?' The person who ordered The Roman Steambath flowers had the last name 'Teeze'."

"My God," Rand said, "where did you send them?"

"To the Royal Albert Hall."

A cold shiver prickled the detective's skin.

Her eyes snapped to the photographs taken of the computer digital map routes which she had earlier tacked to the wall.

One end of the "wild route" came to a halt near the Royal Albert Hall.

"Good Lord," she whispered, about to hang up when the florist said, "I checked what's on at the Hall tonight. That's why I called. The London Choir in concert for an AIDS benefit. The Prince and Princess of Wales are in attendance. Curtain time was half an hour ago."

## 8:54 p.m.

The 150 grams of Teflon were packed in 2½ pounds of thermite. Thermite is a mixture of powdered metallic aluminium and iron oxide which when ignited produces extremely high temperatures. It is used in welding and incendiary bombs. If Jack Ohm's thermite was set off it would depolymerize the Teflon into perfluoro-iso-butylene gas and kill every human being now in the Royal Albert Hall.

The Royal Albert Hall of Arts and Sciences resembles a huge flying saucer come down to earth on the edge of Hyde Park across from the Albert Memorial and Kensington Gardens. Captain Francis Fowke based its design on the Roman amphitheatres in the South of France. It's built from 6,000,000 bricks and 80,000 terracotta blocks. The external colours are dull red, purple, and dirty cream. The dome is of glass.

The Hall was opened by Queen Victoria on March 29, 1871 as a memorial to her husband. In those days the building was lit by gas and its 11,000 burners could be illuminated in ten seconds. Heating was by means of steam that passed from the boiler room below to hiss through five miles of pipe which snaked around all levels behind the arena walls. The water which fed the boilers flowed from the Serpentine in Hyde Park under the Royal Albert Hall and then on to the Thames.

Earlier this afternoon, Jack Ohm had brought his Teflon and thermite into the Hall by means of the underground river, some scuba equipment, and a waterproof container. He had hidden it in the basement masked as a Coca-Cola pressure canister to stock the bar.

When Ohm had first heard several weeks ago that the London Choir was to sing at an AIDS benefit tonight, he had taken a public tour of the Albert Hall. His questions to worm out the facts he needed to know were hidden among innocuous inquiries from others in the group.

The interior of the Hall is a plush auditorium. At one end behind and above the stage is the great organ. With 10,000 pipes it is perhaps the largest and finest in the world. The oval arena in front of the stage platform provides floor seating. Circling the arena are the amphitheatre stalls, then the loggia boxes, then the gallery. Below the roof, 135 fibreglass discs called diffusers hang to create almost perfect acoustics. The colour scheme of the auditorium is maroon and stone.

"Where is the royal box?" someone had asked.

The tour group was then standing on the platform stage. The guide pointed back across the arena toward door No. 6, the main entrance.

"Grand tier boxes 27 and 28 make up part of the royal suite," she replied. "It is reached through a small entrance to the northwest."

"When did the Hall convert to electric light?" Ohm asked.

"It was installed throughout the building in 1897. Electricity had been partially wired in a few years before that."

"How was the Hall heated in the early days?" Ohm pressed.

"By steam. A tunnel used to take warm air to all levels of the Hall back then. In a minute we'll tour the ring route behind the stage, and I'll show you where the entrance is, lower down under the arena on yet another level. There is a gents' toilet under entrance No. 9, which is over there."

The guide was pointing toward the west entrance.

"Behind the toilet is a door that leads to the old heating tunnel in the basement."

"What's it used for now?" Jack Ohm asked.

"Mostly cabling and TV equipment. The BBC has a control room with millions of pounds' worth of electronics up on the balcony near the picture gallery."

As they toured the ring route behind the stage, Ohm took note of the orange walls, the black ceiling, the square lights in the roof—and how to get to the lower level.

When they finally descended to the darker corridor underneath the arena, Ohm asked the guide for water to take a heart pill. He was immediately directed toward the gents' toilet under entrance No. 9.

The lower level was the same as the one above except the ceiling was orange. The door to the men's toilet opened into a room lined with sinks; the door opposite that to a room of urinals. A third door across the urinal room was securely locked. Ohm knew this gave access to the air tunnel which he was working into his plan.

One of the members of the group was a fireman from Ohio. His wife adored classical music and had dragged him along for the tour. He was downright bored.

"What are the fire precautions you take in this fancy place?" he asked. His dumpy wife scowled menacingly at him.

"The main fire panel is at door No. 1, the artists' entrance by which you all came in. That's to the southeast. I'll show you the fireman's cabin under 'K' stalls by the north main entrance, door No. 6. Incidentally, behind the back row of 'K' stalls is the foundation stone Queen Victoria laid on May 20, 1867."

In the fireman's cabin was a cabinet within which was kept a number of keys. It also housed a fire alarm panel.

"Don't you have a master key?" the Ohio man asked, as if Britain had yet to come into the twentieth century.

"Yes," the guide said curtly. "It's that one there. Our electrician has one too."

"Looks too modern to get you into the old heating tunnel," Ohm commented.

The guide frowned at him for questioning her statement.

"That's the tunnel key," she said, pointing toward an old-fashioned one on a ring.

As they walked back through the auditorium toward
the artists' entrance, Ohm noticed the numbers on each
pair of opposite entrance doors all added up to unlucky
thirteen. His mind was always picking up on details like
that. And soon to be true, he'd thought.

All that, however, was weeks ago, and tonight was the
night of his plan.

Earlier this evening Ohm had lifted a security pass
from one of the ushers, stealing it in the crush of people
streaming through the foyer. Warning signs were everywhere announcing that patrons would be searched for
their own protection. The signs made Jack Ohm smile.

Just before the concert began he had gone to the
fireman's cabin to report that a battery had been removed from one of the backup emergency lights. When
the fireman's back was turned Ohm had stolen the master key and the old-fashioned one for the tunnel. In fact
he had taken the battery himself for his own purposes.

Once the concert was underway and both the ring
route backstage and the lower level were deserted, he
had retrieved the Coke canister from its hiding place in
the basement and taken it along with the battery into the
urinal room of the gents' toilet under entrance No. 9.

After checking to make sure the coast was clear, Jack
had unlocked and disappeared through the air tunnel
door. Once inside he'd locked himself in.

Now, crouched on the boards that were slung over the
concrete floor, Ohm took a look around the tunnel passage.

It was stifling hot in here, with only a single lightbulb
burning. Pipes and wires, cobweb-covered, ran off down
the tunnels circumnavigating the building and rising to
upper levels. The dust made him want to sneeze.

Satisfied with what he saw, Ohm unscrewed the top of
the false Coca-Cola container to expose the thermite
packed around the Teflon core inside. He unstrapped the
watch from his wrist which was in fact a miniature timing
device, and set the clock for thirty minutes to twelve. He
ran two wire leads from the stolen battery, then removed
the glass face of the watch and attached one wire to the
minute hand. Next he carefully glued a short wire unconnected to the power source to the metal stroke on the
timepiece that marked twelve o'clock.

Sweating now from the heat and the thrill of his mission, Ohm pulled some steel wool from his pocket and tied the remaining lead from the battery and the short wire glued to the twelve stroke to opposite sides of the wool, which he then buried deep in the thermite pack. Finished, Ohm sat back on his heels to admire his handiwork.

In half an hour when the minute hand struck twelve o'clock, the timer would complete the electrical circuit from the battery, sparking a current through the steel wool and igniting the thermite pack. The resulting heat would depolymerize the Teflon core into poisonous gas which would spread out through the heating ducts to kill every gay and closet queen in the Hall. Plus all their disgusting supporters.

Pleased, Ohm unlocked the door and peeked into the gents' room.

No one around.

Grinning, he left the tunnel and locked the door behind him.

## 8:56 p.m.

When the Commissioner's office called, Rand's line was busy. She was on the telephone to Commander Richard Orr, making arrangements to call out the Flying Squad, the Anti-Terrorist Squad, and elite D11. Then she requested a car.

When the package was delivered downstairs by courier service, the Detective Chief Superintendent had already left the Yard. She was on the radio phone speaking to Special Branch, who were guarding the Prince and Princess of Wales at the Royal Albert Hall.

The note inside the package read: "Bye, bye, baby. You're not smart enough for me."

With it was a picture clipped from a book of the anacardiaceous shrub, *rhus radicans*.

Poison ivy.

## 9:01 p.m.

The Flying Squad is the eighth branch of Scotland Yard's Criminal Investigation Division. Formed at the end of the First World War, it is known in-house as C8, the "go anywhere, nick anyone" force. It consists of teams of detectives with skilled drivers specially trained for high-speed city chases. Over the years Cockney rhyming slang has dubbed the Flying Squad the "Sweeney Todd", shortened to "the Sweeney".

Jack Ohm heard the C8 sirens as he left the Hall through door No. 6. Their wailing was coming from Knightsbridge to the east. He quickly walked down Kensington Gore, turning right into Exhibition Road.

Just as Jack disappeared from sight the first Met cops arrived to take up stations sealing off the Royal Albert Hall.

## 9:03 p.m.

Rushing to the scene down Victoria Street, up Grosvenor Place, along Knightsbridge, Hilary Rand had several serious decisions to make.

The initial dilemma was easy because she was a traditionalist. The future King and Queen must come first so she radioed the royal box. Within seconds, Special Branch officers had pulled two curtains across the corridor separating boxes 27 and 28 from the royal reception area and were leading the couple out of the Hall to safety by the royal entrance.

The real conundrum, however, had two interlinking parts: what to do with the power and with the audience?

If Jack The Bomber had set up an explosive device, was he using the Hall's power in some personal way? For the AIDS clinic bombing he had tapped the current flowing from the London Grid. Therefore, shut off the power and that might shut down the device. Plus leave the audience getting jumpy in the dark.

Should she or shouldn't she evacuate the Albert Hall?

If the Hall was sealed the Bomber might be trapped inside. Moving the audience out would surely allow him to escape. In her policeman's heart, Rand desperately wanted to trap him, but she knew the risk was just too great.

Picking up the car phone, she ordered the Hall evacuated by emergency-power lights.

## 9:11 p.m.

As Jack Ohm waited on the eastbound Piccadilly Line platform of the South Kensington Underground Station he asked someone the time.

"Ten past nine," a tall Kenyan said.

Less than fifteen minutes to detonation, the Bomber thought, smiling to himself.

## 9:12 p.m.

The car squealed into Albert Court and screeched to a halt.

In through the artists' entrance over the years have come many important people in the history of the Royal Albert Hall: Wagner, Verdi, Chevalier, Menuhin, Boult, Sargeant, Sinatra, Bernstein, Laver, Mohammad Ali, and Detective Chief Superintendent Rand. A hundred people in choir robes were streaming out.

The C8 Sergeant who met her at the door informed her the Hall had been searched that afternoon with Labrador dogs trained to sniff out explosives and had come up clean.

"Then he's employing another method," Rand shot back. She was thinking about the water, steam, and electricity Jack had used for the AIDS clinic attack.

"Any flowers delivered tonight?" she asked a Hall employee sitting near the door.

"Lots," he replied.

"Where are they now?"

"Down in front of the stage."

"How did they get there? What's the procedure?"

"There's a security check here before anyone goes backstage. Unless you've got a pass you don't get in. Flowers are delivered and left here at the No. 1 door. We notify the stage manager who notifies the performers. They come down and fetch the flowers. Of course people in the audience sometimes go up and give a single rose to—"

Rand turned back to the C8 Sergeant as the stage manager arrived. Around them surged the pandemonium of evacuation.

"One bouquet reads 'Love Jack'," the manager said. "Is that the one you mean?"

The Flying Squad cop nodded and introduced Rand.

"Ignore the flowers," Hilary said. "Which way to the sewer connection?"

"There are ten men down there already with dogs," the Sergeant replied.

The man at the door who Rand had just questioned about the flowers called out through the din, "Fireman's on the line to say his master key is gone."

"Damn," the DC Supt cursed, turning back sharply to the stage manager.

"List all the ways someone can move around this building."

## 9:18 p.m.

As the tube train rattled northeast, Ohm glanced at the wristwatch worn by the woman sitting next to him.

Six minutes left, he thought, then laughed out loud.

The woman got up and moved to a seat further down the carriage.

## 9:19 p.m.

Assume Jack got in somehow and planted something deadly somewhere, Hilary thought. What might that deadly something be?

It can't be a dynamite bomb since the dogs did not detect it.

The electricity's shut off so if that's his source of destruction we're now safe.

What does that leave?

Gas, she thought.

Turning to the stage manager she asked, "How would you distribute poisonous gas throughout the Hall?"

Blanching, he replied, "I suppose by the tunnels originally used to heat the building. They connect with all levels."

"How do we get to them?"

"There's only one entrance. Through the mens' toilet on the lower level beneath door No. 9."

"Is it locked?"

"Yes."

"Where's the key?"

"In the fireman's cabin."

"Get it," Rand ordered as she turned to several PCs who were ushering people out. "You, you, and you. Come with me."

Just then someone called out above the noise, "The Commissioner of Police is on the telephone. He wants Detective Chief Superintendent Rand."

"She can't be reached. She's in the Hall," Rand yelled back. "All right. Let's move," she said.

## 9:21 p.m.

Jack Ohm changed trains at King's Cross. Standing on the platform waiting for his connection to arrive, he casually dropped the old-fashioned tunnel and master keys in a rubbish bin.

"What time is it?" he asked the person to his left.

Three minutes to go, he thought on receiving the reply.

## 9:22 p.m.

A Flying Squad Inspector was standing at one of the urinals taking a piss when Rand burst into the room.

"Wrong loo, Hilary," he said, zipping up his fly.

The other cops and the stage manager were close behind.

"Tunnel key's missing from the fireman's cabin," the manager said.

"Force that door," Rand ordered.

The first PC hit it hard with his shoulder but the door wouldn't budge.

"Find an axe!" Rand snapped. "Let's get the lead out!"

Beyond the door the timer clicked to one minute before the hour.

The two electrical leads were now less than a millimetre from closing the circuit.

## 9:24 p.m.

All dead, Ohm thought, his penis stiff in his pants. Nine out of ten male killers, they say, have a hard-on when they do it.

Splinters flew everywhere as the lock smashed under the bite of the blade and the door was kicked open.

Rand slipped through the aperture and yanked the wires from the thermite.

Two seconds later the steel wool sparked in her hand.

## 9:52 p.m.

Jack Ohm crossed the graveyard and entered the Wax Museum.

Elaine Teeze would be pleased with him, so he'd demand more time.

Lots more time.

# Boogeyman

"Tell me about your mother," Chandler said.

Deborah sighed. "She suffered, Zinc. When I was very young I used to sleep in her room. My father would get drunk and force himself on her. I'd end up crying in her arms all night. She once told me she suffered so God would let her into heaven, so that He would forgive her for the wrong she'd done. She used to tell Saxon he had haemophilia for the same reason. That's why she used to strip him and search for signs of bleeding. To her that would have been a message from God."

"Deborah, if Saxon really didn't have the disease as you said, what was the effect of your mother's actions on him?"

"I can only guess. Do you know what parasitosis is?"

Zinc shook his head.

"Creeping delusions," Lane said. "The false belief that you are infested with bugs. Some people slash themselves with razors to let the imaginary vermin escape."

"Saxon suffered that?"

"Uh huh. At about the time my father died. He thought his head was infested with worms. Through the wall I could hear him screaming and crying in his room."

"Then what happened?"

"The delusions seemed to stop the day my father shot himself."

Chandler frowned. Shot himself in the garage where he used to beat Saxon, he thought.

"Parasitosis often occurs," Deborah added, "in people who suffer a bad reaction to a drug such as cocaine or who suffer some additional form of psychosis."

315

"Like schizophrenia?"

Deborah nodded.

"How is it treated?" Chandler asked.

"With a tranquillizer called pimozide. The doctor gave my half-brother some the day my father died."

"What happened to you after both your parents were gone?"

"I was put into an exceptional foster home. The same one from which the twins ran away. None of my mother's money was left by then. My father had drunk it all. It was my foster parents who put me through college."

"Good people," Zinc said.

"The best," she replied.

"So that's when Saxon and Rika joined the rock commune as they testified at the trial? And Ghoul grew out of that?"

"Right. Fronting a rock band had always been Rika's dream. The twins had already formed two stage personalities to assume. Erika Zann for her, and Axel Crypt for him. Her wish came true."

The Gates Of Hell was a rock theatre in Camden Town. It had been a music hall during the 1880s when the Ripper roamed the Whitechapel streets to the southeast. Variety shows had used its stage in the twenties, thirties, and forties, then for the next twenty-five years it had been a cinema. Now it was converted to a replica of the *Théâtre du Grand Guignol* in Paris.

The kids in the seats around them were like the crowd that attends a midnight showing of *The Rocky Horror Picture Show*. Most of them were male, for there is nothing more dreadful in this world than the fantasy life of an adolescent boy. There were ghouls, warlocks, vampires, werewolves, and vicious monsters. There were succubi, incubi, raw-heads and bloody-bones. There were boogeys and fiends and hell-hags and savage, brutish demons. The place was a hangout for the children of the damned.

Watching them Chandler felt suddenly, inexorably alone. He had always thought that we are born alone into this life and that any human relationships are but a necessary illusion to keep us relatively sane on the short road to death. It was easy to say that this was a theatre both on and off the stage, but Chandler knew in his heart that it was much more than that. Dark hints of paranoia lurked in some of the eyes.

If everything in horror has a psychological source, he thought, do threats that appear to come from without not actually come from within? Of all our emotional baggage is horror not the feeling that most responds to that which in reality really isn't there? To embrace horror fully as these kids are doing, is that not to begin to break with reality? And will the final step for some not be the slavering, vengeful fury of a Saxon Hyde?

But even as Zinc thought these thoughts he perceived there was something more. For each of these kids both fed on and provided fuel for the fantasy life of the others. Psychiatrists he had worked with called such symbiosis *folie à deux*, when two or more people closely associated come to share delusional ideas. In other words, when insanity passes from one person to another.

That happened in the Manson Family, Chandler thought. Had it also happened within The Ghouls? To Saxon and Sid and Jack and Reuben and any of the others? And had it carried over into the rock band Ghoul?

Watching these kids, what frightened him most was just how closely his own attitude seemed to parallel theirs. Hopelessness. The cancer of the soul.

As the lights within the theatre dimmed, Zinc reached out and took Deborah firmly by the hand.

Unnoticed, leaning against the wall ten rows back, two men from Scotland Yard were also here to watch the show.

## *10:03 p.m.*

The Ghoul was stitching dead skin in The Well, thinking soon it would be time to go get Hilary Rand, when he shot to his feet and let out a frightful scream. The black cat jumped and skittered behind the Iron Maiden. The vacant eyes around him did not blink.

The Ghoul had moved the Poe mirror here on the day he'd abandoned his basement room. All his inspirational pictures, however, he'd left pinned to the walls. No need to go back and take them down once the Old Ones were here, for then the world would belong to them and there'd be no fear of detection. In the meantime he'd put together a different collage for The Well.

Now as he looked in the mirror by the pulsing red light, The Ghoul saw his forehead was wormed with tunnel-bumps underneath the skin. The parasite tracks grew in length every second.

In disgust The Ghoul went to find a razor.

## 10:05 p.m.

The theatre was completely dark except for the exit signs. The whir of the curtain rising was the only sound as a tall, lean, masked figure wearing shabby clothes approached centre stage with a lighted candle in his hand. The mask was grotesque and satyr-like, and almost bald.

The hunched-over figure climbed a set of dark-shadowed, rickety stairs toward a platform built eight feet above the stage, while the audience puffed an assortment of dope, enthralled.

The platform resembled a peak-roofed garret room. The set evoked a sense of barrenness and neglect, the attic furnished with a narrow iron bedstead and a dingy washstand, an iron music rack and one old-fashioned chair. The back wall of the set contained a curtained window looking out over a black panorama beyond. Sheet music was scattered about the attic floor.

The figure reached the platform, setting the candle down on the washstand before he removed an old violin from a moth-eaten case. This he put to his chin as he picked up the bow.

When the first note exploded throughout the hall like an amplified torture scream, the crowd—Zinc and Deborah too—jumped in unison. The screech of the electric violin was like a thousand plastic forks and jagged fingernails being scraped along a blackboard.

Chandler braced himself against the next strike of the bow, while the old musician cast an exaggerated and startled glance back toward the window. As a light night breeze came gusting in to flutter the curtains like sails, the shutters began to rattle and the violinist recoiled with haste.

In a flash and without warning he hit the strings again. Chandler's teeth chattered and he covered his ears as all hell then broke loose on stage.

The wind blew harder, the shutters banged, and the candle wavered wildly. The musician's play grew more cacophonous, the shrieking violin swelling into a chaotic babel of noise. The player began screaming in terrible anguish and fear.

Zinc sensed the rising level of agitation in the hall. A youth down front near the speakers flew to his feet, dancing like a demented puppet, arms stiff at his sides. His head pistoned back and forth as if he were banging it against a wall.

Terrified, the violinist froze, listening. The audience all leaned forward at once in their seats. Then the musician began to shake as if from a nervous shock, and whirled once more to face the curtained window at the back of the stage.

From out beyond the shutters came a low, haunting wail of sexual ecstasy. It grew in pitch, then converted to a bone-jarring fuzztone before it died.

The musician curled over his violin and began to rend the hall with the weirdest playing Chandler had ever endured. Its impact was like a barber's razor stropping at his nerves. Struggling to resist the effect of this aural assault, Zinc suddenly realized just how exhausted he really was. Making love with Deborah had brought him second wind—but that had just run out.

Frantic, delirious, hysterical: the fevered pitch of the music went up and up and up. Louder and louder, wilder and wilder mounted the whining and shrieking of the electric violin. The old man was now continually glancing at the curtained window. He played as if this noise was a desperate attempt to ward off or drown something out.

"Lovecraft!" Deborah shouted in Chandler's ear. "Ghoul's act is based on 'The Music of Erich Zann'!"

Then, shockingly, light exploded behind the garret wall. It was revealed to be nothing more than a transparent theatre scrim. Green laser holograms danced behind it in a three-dimensional orgy of obscene night-gaunts and other monstrous lascivious things, all swirling about in a chaos of lightning and smoke.

From out beyond the window came a hellish scream that mocked the single shrill note now held by the electric violin. The curtains blew in on a howling wind that sprang up in all this madness, sweeping the papers off the floor out into the audience. The shutters slammed to a rock bass beat against the window frame. The candle snuffed out.

Now there was just the silhouette of the tortured violinist against this hologram backdrop of cavorting alien fiends. Then, wrenching a gasp from the audience, a hell-hag harpy, half woman, half luminous skeleton and grinning skull, burst through the scrim and clawed at the man, tearing his face off as the speakers barked out an amplified *riiiiiiipppppp*!

All sound in the theatre stopped as if cut by a knife.

The lights went up on stage as a waterfall of blood rained down from above the curtain.

Soaked red, the harpy woman whirled with a snarl and lunged like a jungle cat towards the crowd. Her lips pulled back from her teeth as she yelled, "Do you wanna rock and roll?"

The audience shouted back a resounding "Yeaaaaah!" as the rest of Ghoul walked on stage and tore the crowd apart with metal mayhem akin to the sound of a chainsaw eating through a human skull.

"That's her!" Deborah cried. "That's Rika Hyde!"

Chandler found himself staring at the same woman he had seen onstage at The Id club in Vancouver. Except that now her hair was short.

The violin player turned to reveal the face behind the ripped-off mask as he slung a bass guitar over one scrawny shoulder. He was the bone-rack in the codpiece who had performed at The Id as Axel Crypt.

"So our boogeyman tonight is your half-brother!" Zinc shouted back.

But Deborah frowned, shook her head and screamed in his ear, "I've no idea who that is! But he's *not* Saxon Hyde!"

# Wax Museum

*Wednesday, January 29, 12:15 a.m.*

Backstage at The Gates Of Hell was the usual groupie scene. The band had disappeared down a corridor that led to the throne room of horror-rock kings and queens. Between here and there were checkpoint barriers manned by indifferent roadies or hangers-on who checked the crowd out according to previous instructions. Luscious young girls in a daze who couldn't wait to get laid by a star were led down the corridor straight to the inner realm. The rest of the crowd—photographers, rock-rag writers, fans without the necessary T&A—cooled their heels at the barriers waiting to be ushered into the party room. The party room was a small cramped space with beer on ice and a table spread with cold cuts. Helium balloons were taped to the walls, each one painted with the band's logo—a guitar fashioned from a human skull with insane red-veined eyes. Here the crowd would wait a whole lot longer until the group deigned to come down to meet its fans.

When the Scotland Yard detectives reached the door that led backstage, a beefy security guard put his arm across the frame. "No one gets back without a pass, governor," he said.

McAllaster flashed his Yard ID and pushed the arm away.

Backstage, he crashed the barriers and moved down the corridor toward the throne room at the end.

He was in no mood to waste time with a lot of shit.

## 12:17 a.m.

Zinc knew he'd fucked it.

The alley outside the stage door was also crammed with kids. Some wore the tour T-shirts of the last metal-mongers to have passed through town, the images all S&M and the subjugation of women. A few had bones through their noses or rings stuck through their cheeks, or hanks of hair hanging from the pockets of their trousers. Leather jackets and steel-capped Doc Martins were the accepted uniform. Chains and studded belts glinted in the moonlight. Marijuana smoke killed the stink of the rubbish from across the lane.

As Zinc and Deborah waited for Rika to come out, Chandler turned the twins' death plot over in his mind.

Carol Tate had told him that Saxon Hyde made a trip from London to Vancouver late last September. Was that a scouting excursion to get the lay of the land? By then Rosanna was living at the penthouse suite in North Vancouver. Thwarted at the probate trial from getting their rightful share of Enoch Keate's estate, the twins must have determined to get it another way.

Did Saxon find out that Rosanna hired models from Fantasy Escort Service to play her sexual games, and that she was then quarantined with glandular fever? Did he also discover that Ray Hengler was both boss of the escort service *and* a man with rock video aspirations as a way to launder dirty money from his drugs and porno films? That Hengler ran much of the sleaze in the town was common underground knowledge, plus he was up before the courts on a fuck-film charge.

Okay, so Saxon made contact with Hengler and offered him Ghoul as a money-laundering prospect. By then he had been replaced in the band by Codpiece, who had assumed his stage name of Axel Crypt. Was that because Saxon needed more time to put the plan together? Or was it all Rika's idea, with Saxon as her yes-man? From everything Deborah had told him, she was the dominant twin. Had The Ghouls club of Saxon's youth become the rock band Ghoul, and was Rika now the dominatrix of all the boys?

That would fit, he thought.

All right, so then what happens? Hengler tells Saxon let's do it, and the twins move into action. A date to bring Ghoul to Vancouver is set for January 1986. Rika has seen a doctor in London on referral by the American Embassy. She knows she has gallstones. Well in advance of the concert date she goes to Mexico where they are removed. Then in January she flies to Vancouver to join Saxon and the rest of Ghoul, bringing the gallstones with her.

Sometime that Saturday morning after the concert at The Id, Saxon and Rika make a surprise call on Rosanna. They enter the building by the door the painters have left open and are unseen by the workmen who are either taking a break or in the manager's suite. Wearing gloves, they get Rosanna to let them in. Did she think it was Reid Driver, the model, at the door? They tie her down on the bed and torture her with strychnine, dose by dose. What did they hope to get from that—the doctor's stolen medical file on Enoch Keate? The one that showed he was mentally unfit when he signed that last will? Rosanna would have obtained it somehow to cover her own tracks, then kept it as a sword over Ronald Fletcher's head should he ever weaken in resolve to keep their fraud and her father's murder a secret. Now the twins have the file to use in blackmailing Fletcher.

Saxon and Rika then kill Rosanna and destroy her body with an acid bath. Rika, disguised as Rosanna, leaves the penthouse for some reason at 2:30 a.m. and is seen by the painters. Was she going to get the acid carboys to bring up?

The gallstones are added to the bath once the body has corroded since they will not dissolve. The twins no doubt got that idea from the case of John Haigh, the forties' killer on show in Madame Tussaud's Exhibition. The gallstones are a red herring to give them time to complete their plan.

Rosanna caught infectious mononucleosis shortly after she arrived on the West Coast. Few people in Vancouver saw her often. Rika is similar enough to pass herself off as her cousin/half-sister in a dash to the airport. So twelve hours after the twins killed Keate, her body now dissolved and Ray Hengler lured to the penthouse as a framed suspect to distract the police, she takes a cab to the terminal and is once more seen leaving by the painters. No need for a passport to travel from Canada to the

States. And that's why her hair at the concert tonight was cut so short.

The result of the twins' deception is that the cops waste a lot of time wrongly identifying the victim and building a case against Hengler, meanwhile giving Saxon and Rika time to steal a fortune.

Rika masking as Rosanna flies to Newport where she confronts Ronald Fletcher with the stolen medical file. It's proof the lawyer was involved in fraud concerning Enoch's will and points a finger at him being a party to the old man's death. Fletcher already has business problems of his own. This could be the last straw. So Fletcher gives Rika access to Rosanna's fortune banked in Switzerland. He also obtains a false passport for her with him as guarantor, as Carol Tate had hinted in her note left last night at Zinc's hotel.

Rika travels to Switzerland, then on to London with Rosanna's money. The gallstone ruse, as planned, has left the North Vancouver RCMP still trying to figure out who the penthouse victim is. Rika had stretched out on Rosanna's bed after the heiress was dead so the singer's hair would further confuse the cops and seem to indicate her as the dissolved body. Meanwhile the twins are gaining time.

Some of Rosanna's money obviously was up on stage tonight. Holograms are high-tech and very expensive to make. A first-class hologram studio rents for $5000 a day. The show at The Gates Of Hell was two hours of dazzling special effects light years advanced from their previous gig at The Id. Rosanna Keate no doubt had financed Ghoul's rise to fame with her life.

The final piece of the puzzle, however, greatly bothered Zinc.

That Rika and Saxon had plotted last night's kidnapping of "Rosanna" Chandler was certain. Saxon had masqueraded as this Sewer Killer who was terrorizing London, and Rika had played the role of the heiress as random victim. It was the final scene to wind down their plot. If Rika was later questioned about what went on in Vancouver, she would say simply that the RCMP were wrong. Hair cannot be perfectly matched and millions of people suffer from gallstones. Without more, that was the end of the case. Particularly now that Ronald Fletcher was gone.

But what really disturbed Zinc was the fact that Saxon fit his new role *too well.* From what Chandler had read of the Sewer Killer in the London papers, this maniac's psychology *was* Saxon Hyde.

Even more disturbing, however, was the knowledge that he'd fucked it. For did it not follow from the evidence now come to light that Ray Hengler was not involved in Rosanna Keate's death? And if the promoter was therefore imprisoned unjustly as Burke Hood feared, was he not stabbed as an indirect result of Zinc stepping over the line? That *would* mean his job.

Zinc could not get around the fact that Hengler was being watched at the time the heiress must have been killed. The call asking Hengler to come to Rosanna's later that Saturday morning, plus his presence at the scene as confirmed by the lobby painters were silly moves to make if the guy was involved in her death. The finding of his wallet beside the bed was just too pat. The glove smear suggested a plant, and Rika could have stolen it back at the club as Hengler's lawyer said. Why was nothing else—like fingerprints—found to connect him to the suite? Zinc had been a cop long enough to know it didn't mesh.

That's what happens, Chandler thought, when you let personal motives interfere with your—

Deborah grabbed his arm. "That's her," she said.

Zinc turned from the stage door which the alley kids were watching to see an old cleaning woman leave the building by a side exit.

"How do you know that's Rika?"

"I recognize her walk. She moves on the balls of her feet. Now what, Zinc?"

"I follow her."

"*We* follow her you mean."

## *12:18 a.m.*

A pretty sixteen-year-old girl had pulled down one side of her top to let Axel Crypt autograph her breast when Sergeant Scot McAllaster and his backup stepped through the door. Crypt was now wearing a black silk robe and a spiked headdress that made him look like a Zulu chief. "Get outa here," he said as the two men walked in.

"Scotland Yard," McAllaster said, flashing his ID.

He pointed at the girl and ordered, "You. Be gone."

She hesitated just long enough to see the look in his eye, then tucked her breast away half-autographed and left the dressing room.

"Let's talk, Mr Hyde," the Scotsman said.

The bass player smiled and shook his Zulu head.

"Wrong guy," the American answered. "I'm not who you want."

McAllaster stared hard in return. He didn't need to speak.

"I replaced Saxon Hyde in the band last September. We're of similar build. They gave me his stage name for continuity."

"Where's Hyde now?"

Again a shake of the head, this time bemused. "Help with your inquiries, huh? I've seen this gig before. Jack Hawkins in *Gideon of Scotland Yard*, right? Sorry, I don't rat on friends."

The Highlander's voice was very low when he replied, "These are troubled times, laddie. You hurt us, and we'll hurt you."

McAllaster turned to his backup and said, "Leave us for a moment."

The cop glanced from one to the other, unsure, then did as he was ordered.

"Close the door," the Scotsman said as the man stepped out of the room.

The moment the lock clicked shut McAllaster grabbed Crypt by the throat, hurling him against the wall with all the power in his massive frame. The musician slammed into the plaster so hard that the ceiling fixture shook. McAllaster whacked his forearm up under the guitarist's chin, nailing him back against the wall so the tips of his toes barely touched the ground. With his free hand the Highlander grasped the choking man by the balls, and gave them half a twist as his face closed in to meet the rocker eye-to-eye.

"Talk, you fuckin' shit-arse, or you'll never sing bass again."

The door to the hall whipped open as he released the man in a crumpled heap.

"Everything all right, Sarge?" the backup inquired.

"Aye. Mr Crypt was just asking if we would allow him to tell us everything he knows."

## 12:41 a.m.

The Commissioner of Police was a political man. One did not rise to the position he held without knowing how to play a situation to one's advantage. He had therefore converted the 10:00 p.m. press conference, the one called originally to announce the sacking of Rand, into a "The-Yard-takes-care-of-London" celebration over the saving of the Royal Albert Hall.

Meanwhile, Rand was still at the site of the attempted crime, personally directing the hunt for evidence. Scot McAllaster reached her there by radio telephone.

"Have you got a coat?" he said. That was Yard-speak to intimate an arrest.

"Who's the knock off?" Hilary asked, her nerves tensing.

"The man we thought was Saxon Hyde isn't," McAllaster said. "A new bloke took his place as Axel Crypt last autumn. But the real Hyde is still in the city. He's in the process of moving from a cellar room in the East End to a North London mortuary. The cellar room is close to one end of the sewer route on the computer disc that ends at the Mayfair suite."

"Where's this mortuary?" Rand asked.

The Scotsman told her.

"That's near the start of the 'wild route' that ends at the Albert Hall. Good show, Scot."

"What do you want me to do?"

"Get a warrant for that cellar room and toss the place. I'll seal off the mortuary and meet you there."

"Don't use the Yard computer," McAllaster warned.

## 12:45 a.m.

There are a hundred graveyards within a nine-mile radius of central London. Most of these have at least one mortuary.

Before 1832 when Kensal Green became the first garden cemetery, the dead were either laid to rest in the local churchyard or interred in one of the many *private* burial grounds. That was a time of drunken gravediggers and second-hand coffins, of illegal exhumations and nauseating smells. As Dickens wrote of the period, "Rot, mildew, and dead citizen formed the uppermost scent in the city."

When the 1830s and '40s brought the cholera epidemics
and a population explosion, Parliament responded with a
number of Burial Acts. These, however, were not finally
rationalized until 1972, and in all this legislative mess
several of the original sites remained in private hands.
Like the one that Zinc and Deborah now watched Rika
enter.

Harsh, stark moonlight shone down on the deserted
graveyard. Pressed in upon by silver-sheened and soot-
stained buildings, it appeared forgotten by all except
those who lived nearby and stared down into it from
smoky upper windows. The tombstones were lopsided,
illegible, or broken. Rust peeled off the spiked gate and
iron fence as did bark from the withered trees within. A
new sign over the entrance read *Necropolis Wax Museum*.

The old Gothic mortuary stood just inside the gate. Its
walls of grey brick with stone dressings were choked with
dead ivy, its gables crumbling. Mounted in alcoves around
the walls were cemetery urns.

From across the mews fronting the entrance gate, Zinc
and Deborah watched Rika reach behind one of the urns.
Then she went to a side door near the back of the
building, only to return to the urn before going inside.

"Wait here," Chandler whispered.

"Where are you going?" Lane asked.

"Inside to find Saxon. To have a talk with him."

"You must be kidding. That's got to be illegal."

"I don't have time to play this any other way. Thirty-
odd hours and I'm out of a job."

"But you're not armed."

"No. I'm in Britain."

"What if he is?"

"I'll take that chance."

"What if Saxon and Rika aren't alone inside that place?"

"Just stay here."

"Don't treat me like a child, Zinc. There's as much of
my life tied up in this as there is of yours. I'm going in
too. And you can't stop me."

## 12:46 a.m.

The Ghoul was in a rage. Where had the time gone?

Already the tunnels burrowed by the grave worms
through his brain were pulsing with cosmic winds gusting

in from the gulfs between the stars. The city of R'lyeh
was surfacing from the bottom of the sea, the tomb of
Cthulhu ready for the ritual of blood to set him free.

How had this happened? Legrasse had not been stopped.
By now Rand should be his captive, his blood sacrifice.
The altar and squid-faced idol were ready, but where was
the time? He had to find a victim fast while the stars
were right.

"Let me out!" he screamed.

## 12:47 a.m.

Zinc and Deborah stepped out of the shadows and ran
across the mews.

Lane found a key behind the urn and handed it to
Chandler.

They entered the side door.

## 12:48 a.m.

Jack Ohm was surprised when a second warning light
flashed on the computer console within that steel-walled
room which was his mind. Elaine had told him to expect
Rika Hyde, and indeed her figure had just passed across
the screen, recorded by the cameras upstairs that watched
the entrance hall inside the mortuary door.

So who in hell was this who'd now tripped the electric
eye?

"Elaine," he called out tensely.

Within seconds the black silhouette of Teeze was standing outside his door. "What's wrong?" she asked. "Let
me in."

Ohm punched the backup release button to slide back
the panel. He'd not had time to fix the faulty main
switch.

"Who's that?" he whispered, staring at the screen. His
mental computer had automatically switched in the security system upstairs.

Elaine Teeze glanced at the image.

"Rika must have been followed," she said. "Or they
figured out the computer."

"What do you mean 'figured out the computer'?"

"Jack, it's fallen into the hands of the police."

"The police!" he said, shocked, his voice rising shrilly.

"A friend of mine dropped it."

"You gave it to someone else?"

"Shut up, Jack. Let me think."

"But you didn't ask me! We didn't discuss that!"

"*We* didn't have to," she snapped. "*I* run this show."

Jack Ohm was furious over what he had just been told. No wonder there was nothing on the radio about mass killings at the Royal Albert Hall. The police had studied the computer with his planned route on it for how long? That, plus the flowers, let them put it all together. Jesus Christ, he could have been caught in the act tonight.

"You bitch," Ohm said, glaring at the black silhouette framed in the doorway. On the wall screen beside it, the image from the camera upstairs panned as Zinc and Deborah moved down the hall.

"You think you can use me any way you want, don't you? Well, you can't, Elaine. That's the last job I—"

Without warning a circuit suddenly blew in the electronic hardware to Jack Ohm's left as the steel wall that was the right edge of his mind bulged in surrealistically.

"Stop them!" Teeze commanded, her silhouette pointing at Zinc and Deborah on the screen.

In a panic Ohm reached out and punched another button.

Chandler and Lane could faintly hear music from somewhere far below. They were in a corridor no more than five feet wide, lined with heavy planks running parallel to the floor. At the far end of the hall was a room lit by candlelight. From what they could make out it looked like an embalming chamber for receiving corpses. They walked toward it.

The intruders were halfway down the hall when Jack Ohm punched the button two storeys below. Alternate planks from the wall to their left swung out to block the way. One caught Deborah in the stomach, knocking the wind out of her. Before Chandler could react, a heavy board to his right swung viciously on a spring and slammed the back of his head.

Everything went black.

## *12:49 a.m.*

As the black silhouette of Elaine Teeze passed the entrance to The Well, The Ghoul screamed at her, "Let me out! The stars! The stars are right! I must find a sacrifice!"

As the slurping worms sucked at the remnants of his brain and the stereo blared "Darling Be Home Soon" from *Slade Alive!*, The Ghoul picked up his chair made of human bones and hurled it at the woman.

The first police to arrive stopped three streets away. They set up an outer perimeter to cordon off the area, then waited for Hilary Rand and the equipment to arrive.

"The stupid cunt was followed," Elaine Teeze snarled. Her silhouette now stood framed in the doorway to Sid Jinks' black-walled room, shattered bones tied with leather thongs scattered about her feet. Jinks reached for his cutlery, grabbing the skinning knife.

"Come here," Teeze demanded, motioning him to the door. "Who's that?" she asked.

Sid looked out through the doorway and across the mouth of The Well into another room where a TV screen glowed. The image on the screen was of two people sprawled unconscious on a floor.

"Well, well, who do we have here?" he said, eyeing Deborah Lane's breasts and thighs.

"Do you know the man?"

"Yeah, I know the bloke. He's a Horseman from Vancouver. A cop, Elaine."

From out beyond the doorway came an unearthly, piercing scream. Elaine Teeze whirled as Sid Jinks moved to leave the room.

"No," she snapped.

"I want that girl."

"You can have both her and the cop as soon as they're softened up."

"Why can't I have them now?"

But she was gone, leaving Jinks staring at the black wall beside the door to his room, where he was planning to lavish his taxidermal skills on Deborah Lane.

*Gonna stuff and mount her tits and cunt at last,* he thought.

His penis hardened.

The Ghoul stalked Elaine Teeze around The Well, a leg bone held like a club in his hand.

"Come here," she said, backing toward the door beyond which was the TV screen. "I'll give you someone as your blood sacrifice. She's upstairs in the mortuary now. But first you must take care of them if I'm to let you out. The man's a cop, I'm told. A Horseman from Vancouver."

The Ghoul's eyes followed her pointing arm toward the TV screen.

"Legrasse," he whispered.

## 1:17 a.m.

When Chandler came around the first thing he did was throw up. Then a few seconds later his subconscious threw up too. The Mountie recoiled in horror as his eyes perceived large hunks of his stomach lining and intestines writhing on the floor. Then his hands began to shake out of control and tears ran down his cheeks.

He closed his eyes for a moment as if to then awake from a dream, but that only began a sickening vertigo that spun him slowly around and around as if he had drunk too much. Opening his eyes to vomit again, this time he threw up skinned snakes and slimy slugs that made him gag even more.

"Oh my God," Chandler moaned, his throat choked dry.

Now his muscles were infested with tiny spiders that crawled between the fibres or poked up as gooseflesh on the surface of his body. Lack of sleep in the past few days had drained his energy. In weary resignation he went to bury his face in his arm.

Zinc's gut, however, turned to ice when he saw the drop of blood. It had welled up from his elbow crease like a glistening ruby. He had seen drops like this on junkies who had just mainlined.

A sharp shiver shook him suddenly and rattled his teeth. Uncontrolled, his limbs reflexed to cover his freezing torso. Chandler looked down with surprise to find his body naked. In white paint someone had circled a three-ring bull's-eye over his heart.

As the implication of this sank in, his eyes pierced his body. Gone now was his skin, and gone were his muscles. His bare heart was exposed to the air all wattled and grey and diseased, the arteries leading away from it caked almost shut with white gunk. Each time the organ struggled to pump it bloated to bursting point, then as he gawked in disbelief it ripped and sprang a leak. Blood trickled down his abdomen as his genitals shrank until they completely disappeared.

When his mind heard a gunshot that wasn't there, Zinc threw himself to the floor. Scampering sideways like a crab he retreated into the darkness, as far away as he could go from the light of the single candle dripping a pool of wax on the stones. His shoulder struck a damp wall as he curled into a foetal ball. Then, totally overcome, he began to cry.

Great sobs racked his body as his emotions flowed out of control. At one delirious point he found himself calling for his mother.

A drug, he thought. Only a drug. Hold onto yourself . . . your self . . . self . . . no self . . . all one continuum . . .

Breathing out slowly, mesmerized, he examined his hand in the dark. He could barely see its outline, or what he *thought* its outline to be. For now his mind discerned an aura around his body, a shimmering flux of dull grey light where the atoms on the edge of his self crossed over to exchange with those in his surroundings.

No self, Chandler thought. I am non-existent.

The sudden infinite wonder of this realization made him feel elated. His world was reduced to a realm of light and shadow, of white and black, where nothing else mattered. He vaguely recalled a journey or quest in some far-off dimension, but of what possible consequence was that to him now? His body so tired, his mind so hollow, he wanted to drift away.

But something was scratching and grating his nerves—a noise from above. Irritated by this intrusion, Chandler slowly looked up.

In the beginning all he could make out by the light of the candle burning fifteen feet away was that he cowered shivering in a crouch on the cold stone floor. Then he noticed the steel shaft that jutted straight up to the ceiling, topped by a platform high above, thirty feet in the air. For a split second Chandler thought he remembered where he was—until the growing force of the drug hit him again.

Without warning his mind slipped as one side of the floor dropped away. All angles in the pit altered accordingly. The walls seemed to lean in and nothing was a square. Fact or drug? Zinc lost all perspective.

He threw up again.

Now each time he gained his feet, he fell back to the floor. The bricks around him had become living sentient things, breathing in and out as if synchronized to his heart.

"Yes . . . dead . . . I love . . . dead . . ." Karloff's voice scratched above.

Zinc could see that square head forming in his mind, all dead-white skin with eyelids heavy, a vision of scars, bolts, and concave brow.

Hallucinating. LSD. All in your mind, he thought. PCP mixed with cocaine too, perhaps.

Hot, cold, numb, burning—sparks and chills inside. His brain now an echo chamber that amplified the sounds down here and sent reverberations back from the lowest reaches of his subconscious mind.

No control, he thought. Can't stop hallucinating.

"You died last night."

Did I hear that with my ears or in my mind?

"Perfect awareness is perfect paranoia. I am listening. I am watching. I am everywhere."

No.

"I kill free will to create a free mind. Listen to me . . . listen to me . . . I am your Master, slave."

Chandler bit into his hand hard, focusing on the pain. His eyes jerked around this pit sunk deep beneath the mortuary building, thirty feet under the embalming room at ground level, trying to pierce the darkness.

Then suddenly he saw it, a door in the wall.

From high overhead more scratching was coming from the speakers.

Unable to gain his feet, Zinc crawled toward the door.

"Inner Sanctum," whispered the old phonograph record transferred to tape. A slow, sardonic voice floated down from above. "Welcome to the dark room of your own imagination."

A hand, his hand reached out toward the door.

*Squeeeeeeeek!* went the recording back above his shoulder as the massive portal groaned ajar on rusting hinges.

Then laughter, madman's laughter as Zinc Chandler crawled on hands and knees through the crack in the wall, the door closing by itself with gravity, the last words from the speakers, "Good night and pleasant dreams."

Blackness, only blackness, as far off Deborah screamed. . . .

Her cry was stifled by a voice that boomed and echoed up from somewhere far below.

"HOOOOOOOORSEMAAAAAN! Come to me! Shall we play The Game?"

## Part Four

# THE
# WELL

"Where lies the end
To this foul way?" I asked with weakening
    breath.
Thereon ahead I saw a door extend—
    The door to death.

—*Thomas Hardy*
    A WASTED ILLNESS

# Worms

Hilary Rand stood by the door to the van that contained
the mobile computer. The programme to coordinate the
assault was being run on the Home Office system and
radioed here. Anyone hacked into the Yard PNC would
not be aware of what was going on.

Basil Plimpton of Thames Water had been yanked out
of bed. He now paced beside Rand, a Styrofoam coffee
cup in his hand. When he spoke he still used his arms to
gesture so the liquid splashed around.

"The sewers around here are complicated," Plimpton
said. "The area was built up *after* the graveyard was in
use."

"They're on the maps, aren't they?"

"Yes," he replied.

"Then we have them covered."

Hilary glanced at the screen which showed the posi-
tions of all the officers underground. There were inner
and outer street cordons to seal off "the sterile area".
Forward and rear operational controls had been established. The Flying Squad, the SAS, and the Special Patrol Group were in use. A Met Police catering van had
arrived to provide food. They were brewing tea by the
gallon.

A Sergeant manning the mobile phone at the forward
operational control rang off. He turned to the DC Supt
and said, "The cemetery was laid out early last century as
a private endeavour."

"Is it still in private hands?"

"Yes. No one's been buried here since Queen Victoria's reign. But an underground tomb belongs to a family

that set up a trust long ago to ensure continuing operation. The trust ran out last year."

"Who then bought it?"

"An English company. They may use the buildings but not dig up the land."

"Who's the principal in the company?"

"A man named Saxon Hyde."

"When was the deal completed?"

"About a week ago. But the sale's been in the works since last October when the downpayment was made. That downpayment was in Canadian funds."

According to the FBI report, Hilary remembered, Saxon Hyde was in Vancouver in September. He must have been paid for doing something there and used the money to begin the purchase of the mortuary. Working for this fellow Hengler trafficking drugs, perhaps? Was that their initial contact before the rock band deal?

"How was the final purchase made?"

"Cash from an account opened recently with a Swiss bank draft."

"What's the layout of the place?"

"Blueprints are on the way. Over the past few months it's been converted to commercial use as a waxworks chamber of horrors. Opening date on the business licence is February 1, three days from now. We'll have the exact contractor's dimensions as soon as the maps arrive. The mortuary has three levels. Ground level is the embalming building down the road. The level below that services several burial chambers beneath the graveyard next door. Railed tunnels provide access. The lowest level is a catacomb passage leading to the bottom of a tiered entombing well. The well is for the family that set up the trust."

An SAS man dressed in nighttime combat fatigues ran up to the detective. They were in a sidestreet next to the graveyard. The angle of the moon cast the command post in shadow.

"All the lights inside are out," the SAS man said. "When do we take control of the incident?"

"Two a.m., I hope," Rand replied. "That's if we have the maps you'll need by then. Let's wait till everyone's asleep in case some of those kidnapped are still alive."

Just then a car pulled up and the hard men scrambled out. A second vehicle arrived from another direction. As one of the hard men approached her Rand clenched her hands. She had gone without sleep for so long that her left eye was twitching involuntarily.

"All right, Hilary," the man said smoothly. "We'll take over here."

"Back off," Rand warned, her lips a thin, tight line.

"No, you fuck off," the man replied sharply. "We're in command now."

A voice from inside the second car to have arrived broke in. "Calm down, both of you," said the Commissioner of Police.

The hard man advanced toward the open rear window. "Sir, we have a rogue on our—"

"Who located the graveyard?" the Commissioner asked.

"Sergeant Scot McAllaster," Rand answered.

"Who's his governor?"

"I am," she said.

"Then it's hers," the Commissioner said, sliding his window shut.

## 1:19 a.m.

Teeze had said not to kill them, so he hadn't. If Legrasse's man had come, could she be far behind? It would be no time at all until the Old Ones arrived, the pulsing down his brain tunnels evidence of that, the sacrifice on the altar at the moment the stars were right all that was needed for them to break through. By the time Legrasse arrived they'd all be waiting for her, and all could have revenge for what had happened so long ago in that Louisiana swamp.

The Ghoul slammed a rubber ball into Deborah's mouth to stop her screaming. Then he touched the point of a knife gently against her eyeball. "One more sound and I'll push it in," he threatened.

Turning from her he approached Rika who was tied down spread-eagled on the altar slab. Her eyes were burned out by acid that ran smoking down her cheeks, her mouth wedged open with a three inch piece of wood rammed vertically between her palate and her tongue. He put down the knife and picked up a hammer and centre punch from the surgical shelf.

Deborah was chained to the floor of The Well by an iron collar locked around her neck on a three foot leash.

Both wrists were handcuffed behind at the small of her back. The Ghoul had stripped her bare.

His back now facing Deborah, he grabbed Rika by the jaw and aimed the centre punch at one of her front teeth.

## 1:20 a.m.

Zinc lay near-paralysed in the dark, listening to the silence. The screams had stopped a minute earlier and now his mind was alive with the phantom humming of its own circuits. The veins on both his retinas formed trace patterns in the blackness. Whatever the combination of drugs surging through his body, Zinc was so exhausted that he was unable to fight back. He could not think. He could not move. His will to survive had shut down.

Chandler lay sprawled on his back with his right arm flopping spasmodically about on the cold stone floor. He had become no more than a puppet controlled chemically by some invisible master. Then his hand cut through the beam of an electric eye, which activated a searing white light which exploded in his face.

Zinc jumped violently as adrenaline flashflooded his heart. He recoiled yelping involuntarily as he covered his eyes.

Towering high above him was the figure of a doomed man. The man was dressed in safari clothes ripped open over his chest, his face contorted by a rictus of terrified disbelief. All over his body were swellings and fresh-bleeding holes, each lump shaped as if something blunt and hard were pushing up through his flesh. A dozen of these boils had ruptured, and through the tears in the man's white skin poked a dozen tiny heads.

Each head was the colour of the blackest African, with miniature teeth, white and straight, behind retracted lips, and clumps of wool on each plum-sized cranium. The voodoo-infested hunter held one of the boil-heads in his hand, and in the other a razor he'd used to slice through the neck of the tiny Balunda fetish-man.

Chandler scrambled back from this grisly tableau as more and more swellings appeared, and the features of the safari man transformed into his own. Then all the boil-heads bleached out to resemble his dead partner Ed, each turning to focus malignantly on Zinc's retreating form. The light he had tripped with his hand began to fade, dimming the plaque on the floor that read "Lukundoo", as the heads in unison taunted him with chittering, falsetto voices: "Chandler, Chandler, the beast within us lies."

Darkness returned for a second before Zinc tripped another light.

He spun around to find a small boy in a public school uniform sliding down the banister of an English manor house. The bottom half of the railing was a gleaming razor-blade.

As the light went down this time, Chandler's mind watched the boy slit apart and his palpitating pink entrails slide down both sides of the steel toward the floor.

## *1:22 a.m.*

The Ghoul hammered the centre punch and snapped off another of Rika's teeth, glancing with an inspired grin at the image of "Berenice" carved into the frame of the Poe mirror.

Deborah winced at the sickening sound of tooth enamel cracking and the gargle of pain that escaped from her half-sister's wedged-open lips. Her own jaws bit deep into the rubber ball.

"It's time! It's time!" The Ghoul snarled, his blazing eyes staring down at the mutilated face. Then he laughed as he sadistically hammered the remaining teeth from Rika's bleeding gums, threw down the tools and picked up the knife and moved it toward the palpitating flesh above her heart.

Then suddenly he stopped as if momentarily frozen solid—before turning toward Deborah who cowered on the floor as he now crouched down above her shaking body. In one palm he held the fractured tooth fragments above her head, as he poked her nipple with the cold steel of the knife.

He turned his hand over and let the ivory pieces rain down on her. Then he reached out and yanked the ball from her mouth.

"I've been waiting a long time, baby," the madman said.

## *1:23 a.m.*

Deborah cried, "Please don't!" from a thousand miles away as Chandler tripped another electric eye to light up

Jack the Ripper at work in Miller's Court. The remains
of Mary Kelly showed the ferocity of his crimes, for there
was not a square inch of skin on her corpse that did not
have a knife slash through it.

"Only wax! Only wax!" Zinc whispered again and again,
as the carved and butchered features of the Ripper's
victim became those of Deborah Lane.

Try though he might, he could not get the hallucinations under control. There was just too much reality in all
this make-believe.


## 1:26 a.m.


She bit him on the shoulder as hard as she could, refusing
to let go even when he punched her.

The sharp cry that erupted from him was more of fear
than pain. Wrenching loose from the clamp of her jaws,
he looked down in terror at the bright red blood now
bubbling out of his skin. "Oh, Jesus, no!" he wailed.

Deborah Lane was thrown back on the ground, her
wrists still locked behind her and the iron collar still
clamped tight around her throat. Rika Hyde was gurgling
and coughing five feet away, rocking her head from side
to side to keep from drowning in blood. Anywhere that
Deborah's eyes gazed around The Well, there was blood
    blood
    blood
    blood
everywhere.


## 1:27 a.m.


"Leave her alone!" Chandler yelled, stumbling across the
room, his limbs convulsing as each of her shrieks stabbed
him in the heart, crying out berserkly, "You bastard!
You fuckin leave her alone!", as around him all the
exploding waxworks images blended into one, until Chandler was tripping off so many lights in such rapid succession that their combined brilliance revealed this hell-hole
for what it was.

Then he saw the well.

## 1:28 a.m.

The image of Elaine Teeze flashed on the wall screen in Jack Ohm's mind. Her vampire teeth extended down into her mouth, their razor-sharp points red from having recently fed on the blood of the body that once was Saxon Hyde.

"Do something!" she ordered. "We'll bleed to death!"

Ohm, however, ignored her request. He had more pressing problems.

For the steel wall that made up the right edge of his mind—the wall behind which he'd heard the scratching he thought was a short-circuit—now throbbed as if imbued with a life of its own, bulging into his cerebral fortress at a dozen places. The force of whatever was out there relentlessly trying to get in was popping the rivets that joined the steel plates of the room together, shooting them like bullets across his mental space. One of these ricocheted off his computer bank and hit the wall screen, shattering the image of Elaine Teeze.

"Open this door!" the voice of the vampire shouted from the speakers, but inside Ohm was frozen immobile with fear. For something had just broken through the bulging wall of his mind.

It was the slimy head of a gigantic worm.

# The Hollow Men

**1:29 a.m.**

The mirror was an antique dating from the 1850s. Its hardwood frame—now jet-black from the grime of so many years—was carved with scenes from the stories of Edgar Allan Poe. Above the mirror, fingerpainted in blood on the brick wall of The Well, were two dripping words—*Poe-tic Justice*— flanked by a pair of red lights synchronized to the pulse-beat pounding from the speakers. The throbbing glow reflected Deborah Lane in the mirror. She felt like she was imprisoned inside a human heart.

The Well was a stone barrel sixty feet in diameter. Left of the mirror a ladder ran up the cylinder's side, soon lost in the darkness high above where the dead slept forever bricked up in tiers of cells.

Her eyes moving counter-clockwise around the pit, Deborah grimaced at the Iron Maiden propped against the wall, its door yawning open to reveal four barbed iron spikes strategically placed to miss the body's vital organs. A victim impaled within its confines would die in slow agony.

Next to the Iron Maiden, the yellow-waxed corpse of the woman attacked in Stonegate Cemetery hung crucified upon the wall. Large rail spikes had been hammered through both palms and the throat of her naked, mummified body. The axe which had split her skull in two was still wedged in her head, her brain bared in the deep Vs on both sides of the steel.

Arranged on the bricks above the woman was a collage of pornographic pictures, some clipped from hard-core magazines, others time-delay Polaroid shots of The Ghoul having necrophilic sex with his victim. The photos spewed from her head like final thoughts set free by the axe.

Under her dangling right leg was a 1940s office water-cooler, its cloudy liquid a light milky-grey. The Stonegate baby drowned within floated like a foetus in the womb.

The strippers from the Soho club had been transformed into a mummified monster, their once-beautiful flesh cut into jigsaw pieces and reconstructed with black stitches. The resulting hermaphrodite was a human travesty, a thing with half a woman's face and half a man's, each arm and leg of a different sex from its partner, female breasts jutting from a muscular male torso.

The head of Detective Inspector Hone hung dangling from a chain six feet above the altar to which Rika was tied. The chain was attached by wires to a horizontal rod rammed through his ears. The neck of the policeman ended in shredded skin. The teeth in his mouth had been sharpened to points and his tongue had been pulled out to form a Colombian necktie.

Hone's head, however, was but one part of a grisly mobile. Eyeballs of human and animal origin had been plucked out and embedded in clear plastic squares. These hung suspended from strings that turned slowly in response to subterranean currents. Right now three of them were glaring at Deborah Lane.

A collection of animal skulls and bones were strung to clink and rattle like a gruesome windchime above the stripped body of Edwin Chalmers QC. The Ghoul had left the lawyer to rot, his cadaver stretched out in an advanced state of decomposition beside the altar. From one end of the glass coffin within which his corpse lay, a five-inch square chute angled into the floor providing easy access for the large rats which now and then ventured up from below to forage a meal. The flesh that had not been nibbled away from the dead barrister's bones was a festering mass of maggots and yellow fat slime. The torso had swollen and burst to expose the jellied organs within. Hair was sloughing away from the tissue in ugly damp wads. The stench was nauseating.

The first of three doors located next to the coffin led into a black-walled room decorated with gleaming butcher's cutlery hanging from silver hooks. The pulse of the blood-light from The Well glinted off razor-sharp edges.

The middle door opened into the mouth of an access

tunnel, the passage curving away to disappear in darkness. Hanging above the entrance were a maroon scarf and a monkey's paw.

The third door pierced the wall of The Well to the right of the Poe mirror. Within the room beyond, which was plated with metal sheets, Lane could see eight large laboratory jars containing floating hearts. In shock she wondered how such a small thing could keep a person alive. On the floor in front of the jars was a glass-domed slab with grooved collecting troughs. The room was bathed in a cold green wash from several unseen computer screens.

Saxon was a kinetic mess of madness and paranoia. Since the moment he'd seized her upstairs in the hall, her half-brother had behaved as if he were caught in a tug of war. Shouts and counter-shouts of an argument out of control now issued from the steel-walled room into which he'd last disappeared.

A furtive movement on the edge of her field of vision made Deborah's eyes flash to a large round hole sunk into the floor several feet from her. It was capped with a wooden plug and resembled a well within The Well in which she was chained. At its edge so The Ghoul could peer down into the pit below had once stood the chair fashioned like a throne which he had smashed to pieces before Deborah was dragged down here. The chair had been constructed from human skulls and bones tied together with leather thongs and decorated with long-haired scalps. Its remnants were now scattered about the floor.

Deborah knew everything in this man-made hell was painstakingly designed. It was but a more deadly version of her half-brother's bedroom back home in Rhode Island when they were young. So what was down that well in the floor that was stoppered with the wooden plug? And why did the chute that brought the rats up to feed on the rotting lawyer angle down to intersect with its sunken shaft? It was the movement of one of these rats that had caught her attention.

Suddenly Saxon burst out of the room with the dull steel walls and ran toward the black room hung with cutlery. He was now cringing as if afraid of attack, no longer all-powerful as he had seemed while torturing Rika. His eyes drifted from side to side and he grasped his cheek as if to confirm his existence. The voice she heard coming from his mouth was a whimpering quiver of fear, as he cried out repeatedly, "Disease! Disease! Disease!"

But less than a minute later when Saxon emerged from the black-walled room, Deborah sensed yet another radical change in his personality. Now he spoke with the English accent he'd used just before she bit him to stop the sex attack, his attitude arrogant as he snarled from one side of his mouth, "I don't care! She's mine! I want her body parts."

Then, with lightning abruptness, Saxon changed again.

His face paled and his eyes glazed, rolling back in their sockets until only the whites remained. As his mouth transformed to a twitching contortion of spitting hate, his eyes rolled back and his movements feminized. Now he parodied a female voice to whisper, "Then I'll do it myself."

Deborah watched aghast as he crossed to where Rika was tied to the altar, picked up the shining knife and viciously slit her throat. With a circular cut he then peeled off her face, sticking the horrid flesh-mask over his own.

That done, he turned and minced toward Deborah Lane.

It was all coming apart.

Saxon's body stood paralysed for a moment on the edge of The Well, Jack Ohm's steel-walled room to its right, Sid Jinks' black-walled lair to its left, the access tunnel behind, while Elaine Teeze made a decision.

Which of the three personalities should she release from the well of the subconscious mind to the stage of consciousness?

As blood from Deborah's bite flowed out of the body that had once been Saxon Hyde, Teeze felt herself getting weaker as her precious lifeforce bled away, and she knew that no matter what the danger the injury must come first.

That meant Jack Ohm got this slice of time.

Jack Ohm punched the console switch to open the sliding door that gave access to his mind. As the silhouette of Elaine Teeze came into view, the lights on the computer cabinet to his left flickered and dimmed. The metal-walled room he perceived as his mind dimmed and darkened too.

"We're bleeding!" the vampire cried in alarm. "Stop the flow, you fool!"

But Jack Ohm was too far gone in disgust at the sight of the giant worms now flopping about on his floor.

"What have you done, Elaine?" he shouted hysterically.

Then his eyes locked on the holes in the wall where the gross things had chewed through, widening in absolute disbelief at what he now thought he saw. For the tunnels eaten through the flesh of the mind next to his within this single brain found their source in the awesome infinity of the gulfs between the stars. Down these cosmic chasms of black interstellar space blew a wind that howled in raging gusts through the halls of time, driving before it a million pinpoints of unnatural spanning light and pouring forth shafts of radiance that transmogrified into monsters.

There were hellish forms with streaming hair, and lean rubbery things. Slavering dog-faced throwbacks that mocked the human form. Fungous, flabby beasts with mould-caked bodies. Great Cthulhu bubbling up from a chasm of water below, all gelid tentacles and vaginal slit for a face. Azathoth and Yog-Sothoth and Nyarlathotep. Lovecraft's Great Old Ones returning to reclaim this dimension as their own while the disembodied voice of The Ghoul cried out for them to come . . . come . . . "COME! Now is the time!"

Jack Ohm gibbered "Disease! Disease! Disease!" and fell cowering to the floor of his mind as Elaine Teeze disappeared and Sid Jinks turned to the door of his mental room to find her standing there.

"Do something!" she ordered.

"Get me a medic," he snarled.

"Transfuse Rika's blood. We'll bleed to death."

"She bit me, the bitch. I'll take it from Debbie Lane."

"No! Rika's compatible. She was his twin."

"I don't care! She's mine! I want her body parts."

These last words were spoken aloud as Jinks was leaving his subconscious room for the stage of consciousness, until he felt himself jerked back and thrown across the floor.

"Then I'll do it myself," the succubus said—and with that Elaine Teeze stole time from all the hollow men, turning on Rika and skinning her face so that Saxon's body could take on female form, now unchaining Deborah to drag her kicking and yelling by the hair across to the hole in the floor. Teeze yanked off the wooden plug and pushed her into the well, tossing her still handcuffed into the pit from which rats ran up the chute to gnaw at what was left of Edwin Chalmers QC.

Replacing the plug, the vampire bent over Rika's body and bit into her throat.

## 1:30 a.m.

McAllaster arrived at the scene and went straight to the weapons van. Hilary Rand was talking to the commander of the SAS strike force team. The Highlander interrupted to say, "A right nutter, this one. We got 'em *all,* Chief."

"What did you find?"

"Our lad's a real Jekyll and Hyde," McAllaster said. "Perhaps a Hyde and Hyde is more exact."

He handed the DC Supt a bundle of papers.

"Found these scattered about the floor of his lair. Until this week Hyde lived in a basement flat in the East End. The flat has one large room divided into three parts. One part is papered with horror pictures, photos, and clippings from magazines. There's a hole in the wall that was once covered by some sort of door, but that's now gone. The hole leads into a tunnel that joins the sewer system. Off the tunnel is an old crypt filled with deer-skinning frames ringed in a circle. There's dried blood all over the place."

"Good, Scot. We've got the Sewer Killer."

"Aye, but there's more. The second part of the room is sheeted with aluminium foil. It contains the remains of a pseudo-scientific lab. The third part is painted entirely black with small hooks in the walls. The papers in your hand come from all three sections."

"How many people lived in the flat?"

"Just one according to neighbours across the road."

"And elsewhere in the building?"

"None. The upper floors are storage."

McAllaster tapped the papers in Rand's hand.

"Chief, Hyde's not just the Sewer Killer but Jack The Bomber as well. *And* the Vampire Killer. *And* some bloke named Sid Jinks, whoever he may be. It's all in these papers."

The Scotsman approached the weapons officer standing near the van and ordered a Heckler and Koch MP5 with a sound suppressor. He'd used this submachine-gun during the SAS assault on the Iranian Embassy in May 1980. Not counting the silencer, the gun was 19 inches long with the butt stock closed. The box magazine held 30 rounds of 9mm Parabellum ammunition which the H&K spat out at the rate of 650 rounds per minute. He clipped the magazine into the well in front of the trigger, then pushed the selector lever down to the three-shot-burst position.

"When do we go in?" the Highlander asked.

"Two a.m.," Rand replied, glancing at the gun. "And if it comes to that, Scot . . . Yes, he's yours."

That was the only time she ever saw Scot McAllaster smile.

. . . until Chandler was tripping off so many lights in such rapid succession that their combined brilliance revealed this hell-hole for what it was.

Then he saw the well.

The waxworks were in an underground vault beneath the embalming room. Opposite the door through which Zinc had crawled, forty feet away on the other side of the crypt, a series of tunnels leading to the burial chambers beneath the adjoining graveyard ran into the earth. Rail tracks for push carts were spiked to the floor of each subway shaft but one.

Across the mouth of the tunnel without the rails was an iron mesh gate with an open padlock hanging from the eye of its latch. Behind the metal grating, a well five foot in diameter was sunk even further into the ground, an electrified pulse now pounding up from its depths.

Chandler was down on his hands and knees at the foot of a waxworks figure depicting Miles Bennell striking out with an axe at a half-formed effigy of himself developing from a pod. The plaque on the floor read "Invasion of the Body Snatchers".

Pain was shooting up and down Zinc's left arm from overexertion, his heart hammering wildly in his chest as the lights began to fade. Using all the will he could muster he fought back the effect of the drugs now transforming Bennell's features into his own and those of the pod-man into his father's. Straining his mind to try and gain some vague sense of focus, Deborah's name uttered again and again from his quivering lips, Chandler reached up and snapped both tallow arms off the waxworks figure. Then axe in hand he staggered across the vault toward the tunnel gate in front of the well.

## 1:31 a.m.

Deborah Lane tumbled ten feet down to the bottom of the pit, landing in a pool of stinking mush that splashed up and rained back on her body.

Stunned by a sharp blow to her head as she'd bounced off the walls of the shaft, she lay crumpled in twilight, slowly coming around. Then the plug was replaced above and everything went black.

## 1:32 a.m.

Stumbling in a zigzag toward the iron gate, Zinc tripped exhibit lights to guide him on the way. Groping the corroded metal of the latch, he pulled hard on the bars to gain entrance to the tunnel. Gripping the axe up near the blade, he dropped to his knees and stuck his free arm into the pit, searching until his wrist hit a metal rung. Then grasping the iron footing, he swung his body into the hole and started down the half-hoop steps hammered into its side.

Sightless and moving by touch alone, his nerves shredded and crippled by his own deceiving mind, Chandler descended the throat of the shaft.

*Boom!* . . . *Boom!* . . *Boom!* A giant heart was beating far below.

Then one of the steps, a hinged trap, gave out below his foot as his hand-hold pulled out of the wall.

He plummeted to the bottom.

## 1:33 a.m.

Her hands cuffed behind her back, Deborah rolled over face down in the muck, then inched to her knees.

The wooden stopper ten feet above that closed off the well had not been properly replaced. Wedged at a slight angle it allowed in some light, but the glow of the red pulse barely reached this far below.

Deborah stood and turned her back to the curved brick wall. Slowly she moved around its slimy surface foot by foot, examining her circular prison. Halfway around her fingers slipped into a hole, and when she crouched to examine it she found a barred cage built into the wall.

A second later she heard a sound that made her flesh crawl.

Something in the cage was moving in her direction.

Suddenly whatever it was lashed out and clawed her across the chest, forcing a stifled gasp from her lips more terrible than a scream.

Slipping and scrambling through the mush she jerked away from the cage, flattening herself against the brick wall.

The grunting thing was reaching out between the restraining bars.

"Food? You . . . food?" she distinctly heard it say.


They attacked as soon as he landed.

For whatever the drugs jabbed into Zinc's arm, their grip on his mind grew stronger and stranger with every second until they pushed him to the edge of chemical psychosis. The heightened flow of adrenaline coursing through his blood seemed to intensify their effect. His eyes were out of focus, his limbs twitching spasmodically from the cold, his fear, and the pharmaceutical overload.

Chandler hit the ground with a jolt and his right ankle wrenched to the side. A scorching pain shot up his calf as his leg gave way. He crashed to the ground in a spray of splintered wood and sharp nails that ripped his naked torso.

The shaft from the waxworks above dropped into a horizontal tunnel filled with open coffins. The coffins had been gathered from the subterranean crypts beneath the graveyard next door, then lowered here and cracked open to arrange yet another grisly tableau. This particular horror, however, wasn't made of wax. For Chandler had reached that point where fantasy blurred into the grim reality of The Well.

Beyond the broken boxes and the bones surrounding Zinc, a thirty-foot passage curved left ahead. An eerie red glow and the amplified pounding seemed to originate just around that bend.

When a skull suddenly opened its jaws and bit off his hand, Chandler's mind gave up. All he wanted now from life was simply not to think, to flee like a frightened animal from anything that might stir his drugged imagination.

Not real! Not real! he told himself over and over again—but his will was powerless to stop the attack.

Bone fingers grabbed at his ankles and teeth sank into his flesh, while around him the mangled charnel mess that spilled from the coffins quickly came to life. Relentless fear and loathing overwhelmed Chandler's mind, weirding and warping it into a nightmare spawning ground. Stretched to its absolute limit by drug pollution and lack of sleep, it conjured up monsters from down the skid to genetic reverse evolution.

One, two, three, four—each subsequent skull that bit him was yet another step back along the scale that led to something vicious in man that had never been bred out.

That's not a man! . . . not a man! . . . you're not a man! he thought, his mind wobbling on the edge of a madness from which you never come back, his spine bending uncontrollably until he couldn't stand erect.

. . . man! . . . man! . . . get . . . man! . . . get your man! the Mountie thought, desperately grabbing at anything to fight back from stepping over that taboo line in his brain, as now they were upon him, this half-human drove of quadrupeds tearing at his flesh, eating him up piece by raw piece as he kicked and squirmed frantically, snapping their ribs apart with his hands and caving in their skulls, trailing red streamers behind him as he crushed and smashed and destroyed.

. . . be a man! . . . take a stand! . . . . must take a . . .

"Stand!" he yelled, focusing every shred of resolve on that one word.

"Stand, you bastard! One last stand! Stand! Stand! STAND!"

With a white-knuckle jerk his hands closed around the wood of the axe.

"STAND!"

Then Chandler stumbled, fell, stumbled, staggered, and gained his feet.

## 1:34 a.m.

"He's here," Elaine Teeze whispered, staring across at the screen that glowed in Jack Ohm's room.

An infra-red camera caught Chandler approaching the

entrance to The Well, limping down the tunnel using the axe as a crutch.

"He's here. He's here," she repeated, lurking to one side of the door just around the bend in the passage.

Her hand raised the skinning knife.

Lane's eyes strained to pierce the darkness. She cowered as far away from the cage as she could. The well was only five feet in diameter. The restraining bars squeaked as they were lifted by whatever was there, grating up and down Deborah's jagged nerves. Then seeping in through the stopper crack ten feet above, the red light-pulse just barely revealed two twisted, taloned hands curled around the bars of the rising cage.

A *crunch* came out of the darkness as if something was bitten. Deborah saw a mouth appear this side of the cage, chewing the head off a rat and swallowing it as the rodent's body continued to claw at two more hands.

When she saw the single body with two heads crawl out under the half-raised bars, bile as bitter as acid bubbled into her mouth.

### 1:35 a.m.

Chandler faltered as he staggered into The Well, gaping at the flayed thing strapped to the altar. What had once been a woman was now no more than butchered meat, her body red from the slash to her throat and her face a raw mess of pale-pink spastic muscles.

Chandler wavered because he thought the horror was Deborah Lane.

Then Elaine Teeze stabbed him.

The scream that issued from her throat bounced back at her in waves. It echoed up the pit and was reflected by the stopper as her feet slipped in the gelatinous muck that slopped about her legs.

Two of the two-headed monster's four hands grabbed her by the throat.

Chandler hit the floor hard as the blade was yanked out of his thigh. The axe clattered from his grasp and skidded across the stones. Other fingers reached for it as he rolled to one side.

\*    \*    \*

Deborah lay on her back with her hands cuffed beneath her. The Thing sat on her stomach, submerging her in the sludge.

It was holding her head under water until she drowned.

Ironically it was the drugs that saved him from the first blow of the axe. For Chandler's nerves had been so shredded by their effect that he reacted to every sight and sound that brushed his senses. The pounding of the electrified heartbeat and the red pulse of the lights seemed to shift his sense of time to slow-motion nightmare speed. He was now running on pure instinct that found its source in the reptilian core of his brain, so as the shadow crossed the floor to the right of his head, Chandler intuitively rolled another turn.

The blade of the axe hit the floor exactly where he would have been, throwing off sparks and chips of stone.

Zinc grabbed the edge of the altar and pulled himself to his feet. Then he swiftly veered to the right as the axe came down again, its wedge biting deep into Rika's chest, making her body jump.

Limping badly and gritting his teeth in almost unbearable pain, Chandler reached for the squid-faced idol as the naked man wearing the skinned face came at him again.

The clay idol smashed beneath the descending steel, hurling a spray of dust and chunks across the circular room. It whammed against the floor with a resounding *clanggg!*

"Kill him, Sid!" a high-pitched voice screamed from the mouth of the female mask, then the madman reached up with one hand and wrenched the sliced-off skin from his face.

"Remember me, Horseman?" Jinks snarled, taking a swipe at Chandler.

At the moment of this abrupt change in personality, Zinc smelled an acidic sweat unlike any he'd encountered before. In this world there's the sweat of work, the sweat of fear, and the sweat of insanity.

The axe came off the floor heading straight for Chandlers naked groin.

He saw it too late and couldn't move in time.

## 1:36 a.m.

With all her strength Deborah arched her body off the floor
of the pit. She bucked the Thing on her stomach up over
her head. Two dull thuds sounded as it hit the brick wall.

When the hands loosened on her throat she squirmed
to one side.

His head was now devoid of hair, the eyebrows shaved
away—but Chandler knew this was the same man who
had attacked him in Stanley Park. The bare scalp and the
pinpoint eyes, the crooked teeth and hollow cheeks and
nostrils flared with hate all made him look like Death
personified.

The slice to Zinc's groin was just a ruse to catch the
cop off guard, the swing aborted six inches from his balls
as the axe whirled in a reverse arc toward Chandler's
skull.

And that was a mistake.

For the split-second shadow of the axe handle crossing
the bald man's head reminded the Mounted Policeman of
Mohawk that night in the slaughterhouse. This blow was
coming from above just as the stab had then, the
drugs causing Zinc to react in advance on reflex memory.

With an eye-for-an-eye fury fuelled by all he had been
through, Chandler blocked the descending swing with his
left forearm. He drove his right fist in an upward arc up
behind the axeman's shoulder, clamping his right palm
over the back of his own left hand, then wrenched forward with all his strength. As bones cracked under the
pressure of the judo power-hold he slammed the knee of
his injured leg hard into the axeman's groin, lifting him
from the ground to hurl him across the room.

Then he lost his balance and tumbled into the hole in
the floor.

Sid Jinks was thrown back with a sickening *whunk*! into
the Iron Maiden, its barbed spikes ripping out through
the front of his chest, spilling the precious, precious
blood on which Elaine Teeze fed.

As Jinks began to scream, the tone of his voice re-
gressed in age.

"Elaine! Elaine! Elena! Mommy! God help me!"

*     *     *

With a crash Zinc hit the wooden stopper which split beneath his weight. He rode it down the well shaft as if it were a disintegrating flying saucer shot from the sky. He landed to the sound of snapping necks beneath the wood.

"Freddie! Reuben! Peter! Dig me out!" he screamed.

The voice of the man impaled on the spikes was that of a fourteen-year-old boy.

In the dark to his left, something moved.

Zinc lashed out with one hand to grab it by the throat as instantly his other hand clenched to a fist.

With a jerk he yanked it from the alcove in the wall.

Deborah Lane fell into his arms.

## 2:00 a.m.

As Chandler was boosting Lane out of the pit Scotland Yard moved in. The booming echo of stun grenades thundered from above. Saxon was gibbering weakly from the jaws of the Iron Maiden.

"Mommy! Mommy! I'm bleeding!" he moaned repeatedly.

Deborah looked at Zinc as he pulled himself up out of the pit.

"What do we do with him?" Chandler asked.

"Let him bleed," Lane replied.

# Copy Cat

They had spent hours gathering the facts, each person adding what he or she knew to the puzzle. Now they were trying to piece it together to form some sort of coherent whole.

The shot administered to Chandler early in the morning to counteract the effect of the drugs had taken hold immediately, but still his nerves buzzed. He sat slumped in one corner of Hilary Rand's office. Cells were dying all over his body, in his head, in his groin, in his bone marrow. Never had Zinc felt so tired in his entire life. Images ran loose through his mind as if they had no master.

"Elaine! Elaine! Elena! Mommy! God help me!" he thought. "Freddie! Reuben! Peter! Dig me out!"

Then what was the final cry Saxon had blurted out? Oh, yes. "Mommy! Mommy! I'm bleeding!" The key to it all.

It's hard to believe my Deborah came from that same family, he thought. Flowers. I must send her flowers at the hospital before I leave.

With a look of wry irony on his face Zinc got up from the chair and crossed to the DC Supt's desk where he picked up a book—*The Language Of Flowers*— found in Jack Ohm's steel-walled room off The Well. The inscription on the title page read, "To Elena, all my love, Hugh, 1958".

Chandler took a deep breath and slowly let it out. He recalled Deborah saying her mother enjoyed nothing more than working a day in her garden. Elena had met and married Hugh Lane in 1958. Happier days, Chandler thought, that soon turned to shit.

McAllaster asked if he'd like a biscuit and a cup of tea. Zinc put down the book and glanced at the Highlander who was passing a tray around. He was dressed in a sweater with a crest, grey flannel trousers, black shoes and the Murder Squad tie. Chandler nodded his head.

"Are you all right?" the Scotsman asked.

"Yeah, I'm okay."

"A day in hospital would do you good."

"Can't. I've a court date in Vancouver tomorrow that won't wait Must leave tonight. Really, I'm okay."

Braithwaite was sitting at Rand's desk, opposite her. He was reading the stack of papers McAllaster had found in the cellar room. Some were scientific notes and ramblings about Elaine Teeze stealing time by Jack Ohm. Others were The Ghoul's own version of Lovecraft's *Necronomicon*. Jinks had kept accounts and plotted his crimes to the smallest detail.

"Saxon Hyde was the sickest man I've ever encountered," the doctor stated, glancing up.

"You were wrong, Winston, that day you told me multiple personality rarely leads to horrific crime," Hilary said.

Braithwaite shook his head sheepishly. "No, I wasn't wrong. I just didn't have the necessary imagination to take the additional step, to consider the possibility that a psychotic might incorporate the content of a *previous* neurosis of multiple personality into his *subsequent* break with reality. There are as many different psychological profiles on this earth as there are people."

"How does a man end up that weird?" McAllaster asked. "Could *anyone* really have worked it out?"

"Hindsight's twenty-twenty," Chandler said.

"True. That's some consolation. But I think I see fairly clearly now what happened to Hyde from reading between the lines of these papers."

The others looked to Braithwaite, anticipating more.

"Saxon began life with two drawbacks," the psychiatrist said. "He was born with genetic schizophrenia as yet undeveloped. That Keate curse was real. In addition, however, his mother developed the unsubstantiated fear that her son had inherited Keate haemophilia through her. That was just a delusion and he never had the disease, but over the years Saxon convinced himself that he did. In other words Elena's delusion became his own, a psychosomatic illness that was all in his mind."

*"Folie à deux,"* Chandler said. "The sharing of delusional ideas by two people who are closely associated?"

Braithwaite nodded. "A common occurrence," he said. "You understand that by Saxon Hyde I mean his core personality, the child as he was actually born to Elena Keate."

"The mental and physical whole," Rand said.

Braithwaite nodded again. "From our point of view," he continued, "there are two pivotal events in Saxon's early life.

"The first, at the crucial age of four to five when a child's personality forms, was the beating and buggery he suffered at the hands of his step-father Hugh Lane. That's what went on in the garage behind their Rhode Island home when Deborah heard his screams. Forced sodomy. Which in turn led to a fracturing of Saxon Hyde's half-formed personality.

"The mental technique of multiple personality neurosis is to split off a traumatic experience from the general consciousness and then construct a separate personality around it. Sometimes different aspects of one traumatic event give rise to several personalities. Thats what happened here. Each personality then develops its own sense of *reality* to conform to its own mental state. In other words each can see itself anyway it likes."

"So Hyde created three mental characters in addition to his own core personality?" Rand said.

"Yes, initially. Then later he developed a fourth in Elaine Teeze."

"The Ghoul he saw as one of this Lovecraft fellow's Great Old Ones?"

"Right. That was his personality of escape."

"Jack Ohm, the scientist, was as paranoid as they come. Buffered from the world by an array of imaginary machines behind an array of real ones?"

"That was Hyde's personality of fear. Fear of homosexuals from the Hugh Lane rape. And fear of haemophilia springing from his mother Elena's transferred delusion."

"And finally, Sid Jinks. He was Hyde's personality of . . . ?"

"Of anger," Braithwaite said. "Jinks was seen as a psychopath who allowed nothing to stand in his way when avenging a hurt."

"Why did Jinks evolve into an Englishman?" Rand asked.

"That was probably a late development, one that occurred after the band moved to London from Rhode Island last spring. Perhaps he turned British simply for variety, which is common in all multiples. Personalities often vary in age, sex, race, appearance, and ethnic background. It's all a question of perspective within the injured mind. Each personality, as I said, sees itself however it wants, unconstrained by reality."

"Escape. Fear. Anger," Rand said. "An identity for each."

"Yes. With who takes the stage of consciousness later determined by Elaine Teeze according to the job to be done. But that's jumping ahead because Elaine Teeze does not yet exist. The important thing to note at this point is that *each personality knows about the others*. The core personality of 'Saxon Hyde'—don't forget that he too exists at this early time—is the common ground among them and the means of access to each identity. Saxon can slip in and out of the personalities at will, but one personality cannot slip into another. His mental illness at this stage is a non-malignant escape device."

So that's why Deborah heard Saxon talking about Sid and Jack back in the summer of '71, Zinc thought. *Before* his initiation into The Ghouls. In her mind she mixed their names up with those of the real boys in the club.

"Now," Braithwaite said, "we reach the second pivotal event."

"The initiation burial," Chandler said.

"Yes. Resulting in the death of the core personality of Saxon Hyde."

At that very moment a distance away, a young man stood at a newspaper kiosk examining the headlines. The papers were full of stories about the Sewer Killer, the Vampire Killer, and Jack The Bomber. That is, full of stories about Saxon Hyde.

The man bought a copy of each newspaper.

Then he walked home.

&ast;    &ast;    &ast;

Out beyond the windows, twilight was taking hold.

"During the burial," Braithwaite said, "Saxon Hyde suffered a full-blown psychotic break with reality. In psychiatric terms, his latent genetic schizophrenia turned florid.

"From a purely professional point of view the result is fascinating. For Hyde's mind fractured along the same lines as his previous multiple personality neurosis, except now each personality was no longer controlled by his conscious mind."

"By his core personality," Rand said, slowly thinking it through. "Because he *thought* that core personality—his conscious mind—smothered to death within the initiation coffin."

"Right. Leaving behind an empty stage of consciousness," Braithwaite said, "with the three male multiple personalities locked up in dressing rooms so to speak in Hyde's *subconscious* mind. 'Saxon Hyde'—the unifying mental force—had ceased to exist, and in his place the break with reality produced a psychotic hallucination. A fourth personality who was the female vampire known as 'Elaine Teeze'. That comes through clearly in The Ghoul's *Necronomicon* which Scot found in the cellar."

"Elaine, Elena. His mother," Zinc Chandler said. "Teeze meaning tease, I suppose?"

"Probably. She was a schizophrenic hallucination of haemophilia personified. She was a blood-sucking spirit that passed from mother to son disguised as a disease of the blood. The stress of the burial was what triggered off Saxon's undeveloped psychotic illness. His horror-fed mind gave birth to a parasitic vampire living inside his body who now controlled access to his conscious will. To the stage of consciousness."

"So," Rand said, "The Ghoul, Jack Ohm, and Sid Jinks were cut off from each other because . . ."

". . . because the common ground of the core personality had disappeared."

"And they no longer knew about each other because . . ."

". . . because Saxon's illness was now not multiple personality neurosis, but paranoid schizophrenia, a totally different disease. These were not the same personalities as before, but rather new psychotic creations who adopted the usable content of the previous mental disease."

That's why Deborah never heard Saxon mention Jack and Sid *after* the burial, Chandler thought.

"Since Teeze, who was now in control, was herself a personification of haemophilia," Braithwaite said, "each subservient male personality came to develop haematomania in its own way. In other words, each of the three became obsessed with the shedding of human blood in order to mask its own subconscious fear about the blood disease—the vampire—who was living within the body they all shared. The net result was that Saxon's mental illness turned malignant and each of the three male personalities became a psychotic killer."

The young man inserted his key in the lock and opened the door to his flat.

He sat down at the kitchen table to read the papers he had bought.

He turned on the radio to get the latest news.

Then leaving the kitchen he walked along the hall to his bedroom.

"Something I'm wondering about is the rooms," McAllaster said. "The cellar in the East End was divided in three parts. Each part was equal in size to the others. But the crypt beneath the mortuary was not like that. The Ghoul's part was three times as large as the others."

"That, I suspect," Braithwaite said, "is because Hyde's subconscious mind was superimposing its internal world over the external one. Jack Ohm lived mentally in a part of the brain that he perceived as a steel-walled room. You'll see that in his notes. So when he occupied the stage of consciousness and moved about in the real world, his living space came to reflect the room that was his mind. Therefore, it was plated with real steel. The same with the others. The Ghoul was getting out of Elaine Teeze's control. Unlike Ohm and Jinks who were human creations, The Ghoul was a supernatural manifestation."

McAllaster shook his head in disbelief.

"To understand a psychotic mind," Braithwaite said, "you must try to grasp its point of view. Assume that 'Saxon Hyde'—the conscious mind—has just died in that Rhode Island coffin. Elaine Teeze, the female vampire, needs the blood of Hyde's body to survive. She's a parasite. If that body dies, she dies too. If you were her, what would you do to save yourself?"

"Animate the body like Frankenstein's Monster," the Scotsman snorted. "She's supernatural. She could do that, I suppose."

"No," the psychiatrist said. "Not according to all Hyde's writings. Because she's a *female* spirit and therefore cannot activate a *male* body."

"Ah," McAllaster sighed. "I see where this is heading. Teeze was required to tap the three *male* personalities cut off from Saxon's consciousness by his mind's death and use them to activate the flesh giving her life."

Braithwaite nodded. "From the moment she came into being at the time of the break from reality, Teeze was the personality in control and the man on the stage of consciousness was the one that she released from the subconscious mind for that particular slice of time. She was the jailor guarding the well of insanity.

"You see," he continued, "once you understand the logic of Hyde's delusional system, everything else follows logically from that."

"So," Rand said, "The Ghoul was the first personality Elaine Teeze tapped."

"Why?" the doctor asked, playing devil's advocate.

"Because he didn't see himself as a human being. The Ghoul was an entity from Lovecraft's other dimension. Therefore he was the personality used by Teeze during the burial trauma since his virile force was not bounded by our concepts of time and space. A Lovecraftian Old One lives by different rules, so he could slip into our dimension through the door of death that opened to take Saxon's soul away and preserve the body's life while still buried in the grave. When The Ghouls finally returned to dig Saxon up, what came out of the ground was—"

"A zombie," Chandler said. "The corpse of a dead person given the semblance of life by a supernatural force."

"Jesus," McAllaster muttered. "A nutter to the bone."

"So why did the killings only start recently?" Rand asked.

"My hunch is they didn't," Chandler replied. "I'll bet within a month of the burial back in 1971, The Ghoul killed Freddie Sterling and that's why he disappeared, shot Hugh Lane and made it look like suicide, and sexually attacked Deborah. We'll never know the full story but that would fit."

"Right," Braithwaite said. "He got totally out of control, forcing Teeze to banish him from the stage of consciousness. But then she had to give him some form of mental release because he was supernatural and if completely thwarted might break free. So instead of allowing him direct access to the real world by granting him time in control of Saxon's body, she let him dream vicariously through the benign stage character of Axel Crypt who had been created by Rika and Saxon shortly before the break."

"Just like Cthulhu dreaming in R'lyeh," Chandler said. "Waiting for the day when he would return."

"Yes. Crypt became a shadow manifestation of The Ghoul and, in a way, a quasi-personality himself. But he was never really more than a living *Grand Guignol* theatre mask. He was an actor's role as distinct from the actor himself, albeit a role that existed even when the actor wasn't present on stage. He was, I suppose, much like the shadow cast by an invisible man. And from that point on he performed The Ghoul's evil acts through the stage show of the rock band Ghoul."

"So what eventually brought The Ghoul back into our world?" Rand asked.

"AIDS," Braithwaite replied.

The young man picked up the paper bag from the floor and carried it to his bed. Reaching inside, he removed the tool he'd been carving from among the others.

Then he grabbed his knife.

"The delusion of haemophilia was at the centre of Saxon's madness," Braithwaite said. "Up until the early 1980s the personality of Jack Ohm was a homophobic recluse who studied medicine and science as a means of dealing with the general threat to Elaine Teeze's blood supply. His safety net was the American and British public blood banks. Then over the last two years he underwent a severe personality change as a result of the AIDS epidemic. For now not only was his life-saving source of backup blood possibly tainted by the disease, but the source of that taint appeared to be of homosexual origin.

"As a result, Ohm, the paranoid, came to believe that all gays were connected in a conspiracy to kill him by means of AIDS. To insulate Elaine and himself from this he required a source of pure backup blood. That's how the Vampire Killer came to be. Then he went on a rampage of revenge and purification, and as Jack The Bomber killed off homosexuals suspected of incubating and spreading the disease."

"Haematomania," Rand said. "It pops up everywhere."

"Yes, because Hyde's entire delusional system was internally consistent until just before the end. Ohm needed money for research to find a cure for AIDS. He also needed money for a sophisticated electronic security system to buffer himself from any gay counterattack. Elaine Teeze, understandably, had her very life depending on all of this—so she activated Sid Jinks to get the required money."

"It was Jinks who plotted with Rika to do Rosanna in?" Rand said.

"Right. Jinks was the personality used by Teeze to deal with the problems of the now. It was also his job to protect the physical body of Hyde from immediate threat."

"Do you think Rika understood what was happening with her brother?"

"I doubt it," Braithwaite said. "She'd always humoured his weirdness and used it to her advantage. From what we know their entire relationship was based on the playing of changing roles."

"So how does the resurrection of The Ghoul fit in?"

"Under the pressure of the AIDS scare and the sudden need for money, Jack Ohm and Sid Jinks were more often called into action. That meant Saxon's body was not available for use as Axel Crypt to meet the growing commitments of the rock group Ghoul. So a new bassist was brought in to assume his stage personality within the band.

"But when Crypt was no longer 'Saxon' by the autumn of 1985, that meant The Ghoul—who was still kept imprisoned in the well of the subconscious by Elaine Teeze—could no longer dream and vicariously play out his evil games through that stage personality. So he went on a mental rampage which is recorded in detail in the papers you found, Scot."

"I've worked it out," Rand said. "Now Teeze was

afraid *not* to let The Ghoul out into the real world because he was supernatural and if pushed to the limit might do damage to everyone's mutual body."

"Therefore," McAllaster said, "she began to release him onto the stage of consciousness as she did with the other two."

"The real world, however," Chandler cut in, "was not a place he liked, so he set about creating a new world of his own—The Well—in preparation for the coming of his friends, the Great Old Ones."

"And because his system of belief was based on Lovecraft's writings . . ."

"He had to seek out the modern Legrasse who might stop him," Rand said.

"And thus the taunts," the doctor completed. "They were designed to draw out Legrasse—namely, you—so he could be eliminated before the stars were right."

"So the plot to kill Rosanna," Chandler said, "which Rika must have also played a part in, was nothing more than a money-raising operation to finance Ohm's equipment, the rock band Ghoul, building The Well, et cetera."

"And the reason The Ghoul occupied so much more space in that crypt than the other two personalities," McAllaster said, "was once again—as in 1971—Teeze was losing control over him. He was like a supernatural tumour."

"Yes. Another external reflection of Hyde's internal fantasy. The Stonegate Cemetery killings were the first time The Ghoul himself—as opposed to his shadow manifestation in Axel Crypt—stepped onto the stage of consciousness since the early seventies."

"So what went wrong?" Chandler asked. "Why'd he break down?"

"The depth of Hyde's delusional system adopting the multiple concept led to an intricate network of overlapping psychotic beliefs. Imagine the energy necessary," Braithwaite said, "to keep all this intact and manageable within his mind.

"In the end, I suspect, the inner logic of his psychotic world collapsed. What probably pushed him over the top was the fact that his system was based on the separation of the three male personalities. Then suddenly all three were required to function simultaneously. The Ghoul refused to leave the stage of consciousness because the stars were finally right. Ohm was needed immediately since the body was bleeding from Deborah's bite. Jinks had to emerge right then to meet Zinc's approaching threat. The breakdown is evidenced by the fact that Elaine Teeze stepped on stage, the very thing she could *not* do during the Rhode Island burial.

"Hyde's delusional system had grown too complex to manage. The unbearable stress of the moment shattered his inner logic to pieces, leaving the personalities screaming and arguing among themselves.

"Then when his body was impaled on the spikes of the Iron Maiden and clearly about to die, the ghost of Saxon's core personality—his dead conscious mind—reappeared. At the end he came full circle to the birth of his psychosis, crying out the names of The Ghouls who had interred him alive."

A pregnant silence fell among the four of them.

After a while Zinc said, "I've got to catch a plane."

"I'll give you a lift to Heathrow," McAllaster offered.

"Thanks," the Mountie replied.

Resigned to his fate, Chandler was going back to face the music.


After Zinc and Scot had left, the Prime Minister called. Braithwaite sat at the desk while Rand received congratulations. The DC Supt hung up and crossed to the bank of windows. Outside, night fell like a mask.

"Vampires, zombies, ghosts, ghouls. I was right all along," she said. "Winston, this case *was* a horror story."

"Hungry?" Braithwaite asked.

Rand's reflection in the glass smiled back at the doctor. "I don't know how to thank you for everything you've done."

"Buy me dinner," he said.

The detective half-turned away from the window, then glanced back.

"You're thinking about the unresolved problem, aren't you, Hilary?"

"Yes," she replied.

"I'm sure it will wait till after you eat."

Rand fetched her coat.

As they were leaving the room she said, "Sometimes I wonder, Winston, if we ever really win. The madmen just keep coming. They never stop."

\*     \*     \*

Off to the east in another part of the city, the young man looked up from his work to stare at the blank wall above his bed. Unconsciously, he ran a finger along the zigzag scars on his face where the shards of the shattered scuba mask had cut him.

At one time he had thought they'd make quite a team. The Sewer Killer, the Vampire Killer, Jack The Bomber, and him. They'd be four of a kind who belonged to the world's elite, part of that dominant five per cent who are heir to The Will To Power.

That's what he had tried to do with his very first crime, show everyone that he too deserved their attention. Be able to paper *his* wall with clippings similar to those he'd collected on the other three.

But then his funfair attack had turned out a bloody mess. Which had made him feel like a failure who didn't belong with them.

Now the papers were telling him that he really was alone.

No more Sewer Killer.

No more Vampire Killer.

No more Jack The Bomber.

The fame could all be his.

If his Tunnel of Love attack had failed, so had Saxon Hyde. Could there be any doubt that tonight he would succeed? That come tomorrow the papers would be coining names for him?

Tingling with anticipation, he finished carving the handle of the icepick into the shape of a monster.

# EPILOGUE

We fall from womb to tomb, from one blackness and toward another, remembering little of the one and knowing nothing of the other . . . except through faith.

—*Stephen King*
DANSE MACABRE

# Genes

"Your friend Caradon is a bit of a sexist," Deborah said.

"At least he's honest," Zinc replied. "I owe him a lot."

"Why do so many men do that?"

"Do what?"

"Look at a woman's breasts before they look at her face?"

"Arrested oral fixation. Weaned too soon. Transferred Oedipus complex. And other such mumbo jumbo."

"Be serious, Zinc. Why do you think?"

"Because men are basically horny, Deborah. It's the nature of the beast. That's how the race survives."

"Still, I'd have hoped the baser aspects would have disappeared by now."

Chandler shook his head. "They never will. Feminism's done little but change the rules of the game. All men still want into a woman's pants, and if that means paying lip service to a philosophy, they'll do it. The dishonest fuckers are those who believe they actually function according to the new philosophy. The world is full of deception, Deborah. Sometimes we deceive ourselves."

"Do we now?"

"Yes, we do."

"Is that Chandler The Cynic speaking?"

"No, The Realist."

"What do you owe Caradon for, that you overlook his faults?"

"I made a big mistake in the case that took me to Rhode Island. I arrested a guy with little evidence and he got stabbed in jail. In my line of work if you make a mistake, you don't get a second chance. The guy's lawyer started a court case to put my ass in the can. That's why I had to leave London so suddenly. Then at the fifty-ninth minute of the eleventh hour, Bill Caradon found a snuff film produced by the guy stabbed in jail. His lawyer was involved in financing the film, and before the case could be heard the Law Society suspended him. The application never got before a judge."

"What happened to the guy who was stabbed?"

"He died."

"How'd that make you feel?"

"Good," Chandler said. "He paid for a woman named Jennie Copp and the victim in the snuff film indirectly. In this world, Deborah, I'll take rough justice any way it comes."

They were standing alone on a glassed-in balcony under a spread of stars. From beyond the French doors of the Hyatt Hotel came the sound of dance music and the RCMP Red Serge Ball. Deborah was dressed in a long black gown that crossed over her breasts and tied behind her neck. Her back was bare to the waist. Chandler wore the mess kit of an RCMP Inspector: a waist jacket of red serge with aiguillettes over a blue vest and white ruffled shirt with black bow tie, blue trousers with a yellow stripe and black half-Wellington boots with box spurs. Golden crowns representing his rank gleamed from the epaulets, while two gold regimental crests sparkled on the lapels.

Deborah looked up at the stars and asked, "Do you see Halley's Comet?"

"No. But I'm sure it's there."

She touched her cheek to his shoulder tenderly.

"When I was a young girl living at home with all those problems, Zinc, I'd dream that Halley's Comet would come and take me away to a far-off perfect world. I'd fly through black velvet space on a streaking silver ball streaming sparks behind."

"Life goes in circles," the Mountie said. "The best and worst of it always return."

"Hey, you're starting to sound morose. Lighten up, Zinc."

Deborah felt Chandler slowly move away from her.

Then he took á deep breath and asked, "Why'd you lie to me about never being to Vancouver?"

"What do you mean?" She frowned.

"You told me the night we went dancing in Providence that you'd never been out here. Just seen pictures and the Expo brochures."

"I haven't," Deborah said.

Chandler reached into his pocket and removed a copy of an airline ticket. "This says you have. You flew here from New York on January 10, returning the next day. A few days later you went back to Providence."

"Zinc, I spent that time in New York seeing publishers about my novel. I don't know what you're talking about. Let me see that ticket."

He passed it to her.

"Where did you get this?"

"That same night in Providence, just before I called to say I had to leave unexpectedly for London, I passed the information you had given me to the FBI and asked a friend to check it out. She checked you out too and sent a report to Vancouver."

"Is that why you asked me to the Red Serge Ball? To confront me with this?"

"Deborah, I never looked at the file after I returned from London. Not until yesterday. I thought the case was closed with the deaths of Saxon and Rika Hyde. I asked you here because I love you."

"Why'd you look yesterday?"

"Cause something's been bothering me and it won't go away."

A sheen of perspiration appeared on Deborah's forehead. "What?" she asked.

"Rosanna made a date with a model the night she died. When he arrived at 2:00 a.m. no one answered the door. I suspect that's because Rosanna's killer was inside the suite. Half an hour later, after the model had gone, a woman came downstairs and was seen by some painters in the lobby. I believe she wanted to distract them into thinking she was Rosanna so she could escape and not be identified later."

"But that was Rika. Pretending like in London."

"That's what I thought too. Because Rika masking as Rosanna was seen twelve hours later leaving for the airport. That was after she and her brother had dissolved

Rosanna's body and their sleight of hand was under way."

"I . . . I don't understand." Deborah's pupils were dilating involuntarily.

"Saxon—Sid Jinks—and Rika went to the penthouse that night to kill Rosanna as part of their plan to get her estate. But what if she were already dead when they arrived? Would the twins have aborted their plan or carried on, knowing the real killer could not give them away without also being exposed?"

"No." Deborah was shaking her head back and forth as if in a trance.

"I went back to the file on the case to see if someone else in Vancouver had a motive to kill Rosanna. That's when I found the ticket attached to the FBI report."

"No."

"What's been subconsciously bugging me for the past two months is something one of the lobby painters said. When Caradon and I interviewed him he went on and on about the cleavage and full breasts the woman who came down at 2:30 a.m. had. Deborah, I saw Rika naked and strapped to that altar while Saxon and I fought it out. I also saw her on stage. She's as flat as a board."

Suddenly Zinc's nostrils were assailed by an acidic sweat he'd only encountered once before. In this world there's the sweat of work, the sweat of fear, and the sweat of insanity.

A dark shadow seemed to pass behind Deborah's eyes, then without warning she yelped and her hands flew up to cover her face.

"The light! The light!" she cried.

A searing whiteness burned her eyes and cracked through her mind like lightning.

Mother! she thought ecstatically, Oh blissful blissful brightness, as white turned red, redder, as red as the fires of hell that await those who will burn below. A vision formed in her mind of Rosanna's damned body writhing and arching up off that waterbed, her spine curling back as far as the ropes tied to her limbs would allow, the strychnine contorting her face into the Devil's grimace as Deborah whispered, You whore! How dare you defile my mother's sacred image! Burn for stealing her money, bitch! Burn for soiling her name! For dragging her reputation through that court of ridicule! You and those other two who soon will share your fate. Whore! Bitch! Jezebel! You who've looked back on Sodom! she thought, as red bleached out to white again and a voice as soft as a lullaby said, Hush! Hush, Deborah! Its all over now.

Mommy? Mommy, tell me you loved me more than you did him! What do you think of your son now that you see all! Mommy, he is the Antichrist, don't you see? Why did you love him more—

Hush, my baby. One day you will come to me. Yes, all the stars in Heaven do outline the face of God. Now sleep, sleep, Deborah. My sweet Avenging Angel.

Deborah slowly uncovered her eyes and looked at Zinc. Tears trickled down her cheeks but when she spoke it was as if nothing strange had happened. The Deborah Chandler knew and loved was the mask of the Impostor.

"I love you, Zinc," she said bitterly. "Love you," she repeated. "Yet you suspect me of murder based on an airline ticket and the size of a woman's breasts? You call that a case, my love? I thought you learned that lesson. Are you going to arrest me, Zinc? Is that why you lured me here?"

Chandler shook his head. His heart felt punctured.

" 'Deborah, I can't get you out of my mind.' That's what you said when you called. 'Please come to Vancouver for the Red Serge Ball.' And I was as giddy as a girl on her first big date. I've never been to a formal dance in my entire life. Then you do this."

"Deborah, please, I had to know. We couldn't just—"

"Well, there's something else you ought to know, my love. I'm two months pregnant."

Zinc couldn't hide his shock. "Us?" he asked, astounded.

"You're the only lover I've ever had."

"Deborah, I . . . Deborah, you . . ."

"No, I won't abort it. I'm going to Heaven, Zinc. That's where I belong. Take a human life unless it's ordained in the Scriptures, and you won't get in. My mother taught me that."

"Deborah . . ." Chandler said, but his throat went dry. All he could think was, You poor kid. You didn't escape the curse. Keate genes. Lane hell. You never stood a chance.

Then he thought of his own genes mixed up with hers.
Thought of *his* child starting life with that stacked deck.

"Deborah . . ."

"Good-bye, Zinc," she said, and turned away.

The last glimpse he had was her naked back disappearing through the French doors that led from the balcony, as the band inside at the Red Serge Ball played Floyd Cramer's "Last Date."

The fantasy was just too good to be real, he thought.

# Afterword

## *"reality"*

The California police say that Richard Ramirez spent many nights alone in a rundown rooming house with nothing but a ghetto blaster playing songs by the rock group AC/DC. He was fascinated by satanic references in the band's music. His favourite cut was entitled "Night Prowler" from the album *Highway to Hell*.

The L.A. cops say he then went on a year-long killing spree that claimed as many as sixteen victims.

His alleged crimes became known as the Night Stalker case.

At 7:00 a.m. on April 12, 1985, a fourteen-year-old youth shot and killed a gambling expert named Bruce Irwin, his wife, and their daughter in Scarborough, Ontario.

After the killings the boy had breakfast at a friend's house where he described the slayings to his buddies and had his ears pierced. He bought records and batteries for his radio with money stolen from the dead man's pockets, then took four of his friends on a tour of the death-house.

The police arrested him fifteen hours later.

At his trial it was alleged that he was a novice devil worshipper who had carved the satanic symbol 666 on his chest with a knife. A psychiatrist stated that he had killed the family to vent anger stemming from an argument with his own family over smoking and girls.

The youth evidently had a violent side to his personality that told him the killings would set him free. This angry second person the boy called Eddie, a name borrowed from the mascot of the British heavy metal rock group Iron Maiden.

Ed McBain wrote *Fuzz* in 1968. This 87th Precinct novel was filmed starring Burt Reynolds, Raquel Welch, and Yul Brynner in 1972.

Later, a young woman ran out of gas in Roxbury, Massachusetts. Walking back to her car from a service station she was set upon by a gang of black youths who doused her with petrol from the can she had just filled and set her on fire.

They had seen this done the night before when *Fuzz* was shown on *ABC Movie Of The Week.*

In 1981, in Washington DC, John Hinkley Jr attempted the assassination of President Ronald Reagan to impress the actress Jody Foster. The inspiration for this crime was Martin Scorsese's *Taxi Driver,* starring Robert De Niro.

In 1984 Farrah Fawcett was in a TV film on wife abuse called *The Burning Bed.* The same night as the broadcast, after watching the show, a husband set his own wife's bed on fire to settle a personal score.

In 1977 Gary Gilmore died in front of a Utah firing squad. He was the first man executed since the U.S. Supreme Court had earlier struck down existing death penalty laws. Norman Mailer wrote about him in *The Executioner's Song.*

Gilmore had once persuaded his girlfriend to join him in a suicide attempt.

His inspiration was the song "Don't Fear The Reaper" by Blue Oyster Cult.

At the Altamont racetrack in California in 1969, a man took aim with a gun at Mick Jagger during a concert by the Rolling Stones. This was just after Jagger had sung "Sympathy For The Devil".

The gunman was stabbed to death by a Hell's Angels security guard.

The Stones stopped performing that particular song in concert.

In 1984 John McCollum shot himself in the head with a .22 calibre pistol. In the lawsuit that followed it was alleged that British heavy metal rocker Ozzy Osbourne had contributed to the youth's depression with his albums *Speak To The Devil* and *Blizzard Of Oz*. The song "Suicide Solution" was said to be the cut that did McCollum in.

In 1985 Raymond Belknap was killed and James Vance severely disfigured when they formed a suicide pact and shot themselves in the head with a shotgun. In the Nevada lawsuit that followed it was alleged this pact was sealed after they had spent six hours listening to an album by the British rock group Judas Priest.

In late 1986 Paul Kutz and his wife were found dead in their North Carolina home, both repeatedly stabbed with their throats slashed. Two U.S. soldiers were subsequently charged with murdering the elderly couple. Found in their truck when arrested were Japanese Ninja warrior clothing and a game of Dungeons And Dragons.

In December of 1986 a Colombian man in Bogota stabbed a woman and her daughter to death, then killed his own mother and five other women, then killed twenty more people in a rampage through a café.

The man, Campos Elias Delgada, was shot to death by police.

Neighbours and friends said he suffered a personality change after becoming obsessed with the novel *The Strange Case Of Dr Jekyll And Mr Hyde*.

Charles Manson let his "Family" believe that he was a messiah. He told them about his vision of the end of the world. This vision he found in songs off the Beatles' *White Album*, especially "Helter Skelter".

The message that Manson found in this music led him to direct his followers on a murderous rampage. Over two nights they killed seven people in two posh L.A. homes. These acts, Manson said, would herald the end of the world. This ultimate annihilation he called Helter Skelter.

The Beatles' song "Helter Skelter" was about a ride on a children's playground slide.

# Author's Note

This is a work of fiction. The plot and characters-in-action are a product of the author's imagination. Where real persons, places, or institutions have been used for background to create the illusion of authenticity they are used fictitiously. Facts have been altered if necessary for the purpose of the story.

It would not have been possible to write this novel, however, without the generous help of certain individuals to whom the author owes a debt of gratitude:

To Dr Maelor Vallance and Dr Joseph Noone (psychiatrists), for pointing out the way.

To Dr Gordon Thorson (surgeon) and Dr James Ferris (pathologist), for help with . . . well, with the gore.

To Harry Beckwith and Les Daniels, who guided me through Lovecraft's Providence, then sat me down in Saint John's Graveyard in the moonlight for inspiration.

To Lewis Clark of Rhode Island Fish And Wildlife, who helped me bury the body in the Great Swamp.

To Janet Ferguson of the North Vancouver Public Library, an Exocet missile of research.

To Pat Shaughnessy of Golden Age Collectables, for the fantasy.

To Mötley Crüe and Iron Maiden, for a look backstage behind the fantasy.

To Bernie Major, late of New Scotland Yard, for the ins and outs of the London Metropolitan Police.

To Ben Nithsdale of Thames Water, who took me down into the sewers.

To The Phantom of the Albert Hall, who took me down into the tunnels.

To Geoff Hilton of the VPD, for help with the ballistics.

To Inspector Mike Cassidy of the RCMP, for aid with the fingerprints.

To Corporal Lloyde Plante of the RCMP, for regimental detail.
To Mary Ashworth and Gary Weinreich, who lit the spark.
To Bill and Tekla Deverell, for the anecdote of epiphany.
And to Lois McMahon, who keeps Slade afloat.

In addition, I must acknowledge the influence of, and the wealth of knowledge contained within, the following nonfiction sources:

Beckwith, Jr, Henry L. P. *Lovecraft's Providence And Adjacent Parts*, Grant, 1979, W. Kingston, R. I.

BSSRS Technology Of Political Control Group, *Techno-Cop, New Police Technologies*, Free Assn, 1985, London.

Consumer Guide. *The Best, Worst, And Most Unusual: Horror Films*, Beekman, 1983, New York.

Daniels, Les. *Living In Fear: A History Of Horror In The Mass Media*, Scribner's, 1975, New York.

de Camp, L. Sprague. *Lovecraft, A Biography*, Ballantine, 1976, New York.

Gollmar, Robert H. *Edward Gein, America's Most Bizarre Murderer*, Hallberg, 1981, Delavan, Wis.

Harrison, Michael. *London Beneath The Pavement*, Davies, 1961, London.

Gaines, William M. (original publisher). *The Complete Tales From The Crypt* (1979); *The Complete The Vault of Horror* (1982); *The Complete The Haunt Of Fear* (1985), Cochran, W. Plains, Missouri.

Gaute J. H. H. and Odell, Robin. *Murder "Whatdunit", An Illustrated Account Of The Methods Of Murder*, Pan, 1984, London.

Haining, Peter. *A Pictorial History Of Horror Stories*, Treasure, 1985, London.

Hart, Bernard. *The Psychology Of Insanity*, Cambridge University Press, 1957.

Holdaway, Simon. *Inside The British Police, A Force At Work*, Blackwell, 1983, Oxford.

Honeycombe, Gordon. *The Murders Of The Black Museum*, Hutchinson, 1982, London.

Keyes, Daniel. *The Minds Of Billy Milligan*, Random, 1981, New York.

King, Stephen. *Danse Macabre*, Everest, 1981, New York.

Laurie, Peter. *Scotland Yard,* Bodley Head, 1970, London.

Lovecraft, H. P. *Supernatural Horror In Literature,* Dover, 1973, New York.

McCarty, John. *Psychos,* St. Martin's, 1986, New York.

McCarty, John. *Splatter Movies,* St. Martin's, 1984, New York.

McNee, Sir David. *McNee's Law,* Collins, 1983, London.

Peat, David. *The Armchair Guide To Murder And Detection,* Deneau, 1984, Ottawa.

Schreiber, Flora R. *Sybil,* Penguin, 1975, London.

Simpson, Keith. *Police: The Investigation Of Violence,* Macdonald, 1978, Plymouth.

Smyth, Frank. *Cause Of Death,* Pan, 1982, London.

Sullivan, Jack (editor). *The Penguin Encyclopedia Of Horror And The Supernatural,* Viking, 1986, New York.

Taylor, Laurie. *In The Underworld,* Unwin, 1985, London.

Trench, Richard, and Hillman, Ellis. *London Under London, A Subterranean Guide,* Murray, 1985, London.

Tullett, Tom. *Murder Squad: Famous Cases Of Scotland Yard's Murder Squad,* Granada, 1981, London.

Wilson, Colin. *Order Of Assassins,* Panther, 1975, London.

And finally, to come full circle, to Howard Phillips Lovecraft for the Cthulhu Mythos.

The king is dead.

Long live the king.

*Mike Slade*

## ABOUT THE AUTHOR

Michael Slade is the pen name of Jay Clarke, John Banks, and Lee Clarke. With a combined experience of thirty years in the trial courts, Jay Clarke and John Banks are Vancouver lawyers who specialize in the field of criminal insanity. They have been involved in more than seventy murder cases, and several major precedents in the Supreme Court of Canada have resulted from their work. Michael Slade is the author of *Headhunter,* available in an Onyx edition.

# There's an epidemic with 27 million victims. And no visible symptoms.

It's an epidemic of people who can't read.

Believe it or not, 27 million Americans are functionally illiterate, about one adult in five.

The solution to this problem is you... when you join the fight against illiteracy. So call the Coalition for Literacy at toll-free **1-800-228-8813** and volunteer.

## Volunteer Against Illiteracy. The only degree you need is a degree of caring.